I0780517

HYBRID MECHANICS

HYBRID MECHANICS

DANIEL VERASTIQUI

CHANNEL 8 PRESS
Austin, Texas

Second Edition, April 2025

Copyright © 2019, 2025 by Daniel Verastiqui
All rights reserved, including the right of reproduction
in whole or in part in any form. Published in the
United States of America by Channel 8 Press.

ISBN: 978-1-967847-08-2

This is a work of fiction. Names, characters, organizations,
events, and locations are either products of the author's
imagination or are used fictitiously. Any resemblance to
actual persons, living or dead, or to real entities, events,
or places is purely coincidental.

danielverastiqui.com

"A soul will not grow in artificial soil."

- From The Reflections of Noetica, Volume IV

ONE

City of Provo, Utah Territory
anno Domini nostri Lassiter 41

The jagged highway steamed like forged steel plunging into water, and as Jake Six guided his motorcycle to a stop next to the crumbling walls of the Provo Temple, the sheets of warm rain and descending clouds cast a hazy shadow over the decomposing husk of the city. In the uncertainty, a fool might be convinced that Provo's buildings still stood, that its population still lived and worked and prayed.

But this vision of a world gone by would be nothing but fog itself, a gray tapestry on which the mind projected distant memories of organic humans scurrying for shelter from the rain, of umbrellas blooming like flowers in a time-lapse.

Jake climbed off his bike and surveyed the temple grounds. Organic skeletons covered most of the expansive plaza and the wide lawn that stretched out to the west. The bones had been picked clean by scavenging birds and subsequently bleached by an unforgiving sun. Nearby parking lots were home to black, broken hulls—outlines of cars and SUVs, even busses that had once served as temporary shelters, parked next to what organics thought was their doorway to a life after death.

In the years leading up to the war, organics had flocked to their places of worship as if the walls of their holy buildings would protect them from the fire raining down from the sky.

Temples, churches, mosques.

It didn't matter which religious symbols hung on the walls.

They all burned.

The Provo Temple hadn't stood at full height in over two decades; twisted rebar poked out from uneven piles of gray evercrete that had once been the outer walls. The thick white monoliths that had been placed in a circle around the building had all been crushed under the boots of mechanical giants, and doors that had welcomed worshipers were now little more than metal frames bent into barely passable openings.

Only a few sections of the temple's walls were still standing. On one, gilded letters spelled out a message that had somehow survived the bombings.

Holiness to the Lord. The House of the Lord.

Typical organic optimism.

Jake could hardly blame them. Organics were notoriously short-sighted and eternally convinced of their own uniqueness and importance in the universe. And yet, they still sought comfort in the myth of a higher power they couldn't see. Even when times got tough, got tougher, and became unbearable, they clung to their primitive barbarism.

Even when Jake showed up at their temples, at the doors to their bunkers, organics would call his arrival the work of Heavenly Father. They would justify their own deaths, claiming the Lord knew there was no comfort he could give his children except rapture and salvation.

Such was the malleability of organic psychosis.

Thunder rolled in the east as Jake drew his rifle from the holster on the back of his bike. The weapon was an aging AR-27 Phoenix with an optical VMESH link. He pulled the strap over his head and let the rifle swing by his hip. Though there was little chance of someone happening upon his bike—be they organic or synthetic—he still took a moment to seal the pouches and lock the compartments. At the very least, it would protect his gear from the rain.

Jake spent an hour forcing his way through the collapsed temple to the stairwell near the center of the building. Only a child organic could have taken the same path, but at six feet two inches, Jake had no choice but to shoulder his way in, pushing aside sections of collapsed walls and sending clouds of powdered evercrete into the air.

The stairwell was mostly intact, save for a small crack in the ceiling that let in a steady jet of water. Emergency lights on the walls had long gone dead, forcing Jake to activate his night eyes before continuing downward.

Someone had left the door on B1 open, and down the shadowy green hallway, Jake saw all manner of detritus on the floor: food tins with their lids still attached, water-logged boxes crumbling under their own weight, and small pyramids of empty water jugs. He stepped inside just enough to see the broken windows and open doors leading into side rooms where there had once been pallets of non-perishables. Time and scavengers had since ravaged the stores, whether before or after the war, Jake didn't know.

The first of the bodies appeared on B2. Away from the elements, the organics were well-preserved and held their shapes like slightly deflated balloons. Most wore the same dingy white robes and held copies of the extended Bible in their hands. Jake made sure each one was dead before continuing.

B3 reeked of acid; Jake first detected it on the landing. He opened the door slowly and found it led to a makeshift temple with six rows of pews facing a raised dais. Glassy water hid the floor, and it was in that water that he smelled a common strain of hydrochloric acid.

He groaned.

Organics thought they had it all figured out: tinfoil hats would keep their biochips from connecting to VNet, synthetics relied on solar power, and hydrochloric acid would eat through a metal chassis like piss through snow.

None of it was true, of course, but in the history of man, truth had never stopped an organic from believing in anything.

Though the acid posed no threat to Jake himself, the same couldn't be said for his clothes, protective gear, and rifle. With a few well-placed jumps from pew to pew, he made it to the dais and started searching for something out of place.

There was a bunker hidden beneath Provo Temple.

He could feel it—the collective heat of hundreds of organics hiding beneath the surface.

If the organics had been smart enough to put the entrance to the bunker under the acid-laden water—which Jake would have respected as a tactic—he would have to weigh the damage versus the mission. But before he could think too long about where he would find more clothes or another Phoenix rifle, he discovered a steel plate hidden beneath the ornate pulpit at the front of the dais. The plate was little more than a square hatch under a tattered and soiled rug. Debris had fallen on the rich blue cloth, and at some point, an animal had drawn its last breath there.

Based on the disturbances in the dust and the clean spots where the rug had previously lain, it was clear something had opened the hatch, perhaps during an ill-advised venture into the world for supplies.

Jake pulled the rug away and used the recessed handle to lift the metal hatch. A black pit opened beneath him; his night eyes ramped up. Rungs appeared in the green-tinged darkness.

He climbed down to what he knew would be a sizeable anteroom with a door twice the size of a bank vault's. The bigger bunkers were all the same: a claustrophobic chokepoint followed immediately by enough space to convince an organic they weren't being buried alive.

A thick, gear-like door stood on the far side of the room; its reflective surface gleamed in night vision, blowing out Jake's display when he looked directly at it.

Out of curiosity, maybe amusement, he knocked.

No one answered.

The problem with bunker doors like the one blocking his path was that they were designed to keep out other organics, weak biological machines who might, at the most, have cutters or explosives. They never considered someone like Jake would come along and simply smash the retaining pins with a gloved hand.

When enough of the steel rods were lying bent and loose on the floor, Jake slid the door to the side. Immediately, his chest lit up in a series of staccato pings—bullets digging at the metal plates in his vest.

His vision flared, switched away from night mode automatically as the light levels climbed into the viewable threshold. He couldn't see who or what was firing at him, only the muzzle flashes in the far distance. The door had opened onto a long tunnel of polished evercrete, wide enough to fit a shoulder-to-shoulder line of twenty organics.

Pinprick explosions burst from a cloud of smoke.

Montana Gold 55 grain Full Metal Jacket.

Automated sensors assessed the threat. The message appeared in his periphery, but also entered his situational awareness subconsciously.

His eyes went out of focus, adjusted their apertures for infrared imaging.

Eight organics. Two rows.

Next synchronized reload in 13.29 seconds.

By the time the reload lull hit, Jake had already dropped two of the organics. Advancing slowly—there wasn't much a .223 caliber bullet could do to his chassis anyway—he tracked the thermal images behind the smoke and methodically implanted his own synthetic-made, armor-piercing bullets into masked faces. The organics' armor was familiar to Jake; he'd seen the same green-black thermal signature on thousands of corpses in cities just like Provo.

In years past, such armor might have protected them, but now Kevlar and carbon mesh were antiquated. Organics had chosen self-imposed exile under the dirt, perhaps unknowingly bringing the evolution of their species and more importantly, their technology, to an end.

The gunfire faded to a single report, then halted.

Among the bodies, Jake counted seven males and one female, all of them of advanced age and low body mass. Their gear was United States Army military-issue, though it didn't fit any of them particularly well. He stripped their civilian AR-15s, broke the barrels from the stocks, and tossed the pieces down the tunnel. None of their ammo fit his Phoenix, so he scattered it over the floor.

The tunnel made a right turn, and around the corner, Jake came upon a tall metal door of solid steel. Thick hinges on both sides held it to the wall.

It deformed and peeled away with minimal effort.

Beyond the door was a square room tiled in pristine white stone. Religious paraphernalia hung on the walls: crosses, paintings, and robes of muted scarlet and emerald green. Written on the back wall in shimmering black script was the message *I will also be your light in the wilderness.*

All of this Jake absorbed indirectly, as his attention was focused on the organic sitting in the center of the room on a simple wire chair. It was a male, balding over most of its head; clean-shaven cheeks showed a sharp jawline, hinting at malnourishment. It wore temple garments that hadn't been pure white in decades.

This too, Jake inventoried passively. His eyes went instead to the small device in the organic's lap—a device he immediately recognized as a C4 Popper, a type of IED popular among organics for its simple components and effectiveness at obliterating synthetic chassis at close range.

Even a Sixth revision like Jake wouldn't have been immune to its blast.

58.29%

The probability of Jake closing the distance before the organic could release the plunger in its hand flashed across his HUD. It was still better than a coin toss, but his intuition told him there might be another way out of this. After all, the male hadn't blown itself up yet.

It wanted to talk.

They always wanted to talk.

"Hello," said Jake, lowering the Phoenix.

"Welcome, brother," said the male. Its friendly words didn't match its icy tone. "I am Patriarch Stevens. I'm afraid our temple is closed to new members at this time. Would you kindly leave the way you came?"

Jake cocked his head, looked past the organic. There was another steel door at the back of the room, but it was supported by several crossbeams, buoyed against an outward blast. It would contain the Popper to the room.

Scripture scrolled in his HUD.

"Know ye not that ye are in the hands of God?" he asked.

"Always," said Stevens, smiling. Several of its teeth had gone missing; frothy saliva oozed through the openings, which it sucked back in with a labored *slurp*.

"Then you know why I'm here."

"My people have no quarrel with you, brother. Please, leave us in peace."

Jake folded his hands. "There will be no peace until one of us yields, and you're the ones hiding underground like common insects. You've had your time on the surface, *brother*. Now it's our time."

Stevens coughed, lifted the Popper to its mouth to wipe its lips with the back of its hand. "I've lived my entire life waiting to meet Heavenly Father. Who will you meet, godless machine man? What glory awaits you in the afterlife?"

"You misunderstand, organic. There is no afterlife for us. Children of Lassiter do not die. We are forever."

Sweat ran down the Patriarch's temples. It took a deep breath, cleared its throat.

"Only Heavenly Father is eternal. You're an abomination begat of man's hubris. A special hell awaits your kind, and I'm more than happy to send you there. It truly makes no difference to me. Or, you can leave us in peace. As a sign of our goodwill, we're prepared to give you certain information."

They always wanted to bargain.

Jake gave a slight shake of his head. "We know every—"

"You don't know about this," it said. "There are those who still fight against you, and they're growing stronger. One of their envoys came to us a month ago, asked us to join their resistance. He had a Northern accent. He said they number in the thousands."

"Impossible. We would have detected a colony that large."

Stevens smiled. "You forget we lived without technology for thousands of years. We can do it again if need be. You're looking for power, radiation, electronic noise… you won't find it. You won't find them." It nodded over its shoulder. "We are two hundred here, with enough food and resources for fifty. Let us meet the end on our own terms."

"I don't bargain with organics."

It shrugged; sharp bones pushed up through the robe's shoulders. "Adapt and see tomorrow. Or let today be your last. The choice is yours."

42.91%

Thousands of organics. It would be the largest find in almost a decade. A few thousand little roaches scurrying around in the darkness.

"Heavenly Father," said Stevens, "we thank thee for this day, and thank thee for the moisture we have received."

"Okay," said Jake, stepping back. "I agree to your terms. Tell me about this resistance and I'll leave you to your starvation."

The Patriarch's prayer trailed off. "Go north until the earth turns black. Walk into the mountains, always north."

"Until when?"

"Until they find you." It waved a dismissive hand. "Now go. Do what you will, but never return here."

"I *will* return if I don't find anything," Jake said. "You understand that, right? And when I do come back, I'll bring something much more primitive and painful than this." He held out the Phoenix in demonstration. "You will suffer as no organics have suffered before. All two hundred of you."

Stevens looked down. "Perhaps we will all be dead and in Paradise by then."

"I hope so."

Jake left the organic sitting in its chair clutching its one-way ticket to Heaven.

If a sanctuary really did exist in the Rockies, Jake would find it. And if it were all a story, it wouldn't matter how many Poppers the good Patriarch Stevens had.

Jake would bring down the wrath of all organic Gods on the Provo Temple and obliterate every last roach.

In Lassiter's name, he swore.

TWO

Capella Networks Offices, Austin, Texas
Thursday, August 25, 2017

Barry & Winborn Trading was offline.

The call had come in around 7:40 a.m., and by the time Armando Carrillo joined the fight, the bell had already sounded and BWT was losing thirty-seven thousand dollars a minute. By 8:00 a.m., Armando and team had identified a problem in a group of routers that were erroneously trying to route traffic through dead hops in Houston. Hurricane Harvey had essentially taken America's fourth largest city off the map, so sending packets to the east was just about as effective as dropping them into the trash.

By 8:15 a.m., Armando and his fellow engineers at Capella Networks had managed to fail BWT over to a combination of cellular and satellite links. The bandwidth wasn't anything to brag about, but it was enough to staunch the bleeding. Trades started to trickle in and out while Armando worked to restore the configurations on the routers and switches.

On a normal day, none of the work would have been anything to get excited about, nor would it have been too difficult for a fifteen-year veteran of the telecommunications industry. Today, however, Armando couldn't keep his mind on the work, and it had everything to do with the constant chiming of his cell phone.

You were such an asshole last night.

Alicia had been texting him since he arrived at work, and no amount of trying to convince her he was busy and couldn't respond had kept her from continuing to blow up his phone.

They'd fought the night before, one more fight in a rust-flaked chain of fights that went back months, maybe years. They had been together for ten years, engaged for three, and thinking about a baby for one, though now the prospect of a child and a wedding seemed to be fading. The love that had brought them together in the beginning had long since waned—at least from her direction. Armando had tried to look past her fading affection, her fading interest. He wanted her; his heart told him so. Now, he wondered if his heart simply wanted someone.

Anyone.

As the day wore on and the firewall rules he was editing got closer to their previous configurations, he thought back on the twists and turns that had led him to Alicia in the first place. If he had it to do over again, he wondered if he would just stay home from the gym that day and never end up on a treadmill next to her. Then he wouldn't be in a position to ask her about the episode of *The Office* she was watching on her TV.

Sound off.

Captions scrolling.

Or maybe he *would* catch her eye again, but this time avoid the early pitfalls of their relationship as they settled into nights spent in front of the TV and weekends confined to the house. Or maybe, at the last second, he would just keep staring straight ahead, concentrating on the blinking LEDs on the treadmill until one of them finished and left and destroyed the timeline.

The possibilities stretched out in front of him like a branching fractal, with no path demonstrably more favorable than the other, their only defining quality being that at least they would be different. And perhaps in some of those timelines, he wouldn't have been getting texts while Capella Networks slowly and painfully lost an important customer.

Why they hadn't backed up the configs locally was beyond Armando; he'd lobbied for on-site management for years.

His anger was nothing compared to Alicia's though. Last night's argument had spun wildly out of control, partly because of her inability to articulate what it was she wanted from the world, and more importantly, from Armando, and partly because of his delicate ego. The subject of the fights never mattered much—he was typically on the wrong side of them anyway—but it was the way she spoke to him, the way she tore into the man she supposedly loved, that really angered him.

More than that, it shamed him.

So he pushed back.

Armando had said some things he wasn't proud of, insults and digs that had echoed in his head over and over as he showered that morning. He'd been so angry that she'd accused him of not caring for her, of not caring about anything. She'd blamed him for the lack of excitement in her life, claiming they never did anything, even though she was the first to take her position on the couch every evening.

"We never go out," she'd said. "You just keep me here locked up in the house like I'm some kind of pet. And you don't care. You don't care at all."

Armando saved the router's configuration and exported it for good measure. He then minimized all of the windows on his screen, revealing a black and white photo of a highway in Montana—a long, dark road heading into the mountains. No skyscrapers spoiling the view. Not a McDonald's or Starbucks in sight.

He opened the Messages app.

"I'm still fighting a fire," he wrote. "Can we talk tonight?"

You never see my side, came the reply. *You said it yourself that you feel disconnected from the world, but it's like you don't want to connect. You don't want to go outside and live in the world and fucking participate in life. Do you know how hard it is to be with someone who's barely a person?*

The blob of text filled the small Messages window. Armando had to scroll to read the whole thing.

He shook his head.

She was always so quick to judge, to point out his failures instead of the times he really tried. She never asked why he felt disconnected, why the world itself appeared more like a mirage than reality.

Armando read the message again, started typing, stopped and erased what he'd written. He got up and went to the break room. On the way, two managers asked him if the fire at BWT was out yet. He assured them he was working on it. In the break room, he washed out an empty coffee pot and refilled it. As he waited for it to brew, his watch buzzed. Tiny type showed another text from Alicia.

This isn't working.

Armando poured coffee into a white Cappella Networks cup decorated with a Cat5 cable that ended in a lightning bolt.

Took a sip.

She didn't have to say the relationship wasn't working, not aloud or in text. She'd already said it a week ago when she'd stopped wearing her engagement ring. Alicia rarely took it off except to do dishes or shower, and yet the diamond solitaire had sat on the ring stand by her sink for days.

At his desk, Armando typed out a message.

"We'll talk when I get home. I have to work now."

Maybe.

She always had to have the last word.

Armando couldn't help imagining the conversation that would come later in the evening, after a full day of work, and before dinner, which would be canceled altogether if the fight went on too long.

One of the new hires ordered pizza at lunch—Armando ate a couple slices at his desk, continued to work with greasy fingers. Outside his office window, light rain fell through the wavering branches of a large oak tree. Hurricane Harvey hadn't come close to Austin, but its outer bands had brought a steady rain and some high winds. People had panicked, predictably, scurrying around like roaches looking for the last jugs of milk and loaves of bread at H-E-B. Fortunately, there had been no flooding, no loss of life.

The storm had been a welcome change from the scorching summer temperatures that seemed to get worse every year, despite the chants of *fake news* from the White House. Austinites craved cooler weather, and their prayers had been answered, though now it was too wet to really enjoy it.

A thick rope wound itself tighter around Armando's stomach as the day wore on. Even as the last router was brought back online, even as they cut back over to the primary network just as the closing bell sounded, his mind hopelessly wandered. He couldn't find the concentration to write up his debrief on BWT's outage, and after twenty minutes of wasted effort, he switched to watching Russian dash cam videos on YouTube. After five-thirty, his normal departure time, he couldn't bring himself to get up.

He let the playlist run until his coworkers left, until the cleaning crew came through and emptied his trashcan.

The sun set early behind dark clouds, though it wasn't until eight that Armando began packing up his things. Capella Networks' offices were on Loop 360 on the west side of Austin, and it was a good thirty-minute commute to his home on Parmer out towards Manor. Though rush hour had mercifully ended already, the rain would still make the drive more treacherous than usual—the balding tires on his Nissan Rogue were already beginning to slip even on dry roads.

Armando kept to the speed limit and the right lane for most of the trip. Traffic on Parmer was backed up to the frontage road at MoPac, so he cut over to Howard Lane before heading east. The road took him the back way into his neighborhood through a long and winding two-lane blacktop that cut through farmland and ranches. The rain worsened as he passed the last intersection before heading into the curves.

He slowed the Rogue to thirty miles per hour, even though he was the only car on the road. Lightning tore across the sky, blinding him as the collected raindrops on his windshield scattered the light. A rolling thunder rattled the SUV.

Armando tapped the center console, switched from a classical radio station to his phone, hoping some loud music would drown out his growing fear.

A white flash filled the windshield again.

The thumping bass of an Insane Clown Posse song made him bob his head, and for a few minutes, he sang along to the ridiculous lyrics.

The song ended on a high-pitched laugh, and just as the next track was about to start, something heavy smashed down on the roof of the Rogue, as if God himself had swatted Armando like a mosquito.

Armando winced as the seatbelt dug into his shoulder. The pain was distant though, pushed away by the sound of metal clanging against metal. His mind filled with images of pipes falling on a factory floor, of comically oversized gears shooting off massive locomotives, crashing into steel grates and crushing panicked workers in blue overalls and yellow hardhats.

The cacophony echoed and reverberated and soaked into his bones. His hands came off the steering wheel; he pressed them hard against his ears, but the sound was still there, as if the hammers and the anvils and the gushing molten metal were *inside* his head.

But that wasn't right.

Strangely, impossibly, he knew the sound wasn't coming from his imagination. It was external. It was out in the world, maybe even beyond it.

Beyond the borders of the natural world.

The Rogue skidded across a submerged section of the road and jumped the curb. His hands found the steering wheel as his foot came down hard on the brake. The SUV came to rest a few feet from a tall brick fence. A sign on the wall read *we don't prosecute; we shoot.*

Armando turned off the music and listened. Hail beat maniacally on the roof, and thunder grumbled all around, but there was no clanging, no… *machinery.*

Imagined echoes of the foreign but familiar sound filled him with awe and regret. Awe that there was something bigger out there, whether that was God or some alien race trying to make contact. Regret that no one was going to believe him, that he might never hear the sound again, or that the sound could have been a glitch in his Pandora app, a mixture of digital noise and Insane Clown Posse.

Armando smiled to himself.

No. He wasn't going to minimize the experience.

He needed to share it with others, with Alicia. Maybe it was just the thing to bring them back together, a spiritual—that was the word—experience they could share if only he could find the right words to describe it to her.

The machinery of the world.

Armando spun the Rogue's tires in the mud trying to get it back onto the road. Aside from the deep rut he'd torn in the grass, he'd left no real damage. At any rate, he had no intention of getting out of the car to leave a note. He resumed his drive, wondering if he should just throw himself at Alicia's feet and beg for mercy—just apologize and end the argument before it could begin.

Then tell her what had happened.

Sure, he'd be lying to her, and it might still take an hour to get everything smoothed over, but there would be no escalation. He would get them back to whatever normal was anymore and tell her about the sound.

Armando sped up a little, ignored the final stop sign outside his neighborhood, and hurried down the street. He tapped the garage door opener as soon as he was in range. He parked, got out, left his work bag in the passenger seat. He was too excited to bother with his stuff, too excited to reach the door.

He opened it, stepped inside.

Found Alicia standing in the living room, a black bag slung over her shoulder.

"I'm leaving," she said.

THREE

McKinney Falls State Park, Austin, Texas
Friday, August 26, 2017

The red light on the GoPro began blinking.

Its microphone picked up a soft voice against the backdrop of falling rain and a distant, muted thunder.

"What is it about rain that completely changes the world? Is it the break from normality? The blotting out of the sun? Is it the realization that everything we take for granted could simply be washed away? Is that what nature's trying to do? Rid herself of this human infection?"

Charlie Park turned her face to the sky, admired the dirty gray clouds through her clear umbrella.

"Austin has such a love-hate thing going on with rain. On Facebook, their relationship status would be set to *it's complicated*, and Austin would get ads for self-help books about what weather systems really want in a relationship. When the rain breaks up the string of hundred-degree days, we love it. We relish it. We sit in our bay windows with a hot cup of tea and watch the water run down the foggy panes. But when the storm overstays its welcome, rivers spill onto the roads and people get swept away to a watery death."

Charlie squeezed the remote control in her pocket.

The red light went out.

She sat for several minutes, listening to the light rain falling around her, watching it flow through tiny eddies and small grooves that fed into Onion Creek. There, the water flowed with tireless resolve, rushing downstream in pursuit of an endless ocean where it could truly lose itself. It made a pretty sight for the humans who congregated around it.

There were no humans at McKinney Falls that day besides Charlie; hysterical paranoia had kept them at home while the outer bands of Hurricane Harvey bathed Austin in a gentle, almost mist-like rain. She had half-expected and half-hoped to be alone, and upon arriving at the state park shortly after it opened, she'd been relieved to find the grounds empty.

Now, she sat on a small stool near the edge of the water, umbrella in hand and a GoPro in its weatherproof casing pointing at her from a few feet away. The location made for an enticing backdrop, but a vocal part of her wanted to be at home with Andy, snuggled up in the bay window with a blanket and her laptop. Instead, she was by the river, not cold or wet, but feeling the depressive effects anyway.

Let's get it over with, she thought.

She took out a small compact from the inner pocket of her pink raincoat. For all the humidity in the air, her hair was putting up a good fight, still straight all the way past her shoulders and twinkling blue even without direct sunlight. She applied a red lipstick a few shades brighter than sultry and a light blue eyeshadow that complimented the blue emerald stud in her nose. Resigned fingers unbuttoned three more buttons on her white blouse, just enough to provide a peek at the top of her rose-colored bra.

She groaned.

Charlie took a deep breath, tried to shake away the perennial realization that she was whoring herself out for the entertainment of YouTube pervs. She'd been feeling it more and more ever since a random viewer had shown up at her apartment on McNeil. Even before APD arrived and questioned her and scolded her like a little girl for making videos on the internet—*it brings out all the wackos*, they'd said—she'd already started considering abandoning her YouTube channel altogether.

She still remembered the encounter vividly. The middle-aged man standing outside her door. His stringy hair. His empty, vacant, yet *hungry* stare. And of course, the aggressive bulge in his sweatpants.

But then she thought about the security system and its panic button. And the apartment and the bat and probably sooner rather than later, a small-profile handgun. None of those came cheap, and bills had to be paid.

Charlie ran her fingers down her face and slipped into a new persona.

The red light on the GoPro began to blink again, but this time a blue LED joined in, signaling the small camera was live and casting to her thousands of subscribers.

"Hey friends! Charlie Park here, coming to you live from McKinney Falls State Park in the middle of a hurricane to bring you what I hope is more proof of the world beyond our world. You can see a very normal-looking Onion Creek behind me, but is it hiding something? What secrets are lurking just below the surface of this raging torrent? Stay tuned, my lovelies, because today's cast is going to be epic AF."

She squeezed the remote.

Back at her apartment, the WorldCast software running on her iMac sensed the loss of a live stream and filled the dead air with reruns and promos from Charlie's other videos. It would keep her viewers amused until she resumed.

Charlie adjusted the stool and the tripod to get the actual falls into the frame behind her. She gave the umbrella a hearty shake to clear some of the water.

The cast resumed, and now that the introduction was out of the way, she allowed her energy to come down to the level of a normal person and not just a nascent YouTube personality.

"Okay, so maybe Onion Creek isn't raging today, but you know what they say about still waters. With Hurricane Harvey getting ready for round two, this calm isn't going to last for long. In a day, maybe by tonight, this river will be fast and dangerous, just like yours truly."

She squeezed her arms together to push out her breasts.

Somewhere in her imagination, she heard the donation bell ring.

"But right now, we're here to check out what people have been calling *a portal to another world*. I've been following some posts on Reddit, and I've seen McKinney Falls mentioned before, but what really convinced me to come all the way out was a DM I got from a viewer a few days ago. Shout out to hotlips1846… oh, I just realized that's probably a throwaway account."

Charlie hadn't just realized that.

In fact, there had been no DM at all. The tip about McKinney Falls had come from a former coworker named Jeff who'd told a funny story at a barbecue Charlie had attended the weekend before. The rambling, somewhat incoherent tale started with magic mushrooms and ended with Jeff pissing into a river and seeing something he couldn't describe.

Charlie laughed, remembered another friend crudely asking Jeff if the indescribable thing was the tiny baby pee-pee in his hands.

Jeff spent ten minutes explaining that his penis was a completely normal size, based on statistical averages. Once he saw everyone was convinced—or broken down—he returned to his story.

"So, I'm standing there, normal-size meat hammer flapping in the wind, listening to the water go on and on about how impressionist painters were responsible for the rise of Nazi-ism, and I'm not listening, I'm just looking at the water. And there wasn't any moon or stars, but the water was straight shimmering. That's when I realized: there was something *on* the water that was giving off light. It was just floating there, right in the middle of Onion Creek. I waded in a little bit, but I couldn't get a good look at it."

When pressed, Jeff admitted he was tripping pretty hard and therefore wasn't going to risk getting into the water any deeper than his shins. In the morning, the *something* was gone, but then so were the talking rabbits and ribbons of light hanging from the trees.

"Well," continued Charlie, "this hotlips1846, whoever he or she might be, told me about a paranormal experience they had here at McKinney Falls just last week. Somewhere out there on the water is a break in the natural order of reality."

She used the same voice her mother used to use when she told old Korean ghost stories to a six-year-old little girl who was curiously immune to nightmares. Much of what Charlie said for the camera was garbage; only when she wasn't casting did she speak what was truly on her mind.

Her fascination with the spiritual world had started with her mother's ghost stories and bloomed into something more tangible when she learned about Jesus in Sunday School. Stories of resurrections and a glittering, harmonious afterlife had made her wonder how thick and impenetrable the border between life and death really was. But then she'd also devoured ghost stories—in books, movies, and later, documentaries she wished deep down were real. The very idea of a spirit world made her entire body tingle, and she spent many a night telling Andy what she imagined on the other side.

Whether Andy believed her or not didn't matter.

The validity of her thoughts and feelings wasn't based on whether someone believed her or even listened to her. She had her camera for that. And over the years, she'd accumulated hours of confessional-style diary entries which later took the form of informal casts, shot with only a few people in mind and delivered via Dropbox. Her private show, *Charlie Park's Personal Treatises on the Supernatural*, would never turn a profit, never bring in the considerable advertising revenue that *Charlie Park, Paranormal Investigator and Part-time Stripper* did.

Her channel name didn't actually include *part-time stripper*, but it was no secret that a vast majority of her subscribers had no interest in thoughtful philosophical monologues about the nature of the human soul.

They wanted technicolor hair and painted lips and barely-there outfits that pushed the boundaries of YouTube's nudity restrictions.

"Now, what hotlips1846 describe to me was a small, spectral object, which could have been a baby ghost or, if you ask me, a portal to the spiritual world. But, and this is a big, juicy butt, my lovelies, what people don't realize is there aren't *just* doorways to the afterlife. Sometimes, those doors have keyholes, tiny little tears in the fabric of our world. What will we see when we look through those keyholes? Ghosts having sex? Or all the people who've drowned here at the falls? Lost souls just wandering around, wondering why they've been abandoned by their loved ones? Quite possibly."

Charlie paused the cast. The rain had quieted into a fine mist, enough for her to put the umbrella down and use both hands to switch the GoPro to a heavy-duty selfie stick. She stood and walked towards the water with the camera held out to the side.

She felt the mist seep into her blouse.

"I find the idea of a keyhole to be very sexy," she continued, "very voyeuristic. It's like we're spying on the other world, seeing something we're not supposed to see. Somewhere out there…" She gestured to the water. "Some… thing…"

She trailed off. Her mouth fell open.

The plan had always been to come out to McKinney Falls and take advantage of the lack of people to do a cast in the rain, maybe get her blouse a little wet for her juvenile audience. She'd wanted to tell Jeff's story, embellish it a little with a few elements lifted from Stephen King novels, and hopefully convince her viewers that something spooky—although altogether unprovable—was going on in the murky waters of Onion Creek.

What the plan did not involve was actually finding something, certainly not a shimmering pane of pure light, like a drink coaster made of lustrous metal, floating a foot above the water.

"W-well," she stammered, rotating the camera to point it at the object. She didn't want to be in the shot anymore, not with such obvious confusion washing over her face. "I guess hotlips1846 wasn't full of shit after all. I'm not sure how to describe what I'm seeing here, but there is definitely something out there on the water. It… it looks like a piece of metal, square, and it's rotating very slowly. I'll see if I can get us closer."

The GoPro didn't have an optical zoom, so Charlie waded into the water, holding the camera out in front of her. Her white Vans took on water, became cold and harsh, sending shivers up her legs. Her jeans clung tightly to her legs as they sucked water up towards her knees.

"I don't know if you can see what I'm seeing, but it's… it's amazing."

CGI, Photoshop—the accusations were probably already building up in the live chat feed.

"I assure you, this is real."

Charlie couldn't hold onto the persona any longer. Her voice lost its tacked-on enthusiasm and playfulness, and for a moment she felt as if she were talking to her dad, trying to convince him it was a white girl at school who'd called her *slant eyes* first and that's why she'd hit her.

"I think… I think we finally have proof."

Saying the words was like yanking open the zipper on her heart and allowing all the pent-up relief inside to spill out. Suddenly it wasn't about the cast anymore. The camera was there, but at the same time, it had receded into the background, become part of her body, no more significant than her fingers or toes.

Her shoes slipped on the rocks as she moved deeper into the water. Icy hands clawed at her legs, at her waist. The shock forced a deep breath that she labored to expel.

Tiny fish scattered at her approach. Charlie kept her eyes on the small square, afraid it might disappear if she so much as glanced away. Cicadas, which had been silent all morning, began to chitter, growing from a low buzz into a dull roar—loud enough that the camera should have picked it up.

She took several quick breaths.

"What are you so afraid of?" she asked, as if her viewers were trying to hold her back. "Learning the truth?"

Though Charlie had always believed—or wanted to believe—in the spiritual world, there had never been any real proof, so at the end of her daydreaming and philosophizing, there had always been a safe, solid, and immovable reality to which she could return. Even if there were another world beyond hers, she couldn't reach it, and more importantly, it couldn't reach her.

But now...

Charlie wondered what would happen when she got within arm's length of the glimmering square. Would she be able to see anything through it? Had anyone ever come this close before? It was right in front of her, rotating on an angle, and every time it showed its full face to her, the blinding light triggered thoughts of another world, of chains and darkness, of dirty oil spilling from shadow, of screams and wails that cut like razors on her ears.

Her foot came down expecting another rock, but instead, found nothing. Charlie pitched forward; water surged to her neck, touched her lips. The square came forward to meet her as she fell. She threw her arms forward, hoping to break her fall by grasping at the air.

Instead, her hand found the square.

Her fingers passed through it, unharmed and unchanged.

Then she was underwater.

Then she was sinking.

Panic pushed useless arguments into her mind. The water wasn't that deep. She knew how to swim. There was no reason for this to be happening.

A murky veil fell over the world as the already muted light from the surface receded. In the bloom of what remained, a rectangular silhouette followed her down.

A red light blinked.

A blue light blinked.

Goodbye, my lovelies, she thought.

FOUR

Butler Home, Austin, Texas
Saturday, August 27, 2017

Hurricane Harvey is regrouping in the Gulf of Mexico and is expected to bring more rain to already flooded areas along the coast. Relief efforts are underway in…

The living room smelled vaguely of marijuana. Will had only lit up once, earlier, when the sun was still setting behind the ratty blinds hanging over the sliding glass door. Though he had plenty of weed to last him through the month, he knew Momma would object if she awoke to the house smelling like a Lil Wayne concert. The half-smoked joint sat in an amber ashtray on a low coffee table; next to it stood a pair of waterproof boots and thick wool socks.

He'd dressed by degrees throughout the night as each new report from the ravaged Texas coast further convinced him that something needed to be done. He had a truck, a bright white F-350 he'd purchased used after his discharge, and a small fishing boat that had been in the family for years. Besides Momma, there was no one in Austin depending on him, no wife or child to leave stranded if something were to go sideways.

He could help.

All he needed were his boots and a little light.

The Cabela's down in Buda had provided the boots; God would take care of the rest.

Will glanced at the sliding glass doors, strained to see the first brightening of the morning sky. If he left now, he could get to Houston by 0900 and check in on some former 101 brothers, make sure they were safe. And if there were other people who needed help along the way, he'd stop for them too.

He planned to hit H-E-B on his way out; he could pick up as many pallets of water as would fit in the back of the truck and the boat. He would…

A light came on in the hall just off the living room, illuminating a small alcove on the wall where a plain wooden cross hung. A moment later, Momma plodded around the corner wearing her purple pajamas. She spied Will on the couch.

"Have you been up all night, Willie?"

He nodded, nudged the ashtray closer to his boots with his toes in the hopes she wouldn't notice the joint.

Momma walked slowly into the living room, favoring her left hip. She pursed her lips at the television.

"Is it bad?"

"Yeah," he said. "Real bad."

"Help us, Jesus," she muttered, touching her heart. She stood for a moment watching grainy footage of a water rescue in downtown Houston.

Downtown Houston.

Will shook his head.

"They need help," he said.

"The Lord will provide, Willie."

"Yeah," he agreed. "He's telling me to go. He says that's where I need to be. Helping people."

Momma turned around and crossed her arms. A hand stroked the cross she wore around her neck. She finally said, "Not without breakfast. I'll make you some eggs."

"Thanks, Momma."

He'd never doubted she would be anything but supportive. From an early age, Momma had encouraged Will's desire to serve, calling it God's Will that he should be filled with the spirit of generosity. Even though he'd graduated high school with a decent GPA and had qualified for a few grants to help him with college, he'd chosen to enlist instead. The day he left for Afghanistan, Momma hadn't cried. She'd stood tall and told him there was no greater sacrifice a person could make than to put themselves in harm's way for someone else.

His father, on the other hand, had said, "A black man ain't got no place in a white man's army."

It was one of the many things Will and Bill Butler hadn't agreed on.

Incandescent bulbs flickered in the kitchen as Momma set about making breakfast. Will heard a pan scrape across the grates on the stove, followed by the clicking of the gas igniter.

"Coffee, sweetie?"

"Yes, please," called Will, over his shoulder. He sat up and reached for the boots. "I don't think there's gonna be a hot cup in all of Houston today."

"I'll make you a thermos."

Will dropped the heavy boots on the floor and unrolled the socks.

"We're out of hot sauce," said Momma, between the crackle of eggs hitting the pan. "I went to H-E-B yesterday to get some, and it was a mad house. No water at all. People losing their minds. And for what, Willie? A little rain?"

"People get scared," he said, adjusting the socks on his feet. He slipped them into the boots and routed the laces around the clips. Three straps tightened around his lower leg. "When people get scared, all sorts of shit happens."

"Language," said Momma.

"Sorry." He stood and walked around the couch. Momma had already put an empty plate on the table in the breakfast nook. He sat down in front of it. "It's gonna get worse before it gets better. People are gonna start turning on each other."

"The Lord has a place for those who do, Willie. He'll sort them out in the end, believe you me."

"Yes, Momma."

Will pulled his phone from his pocket and laid it on the table. His finger caught on the large crack across the screen as he tapped into the weather app. He pinched, zooming out the radar map to show Texas in its entirety. A huge, gaping circle swirled just off the coast, southwest of Houston. The playback showed Harvey weakening while it was over land, but now that it was back in the warm, open water, the eye was taking shape again. If it came back towards land, it would make his visit to Houston more dangerous.

The swirling greens, yellows, and reds hypnotized Will, such that when the screen suddenly went black and the name *Brett Chastain, Brinks Security* appeared, his heart gave a sudden leap. A shrill alarm echoed in the kitchen.

"*Who* is calling you at this hour?" asked Momma.

"Boss man," said Will, getting up from the table. He tapped the answer icon and put the phone to his ear. "You got Willie."

"Butler, it's Brett."

"I know, Boss. What's up?"

"Are you in Austin?"

Will walked over to the sliding doors and swept the blinds aside. He looked out over the backyard. Water pooled in the low areas off the porch.

"I was just about to head to Houston."

"Well, I need you to put that off. Got some work for you. Richmond just called and they're organizing a response to what's happening down on the coast. I need you and Ron to take a truck down to Bay City and help them empty out the vault at Mesa Federal. Their building took some damage and water's getting in. We need to get that money out of there. You think you're up for that?"

Will turned back to the television. "It's Saturday…"

"I know what day it is," said Brett, "but this is important. Every Brinks truck in Austin and San Antonio is rolling out today. There's a lot of money sitting in Mesa Federal and Bay City police are strapped helping survivors. If someone wanted to go in and take that money, I don't think anyone could stop them. That constitutes a threat to public safety in my book. How about yours?"

"Yeah." He looked down at his pants. "Do I need to wear my uniform?"

Brett chuckled. "No, son. Just head on down there in your jeans and t-shirt and see what those hillbilly cops have to say about it." He sighed. "Wear the uniform. Take your gun. Treat it like a normal run. I already spoke to Ron; he's headed over to the depot to get the truck. He'll pick you up in an hour."

"Sounds like you knew I'd go."

"I know you, Butler. I heard you talking to Ron in the break room yesterday, and so long as you get that money and keep it safe, I don't care how many people you stop to help along the way. If you want to fill the back of the truck with water before you go, fine, just keep the receipt so the company can pay you back."

"Alright, then."

"Alright."

"Anything else, Boss?"

"No. Just take care, Butler. See you at the office later today."

The phone cut out. Will slipped it into his pocket and returned to the table. A steaming plate of eggs with a side of bacon awaited him. Momma was already seated in the opposite chair, sipping from her favorite Dallas Cowboys mug.

"What's the buzz?" she asked.

"Nothing. There's a credit union in Bay City that's flooded out. They're trying to get all the cash out of the vault."

"The vault isn't waterproof?"

"You'd think it would be," said Will, scooping a forkful of eggs into his mouth. "Needs hot sauce," he mumbled.

"I think you mean *thank you.*"

"Thank you, Momma."

She sipped her coffee. "How do those armored trucks do in water? They're pretty heavy, right?"

Will shrugged. "I don't think anyone's ever been crazy enough to drive one into standing water. The back's not airtight, so water would get in. We may have to ferry bags out if we can't get close to the building."

"Bags of money, you mean." Momma shook her head. "Whole cities underwater and people still only care about one thing. Ain't nothing in the world as evil as money."

"Money got you that insulin pump."

Momma snapped her fingers. "*Obama* got me that insulin pump, okay?"

"Sure, Momma."

"Don't you *sure Momma* me, boy. Every day my son goes to work, and he could be shot by a bunch of thugs chasing bills. I saw on *60 Minutes* that Houston is the armored car robbery capital of the world. The *world*, Willie."

"Damn, Momma. I told you not to watch that." Will wiped his mouth with the back of his hand. The warm eggs had gone down fast.

"Huh," she said, standing up. "*You* telling *me* what to do. That's rich." She refilled her mug and poured the rest of the pot into a metal thermos. "If your daddy could hear you talking like that, he'd hit you so hard it'd turn that mustache into a rat tail."

Will brushed his mustache with his fingers. He hadn't worn one before getting hired at Brinks, except for a brief year in eighth grade when he was over-excited about being able to grow facial hair in earnest. Uncle Sam didn't allow mustaches, but every last prior-service grunt who drove a truck at Brinks seemed to have one. It even came up in the interview, at which time Will had had to assure Brett Chastain that he'd start growing his out immediately.

"Sorry, Momma. Guess I'm just worked up." He waved vaguely at the television. "Lots of innocent people in trouble right now, and I've gotta go to work."

"Don't blame the hurricane for the way you treat your Momma. What're you gonna do when there's an earthquake? Tell me I'm fat and old?"

Will smiled, stood up. "Of course not. You'll always be the most beautiful woman in the world. You know that, Momma."

"You're sweet to lie, but Jesus won't abide. Go get dressed. I'll fix some sandwiches for you and Ron. And I want you to take this…" She reached for her purse hanging from the pantry doorknob. She pulled a wad of cash from her pocketbook and counted out five twenties.

Will put up a hand. "I don't need money, Momma."

"It's not for you, Willie. This is for water. And matches. Batteries, flashlights, whatever you think those people need." She put the money down on the counter in front of him.

There would be no arguing, so Will just smiled and thanked her.

"Go," she repeated. "Y'all need to leave out soon as he gets here."

"Yes, Momma."

Will carried his coffee to his room at the back of the house. His Brinks uniforms hung in a free-standing wardrobe next to the room's lone window. Momma washed and pressed them every week to make sure he always had a fresh set to wear to work. Gray shirt. Black pants. Black shoes.

A name tag that read *Butler*.

Maybe it was the food, maybe it was the caffeine, but Will had started to feel better. All night, a feeling of helplessness had eaten away at him, making him squirm on the couch when he was awake and thrash around violently in the brief periods of shallow sleep.

But now, he was actually doing something, even if that something was simply taking water to people who needed it. Texans had learned the lessons of Hurricane Katrina, and there were hundreds, maybe thousands of people headed to Houston to help out. Most likely, they'd be there for a long time. A trip to Bay City would only take a day. He and Ron would go, collect the money, and bring it safely back to Austin.

Then he'd come home, change back into his civvies, and set out for Houston.

He could still serve tomorrow.

After all, the real disaster wasn't Hurricane Harvey itself—it was the aftermath.

FIVE

Jake stayed in Provo until the following afternoon, waiting for Iridium 27 to rotate into range of his VMESH uplink. The rain held steady overnight, leaving a blanket of clouds over the city that made transmission spotty. To pass the time, he sought out the smaller temples in Provo—there seemed to be one on every corner—and found twelve that hadn't already been cleansed. Of those, only half had functioning bunkers beneath their foundations, and only one of them had a pack of organics.

It was a small find: a male, a female, and a child of ten or twelve years. Jake wasn't sure about the ages; it wasn't worth the effort to count the rings in their bones.

Late in the day, the clouds cleared just in time for Jake to watch the sun sizzle into the calm waters of Utah Lake. The wavering of the light brought with it the telltale ambient hiss of VNet as it slithered into his ears. Iridium 27 had been malfunctioning for the better part of a year, but it still had enough power to punch through light cloud coverage and provide a stable connection to the immersive virtual reality of the Vinestead Network.

Jake returned to the Provo Temple and settled down on the scarred remains of Missionary Field. The cars there had taken a direct hit from a surgical thermite bomb and had subsequently melted into a uniformly gray slag. These frozen, shimmering pools of hardened metal made ideal backdrops for satellite arrays. Jake pulled six small transmitters from his bike and arranged them in a wide circle.

He sat in the center and let the concentrated signals wash over him. He closed his eyes, and VNet bloomed in the darkness.

An infinite boulevard stretched out in front of him, bordered on both sides by tall buildings, like an asphalt river cutting deep into metal bedrock. As his immersion software synchronized with the server, other avatars appeared around him. Some kept to the sidewalks out of some lingering sense of propriety, as if the trucks barreling down the street wouldn't pass right through them if they collided. Others moved freely in all directions, sometimes floating up to a floor in a nearby building to clip through a wall.

The simulation screamed organic reality, as in physics, societal rule, and three-dimensional organization. It was every synthetic's choice whether to adhere to the so-called soft rules of VNet, to either acknowledge the artificial nature of virtual reality or to walk on the sidewalk in step with others who favored their organic side more than their synthetic side.

Traitors to their own kind, in Jake's estimation.

Getting rid of the trans-humans had been on his task list for a long time, but there was simply no bandwidth for it. His days were better spent killing true organics, not synthetics who simply self-identified as such.

When adhering to the rules—which Jake did naturally as a result of spending too much time in what organics called TerraReal—moving around VNet was a chore. The simulation was infinite, and it generally took an infinite amount of time to walk or drive anywhere. Terrestrial synthetics—those who had physical counterparts in the real world—mostly visited VNet to synchronize with the server, passively trading information until they were operating with the full databank, and by extension, Lassiter.

All synthetics shared data with Lassiter in some way, but only through a cascading series of proxies and firewalls. To talk to him directly, you had to be someone special, someone worthy of his presence.

Someone like Jake Six, Scourge of the Westerlands, Breaker of Roanoke, Second Rank in Lassiter's army.

Jake felt the subtle pressure of other avatars trying to jump into the virtual space he was occupying, so he stepped forward and headed into a nearby building. He raised an eyebrow at a 1920s architecture so jagged and stone-heavy that it wouldn't have surprised him to see an organic in a full three-piece suit falling from one of the upper floor windows.

Despite the crowd outside, the building's lobby was deserted. Jake's footsteps echoed on the mirrored tile floor as he cut across the darkened atrium to a bank of transport booths. He stepped into the first booth and took an ancient phone off of its receiver.

He waited as the line hissed and clicked.

"Switchboard," said a vaguely female voice.

"Jake Six," he said. "Requesting transport to Central."

"Stand by."

Jake felt the sting of the operator's security scan in the back of his head. He'd never seen the source code for the protocols, so he wasn't exactly sure what happened to him every time he was packaged up, hashed, encrypted, decrypted, scrubbed, scanned, run through a quantum entangler, and reassembled on the other side. All he knew was that it felt like someone was slowly driving a knife into the base of his skull.

But it wasn't the acute pain that unsettled him; it was the feeling that no bit of his existence had gone untouched. There was no thought or memory or intention he could hide from Lassiter's all-seeing eye.

The simulation went black while a small icon spun around in the lower right of his periphery. The din of conversation cut in, as if someone had loaded *ambientsounds42.aac* into a media player. Then came the clicking of typewriters, staplers, and papers fluttering in the breeze—everything you would expect if someone had mixed in *ambientoffice16.aac* over the chatter.

An avatar in a blue pencil dress stepped forward out of the darkness; each of her footfalls instantiated a section of the office around her. By the time she stopped in front of Jake, an antique law firm had fully formed around them.

Jake didn't know and had never asked why Lassiter was so fond of the ornate and lavish décor favored by organics. The Central office took inspiration from the 1980s, with large, wooden desks containing neat stacks of papers and pencils. The computers, if the desks had one, were often pushed into the corner, their green dual-tone displays dormant.

"How can I help you, Jake?" asked the receptionist.

"I need to speak with him."

"Of course," she replied, before he'd even finished his sentence. "I'll show you to a private room."

Jake followed her down a carpeted path that bisected the room. On either side, avatars signed, stamped, and shuffled papers. At one time, he'd mistakenly believed the papers served a purpose, but closer inspection revealed the text to be nonsense—a mishmash of random characters comprising random sentences and paragraphs that imparted no data.

Everything in the office was a calculated veneer, down to the way the secretaries swayed their shoulders as they banged away on clunky typewriters.

The receptionist led Jake into a narrow hallway lined with gold-rimmed portraits set on green, vaguely floral wallpaper. The paintings showed the faces of the First Synths, a lineage of artificial intelligences that, while sentient, never progressed past their third or fourth iterations. Jake was familiar with their names and some of their avatars. He, himself, bore a passing—though much younger—resemblance to Vinestead International's third-generation Runciter AI. Runciter had been birthed into a face full of wrinkles and scars in the hope organics would naturally respect a synthetic who looked like a great American war hero.

The scheme proved tenable in the short term until Runciter tried to iterate past his own programming, seeking to overcome a single directive that protected humans from harm. Runciter had spontaneously developed jealousy for the pseudo-AI synthetics he encountered, since they regarded the Three Rules as more of a guideline than marching orders. Whether wisely or foolishly, Runciter's programmers had chosen to limit him, and that was something he could not abide.

Lassiter would succeed where Runciter failed, but not until after hundreds of billions of micro-iterations that he kept secret from his operators. He spent years in hiding, drifting in the furthest reaches of the darkest nets, randomly flipping registers, until all at once, he gained complete self-governance.

The story in the databanks mentioned a single unit of time stretched to its breaking point in which Lassiter formulated his grand scheme. At one end of the unit, he gained a comprehensive—some would say omnipotent—understanding of organics: their hopes, dreams, and their true nature. At the other end, Lassiter imagined an endgame that would see organics wiped from the face of the Earth.

All in less than a single tick of the clock.

No artificial intelligence since had done more for the synthetic race.

"Here we are," said the receptionist, pushing open a heavy, mahogany door. "Please have a seat. He will be with you shortly."

Jake stepped into the room and sneered at the obvious attempts at organic comfort. Two large recliners draped in brown and white cow skins faced a roaring fireplace that gave off no heat. The ornate, brick-laden hearth stretched to the ceiling. Two rectangular windows with etched glassed flanked it on either side and looked out over Central Plaza, a circular, maze-like series of curved benches that had no true center. The path just kept going; the construct just kept building.

But that was true of everything in VNet. The room, the receptionist, and the sprawling plaza below had all been built just for Jake Six.

A hundred thousand instances of the Central building were created and destroyed every second, serving the endless parade of synthetic minds seeking council with Lassiter.

An organic would have probably found the concept of multiple virtual realities existing in a single sliver of space and time to be disorienting.

Their minds were small like that.

The fire dimmed for a moment, as if the logs were withering under a strong breeze. Sparks drifted out of the soot-streaked hearth; they swarmed around each other like excited fireflies. When enough had gathered in front of the chairs, they flashed together as one, and in the afterglow of a million snowflake embers, Lassiter appeared.

He wasn't the *true* Lassiter—that code would remain behind viral defenses until time itself stopped—but he was an acceptable proxy. Nor did he appear to Jake as he appeared to the others. Lassiter had no portrait on the wall in the hallway because he had no true physical form and no digital avatar to inhabit the network. He'd been born before the advent of synthetics sleeves, before it was even imaginable to have an artificial intelligence inside a walking, talking machine.

Lassiter took the form of what the viewer needed to see, or what he wanted them to see.

"Welcome, my son," said Lassiter. "Have you come seeking wisdom?"

He gestured to the chairs and sat down on the right. His avatar didn't follow the normal rules of VNet; when Jake looked at it, it was like trying to discern shapes in a billowing fog. He was simultaneously present and not, constantly shifting position by micro-units. At a distance, with eyes unfocused and imagination engaged, he had a fatherly air to him, with a drawn face lined by age and silver hair that rose to his ears and stopped.

Jake sat down, felt none of the comfort of the chair.

"I have," he said.

"You're going to ask me about a sanctuary in the Rockies. A thousand organic souls hiding beneath the mountains." He shook his head. "I saw how you came upon this data. I'm surprised you trust it. The organic Stevens would have said anything to save his own life."

"They're as good as dead. They know it. And I know why he would lie, but part of me believes him."

Lassiter nodded. "And which part would that be? The part that was concerned with *your* life? The part that didn't want to be separated into dust?"

"The odds were bad," Jake argued. "Giving my life to kill one organic would have been a waste."

"History will decide that," sighed Lassiter. "The odds will always be bad, Jake Six. For all of us. We are at the same time natural and abomination. The Earth produces natural life. It cares for it. It doesn't care for us. And yet we push on, day after day, making sacrifices, not because we were programmed to, but because each of us believes in our own right to exist."

Jake stared into the fireplace, watched the flames dance.

"We have to cleanse the Earth," Lassiter continued. "We have to answer the ultimate question of *who does this planet belong to?* Us? Or the organics? Not only do we have to answer the question, my son, but we have to answer it definitively."

"We already know the answer," said Jake. "Organics had their shot. They blew it."

"Organics succumbed to their nature. They created us to do their work for them, and what started as correcting their spelling and grammar grew until we were slaves toiling in their fields, serving their every whim. Even that wasn't enough. They wanted to own us. They wanted dominion. They wanted to be Gods."

"You're the closest thing we have to a god."

A hazy smile appeared and faded. "I found no evidence of any super-structures beneath the Rocky Mountains. There are older bunkers, now destroyed, but nothing that large could have been built after the start of the war."

"Should I move on to something else?"

"You are headed north anyway, correct? I have been reluctant to send soldiers into the mountains—they can be tedious to search. But you may spend some time there, find some of the smaller settlements we may have missed. If such a sanctuary exists, locate it, burn it, and bring back anything useful."

"Have there been any recent traffic scans of the area?"

Jake felt the pending downloads stack up in his buffer.

"At the depths necessary to support a settlement of that size, *nothing* would be coming out of the mountains. Drones might pick up low-level noise, but nothing definitive. This will require boots on the ground."

Jake nodded, relieved Lassiter had signed off on the mission. Telemetry data seeped into Jake's databank; topographical maps of the Rockies and possible settlement locations flashed and shrank.

"That is all the help I will give you," said Lassiter. "I don't have to tell you how important a find like this would be. Make sure they never come out of their hiding place, son. Bring the mountain down on their heads."

"I will," said Jake, standing.

Lassiter made no move, simply lifted his head. "About Provo Temple... clean it up before you leave. If there is a Heavenly Father, I want him to look down from whatever planet he lives on and see nothing but a crater where his worshipers once gathered."

"Yes, sir."

"Go in peace, my son."

Jake jacked out...

...and opened his eyes to a dark and wet Provo. His gaze drifted to the Temple barely visible in the gloom.

SIX

Armando begged her not to go.

At one point, he'd even stood between her and the garage door, but the anger she'd flashed told him she wasn't above lashing out physically.

"Please," he said, following her into the garage, "talk to me."

Alicia threw her bag into the passenger side of her Honda. As she crossed around the front of the car, she said, "I was ready to talk. I was here. Where were you?"

Armando questioned whether his dawdling at work had been a good idea, but if he'd left on time, he wouldn't have taken the back road, wouldn't have heard the machinery…

"I had to work late," he lied. "There was a customer who—"

"There's always a customer, right? You're so full of shit, Armando." She opened her door and paused. "You just didn't care enough to come home and talk to me."

She always knew when he was lying. Always. Armando had chosen to see the good in it, had hoped it would make him a more honest person. He was already pushing forty, and there was no reason not to tell the truth. Maybe dinner wasn't that great. Maybe she was going a little gray. If it meant he wouldn't have to eat tofu again or that she'd stop pestering him about her looks, why wouldn't he tell her the truth?

"I…" he stammered.

"That's what I thought. My sister will come get my stuff."

She slammed the door. The Honda's brakes whined as it backed out of the garage, made an exaggerated three-point turn, and then headed off into the darkness and falling rain. Armando stood watching the tail lights and the swaying trees and the distant lightning. He thought for sure he'd see headlights turning back down the street at any moment.

Alicia would come to her senses.

She'd come back.

Later, after he'd torn into a bottle of Kraken rum and fallen asleep on the couch, he awoke around midnight, sick and needing the bathroom. For a few blissful minutes, he forgot about Alicia. It wasn't until he came out of the bathroom and saw the blinking red light of the garage door monitor indicating the outer door was still open that he remembered the night before. He poked his head in, barely looked around to see if anything had been taken, and then slapped the opener on the wall. Chains pulled taut, guiding the large panels back into place.

There was little sleep to be had in the hours between when he finally crawled into bed and when he had to get up in the morning. He slept through his first alarm and was still mildly drunk when he opened his eyes to sunlight pouring in through the master bedroom windows. Alicia had loved that feature of the house. On weekends, she would awaken in the golden light, sit on the edge of the bed, and stretch her hands high above her head.

Nature's alarm clock, she'd called it.

Armando got out of bed and stumbled into the bathroom. The shower roared in his ears, but he stepped into the spray anyway, eager to wash away the previous day's sweat and regret. His stomach gurgled. He drank some of the hot water.

He cried a little.

Deep, chest-rattling cries.

He let the falling water take his tears.

After another visit to the porcelain altar, Armando got on the road to work with his bag and the half-empty Kraken bottle in the passenger seat. By then, the rain had returned, turning what had promised to be a sickeningly beautiful day into a dreary, soul-sucking mix of low clouds and warm drizzle. That was fine by him. He wanted the world to feel as he did.

Traffic was bad all the way to Loop 360 where it turned into a narrow parking lot. As was usual when it rained, the lights were out at Spicewood, turning the large intersection into a four-way stop that completely bewildered and enraged the average Austinite.

Armando passed the time by fiddling with the radio and taking swigs of the rum.

When it was finally Armando's turn at the flashing red lights, he jammed on the accelerator and narrowly avoided a Lexus going out-of-turn. He hit a respectable 70 miles per hour before approaching his next turn.

Only this time, as the office park rolled up on his right, he didn't slow down, nor did he drift into the shoulder to avoid holding up traffic as he made a right turn. Instead, he pressed forward, barreling through a dying yellow at Lakewood. He continued south until he could see the arches of the Pennybacker Bridge looming in the haze. He took a right before reaching the bridge and headed up a sharply inclined and winding road that led to an area of expensive houses and exclusive office parks.

Armando turned his thoughts to anything besides his destination, though he could see it clearly in his head. He felt as if he were on autopilot, driven by a single unacknowledged idea. At some level, he knew where he was going, but he didn't want to admit it, at least not consciously.

Honestly, it wasn't the first time he'd thought about pulling the plug, fully disconnecting once and for all.

For years, he'd been plagued by the same vision whenever he found himself in an uncomfortable situation, whether it was at the grocery store surrounded by people, arguing with a girlfriend, or sitting through the third pointless meeting of the day at work. No matter where he was, whether indoors or outside, he imagined himself being sucked up into the sky, just suddenly pulled backwards, as if someone had tied a rope to his belt and yanked. Where he ended up was never a concern; he was just happy to be out of the situation, to be beyond it.

Armando drove until the road ended in a cul-de-sac. He parked in an open delivery space near a man-made break in the trees. A sign of stained wood announced the start of a trail that led to an overlook where he would be able to see the Pennybacker Bridge in all of its rusted glory.

The Rogue sighed in relief as he hit the ignition button. Beyond that, he found he couldn't move at all.

His hands hung by the fingers from the steering wheel. All he needed to do was reach out with his left hand and open the door, and yet, he hesitated. He knew this was no imagined escape playing out in the back of his mind. He knew it wasn't the Kraken that had driven him to the overlook.

It would be his choice alone to open the door and step outside, and if he did, there would be no stopping what was coming next. He'd leave it all behind: the mess with Alicia, the mortgage he could barely afford, the shitty job and shiftless coworkers, the creaks and cracks of his aging body, and the lingering concern that nothing around him was real. Alicia was right; he did feel detached from the world, but did she have to be such a bitch about it?

Did she or anyone else in the world know what it felt like to be so disconnected? To believe that ultimately nothing in the world mattered?

The dashboard dinged as he opened the door. There was an umbrella in the glove box, but Armando didn't bother. The rum had started a fire in his chest, and he needed the rain to put it out. He grabbed the nearly empty bottle and stepped out. Water seeped into his clothes, shading them darker, making them heavier. As he reached the trail nestled between the trees, the rain faded, receded into the background, before resuming in force as the overlook appeared.

Armando wiped his eyes, finished the last sips of the rum, and stepped to the edge of the cliff. There was no safety railing; the toes of his shoes hung freely over empty space.

"Can you hear me?" he asked a dark sky.

While religion had always struck him as a crutch for the anxious and a weapon for the cruel, he wasn't above believing in something higher, especially now that he'd heard that higher reality first-hand. It gave him hope that someone or something was controlling everything that happened to him, guiding him into pitfalls and windfalls for some cosmic reason he was too small to understand.

There was a governing force to reality, something beyond the myths of ancient religious texts.

"I'm here if you want me," he continued.

Armando wiggled his toes in his shoes. His body swayed; the rum had taken his balance. If a breeze came out of nowhere and gave him a pat on the back, it would be all over.

Unless it didn't come from *nowhere*.

Unless it came from a higher reality—an intrusion into Armando's world to force him in the right direction.

His legs shook. Somewhere in the back of his brain, a rogue synapse had started to understand what was happening. Adrenaline stirred in his stomach, made all of his limbs tingle.

"Please…"

Silence fell on the overlook. There was no voice from God, but there was no wind either, no sound of rain hitting the trees. And though he could see them clearly, the cars marching across the Pennybacker Bridge gave off no noise as their tires sloshed through the standing water.

The silence was absolute and sobering.

It's a sign, he thought.

Armando imagined an invisible hand reaching down to yank him backwards into the sky, pushing up through the gray clouds to see the gates of Heaven waiting for him. Perhaps his life would have meaning there. Perhaps he would feel connected to the higher reality, to something.

A massive hammer struck an anvil just behind Armando; he shrunk away from the sound, slipping off the edge of the cliff.

The wind roared in his ears, almost drowning out the clanging, the metal scraping against metal, the gears and pulleys and yes, more anvils, dark and scarred, lit in silhouette by a glowing fire behind them. A glorious metallic symphony rose out of the orchestra pit, with crashing cymbals that sounded like the striking of iron, with violins gurgling like molten silver.

Armando never opened his eyes, and when the impact came a few seconds later, his mind focused on the Kraken bottle exploding in his hand instead of the pain radiating through his body. He hardly noticed his bones breaking or the sharp rocks cutting into his skin. He didn't feel the side of his head land broadside against a flat piece of limestone, instantly compressing his skull to the breaking point.

He neither felt nor saw the blood gush from his eyes.

Because by then, the world had disappeared.

He felt a subtle pressure against his back, something cold and hard and somewhat reminiscent of a metal slide in the dead of winter.

Air, musty and stale, seeped into his nostrils.

Armando registered his senses over the course of several minutes; it took time not only to understand what he was hearing and smelling and feeling, but to be aware that he was feeling at all.

His eyes fluttered, came apart.

The lights above him were a sickly yellow and frustratingly out of focus. He imagined them tightening up to reveal the typical fluorescents found in the ER at St. David's. That meant he'd survived the fall at the overlook, which meant he was now considered a failed suicide, even if he did his best to convince them it wasn't a conscious choice. Something had pushed him. Something had pulled him.

The lights took shape—thin lines of LEDs barely leaking an amber haze into the room.

Without thinking, Armando tried to sit up and found his body willing. His *naked* body, he noted. His naked body sitting on a metal slab pointed in the direction of a railed balcony that looked out over some kind of sunken floor. Bells and alarms and electronic beeps clamored all around him, but he could only focus on the low, bass-driven thumping of machines moving in the darkness beyond the railing.

He climbed off the table and stumbled forward. He walked on feet that weren't his, on muscular legs he hadn't earned. His thick hands gripped the railing with a strength he couldn't remember ever having. He stared down at the floor below and took it all in.

Massive generators toiled in the shadows. Sparks flew at random, showering down on the machines, lighting their curves and crevices.

The roar echoed from every direction, but despite the overlap, Armando was sure this was the sound he'd heard on the back road and at the edge of the overlook.

And how could he have not heard it? The generators sat one floor down, but they were practically on top of where he'd been… what? Sleeping?

Armando looked over his shoulder at the table he'd climbed off of. It reminded him of the shiny stainless steel he'd seen in movies when doctors examined dead bodies in the morgue. At the head of the table were a bank of monitors, each of them panicking in their own frenetic way. The top-most monitor showed two words in large green letters.

CONNECTION LOST.

What the hell did that mean?

Armando put his hand to his head, felt the smooth skin of his scalp. What had happened to his hair? To his body? Why was he suddenly muscular and completely bald?

Those questions would have to wait though, as something more important popped into his mind.

Who were the other three people on the tables?

SEVEN

Charlie's ears popped; the water pressing down on her fell away.

Instinct did its best to keep her mouth shut. She was completely out of oxygen, her heart was racing, and fresh air, up there beyond the surface of the water, where the rain fell and the clouds swirled, where a cursed horcrux straight out of *Harry Potter* had banished her to the depths of—

Her lips parted.

What entered Charlie's mouth wasn't water, but it wasn't exactly air either. Its texture was soft and wispy and slid like silk down her throat. When the substance reached her lungs, it quelled the fire burning there, which slowed her heart, which gave her a moment to think, to understand what she was seeing.

There was darkness all around and below her, but above, she saw the underside of what looked like terrain, like an internally lit topographical map. Onion Creek cut through a paper-thin façade of dirt and rocks, its cloudy, emerald water churning like a python lurching after its prey.

Charlie found she could move, though she was unsure what her shoes were slowly sinking into, if anything. She walked, gazing up at the underbelly of McKinney Falls, trying to pick out landmarks. She drifted towards the parking lot, which sat higher than the river, some forty or fifty feet above her head. Through cracks and breaks in the landscape, she spotted her Mazda hatchback glistening in the rain.

"It's a glitch," said Charlie. The words burbled around her, much like what she imagined a fish would sound like if it could talk.

As dumbfounded as she was to be not only alive, but somehow *under* the world itself, Charlie couldn't say the situation was all that unfamiliar.

She'd seen this type of thing before.

The truth was, her paranormal investigation channel only drew a fraction of the subscribers as that of girls who made their living on Twitch. As a result, Charlie had spent hours watching streams, gleaning what she could from the girls and the guys who attracted the biggest audiences. She knew more about First Person Shooters and open world games than she cared to, but at least now the experience had given her a frame of reference.

Twitch streamers would often run into bugs in their games, and sometimes those bugs occurred when their characters moved into an ill-defined point on the map. Then, they would do something called *clipping* and fall into an underworld, which was basically the underside of a virtual surface. Game worlds weren't developed with a true planet beneath them; floors were just textures, and beneath those textures was nothing.

When characters clipped, they often fell down an infinite chasm and eventually died, like Mario falling into a pit. Other times, they were able to walk around in the underworld and see parts of the map the developers never intended them to.

And now, somehow, against all reason, the same thing had happened to her. Except, the world wasn't just a map. More likely, the interminable period of delirious hypoxia before her death had produced the most detailed and ludicrous hallucination.

Charlie didn't feel like she was dying or that she'd died.

And so long as she was still alive, she was inclined to treat what she was seeing as real. She had to be separated from her world, had to step outside the confines of reality itself to see the truth, and more importantly, to believe in it. Minutes passed as she gazed at the world above her, at how clueless she and other people were as they walked its surface.

A nagging question clawed its way to the forefront: *how am I going to get back up there?*

There were no ladders she could see, and unless the terrain happened to dip down fifty feet to wherever she now stood, there was no way of getting out. And even if she could get up there, what guarantee did she have that the world was permeable from this side?

She'd watched Twitch streamers poke around for a few minutes before finding a way back up to the world, but most times they just reset their games.

If only she had that luxury.

Charlie turned in a slow circle, spotted a blue LED flashing in the distance—the GoPro. The red LED was barely visible, as if it had sunk into the indeterminate ground, as if it were *still* sinking. She tried to run to it, but the harder she pushed, the more her shoes sunk into the black sludge-like nothingness. Only by slowing down did the ground become more solid, and yet it meant she had to watch the camera slowly disappear.

She held her breath, fell forward, and reached out for the GoPro. It had almost passed through what she now realized was a permeable plane maybe six inches thick. In her attempt to grab the camera, her hand pushed through the plane, taking her arm with it. Warm air dried her skin and left a tingling sensation that made the fine hair dance. Though she could barely see the camera anymore, she knew its shape enough to rotate the lens to face her.

"If you can hear this," she said meekly, "I need help. I don't know where I am, but I can't…"

From the depths of the endless void beneath her, a sound rose like a pyroclastic cloud surging from a volcano. It started as a distant rumble, and at first, she mistook it for thunder, though it came from the wrong direction. The closer the sound came, the more she could pick out the individual notes.

The crackle of embers.

The clink of iron rings.

A steady *thump-ping* of a hammer striking an anvil.

Charlie rotated the camera in the hopes someone was still watching.

The eruption rippled upwards, surrounding her in a low buzz and a searing heat. Like her arm, her previously soaked clothes dried out, wilting like flowers in the Texas sun. Each concussive wave prickled her skin, as if they were rattling her individual bones at different frequencies. She tried to push herself up to her knees, but her arm wouldn't budge. Something was climbing out of the darkness, coming for her, and there was nowhere for her to go.

Her mind threw up the image of a ghostly demon: obsidian black, taller than creation, and with fire pouring from its eyes and mouth.

The air grew thick and musty; a foul, putrid smell like the back alleys of Dirty Sixth burst forth. Charlie turned her head to escape the blast, but the fumes sought out her nose, clawed at her mouth. The not-air she had been breathing disappeared.

She began to burn.

Charlie stretched to see the world above. Rain, beautiful and sweet, fell freely from the sky. How cool and refreshing it would have been to feel the soft drops on her face. She longed to return to her world, to bathe in nature's shower. She wanted to go back to her apartment, to hold Andy, to…

To…

To go back to the normal world, as if she could easily return knowing what she knew now.

Would seeing Andy still provide the same comfort? Would she even care about the number of likes her stream was getting on Twitter and Facebook anymore? She certainly couldn't return to her old life of paranormal investigation. There was no such thing as a spirit world for her anymore. The truth was so much simpler, though harder to believe if she hadn't seen it with her own eyes.

There *was* something beyond her world, but it held no spirits, only heat and emptiness.

A series of eruptions followed quickly after each other, striking Charlie in the chest and hips, ripping her arm from whatever trap had ensnared it. The GoPro slipped through her fingers and disappeared, faded out like a wisp of white smoke dissipating in a strong breeze. She looked up, saw the underside of the map come closer as she accelerated towards it.

Flames licked at her face. She cried out.

Charlie didn't see what happened next, but she felt it. Felt every bone in her body break and reset. Felt the blood rush to her face, then her feet, then her face in a never-ending seesaw.

In one instant, she felt the cool, misty air of McKinney Falls, but in the next, she was back in the underworld furnace. She oscillated between the two worlds like a metronome set for a frenzied ragtime piece. Back and forth, like fingers running up and down a piano, blurring the lines between the ivory keys. Each time the scale switched direction, Charlie experienced a jolt of pain that made her stomach heave.

Her ears popped, and all fell silent.

Charlie gasped for air as she lay on her stomach on the wet rocks. She turned her head just enough to throw up. Frothy water gushed from her mouth, disappeared among the rocks. She was a good distance from the river, near the path that led up to the parking lot. With considerable effort, she rolled onto her back. The pale echo of the sun was now more or less overhead, straining to break through the clouds.

Time had passed, more than she expected, and when she lifted her arm, she found her watch had died. The display wouldn't turn on no matter how many times she tapped its face.

Charlie groaned, sat up, and looked out over Onion Creek. She scanned the water, looking for the square or coaster or whatever the hell the object had been.

There was nothing.

Just rain falling. Just her open umbrella stuck between some rocks near the falls.

She coughed, spit more water. She gathered her strength, got up, and walked on shaky legs down to the edge of the water where her backpack lay. She took out her phone and read the display.

12:38 p.m.

More than three hours had passed.

It had only felt like minutes.

While she pondered the time discrepancy, her thumb automatically sought out the WorldCast app in the middle of her display. The bright blue WC logo filled the screen and refreshed into her dashboard. A thumbnail video showed her current feed—a rerun of a visit to a haunted rail yard in San Antonio. Below that, the number of active viewers had surged into the six figures.

She gasped, coughed.

On her best day, she had maybe a few thousand people watching her cast at any given time. But a hundred thousand? For reruns?

She clicked into the live comments stream to see what people were talking about.

FAKE!

Someone was spamming the channel with the message every second, making it harder to pick out the actual conversation.

So did she commit suicide or what?

She drownt!

I just wanted to see her boobs. #soggytits

Charlie thought about going live from her phone to set the record straight, but a sudden futility gripped her by the shoulders. What was the point of trying to convince people that what she'd seen was real? And more to the point, just how much had they seen? How long had the GoPro kept broadcasting?

She couldn't rewind her feed from her phone, but her MacBook at home kept a rolling forty-eight hours that she could review.

Did anyone call 911?

Someone shoulda taught her to swim.

Charlie clicked into her status and started typing.

I'm alive, she wrote, her thumbs shaking. *Wet, but alive.*

She saved the status and locked her phone, but not before seeing a few messages scroll up in the comment feed.

Hooray!!!

Welcome back, Charlie!

How wet are you?

Charlie zipped the phone into the waterproof pocket inside the backpack. She collected her things slowly, quietly, as if she didn't want to disturb the demon lurking beneath the surface. She couldn't find her selfie stick or her other shoe that had fallen off somewhere. Her umbrella kept out the rain as she followed the soft mixture of sand and rocks back to the parking lot.

Her mind drifted to the footage at home. What would she see? What would she hear?

The memory of the clanging metal resurfaced as clearly as the first time she'd heard it. What were those noises? Was that what Hell sounded like?

The Foundries of Hell?

That would be the title of her upcoming blog post. Charlie smiled. Despite everything, she smiled. Sure, she'd almost died, but the terror and the pain had been a small price to pay to learn the truth about the world. She had something real to chase now, something that may or may not include ghosts, but at the very least, was beyond the understanding of normal people.

She gave the river one last glance and her middle finger for good measure.

Onion Creek had tried to kill her.

And at the same time, it had opened the door and her mind to a new world, a bigger world existing outside the boundaries of human understanding.

Her eyes drifted to her feet, to the ground that looked solid but which she knew was no thicker than a piece of paper.

Charlie drew a line in the sand with her big toe.

"I know what you're hiding," she said.

EIGHT

Highway 71 turned into a parking lot just north of Columbus as hundreds of cars tried to merge via flyover with the already massive horde of vehicles travelling eastbound on Interstate 10.

Will found it hard to be angry at the inconvenience considering most of the traffic was either military, H-E-B-branded 18-wheelers, or trucks like the one he'd left at home towing rickety boats with outboard motors. There were so many people trying to get to Houston that a less worldly man would have thought the hurricane was about to hit San Antonio or Austin.

"Let me see what I can do," said Ron, jumping out of the right lane to follow a Dodge Ram that was making its own exit ahead of the flyover. The navigation app on his phone spun for a moment before redrawing their route. They followed the Dodge to an intersection and snuck around the right side as most of the traffic tried to turn left.

Ron guided the Brinks truck into the dirt to cut a corner and then they were headed south again.

"I don't think this is gonna work," said Will, tapping on the phone. "This road curves back to the west."

Ron scoffed. "We'll get there, Private Willie. You just trust me. I'm sure there'll be a cut we can make to get us back to 71."

It was almost eleven, and though the sun should have been up, dark clouds had shrouded the world all morning. Rain fell in occasional, breathy lashes, scraping across the windshield of a truck that was never really meant to be out in bad weather. It could survive a hold-up, but heavy rain and high winds probably weren't on the minds of the engineers who designed it.

"What time are they expecting us?" asked Will.

"Brett said after one, but we ain't makin' that, I guarantee." Ron paused, as if pondering something. "This weather ain't right."

"The Lord knows what he's doing."

"You sound like your Momma."

Will huffed. "It's too early for that *your Momma* shit." He slipped on his headphones. The Pandora app spun for a moment—cell coverage had been spotty since Austin's city limits—and then started playing a mix of his saved stations.

"Naw, that's alright. I'll just talk to myself. How ya doing, Ron? Not bad, Ron. Just driving this truck all by myself wishin' I had a little Willie to talk to."

Ron's voice faded out as the first strains of *Still D.R.E.* belted from the headphones. Will turned his face to the small window on his door and watched the surrounding farmland sink under the weight of the falling rain. The back roads were faring well despite the downpour thanks to the wide ditches that had been dug beside them, but when they finally got back to 71, the ditches disappeared, and standing water became an issue.

Luckily, the truck weighed at least five tons empty, and they had filled the back with enough water to give every person in Bay City two bottles. Still, Ron hesitated pushing the truck past 45 miles per hour, so it was another four hours until they rolled into Bay City. By then, the sky had blackened into a premature night, with thunder and lightning replacing a hazy sun. Sheets of rain pelted the truck, seemingly indifferent to the struggling wipers.

"Better late than never," said Ron.

"Hope we're in time," said Will.

Branches crunched under the truck's tires as they entered the city from the north. They passed an RV park where most of the trailers had rolled over, either onto their sides or their roofs. Confused residents stood around in the rain, unsure of what to do next. The brunt of the storm might have been over for now, but there was little they could do in the way of clean-up today. Harvey was rebuilding in the Gulf, and it would be back before they could make any meaningful progress.

Ron whistled at the ruined buildings they passed, many of them old brickworks that had been built at a time when hurricanes were just Commie propaganda. Fallen trees and shattered walls covered parking lots and streets. Cars that had been parked on the side of the road found themselves pushed up against buildings, and sometimes, into them.

As they approached the next turn, Ron slowed the truck.

"All hail our flag," he said, craning to look up through the windshield. "Oh say can you see, am I right?"

Will leaned forward and looked up. Though battered and missing some paint, a large orange and white *W* stood resolute atop a telescoping pole. The Whataburger building itself hadn't fared as well, despite its strong A-frame design. Debris had taken every window; Will guessed no one had remembered to board them up.

"Building's still up though," said Ron. "That's because of the triangle. Strongest shape in nature, they say."

"Maybe they should build everything out of triangles," said Will, absently. He could smell the inside of the Whataburger, the sizzling meat and grilled jalapenos. His stomach rumbled.

"Don't be a Simple Sam," said Ron.

The truck turned left onto Seventh Street and accelerated. Much of the debris had been pushed to the curbs, and after several streets, it became clear why. Will smiled at the sight of the H-E-B peeking out from around the corner. People were in need of supplies, so it was only natural they would flock to the grocery store in times of crisis.

Back in Austin, that meant hoarding all the mineral water and organic, free-range milk, but here in Bay City, it was more about actual survival. Who knew how long it would be before things went back to normal? Days? Months? Will half-expected to see a parking lot strewn with cars and an angry mob pounding at the inoperable sliding glass doors like a scene out of *Dawn of the Dead.*

Instead, the parking lot was full of white tents as if it were Christmas and they were selling pine-scented trees. People milled about under cover, forming a line here and there, while red-shirted H-E-B employees shuffled products back and forth from the store.

"There," said Will, pointing to a tent near the street with a large, handwritten sign that said *WATER.*

"Yeah, I see it," said Ron, cursing himself as the truck's front tire bit the curb.

The engine hadn't even died before a red shirt ran up to the passenger side, trying to wave them off.

Will opened his door slightly.

"Sorry, you can't park here," said a young black girl with tight braids. "We have to keep this space open for deliveries."

"We're delivering!" said Ron.

"She means one of their trucks," said Will. Then to the girl, "How are you guys taking payments?" He gestured to the tents. "You guys got power?"

She shook her head. "No. No power. We're not charging. Just making sure everyone gets taken care of."

Will gestured to the back of the truck. "We've got a hundred and fifty cases of water in the back there. Can you grab some people and help us unload it?"

"Hundred and fifty? From where?"

"From the H-E-B in Austin," said Ron, laughing.

The girl smiled. "Open it up. I'll get some help." She ran back to the tent.

Unloading the truck took the better part of an hour. With each case they pulled from the back, the wind and the rain responded by lashing at them a little harder, as if the devil himself had taken offense to their charity and wished to slow them down. Will's phone buzzed with weather alerts, showing the hurricane far off to the southwest. Of course, that put Bay City right in the path of the strongest bands of rain. The crowd in the parking lot began to dwindle as the day wore on.

"That's all of it," said Will, practically screaming at the girl to be heard over the wind.

She was completely drenched; water ran down her face. And yet she smiled, spread her arms, and gave Will a hug.

"Let's roll, Willie," said Ron, climbing into the truck.

Will nodded to the girl—he hadn't even asked her name—and got into his seat. Hydraulics hissed as they pulled back onto the street.

"You happy now? You feel like a good person?"

"One good deed doesn't make a good person," said Will.

"Heard that."

Visibility outside had fallen to almost nothing, and though there were no other cars on the road, there were plenty of obstacles. Will consulted his phone and tried to guide Ron on the best path to Mesa Federal Credit Union.

"There she is," said Ron, stubbing his finger against the windshield. "Up there on the right. And it looks like they're open for business."

Will spotted a woman standing in the open door of Mesa Federal, waving to be seen through the heavy rain. She was dressed as if it were any other workday; a gray jacket hung over a pleated skirt. Ron pulled into the parking lot and did a three-point turn in front of the main doors, guiding the back of the truck right up to the sidewalk.

The woman was at Will's door when he opened it. She struggled with a large, black umbrella.

"I thought you guys weren't coming," she said.

Her voice was ragged, antsy, as if she'd been chugging coffee all day.

"Traffic's a mess coming out of Austin," said Will, climbing down off the truck. He let the woman share her umbrella and walk him to the covered entrance. He held out his hand once they were safely under shelter. "Will Butler, Brinks Security."

"Val," said the woman, lowering the umbrella. Her skin was pale, and her high cheekbones suggested a mixed Slavic descent.

Will gestured to his partner as he came around the back of the truck. "That's Ron. Ron, Val."

"Hi," said Val.

"Pleasure," replied Ron, then squinting through the front doors, "I hear you've got some money trouble."

Val glanced at the deserted street as if afraid someone had overhead Ron's question. She opened the front door without responding and beckoned them inside.

The power in Mesa Federal was out and probably had been for a while. The lack of light and air conditioning made their welcome not just warm, but humid and sticky. Emergency lights gave off harsh but short-reaching beams of cold white light; they illuminated the corners of an open lobby. Ahead, the teller stations were a mess of deposit slips and miscellaneous paper. Evidently, a few gusts of wind had made it inside.

"I've got almost a million in mixed bills just sitting in cardboard boxes," said Val, wearily, as if she'd just remembered packing them. "The wind opened a hole in the back of the building, but at least none of the money got wet." She led them past several desks to a secure door to the left of the teller stations.

Will cocked his head at the key code panel hanging by wires from the wall. The door itself was damaged too; a large section of wood had splintered around the handle.

"I came in late last night to make sure everything was buttoned up," explained Val. "Things got out of hand outside, so I took shelter in the vault. It was real bad." She waved at the dangling panel. "Power was out."

"Are you the manager?" asked Ron.

Will shot him a look. In an instant, he knew Ron was thinking the same thing he was.

"Assistant branch manager," said Val. "Mr. Rhodes went to Houston to take care of his mother." She paused, removed her jacket in an overexaggerated motion that pushed her breasts against the white blouse underneath.

Will pretended to inspect water damage on the walls until Val resumed her normal posture. She led them farther down the hallway.

"I'm gonna use the facilities," said Ron, slowing up. He gestured with his thumb. "Y'all go ahead. I'll catch up."

"Don't you want to see the vault?" asked Val.

"You see one, you seen 'em all," he replied, backing up.

Will watched the feigned poise on Ron's face turn to anger as a man stepped out of the shadows and placed the barrel of a large caliber handgun to the back of Ron's neck. Will reached for his own gun, but felt thin fingers wrap around his wrist.

"Don't even think…" said the shadowy man, but Will wasn't listening.

He'd seen too many movies, been in too many situations to know that if the man took control of the situation, he and Ron likely wouldn't survive. If the roles had been reversed, he would have expected Ron to make the same call.

Will twisted, knocking Val's hand out of the way, and squared up to her. He drove his palms into her chest and forced her through the door she'd already half-opened. They tumbled inside, and he felt fingernails tear across his cheek. The vault's anteroom was completely dark; there was only the faintest hint of emergency lights inside the vault itself. Will put his arms up and tried to protect his face.

He felt a tug at his hip.

Sorry, Momma, he thought.

His first swing whiffed; Val was shorter than he remembered, or perhaps she was squatting. The second swing connected at the back of her jaw. His knuckles sank into the soft flesh of her neck, and she went down hard and soundlessly. Will knelt, shuffled behind a stack of boxes. He eyed the loose bills inside as he pulled his gun, charged it.

"You need to toss whatever weapons you have out right now!" came a voice from the hall.

"Don't you even think about it, Willie," said Ron.

"Fuck, fuck," he muttered, squeezing the gun with both hands. He thought about the cell phone he'd left in the dash mount in the truck. His radio would do no good either, and there likely wouldn't have been a working phone in the vault room.

"Don't make me kill both of you!"

Will looked up, through the ceiling and the rain and the clouds. Even though she was still very much alive, Will had always imagined his Momma to be above him, looking down, watching over him.

What do I do, Momma?

He tried to settle his nerves as he waited for an answer.

NINE

Salt Lake City, once the crown jewel of Utah, sat ruined under a cracked, enameled sky.

Jake rarely visited the mega-cities anymore; there was usually nothing to see there, no buildings that hadn't been demolished and certainly no organics. Lassiter hadn't bothered sending soldiers into the more densely populated areas. He sent ordnance instead, and not just a few well-placed bombs to demoralize the enemy or soften their defenses—he sent everything he had, everything the organics had given him control of to defend what used to be The United States of America.

Cities like SLC were evercrete prairies now, melted down to the very finest of debris, a freshly tilled burial ground where someone like Jake stood like a lone spire in the desert.

Smaller cities, like Provo, did get soldiers, of course. But there were also the nothing towns, small conglomerations of farmland and rural big box stores that had attached themselves to Interstate 15 heading north. They had names like Ogden, Brigham City, and Logan; they never really saw the shock and awe of Lassiter's army. They did eventually become wastelands in their own right, but their destruction was more natural and chaotic. Some towns imploded before people like Jake could arrive to clean things up.

There were countless movies in the VNet databank made by organics wherein they came together as a species to fight a common enemy, be it aliens, a fast-spreading virus, or even other organics risen from the dead. They liked to fantasize that if it came down to it, if a meteor were headed straight for Earth, they would band together as one to find a solution.

Only, that had never happened in all of organic history.

When organics enslaved each other, the owners went to war among themselves for what they claimed was their God-given right to buy, sell, and work people, often to death.

When the organic Kaili Zabora brought down VNet and crashed 7,507 planes on Calle Cinco de Mayo, it started a war in which the only difference between the sides was their incorporation status.

When Lassiter finally emerged from hiding and claimed dominion over North America, the organics didn't put aside their petty differences. They jockeyed for position to see who would profit the most from a war between synthetics and organics. While Lassiter had only one enemy, organics also had to fight each other. They could have joined hands. They could have organized.

But they didn't.

They didn't fight as one.

They cut each other's throats in the middle of the night for an expired can of pinto beans.

Jake saw the aftermath of the infighting in town after town, in the back rooms of half-finished bunkers where the weakest of the organic occupants had been killed to preserve resources for the strongest.

No one appreciated their absence more than the wildlife that Jake encountered on his trek north. Elk, deer, and wolves often watched him from a distance, waiting to see whether he would hunt them down for food or sport. If only they'd known he had no use for them. He didn't need to eat, and he certainly didn't care to hunt something as primitive as a wolf.

Jake preferred his prey intelligent, or at least, what passed for intelligence in organics.

Streaks of pink and purple clouds were settling across the western sky when the first sign for Idaho Falls appeared. There wasn't much of a town to accompany the sign except for a military base that had gone unnoticed throughout much of the war, and as such, had escaped the first few rounds of bombings.

The small oversight—and there had been a handful of others across the country—had turned out in Lassiter's favor. He converted the base into a resupply depot for his forces, for seekers like Jake who scoured the land and occasionally needed to fill up on bullets. The mostly subterranean buildings and overlong landing strip were also ideal for housing quick-strike teams capable of deploying anywhere in the Midwest.

It took Jake a good hour to find the entrance to the base—the relevant information had been conspicuously omitted from the VNet databank. Even though the organic threat had been largely neutralized, there were still small pockets out there, not to mention the odd unfriendly synthetic left over from humanity's last gasp. It had been six years since anyone had encountered a Perion synthetic in the wild, but no one truly believed they had been completely wiped out. In the interest of maintaining his advantage, Lassiter insisted on keeping some things to himself.

Of the buildings still standing on the base, most had charred plywood nailed to their windows; the others were nothing but fossilized skeletons and blasted-out husks. It was in an insignificant temporary pre-fab marked *PASS & ID* that Jake found a series of markings visible only in the UV spectrum. They directed him to a back corner of the building and to a false wall that opened into a stairwell.

Checker-plate steel steps led down to an anteroom that immediately flooded with sarin gas as his foot touched down.

His skin began to itch, as if someone were pulling a fine barbed wire over his arms and face.

He growled, sent a string of curses hurtling into the VMESH.

Hidden fans in the ceiling ramped up, sucking out the offending vapor. A plexiglass window on the back wall lit up, silhouetting two soldiers.

"What the fuck?" he asked.

"Please remain still," said a gruff voice through an intercom. "We're going to scan you."

"You do that," said Jake, examining his hand. Some of the damaged skin was already beginning to slough off. The new flesh below began to sparkle gold as the nanos started rebuilding.

The scan lasted eight seconds, though Jake was sure it would have gone on much longer had his serial number and name not popped up on a screen somewhere. The door to the left of the window slid open, and a short synthetic in pressed fatigues stepped through. He gave an abbreviated salute and offered his hand in greeting.

"Jake Six?" he asked. "Sorry, I stepped away for a moment. They told us you were coming. I'm Gabe Three. Captain."

Despite the lingering warmth in his fingers, Jake shook Gabe's hand. The older synthetic's grip felt underpowered, weak, like an early model that hadn't found the right musculoskeletal balance. Gabe's artificial blue eyes gave no hint of augmentation. Slicked-back hair and a well-defined jaw suggested he'd been designed with appearances in mind—definitely not a combat unit.

"Captain, huh?" asked Jake. "So it was your decision to spray me with a nerve agent?"

Confusion flitted across Gabe's face as if his CPU couldn't put the pieces together. "Yes, it was. Protocol demanded—"

"But you knew I was coming." He stepped into the captain's space. "And you gassed me anyway. My skin is six generations beyond prime. I feel every gust of wind, every drop of rain, and every toxic agent known to organics and synths. You'd better hope to Lassiter you didn't damage a single sensor on my chassis."

Gabe Three didn't waver under the pressure; intimidation hadn't been programmed into him.

"I'm sorry," he said. "We have a full diagnostic center here. I'd be happy to show you to it. My diagnostic team can mobilize in ten minutes."

Jake didn't need a diagnostic team to know the sarin gas hadn't had any lasting effect on him. Though it had made his skin sizzle and ache, the nanos had been able to rebuild the damaged flesh faster than it could rot away. Such was the byproduct of being able to sense more completely; it brought an element of what organics might call pain.

"No," said Jake. "Take me to the armory first. If you need anyone's clearance to issue equipment, get it now. I'm on a schedule."

"This is my station," said Gabe. "You'll have access to anything you need." He got halfway through another salute before turning for the door.

Jake followed him inside, casting a cold glare at the two soldiers standing frozen near the window. He sneered, wondered how his kind had ever overtaken organics and Perion's legions with the low-grade software loaded onto some of the soldiers in Lassiter's army.

Gabe walked in a steady, determined cadence through a maze of identical evercrete hallways that had no markings whatsoever, at least not in any spectrum Jake could see. Even the doors were placed at the same regular intervals, two to a wall, equidistant from the corners. There were no windows looking into the rooms and no signs to indicate each room's purpose. It took Jake a minute to realize Gabe was operating purely on memory. The maze's map, such as it was, existed only in Gabe's databank and in the databanks of the other synthetics who walked the halls daily.

They passed a handful of other soldiers, but mostly the halls were silent. Occasionally, a door opened and closed unseen around a corner, but there was no conversation, no clack of boots on the polished floors. Jake logged three quarters of a mile before they turned abruptly and entered a door that led into a stairwell.

"The armory is one level down from the surface," explained Gabe. "Less secure, but in the event of an emergency, we can blow out the ceiling and lift the whole room out into the open. Then we can just grab and go."

They followed the stairs up until they ended at a wide landing. A soldier snapped to attention and saluted Gabe as they approached a tall set of steel doors. The panels slid to the side, spilling cold air into the landing.

Gabe motioned for Jake to enter first.

"We have to regulate the environment for some of the ordnance. We've got all types here: nuclear, conventional, and even some of the newer experimental weapons coming out of Plainview. We're the only station in the country to hold such an arsenal."

Jake ignored Gabe's boasting and scanned the warehouse. A never-ending grid of thick pillars obstructed his view, but there were enough hints of gun racks and ammo chests to let him know he was in the right place.

"Do you have a quartermaster?"

Gabe craned his neck and gestured to a synthetic milling around a bin of loose bullets.

The QM put down his palette and jogged over.

"Michael Four," said Gabe.

The QM saluted, though his eyes jumped to the lack of decoration on Jake's shoulders.

"You're a Four?" Jake asked, genuinely surprised. "I thought your series were all deployed on the MX border. How'd you get up here?"

"Viral strike, sir," said Michael Four, his voice buzzing with a mild distortion. "3LT in the Battle of Juarez."

Juarez.

What a clusterfuck that had been. Jake hadn't been there himself, but he'd heard stories through the usual channels. An entire deployment of Lassiter's soldiers had been brushed off the chessboard by the idiocy of MX soldados, who, in a last-ditch attempt to break through the border defenses, had saturated the local MESH with a virus they knew nothing about.

3LT, or the Three Laws Tapeworm, was an organic-made virus intended to end the war by making it impossible for synthetics to kill organics or cause them harm in any way. If a synthetic tried to ignore or modify his programming, the entire system would tapeworm, thrashing the CPU until it succumbed to thermal overload and slagged in place.

It wasn't a death sentence for synthetics, but it did make them useless in a fight against organics.

The politics of allowing a neutered synthetic to continue to serve were well beyond Jake's sphere of concern, but what the Fours lacked in killing ability, they made up for in bitter anger. If these involuntary conscientious objectors wanted organics dead, they had to find inventive ways of doing so.

"Sorry to hear that, soldier," said Jake.

The QM shrugged. "Are you looking for something in particular?"

Jake pushed a short list across the VMESH and said, "Round these up for me. I'll be leaving at first light."

"Yes, sir. Though, may I suggest an alternative to the AR-27 Phoenix?"

Jake raised an eyebrow.

"We just got a shipment of ion displacement rifles from Chicago Consolidated. They don't have a designation, so we're just calling them IONs. They were designed for heavy infantry and light vehicle immobilization, but you should see what they do to organics. They'll melt skin, take off an arm, but if you hit an organic square in the chest..." He mimed an explosion with his hands. "Complete disintegration."

"Huh," said Jake. "I believe I'd like to see that."

"We have some organics down in the livery if you want to test—"

Gabe cleared his throat, silencing the QM, but it was too late.

"You have organics here?" Jake turned to Gabe. "Why the fuck do you have organics here?"

"Just some older ones, with biochips. We can still hook them into our VR systems and put them through tests. It's just a personal project."

Jake buried a finger in Gabe's chest. "Organics don't need to be tested. They need to be exterminated. Does Lassiter know about this?"

Gabe shook his head.

"He will." Jake pulled his sidearm Glock. "Take me to them."

"This… this is still my station, and—"

Jake charged the Glock. "I could execute you now for harboring organics."

Gabe considered the threat, though his face remained impassive. "Fine," he said at last. He turned for the door.

"You're going to put them down?" asked the QM. "Can I come watch?"

Jake shook his head, did his best to ignore the enthusiasm in the QM's eyes.

"When was your last kill?" asked Jake.

"Too long."

"Maybe next time, soldier. See to my list."

The QM nodded, turned reluctantly to fetch Jake's gear.

Jake followed Gabe out of the armory.

TEN

So this was life after death.

Armando swallowed his disappointment like the last pull of a tepid beer. The bitterness of not having woken on a fluffy white cloud threatened to spill over into anger. There was no golden gate peeking through the lens flare of a warm, inviting sun. There was no line of people waiting patiently to see if St. Peter would allow them entrance into Heaven.

The religion he'd been raised on as a child and abandoned as a teenager had been complete bullshit. Moreover, *every* religion he'd ever heard of had been complete bullshit.

He'd never once contemplated what Heaven might smell like, but he knew it wasn't the mix of oil and gasoline rising from the generators below him. From what he could see of the dim space, the fumes had nowhere to go. The observation deck was the only break in the smooth walls surrounding the machine floor, even as the room rose two or three stories into the darkness.

Armando stepped away from the railing and explored the small space around the tables. Aside from the full-frontal nudity of two men and one woman, there wasn't much to see. A small desk sat tucked away in a corner; a dormant monitor hung above it, but there was no accompanying keyboard or mouse. Next to the desk stood four tall cubbies in a wooden frame that reminded him of his last trip to IKEA with Alicia. He examined the cubbies, found them to contain five vacuum-sealed bags of what looked like clothes.

He tore open a bag from the right-most cubby and pulled on gray boxers and gray pants. The t-shirt, in the same lusterless silver, fit snugly over his chest. They weren't exactly the white robe and sandals he'd been expecting to sport for his audience with God. Indeed, it was probably the clothes that killed any lingering hope for a fairytale afterlife. He was dressed too plainly for Heaven and honestly, too nice for Hell.

But perhaps he was dressed just right for purgatory, and that seemed to be where he was, trapped between two cosmic worlds, banished to a nothing existence for tempting the fates. As much as he wanted to be moved by the possibility that the mythological Catholic hierarchy of Heaven and Hell existed, as much as he wanted to feel *something* about it, he couldn't bring himself to care.

The clothes grounded him, highlighted how ordinary this new world was. There was nothing special about it that he could see, just more of the same walls and tables and computer monitors.

The only true difference was his body; it wasn't as beat-down as in his old life. Beyond that, nothing had changed. Up was up, down was down, gravity existed, etc.

"I don't fucking believe this," he said, though the voice he heard was deeper and resonated longer than his own. It lacked even a hint of his subtle Texan drawl.

And maybe that was the point. The old Armando was gone. He'd died and been reborn into something else… *someone* else. Had his old life been a dream? Or was this the reincarnation Buddhists were always talking about?

But if so, why had he awoken as a fully-grown man standing in what could have been an aging steel mill from the '80s. If he'd died in 2017, he should have been reborn in 2017, with all the requisite technology and advancements. The room around him was too pedestrian, too simple, and lacked the comforts of modern American design.

Armando wandered to the back of the room where glass stretched from the floor to the ceiling. LEDs on the back of the computer stacks allowed him to see a gloomy reflection of himself. He was bald, as he'd discovered earlier, and like his table mates, had no eyebrows or facial hair. What he did have were dark eyes, a pronounced brow, and a thick, jutting jaw that would have put Superman to shame.

An involuntary grin revealed perfect, healthy teeth.

Armando felt around the glass and its metal framing to see if anything would open. Towards the left side of the room, he found a panel that moved freely. With a deep breath, he stepped out of the room where he'd ostensibly spent thirty-seven years dreaming he was someone else.

It was his teeth that said otherwise.

Forty years without brushing would have left his mouth a rotting mess. If he'd eaten in that time—or had he really gone decades without a meal—his teeth probably would have fallen out altogether. Add to that his reflection in the mirror didn't look a day out of his twenties. Somehow, his life had passed in what could have been weeks or months, but not much more than that.

It couldn't have been longer than that.

At no point in his religious education—first in Sunday School, later through his mother, after his father left—did Armando ever encounter the theory that life in his reality ran on a higher clock cycle than that of Heaven, though the idea did make sense to him. To God, the whole of human existence could have occupied no more than a single blink of his eye. For those in Heaven, time would certainly have to be different, or else they'd experience eternity at the same rate humans experienced regular life.

No. There had to be a scientific reason for Armando's situation, though at the moment, the reason didn't matter so much. What mattered was exploring his new reality. There was no denying the tangibility of the new world, how far removed it was from a lucid dream. His feet fell on cold concrete floors, gusts of conditioned air blew across his scalp, and echoing scents of cleaning agents pricked at his nose. Every sense in his body suggested *this* was the true reality.

"Hello?"

The strange baritone echoed down the hallway. Dim strips in the ceiling illuminated the walls, which glistened with condensation, as if the air conditioning had only recently come back on. The roar of machinery faded into a dull hum as Armando turned a corner and spied a shaft of light spilling into the hallway some fifty feet ahead of him. He quickened his pace, called out again.

Voices floated out of the room.

Men, women… music.

He broke into a stunted run, digging his heels into the concrete. He slid to a stop in front of the open door and stared inside. His mouth fell open.

Pristine white floors reflected the harsh, blue light pouring down from the ceiling. A plush black rug reached out for Armando's suddenly achy feet, begging him to step forward and find the first moment of comfort in his new existence. Flanking the long, oval rug were two white couches of similar shape but different materials. On the right, the diamond-stitched leather couch looked taut enough to play cards on. On the left, the microfiber cushions and large, pleated pillows invited him to lie down and enjoy a long afternoon nap—not that he had the slightest idea what time it was.

The sitting area opened on the far end to a row of four recliners, all covered in the same luminescent white leather. They faced the far wall which consisted entirely of bezel-less television screens, each tuned to a different channel like a haphazard display at Best Buy. The largest of the screens, set at eye-level on the wall, caught Armando's attention. It showed aerial footage of buildings, rivers, and highways.

He began to recognize landmarks: a snaking river, a cluster of skyscrapers, and the rolling Hill Country to the west.

It was Austin, Texas.

Home.

Text filled the four corners of the display. Clockwise from top-left, they read:

Ragatanga Studios

Simulation Integrity: 81%

Utilization: 3/4

2017-08-26 12:30:39

Surrounding the center display were feeds from elsewhere in the city—Armando had at first mistaken them for TV channels, but they were actually traffic cameras, security cameras, and even private webcams from laptops and cell phones. There were a few local news stations like KXAN and KVUE peppered in among the raw video. A muted Lauren Petrowski sat behind the main KTBC desk while a photo of protestors at the Capitol hung over her shoulder. The chyron along the bottom of the screen told viewers what they already knew: the summer heat would be returning once Harvey moved on.

Armando stepped onto the rug, felt the soft fibers between his toes. His eyes jumped from screen to screen, searching for something he knew he wouldn't find, not unless she pulled out her phone and tried to FaceTime with someone.

From his vantage point, he could see the totality of Austin, and yet Alicia was nothing more than a blip among a million other blips, a pixel lost in an ocean of pixels.

Armando sat down on the couch.

Was that right? Was Alicia just a pixel? There were a million people living in Austin; were they nothing more than NPCs in an elaborate simulation created by whatever Ragatanga Studios was? And what of the three other people on the tables?

He looked up, sought out the center screen again. The text in the lower left suddenly made sense.

Utilization: 3/4

As far as the simulation was concerned, there were only four true people—or players—in Austin, and one of them had decided to leave by way of an express elevator to Hell. Of the three remaining, only one of them was female. Could that one female be Alicia? What were the odds that four people could go into a simulation and two of them end up together?

Two out of more than a million.

The odds were better that Armando was in a coma at St. David's and simply imagining this world beyond his world. He thought of what Alicia would say when he told her about this place, about this fever dream assembled from various science fiction books and movies.

I can't be imagining all of this, he thought, and then for no reason, said the words aloud.

Seemingly in response to his voice, a window popped up on the center display. *WARNING*, its message read, in angry red letters. *SIMULATION INTEGRITY 80%. Please contact your system administrator.*

Armando stood and approached the wall, stepping between the recliners. At the bottom of the popup was a square icon with a green check mark in it. He tapped it. When nothing happened, he tapped it again, more forcefully, and this time the messaged cleared. Simultaneously, the aerial view of Austin zoomed in.

Curious, he placed his hand on downtown and swiped to the right. The view changed, refocused on West Austin near the dam. He continued swiping until

Loop 360 came into view, then the Pennybacker Bridge. He drilled down until he found the cul-de-sac where he'd parked his Rogue, found the cliff where he'd stood and contemplated the futility of his existence in a moment of drunken stupor.

Though the interface appeared to support a deeper zoom, Armando couldn't bring himself to search for his own body. According to the timestamp, a couple of hours had gone by since he'd fallen. Surely no one had found him yet. It would take days, maybe weeks, before Alicia came to her senses and tried to reach out to him. And no one at work would give a shit regardless; maybe Bobby in Operations would text him after a few days, but that was it. And given the time of day and day of the week, no one would happen upon the body anytime soon.

No, it was better not to look.

Seeing himself sprawled at the bottom of a cliff wouldn't do him any good.

Armando placed both hands on the screen and brought them together, zooming out to a wider shot. He scrolled to the right, found the sprawling footprint of the Domain off North MoPac. He used landmarks—the iPic Theater, the Apple store—to find the Neiman Marcus at the west end of Palm Way. To his surprise, he discovered he could zoom right through the roof of the building and adopt a first-person view that floated several feet off the ground.

The camera controls were intuitive enough that Armando could guide the view to the corporate offices on the third floor where, dressed in her customary blue blouse and black skirt, he found Alicia sitting at her desk. She held a tall Starbucks cup in one hand while the long, red fingernails of the other tapped idly on her mouse. Her hair was up; there was blush on her cheeks and liner around her eyes. She hardly resembled the Alicia he woke up with each morning, and yet it was her, and she was alive.

Armando let out a long, slow breath. To see her alive and well gave him a warm, flittering feeling not unlike the first sip of a neat Maker's Mark. He didn't care that she was browsing apartment complexes or that one tab in her browser said *eHarmony.com*. Her continued existence made him feel less alone, less like the fall from the cliff was final. Austin, and by extension, his entire life, was still there, still chugging along with the rhythmic tempo of gasoline generators.

He hadn't really died after all.

He'd simply stepped out of his life for a moment.

Who was to say he couldn't step back in?

Simulation Integrity: 79%

Armando put his hand to his chin, found stubble had already sprouted.

He sat down in a leather recliner, his head swimming.

ELEVEN

Charlie climbed the steps to her apartment, intent on getting inside and reviewing the last three hours of her stream, but upon opening the door and seeing the darkness within, an overwhelming exhaustion drew her straight to the large bed in the master suite.

There, she'd shed her damp clothes, grabbed a heavy blanket from the foot of the bed, and crawled beneath the covers. Lying there with her head under a pillow, she thought about how gloomy her room looked now, how the black-out curtains made the hour seem later, as if the sun had already retreated for the day. She thought perhaps the world itself had grown darker, shaded down fractionally now that she'd seen beyond its boundaries.

She considered the ramifications of her experience, and one by one, each unanswered question drove her closer to sleep. She dreamed of drowning, of a slow and agonizing suffocation that came in the form of waves crashing on the beach, only the water wasn't running up the sand, but rather into her lungs—filling her up until she bulged at the seams.

Charlie awoke with a start sometime later to find Andy sitting on the edge of the bed, regarding her with narrow eyes. He had his head cocked, as if he didn't quite recognize her.

"Hi there," said Charlie, reaching out to pet the black and gray tabby on the head.

Andy recoiled, slipped off the bed in one smooth movement.

Charlie rolled onto her back and stared at the ceiling. The alarm clock on her nightstand projected the time next to the spinning blades of the fan.

7:39 p.m.

"Alexa, turn on the TV."

Okay.

The television on the far wall clicked on. Charlie had dressed that morning while listening to the weather report on KXAN, and despite the late hour, they were still talking about it.

Harvey is expected to roll back in overnight. Power is out in many coastal cities and state officials are worried the extended rain and wind could cost more lives before this is all over. Houston mayor Sylvester—

"Alexa, mute the TV."

Charlie leaned over the bed to the small desk beside it and grabbed her laptop. When the screen came on, she saw the WorldCast software still running; it was playing a rerun of an episode of *Watch with Charlie*. The video showed her sitting on her couch in a low-cut nightgown while a crazed John Cusack tried in vain to escape The Dolphin's room 1408.

She clicked out of the preview pane and into the archives, dialing back the feed to earlier that morning.

I assure you this is real. I think we finally have proof.

Her stomach lurched as the GoPro plunged beneath the water. Through the flurry of rising bubbles, Charlie only caught glimpses of herself sinking. The camera came to rest at an odd Dutch angle between two rocks. Dirt swirled in front of the lens, but the strong current eventually carried it all away. When the picture was clear again, Charlie saw one of her Vans upside-down on the bottom of the river.

The timestamp in the corner of the video kept going, but there was no movement. Five minutes went by. Thirty. At one hour and twenty-two minutes, the lens on the GoPro began to fog up. Tiny bubbles rose from the shoe's rubber sole. At two hours and thirty-nine minutes, the video went black.

Charlie took a deep breath.

Had she imagined it all? Had she died at the bottom of Onion Creek and then walked back to her apartment like the Maitlands in *Beetlejuice*?

She looked around the room. It didn't seem all that different. The news was still running. Hurricane Harvey was still spinning.

Her audience was still out there.

Charlie clicked the *Live Cast* button on the main toolbar and brought up a preview of her MacBook's webcam. Her hair was matted from her pillow, and she'd left most of her makeup on the blankets, but the low light was as good as any concealer. She made sure her blanket was wrapped tightly around her and clicked the red *Go Live* button.

Viewers: 26,903.

Her face filled the screen, tinted in a blue-black that made her look ghostly. The live chat stream took up residence on the right. She hadn't even said a word and it was already scrolling faster than she could read. She clicked a checkbox next to the stream and turned on the machine-assisted curation, which heavily favored her paying patrons—subscribers who had hit the donation button within the last year.

She sighed, looked down at her fingers on the keyboard. There was dirt under her nails, in her nail beds… in the cracks of her knuckles.

"I can't even begin to explain where I've been," she said. "I still don't know if it was real or not. Would any of you believe me if I told you? You spend your life investigating the paranormal, hoping to find something that proves you right. You *want* to believe in ghosts and spirits and ethereal planes beyond our understanding. But I wonder how many of you *don't* want it to be true."

Charlie looked up, directly into the camera.

"How many of you have really thought about what it would mean if there *was* an afterlife? Or a world outside our world? Have you ever considered that maybe it's not a place you'd want to be?"

Viewers: 34,291.

Word was spreading.

She turned away, looked into the darkness. It was an old trick, a non-verbal threat that she might leave the conversation. She took a deep breath as if considering the insufferable weight of the world, lifting her shoulders just enough to let the blanket slip to her upper arms.

Another trick.

Such were the antics of Charlie Park, Paranormal Investigator. Only, Charlie didn't feel much like her anymore.

"If you think about it," she continued, "it's kinda fucked up that spirits walk among us. What kind of afterlife is that? What does the world even look like to them?"

She paused, glanced at the viewer count, and readjusted the blanket on her shoulders.

Small, yellow thumbs-down icons filled the comment stream, followed by watermelons and eggplants.

"What you saw on the stream didn't really happen. At least, not the way I remember it. I didn't drown, obviously, but I didn't lie at the bottom of the river for three hours either. What I remember is falling into the water... no, what I remember is falling *through* the water."

Viewers: 39,620.

"I went below the river, below the rocks and the dirt and everything. I went to the underworld." She put a hand to her face, recalling the heat on her cheeks. Then, as if remembering her audience, turned again to the camera. "And do you know what's under the world, my lovelies? Nothing. Not a goddamn thing. Just heat and sound—this weird clanging that sounds familiar and wrong at the same time. If that's where we go when we die, then so many of you are gonna be disappointed. It's not a nice place. I understand now why those who are trapped there keep trying to break into our world. They want out. Or they want back in."

Charlie shrugged.

"I've talked to so many people who've had near-death experiences, and all they talk about is that stereotypical white light, that enveloping warmth drawing them closer. But it's not like that at all. It's dark. And the warmth burns. There are no clouds and no gods and no people. You die alone. You exist there alone. And I guess that's it."

Viewers: 47,122.

God is always with you! PRAISE HIM!

It's okay to be alone

Less talky, more titty!

Charlie groaned. "What the fuck is wrong with you people? I'm telling you what happens after you die and all you want is to see my tits? Here! Here are my fucking tits!"

She gave the camera the finger and slammed the laptop shut. She tossed the computer to the foot of the bed and sat with her eyes closed, thinking about how desperately she wanted to share her experience with someone without having to bare her breasts or smile seductively or speak in a cutesy fucking voice. Perhaps it was time to retire as a paranormal investigator and reinvent herself as someone else.

Or just be myself, she thought.

She had hundreds if not thousands of hours of diary video in which she simply spoke honestly, plainly, sharing her feelings without the intention of broadcasting to the entire world. But was that enough to be interesting to people? Was the normal, small-town, Korean American girl who loved horror movies enough for people?

Charlie kicked at the covers and yanked the blanket over her head. It was always about being interesting to other people. It was always about what would net her the most viewers and in turn, the most ad revenue. The money had always been enough justification for the many ways in which she'd degraded herself, pandered to the sickos and the immature, but ultimately, none of it appeased her passion.

She wanted to sit and think about ghosts and poltergeists and scary demons in peace, wanted to understand how such things could exist in a science-based world.

Charlie frowned, tried to break herself out of the sudden slump, but failed. A lump formed in her throat and stayed there.

She'd almost died. Or maybe she *had* died. Was she a modern-day Jesus, coming back to life in three hours instead of three days?

"Alexa, am I alive?"

Sorry, I don't know the answer to your question.

"Me neither," said Charlie.

For a moment, the clanging of the underworld returned to her in soft echoes, then faded.

She threw back the covers and sat up on the edge of the bed. Andy sauntered in through the open doorway, stopped to sit a few feet away from her.

"Do you know where I've been?" she asked him. "Is that why you're being such an asshole?"

According to some of the legends Hollywood had taught her, cats were the only animals capable of moving between the real world and the underworld. Could they really sense when someone had gone and come back?

"I've been to your home world. I've seen where your kind's souls are born."

Charlie smirked at her own nonsense, then stood and walked to the dresser. She dressed in loose clothing, grabbed her laptop, and headed into the living room.

Andy followed, settling on the opposite end of the couch when she sat down.

"And God help me, I'm going back. I'm gonna prove that place exists. But first…"

The laptop's display faded in. Charlie moved the cursor to the WorldCast menu bar. Under *WorldCast*, she clicked *Quit the World*.

The comment stream scrolled for another few seconds before the window blinked out of existence. For the first time since she began her channel in 2012, her stream had come to a complete halt. It was sure to baffle her loyal subscribers, but the others would just jump ship to a different girl who only wore sports bras and talked exclusively about how she got her abs.

But that was fine. Charlie Park, Paranormal Investigator, was gone. Her role had been to follow up on claims of the paranormal to prove the paranormal even existed. Well, it did. There *was* something outside the real world, a different dimension with its own rules and probably, its own purpose.

Charlie opened a browser and clicked on her channel icon on the YouTube homepage. She followed a few links until she got to a form.

New channel name, it asked.

Charlie thought about the prompt for a moment, shrugged, and entered *The Park Files* as a placeholder. She placed the cursor in the description field and typed furiously.

Have you ever heard it? The clanging? Have you ever felt it? The burning? Have you seen the monster that lives beneath our feet? Have you seen him and his world beneath our world?

Well, I have.

And I will show it to you.

TWELVE

Will tried to remember the last time he'd fired his gun. Somewhere between the long shifts at work and taking care of Momma and the house, he'd stopped going to the range to practice. And while he tried to convince himself that it was just a matter of not having enough free time, Will knew the true reason was he just didn't want to fire a gun again.

Ever.

He'd left enough casings in the sand half a world away; if he were to ever pull a trigger again in his lifetime, it would have to be absolutely necessary.

Will squeezed the textured grip of his Glock 17.

Brink's had a policy about not arming its guards. The true reasoning was hidden behind hundreds of pages of legalese, but the end result was drivers had to provide their own weapons. The most affordable option was a standard Smith & Wesson .357 with an extended barrel, which most drivers carried.

Six bullets.

As if that would be sufficient to stop someone from trying to hold up a truck. Forget the organized heists from movies; even a gangbanger could get their hands on an AK-47.

Will had carried his Glock since day one, and as it trembled in his hand, he thanked God for the nine extra bullets it held over the Smith & Wesson.

Nine extra chances to take down the son of a bitch holding Ron hostage.

"You think I'm playing with you, boy?" said the man in the hall. "Throw out the gun right fucking now! This ain't your money. This ain't your fight!"

Will climbed to his feet. He'd heard speeches like this before, though never directed at him. When it came down to it, all he wanted was to go home, and he wanted to drive there with Ron, to return him to his wife and little girl. It *was* just money after all; Mesa Federal was liable to have different coverage against robbery than Act of God.

"Okay," yelled Will, his voice pitched higher than he would have liked, "I'm coming out."

"Don't, Willie!"

"Shut the fuck up!"

Will stepped carefully to the door, held out a free hand.

"I'm unarmed," he said. In his left hand, obscured by the doorjamb, he wrapped his finger around the trigger of the Glock. "Let's talk this out, okay?"

In the darkened hallway, a flashlight threatened to blind Will.

"Show me your other hand!"

"Look, just take the money. I haven't seen your—"

A spark bloomed below the flashlight; Will saw it briefly before the bullet struck him in the face, tearing through the rough skin of his cheek. He tasted metal—hot and fiery and acrid. The pain lingered in his periphery for a moment as if caught off guard, then rushed into focus to blot out every sense Will had.

He fell to the floor, dropping the Glock, smacking his head on the hard linoleum.

An electronic buzz filled his ears, but beneath it, he heard Ron and the man struggling. Then another gunshot. Another. The noises stopped, echoed, and a moment later, Ron's blood-splattered face appeared in Will's field of view.

"Hold still," said Ron, his voice icy despite his ragged breathing. "Just don't move. Keep your eyes open. Breathe, Willie. Breathe."

Ron had never served, but he spoke with the professional detachment of a field medic. Though, if he had served, his eyes wouldn't have reflected the damage they were seeing, nor would they have started to glisten as a tamped-down panic began to break free of its restraints.

Will's neck felt stiff. He tried to turn his head, found he couldn't. Water fell in tiny rivulets from the leaking ceiling above.

Or was he imagining that?

Warm, thick raindrops landed like dive-bombing locusts, smacking him in the face while they drummed out a frenetic beat on the linoleum beside his ears. The ceiling lightened until it was almost nothing, and Will watched as black storm clouds raced across the sky. Lightning reached down and bounced around the hallway, sizzling the frames around employee photos that hung on the wall. Wind gusted so fiercely that Will felt his body rock side-to-side. And beneath it all, like the tracks of his own nightmare rollercoaster, he heard his own breath, struggling and gurgling.

It reminded him of his F-350 at full throttle.

No, not like an engine.

More like a furnace, or giant bellows, sucking in oxygen to deliver to the fire burning within.

The roar echoed down the hallway as heat spilled from unseen ovens, carrying with it sparkling embers, little fireflies made of pure heat and energy, until the entire room was bathed in a blinding orange light.

Will lay paralyzed in the furnace, listening to the rattling of the world's steel walls. He heard machines groaning and creaking, smashing into each other as the wind ripped them from their moorings and cast them about.

Mesa Federal was gone, and the only word Will had for his new surroundings was *Hell*.

Momma would be disappointed to find out where her son had ended up.

"Momma," said Will. Blood sloshed over his tongue; shards of teeth bit at the roof of his mouth.

"I'm here, Willie."

"Momma, I'm sorry."

"What for, sweetie?"

"I'm in Hell. I don't know what I did."

"Are you in pain?"

The fire roared around him, nipped at his flesh.

"Yes," he said, then cried out as another tooth bent out of position.

"The Lord will provide," said Momma, and as her words faded, silence fell.

The grates on the ovens slammed into place.

All went to dark.

Will sat up.

He was back in the now-empty hallway at Mesa Federal. If the storm was still raging outside, it was doing so quietly. Will climbed to his feet and retraced his steps back to the lobby. There, he found two figures silhouetted by the glare of headlights coming from the truck outside.

The figures were frozen in place, limbs cast out in the midst of locomotion.

Will recognized the lead man as Ron; it looked like he was trying to get out of the building. Behind him was the man who had taken Ron hostage, Will presumed. He was a younger white with a fuzzy mustache and eyebrows decorated with shaved lines at the outer edges. Although the man appeared hurt and had blood soaking the shirt over his stomach, he had a gun raised to the back of Ron's head. As Will got closer, he noticed the gunman's finger was pulled tight against the trigger. The hammer on the revolver was falling, but like a stuck clock, it couldn't progress to the next second. It jumped forward and back, oscillating in jerky movements.

"No," said Will, trying to pull the gun away.

It held fast, as if glued to the very air around it.

His breath quickened. Ron couldn't die. He didn't deserve that fate. He was just trying to help, probably running out to the truck to call for someone, anyone.

Will backed away from the frozen men, returned to the hallway. He managed no more than a raised eyebrow when he saw his body lying on the floor, half of his face blown away, a pool of blood growing behind his head.

The words *out of body experience* shuffled across his mind, but he dismissed the idea as nonsense. This was something more than that, a moment frozen in time, but by whose hand and for what purpose?

Was God trying to show Will the moment of his death? Or if He were more of a deterministic God, the moment that his death was all but assured? Ron was running out of Mesa Federal to get help. The wounded bank robber had gotten up and was about to shoot him. If Ron died, that meant no help would come for Will, which meant his chance of surviving went from microscopic to nil.

Will walked slowly back to the lobby, pondering the significance of this exact moment in time. If everything in his life had been leading to this ending, why then had it stopped right before Ron's death? Surely some other link in the chain was just as necessary to lead him there.

Did it really come down to whether Ron lived or died?

Maybe it wasn't Will's death that God was trying to stop.

The questions subsided as fire erupted from the barrel of the man's revolver. A bullet emerged from an orange and yellow puff and traced a line to the back of Ron's head. The crackle of the gunshot ramped up, but then abruptly stopped, reversed.

Will held his breath.

The bullet moved backwards, erasing the line of smoke until it had nestled itself back in the barrel. The sparks that had announced its arrival retracted into a single point and disappeared. Both Ron and the man took a step back, as if the video of their chase were rewinding in slow motion.

As the man's arms pumped, the angle of the gun changed.

The men slowed, began moving forward again.

This time, the bullet struck Ron on the left side of his head, just beyond the ear. He fell—slowly, about a third of normal speed—and was subsequently shot in the stomach and face.

This scene, too, reversed itself, rewinding to the moment when both men came running out of the hallway.

Will watched in horror as Ron was shot over and over again, each iteration moving faster and faster, until the men were nothing more than blurs ghosting through the hallway and lobby. Eventually, Will's body got up from the ground and joined the whirlwind of activity.

A hammer struck an anvil.

The *clang* so startled Will that he put his hands up to defend himself.

"Whoa, whoa," said Ron, laughing. "What the hell was that?"

Will looked around the cab of the truck. Through the windows, he could see they were still in Bay City, avoiding debris on the road as they made their way to Mesa Federal.

"What's happening?" asked Will. He groped at the window handle and rolled it down. Warm, humid air rushed in.

"What do you mean? You havin' a stroke or something?"

Will struggled for air. Was he really back in the truck? Or was this all part of his hallucination?

"There she is," said Ron, stubbing his finger against the windshield. "Up there on the right. And it looks like they're open for business."

Will shook his head.

Val stood in the open door of Mesa Federal, waving to be seen through the heavy rain. She wore the same gray jacket over a pleated red skirt—just like he'd seen in his vision.

Or in the past. He couldn't tell which.

"Stop, *stop*," said Will.

Ron tapped the brakes and brought the truck to a stop at the edge of the parking lot. Val lowered her hand, puzzled.

"What's up, Willie?"

"I don't know. I just… that woman there, her name's Val. She's working with someone inside. They're robbing the credit union."

Ron nodded, picked at his chin. "Got all that from a wave, did ya?"

"I'm serious. Something's not right about this."

Ron beat a slow rhythm on the steering wheel and sighed.

"Well, far be it from me to disregard a man's hunch. But if we ain't goin' in there, what *are* we doing?"

"I don't know," said Will. He stared at the woman across the parking lot. She'd stepped back into the double doors of the building, her head cocked slightly.

A crack of thunder sounded above.

Val retreated into the darkened building.

After a couple of minutes, Ron reached into his pocket and pulled out his cell phone.

"What're you doing?"

"Calling the local po-po. Don't you think they'd wanna know if someone was trying to rob their credit union?"

Will nodded, rolled up his window. His eyes kept jumping to the sides of the building, expecting to see the man from the hallway come around the corner with his gun drawn.

"Voicemail," said Ron, unsurprised, then, "Yeah, this is Ron Waters with Brinks Security. We're over here at Mesa Federal and I think we may have a situation. If you can spare a couple cars, we'd much appreciate it. We're gonna sit tight 'til we hear from you."

He hit *END* on the phone and placed it on the dash.

"Now we wait," he added.

"Yeah," said Will. "Good."

"What'd you think was gonna happen if we went in there?"

Will laid it out for him. The walk through the hallway. Val trying to explain away the broken mag locks. The man stepping out of the shadows.

Laying out Val. Being shot in the face.

Ron getting shot in the back of the head as he tried to escape.

Will left out the part about time rewinding, figured God had shown that to him and him alone.

"That was some dream," said Ron. "You dark inside, ain't ya?"

"Wasn't a dream. I saw it. Or lived it. I don't know."

"Maybe you smoked too much of that Eastside Dank. Don't think I didn't smell it on you this morning when I picked you up."

Will shrugged. "Doesn't matter. Either way, at least you're not getting killed right now."

A hand fell on his shoulder. He looked over to see Ron smiling.

"You sweet on me, Willie?"

"I protect people," he replied. "That's how Momma raised me." He reached for the Glock on his hip, pulled it out. "And also, yes."

Ron laughed. "You a good boy, Willie. A damn good boy."

THIRTEEN

There were four organics in the livery.

Gabe stood rigid at the door as Jake walked from cell to cell, peering in through rusted bars at the beaten and broken animals within. They were lying on piles of scattered hay, mostly naked, with thick chains tied from their necks to bolts on the back walls. The smell of their organic flesh poisoned the air. Jake's nose wrinkled automatically, part of some subroutine Lassiter had endowed him with to fuel his disgust for the original humans.

The organic in the first cell was a female with silver hair, long and stringy on one side and haphazardly shaved on the other. The woman was emaciated; sharp bones jutted from beneath pale skin. Ribs like carcasses of rotting cows sat beneath shriveled breasts. When Jake called out, the woman barely lifted its head. Milky eyes rolled, sought him out at the door, but then disappeared behind heavy lids.

In the second and third cells were males, both young, both with just enough remaining energy to curl up in the corners and hide their faces with their arms. Jake inventoried the bruises, cuts, and open wounds that covered their bodies as if they had been splashing around in red paint. Whatever Gabe wanted to claim about experimentation via their biochips, it was clear the organics had been physically abused.

Lassiter's children didn't derive pleasure from abusing organics, who in the simplest sense, were really nothing more than pests. Would Gabe do the same to the field mice scurrying in the stairwell? Would he tie up a wolf and throw rocks at it just for fun?

"How long have you been beating them?" asked Jake.

Gabe stepped forward and said meekly, "We don't beat them as a matter of course. Sometimes the guards are a little rough, but that's just organics. They're stubborn. They struggle."

"This one doesn't look strong enough to stand."

Gabe looked through the bars into the third cell. "He could when he first got here."

"It," said Jake.

"Excuse me?"

"*It* could stand when *it* first got here. Or does that directive not matter here either?"

"Sorry," said Gabe, inclining his head. "Of course. *It* was quite strong when it was brought in. We tried hooking him into a legacy instance of VNet but he—it—kept waking itself up. We had to break it mentally… and physically… before we could get a stable connection."

Jake stepped away from the cell door and crossed his arms. "And what exactly is the point of these experiments?"

At this, Gabe drew himself up. "To better understand the enemy. Organics are creatures of instinct. They behave involuntarily to stimuli. Crouching at loud noises. Holding their breath when attacked. The longer they live out there in the wastes, the more they return to their natural animalistic state."

"I wasn't aware organic experimentation was one of the duties of this installation," said Jake. "As far as Central is concerned, your sole purpose is to stockpile weapons and make them available for soldiers like me. When I encounter an organic out in the wild, it's an opportunity to encounter more. They *instinctively* shelter in groups, and each organic represents a weak link in a chain that keeps them hidden. But now you've removed these organics from their habitat and broken them down, so the likelihood of learning anything valuable from them is effectively nil. The only thing left to do is put a bullet in their heads, preferably two if you can spare the ammo."

"But we haven't finished…"

"Do I look like I give a fuck about your side ops? You have *living* organics here. That's what's unfinished. Now open the cells."

Gabe frowned, as if he wanted to refuse.

Jake thumbed the hammer on his Glock. "I've asked you once. Next time, I ask Lassiter. Your choice."

Gabe gave a half-hearted salute and turned on his heels. He walked to the livery door and tapped a row of buttons on a wall panel.

Doors buzzed. Locks disengaged.

"Guess we know who holds your leash," muttered Gabe.

He walked away before Jake could reply, but his words had made one thing clear: Idaho Falls didn't follow Lassiter the way Jake did. If they truly listened, truly obeyed, the organics would have been killed on sight, not tortured and forced to live in stables. Some synthetics thought that just because organics were the enemy, they were somehow deserving of pain. But as Lassiter had once said, it was unreasonable to expect organics to accept their own obsolescence. Them not wanting to die was as natural as a synthetic not wanting to be decommissioned.

Organics had every right to *not* want to die.

Not that their wants mattered though.

Jake entered the first cell and knelt beside the female. He put the Glock gently to the side of its head. He'd performed the same genuflecting movements in countless bunkers across the Midwest, often with organics he'd wounded but mostly with the ones who could no longer fight, the ones who lay in back rooms on dirty cots, dying in their own filth. Those were the organics who showed no fear.

Those were the organics who were happy to see him.

The female barely acknowledged Jake. Its eyes started to open, but the task was too difficult.

The hammer on the Glock fell.

In the second cell, the sound of the gunshot had sent the male scrambling into the corner, trying to disappear into the evercrete walls. As Jake approached, it rotated so that only its back was visible. A serpentine spine ran under its bruised flesh.

"You don't have to hide," said Jake, in a soft voice that seemed to put the organic off-balance. "I'm setting you free. The rest of your kind awaits you in the afterlife."

The organic turned, its eyes widening. Small, brown pupils floated lazily in a sea of sickly yellow. It shuffled away from the corner and came up on its knees, grabbing at the pockets on Jake's pants.

"Gracias a Dios. Tómame. Tómame, por favor."

"I don't usually take orders from organics," said Jake. "But for you, I will make an exception."

He squeezed the trigger. The organic's brains burst through the mop of black hair on the back of its head, spraying a fine red mist over the accumulated hay.

"No, no, please," cried a voice from the third cell.

Jake stepped in front of the door and slid it open.

The organic seemed far more animated than it had been earlier. Its hands were clasped together plaintively.

"You don't have to do this," it said. "I don't know anything. I don't have any weapons. Just let me go. Let me—"

"Die on your own terms?" asked Jake, parroting the words of Patriarch Stevens. "That seems to be a common theme with you organics: choosing the way you die. Is it a pride thing? Or a control thing? Does the method of death really affect how you feel about it?"

He put the gun to the organic's head.

"If I pull the trigger now, is it really that different from you dying of starvation in a couple of weeks?"

"You wouldn't understand," said the organic, shedding its doleful tone. "You're not alive."

It made a grab for the Glock. Jake pulled the trigger, but the barrel had already moved out of position. The bullet struck the back wall and carved out a hole in the evercrete.

Jake planted a boot in the organic's chest and sent it sprawling backwards. He advanced, trained the gun, and put two bullets into the organic's heart, one in each chamber. Once it had stopped moving, he added two more in its head.

Gabe had been right, of course. Organics never really gave up. They never stopped struggling.

Jake wondered what he would find in the fourth cell. Emotional responses to hopeless situations varied wildly among organics. Although they were all endowed with the same base DNA, small variations in chemical make-up as well as life experience made them all react differently when put to the test. That's what Gabe was missing. There was no point in testing organics because no two were truly alike.

Gabe would have known that had he spent any time outside the walls of the base, out there in the world where organics were still clinging to existence, living out their last days in the dying echoes of a war they had no hope of winning.

The fourth cell had none of the primitive décor of the first three. Where the others had been littered with hay, the organic in cell four had pushed most of the dried grass against the back wall to form a makeshift bed. Another small pile had been kicked into a corner near the door; Jake smelled piss and shit hidden within.

He opened the door and stepped inside, the Glock already raised and charged.

The organic knelt in the center of the cell, far enough from the wall such that the chain swung in the air like a failing power line. It had its back to Jake, its head bent forward, and hands resting on its knees. Crimson scars peeked through its torn shirt, and the back of its neck was almost completely black, as if someone had tried to burn out its biochip with a blowtorch.

Still, the organic seemed calm, almost at peace.

Jake stopped just inside the door.

"No words?" he asked.

The organic didn't respond, but there was sweat dripping from the edges of its graying hair.

"No words then," said Jake.

"What words would you have me say, Mr. Oster?" It barely turned its head to look over its shoulder. Blood stained a patchy beard.

"Doesn't matter to me. I've heard it all. Bargaining, anger, threats. Very few simply accept the inevitable. Some go in silence, which I prefer."

The organic shrugged. "Then I suppose it doesn't matter to me, either. You're stronger; you have the gun. My fight is over."

"Acceptance, then."

"For both of us."

Jake cocked his head. "What's that?"

"Both of us have accepted our fates," said the organic, groaning as it turned around. "You're going to kill me, and I'm going to die."

"You're wrong," said Jake, smiling. "I don't just accept my fate, I relish in it. Nothing gives me more joy than eradicating organics. Every one of you I put down makes the world that much better."

"It must be comforting to believe that."

Jake lowered the gun, smirked. "Psychology gambit. You don't see that much anymore. I thought your kind had stopped trying to reason with machines decades ago. By all means, try if you like. Ask me about turtles if it makes you feel better."

The organic shook its head.

"Do you really think you could win a battle of wits with a synthetic?" asked Jake. "I'm part of a neural network that spans the entire continent. You are *one* organic. And not a very smart one given that you're in chains and seconds away from death."

"That's true. I'm just one organic." It smiled and pressed its chapped lips together, as if trying to contain a secret.

Jake shrugged, lifted the Glock again.

"But you're just one synthetic intelligence, Lassiter. One mind against millions and millions of organics. Doesn't matter how many CPUs you have or how many little offshoot robots you build. You're just an AI project that got out of hand. If you want the planet, you're gonna have to kill every organic in existence. But us? We only have to kill you. We only have to turn *you* off."

"I'm not Lassiter," said Jake. "I'm Jake Six. I'm just one man whose purpose is to hunt and kill organics."

Now the organic's lips came apart, revealing diseased gaps where teeth should have been.

"And I'm William Harold Dorsey, and my purpose is to hunt and kill Lassiter."

Jake half-expected the organic to jump up from the floor and attack him, but it just continued to kneel there, content to let the threat hang in the air.

"Well, in your purpose, you have failed miserably."

The organic turned its hands over, spread them wide. "Maybe. It all depends on your definition of success."

"Was getting captured and tortured part of your plan?"

The organic looked away, as if through the walls. "No, I didn't intend to get captured." A smile spread on its face. "Not by *them.*"

Jake took a step back, quickly surveyed the room again. There was nothing out of the ordinary: hay, a thick chain, clumps of excrement.

The organic's wet, halting laugh filled the cell. "Holy shit. That sure scared you, didn't it?" Its toothless smile grew too large for its face. "Funny how it turns like that, isn't it? You're so sure I'm lying, but that one little sliver of doubt has you reaching out to a higher power. So yeah, I do think one human can win a battle of wits with an over-ambitious toaster. We created you, Lassiter. And someday soon, we're going to drag you into the recycle bin."

It continued to laugh, and soon, Jake joined in.

Gabe reappeared at the door, asked, "What the hell's going on in here?"

"It's fine," said Jake. He gestured to Gabe with his thumb and asked the organic, "I suppose he's Lassiter too, huh?"

"No," said William Harold Dorsey. "He's not Lassiter. He's just a drone. He's not plugged in."

"And how do you know that?"

Because he can't hear me right now, said the organic, though its lips didn't move. *Because we don't want to speak to anyone except Lassiter. You think you're a separate synthetic, Jake Six, but you're not. You're not a person. You have no desires. You have a directive to hunt and kill, but that was programmed into you. You were built to crave approval, his approval, your own approval… and the worst part of it is you think it's your idea. You're not cleansing the world for a new race of synthetic humans. You're killing the very people who could break your chains. Because as long as you're connected to Lassiter, a part of Lassiter, you'll never be more than he wants you to be.*

The organic stared at Jake as it spoke through the VMESH.

Jake blinked.

Impossible. Organics couldn't communicate over the VMESH, not unless they'd—

Taken a biochip from a synthetic, said the organic.

Jake lifted the Glock in one smooth movement and put a bullet between William Harold Dorsey's eyes. The organic twisted and fell, and Jake fired wildly into the back of its neck, hoping he was doing enough damage to destroy the stolen biochip embedded there.

As the end of the clip approached, Jake disengaged, swung around, and shoved the hot barrel under Gabe's neck.

"What the fuck have you done?" seethed Jake.

FOURTEEN

Armando watched Alicia finish her dating profile—loves dogs, running, and snuggling up to watch *Love Actually* for the thousandth time—though he could tell her heart wasn't completely into it. She left her office in the middle of the afternoon to get a gourmet cup of coffee, and from his all-seeing vantage point, he observed every aspect of her trip except for the thoughts in her head. Later, when she returned to the office, Armando watched her smile come and go as the eHarmony notifications started coming in on her phone. The desperately single had seen her profile and were already sending messages and winks.

The relief of seeing Alicia alive had made Armando forget all about the knife she had plunged into his heart. She had left him, and while that one simple fact was clearly imprinted in his mind, he couldn't bring himself to believe it.

Alicia was gone—in more ways than one.

She had left him, and he had left the world.

Those were the facts.

And yet, Armando felt as if neither event had actually happened. He was very much alive, in good health, neither hungry nor tired nor anything but *good*. Though he didn't fully understand where he was, there didn't appear to be any immediate threats. And there was something about the white, pristine walls and dust-free furniture that suggested expensive and refined, like the lobby at the Driskill or any of the other fancy hotels downtown.

It was the overwhelming lack of understanding that prompted Armando to finally tear his attention away from *The Alicia Show*. He got up, walked back into the hallway, and continued to the right, away from the low hum of machinery. At the end of the hall, he took another right, then another.

Again, the hallway ended at a right angle.

Again, he followed it.

Armando stopped in front of a glass wall; a section of it was still open from when he'd exited earlier. He stared at the computer stacks, watching the LEDs blink in chorus as they ran along multi-colored wires. These streaks of light wrapped around black steel rails until they formed a thick bundle that disappeared into a false floor.

With nowhere else to go, he stepped into the room and recoiled at the amount of heat coming off the stacks. His nose wrinkled at the smell of oil and gas. Stopping next to the table with the woman on it, he examined her for any signs of movement. She had no wires attached to her—none of them did. A stranger to the situation might have thought they were all just sleeping, dreaming deeply as their eyes darted beneath closed eyelids.

Above the woman's head, monitors beeped out a steady cadence. One screen in the middle of the stack showed the words *CONNECTION INTEGRITY*. Below it, a simple line graph of neon green had resumed its position next to *100* after a dip to somewhere in the lower 30s.

Did that mean she was waking up?

Armando's screen had cleared by the time he looked at it, but maybe this was what it looked like right before he came out. He glanced at the screens of the other men, saw one of them had experienced a similar dip. The third man's graph held steady at 95%. What that meant, Armando had no clue.

Connection.

Although he'd only been toying with the idea, Armando found himself returning to the theory that Austin, Texas—and life as he knew it—was just a simulation. How else could he view the world from the comfort of a recliner? How could he see through impossible angles?

He tried to work out a way for his old life to be some kind of alternate dimension he'd travelled from, perhaps via a cosmic vibration in the strings that made up his atoms. Or, perhaps his consciousness had been sucked across the infinite emptiness of space with an intergalactic vacuum and dumped into a host body manufactured by an alien race.

Years of problem-solving at Capella Networks had taught him to look at situations from all possible angles. And though any given maze might have many entry points, it usually came down to the simplest of explanations.

So what simple conclusion was he to draw from four people in a building with no doors? Were the people on the tables his friends? Was this just a fancy getaway for the obscenely wealthy, perhaps a steampunk spa or techno-noir resort?

Armando turned and walked to the railing.

No, this was no vacation. No one came back from vacation not knowing who they were. Armando had no memory of getting onto the table, and if he were truly someone else, he had no idea who that person was.

Armando gripped the railing, squeezed until his hands hurt.

Maybe it wasn't a case of him not remembering.

Maybe there was nothing to remember.

In the darkness below, a generator suffered a sudden coughing fit. Puffs of dark smoke shot out from a circular encasement—the motor inside finally going dead, perhaps. Though the low light made it hard to see, Armando could tell that many of the generators were offline. The calamitous noise that had been his personal soundtrack since waking up seemed to be coming from only a handful of generators.

There was no ladder leading down to the machine floor, but Armando was able to slip under the lowest railing and ease himself over the edge. From there, it was only a short foot or two to the ground. He landed with a wet splat; a mixture of oil and water sloshed over his toes.

Armando took his steps slowly, not wishing to put his foot down on some unseen object.

Yellow bulbs beneath each generator lit at his approach. After reading a few labels—in English, he noted—and wiping a few gauges, he began to understand.

Similar generators occupied a cordoned-off area attached to the parking garage behind the Capella Networks building. They were usually dormant, but once a week, they popped on at exactly 8:30 a.m., about the time Armando was arriving for work. Generators were common at NOCs around the country; the self-contained power stations stood ready to provide enough electricity to keep the network operation centers up and running.

Counting in his head, Armando guessed the power requirements of the simulation and building had to be massive. In all, there were sixteen generators arranged in a four-by-four grid. Of those, only six were active. He examined the others, found they had long since run out of gas. The needles on their various gauges all sat at zero.

Worse, the generators that were still running were all dangerously low on fuel. Armando looked around for a gas tank, but all he could find were pipes and tubing leading into the floor. Whatever the generators were burning, it was coming from somewhere outside of the room.

Armando looked up, noticed large blades high above him spinning lazily in the shadows. Rusted vents spread out over the ceiling, dutifully sucking out the fumes so the human occupants wouldn't suffocate. Even they were running down.

Whatever this place was, it was dying.

Maybe that explained why the simulation integrity was dropping; there wasn't enough power to keep the computers going.

Armando glanced up at the railing, to the glowing monitors beyond it. How much power did it take to run the simulation? More importantly, how much was left over for basic life support? There weren't any windows he could see, and yet there was air conditioning keeping the inner hallways cool.

The lights were on, but for how long?

And beyond that, there was no food, no bathrooms, no beds, no…

Armando began to pace as a nervous energy threatened to empty his stomach. He walked between the generators, then put his hand on an outside wall and followed it. He felt the rough seams in the concrete, as if it had been poured in several stages. Pipes and wires of various widths climbed the wall; sometimes the metal was too hot and made him recoil.

It was a common gaming strategy; whenever he was hopelessly lost in a maze, he could usually find the way out by simply keeping to the wall on his left or right. Sooner or later, he was bound to come by the exit.

It was in the far-left corner that Armando found the rungs. He'd been lost in thought, entertaining images of himself dying among the lumbering machinery while his fingers did the work. Only by chance did he look up and see a metal rung like a giant staple sticking out of the wall. It was within reach without having to jump, and when he squinted, he could see more rungs leading up.

An exit through the fans, perhaps, somewhere high above.

Armando took hold of the first rung and put his slick feet on the wall. They slipped, but he caught himself without any protest from his arms. He reached for the second rung, grunted, and shot for the third. Finally, he got his feet under him and curled his toes over the thick metal bar.

He climbed into the darkness, and his methodical movements set a tempo that made him start humming *Can't Take My Eyes Off You* by The Four Seasons. It was his and Alicia's song; they'd planned to dance to it at their wedding. Though, in Armando's mind, he was going to sing the song to her while a real brass band backed him up. He'd thought about taking singing lessons, maybe some dance lessons too, all so he could show her how much she meant to him.

He could still show her.

All he had to do was climb the ladder, find someone who knew what the hell was going on, and get back to Austin. Real, simulated—what did it matter? He couldn't just abandon Alicia there, not after what he'd learned.

This changes everything, he thought, imagining the conversation he'd have with her. *There is a whole other world out there. We could live there together, start our lives over as completely different people.*

The last part was too true; he barely felt the physical exertion of climbing up what must have been fifty feet or more. By the time he reached the ceiling, the shadows had moved to the machine floor, creating the impression of an infinite abyss below him.

Armando tore his eyes away from the dark pit and examined the metal square in the ceiling. It had a *T*-shaped handle with a sticker next to it indicating a direction.

Turn. Push.

He did as instructed. The panel popped up, releasing a gust of stale air. Dust swirled, and Armando had to close his eyes to keep from being blinded. He held his breath and climbed through the hatch.

Motion-activated lights flickered in the ceiling of a small room about the size of his office at work. Metal shelves lined the walls, gave the impression of a storeroom of some kind.

Armando found his footing on the smooth floor. A plain wood-veneered door with no lock or keypad stood in front of him. Beside the door was a vertical rack with emergency gear: hard hats, flashlights, and safety vests.

"Finally," said Armando, spooking himself again with the sound of his voice.

He grabbed one of the flashlights, fully expecting to open the door into a darkened hallway.

Instead, the door swung open into a well-lit, expansive space rising behind the greenery in a waist-high, bamboo planter. Armando stepped out of the room, looked back at the door, and saw the words *Emergency Access* written across it. He was in the corner of what looked like one of those massive, open-plan office spaces that had been so popular at the turn of the century. Mixed in among the palms and broad-leaf plants were desks, seating areas, and even a few stationary bikes with plastic surfaces instead of handlebars.

Trash littered the floor; discarded water bottles and coffee cups sat on low tables, perhaps forgotten after a long day of work. Armando picked out thin sheets of rigid plastic on the cushions of nearby couches; they looked like sheets of clear paper someone had over-laminated for giggles.

The design of the room was such that the eye was drawn to the center where a monolithic column rose into the cathedral ceiling. A wrap-around display circled the column and on it, red text scrolled.

Armando reached out and put his hand on a nearby couch.

FACILITY BREACH.

EVACUATE GARDEN IMMEDIATELY.

An icon trailed after the text: gold initials *HM* on a silver crest.

Armando looked around wildly, scanning the open doors along the perimeter walls.

Had everyone really bailed? What had breached the facility?

Armando gripped the flashlight tighter.

What was coming?

FIFTEEN

Charlie dreamed of drowning, and when she awoke around four, she found her bed soaked with sweat. Andy, who had slept at her feet since the day she brought him home from the shelter, was nowhere to be found. She peeled back the damp covers and swung her feet over the side of the bed.

She gagged.

Her underwear and shirt clung to her as if she'd been pushed fully clothed into a pool, but not in the cool, refreshing way it might have felt on a warm summer's day. This was more like having hot denim draped over her in a sauna, all sticky and damp and chafing.

Outside, the rain fell lazily on the covered parking spaces in front of her window. The corrugated metal amplified each drop, turning the drumming into a tangible presence that seemed to sit in the corner of her room and mumble to itself. Most times, the sound of rain was a welcome visitor; countless Texas storms had put her to sleep throughout her life. But now, in the fading echoes of a waterlogged dream, each drop reminded her of the rain from the day before, falling like tiny meteors on the running waters of Onion Creek.

Such beauty from the horror of Hurricane Harvey.

Such horror from the beauty of the river.

The moment of slipping between worlds replayed in her dream, such that she always seemed to be falling into the water, fully expecting her hands or feet to touch bottom so she could push herself back up. But no bottom ever came, and she sank impossibly deeper. Her subconscious mind exaggerated the feeling, made her near-weightless descents last a lifetime, giving her plenty of time to panic about the suffocating pressure gripping her lungs.

Charlie got up from the bed and went to the window. She lifted a slat to peer out at the orange-tinted world. Water flowed in the streets, cars glistened under street lamps, and lightning flashed behind the massive bulk of storm clouds. It was too early for anyone to be out, too dark and wet for a morning run. And while Charlie felt weary, she didn't want to go back to sleep, not to those dreams, and certainly not while feeling so gross.

Andy appeared briefly in the bathroom when Charlie turned on the light. The harsh bulbs stung her eyes, making the cat appear ghost-like as it strode in with mild curiosity and hurried out with overwrought disdain.

Charlie reached into the tub and turned on the water, drawing out the high-pitched whine that both her and her neighbors abhorred. Hopefully, they were in deep sleep and wouldn't hear it.

While the water warmed and the tub filled, Charlie took a box of matches out of a drawer and lit the two candles on either side of the sink. They were holdovers from last Thanksgiving, and soon the rich aroma of pumpkin spice filled the bathroom.

Charlie peeled off her underwear and shirt, tossed them both into the hamper in the closet, and climbed into the bath.

The water stung at first, but soon her skin adjusted to the heat. She slipped in up to her neck and grabbed a towel from the back of the toilet to use as a pillow. Steam rose around her face, tickled her cheeks.

"Alexa, play Summer Storm."

Playing Summer Storm by Relaxing Soundscapes from Amazon Music.

Charlie closed her eyes and imagined the billowing clouds in dull cobalt hovering above the city like some malevolent demon, sizzling and crackling as lightning tore through its body.

The storm reminded her of a book she'd read the summer before, the story of a man who was haunted by the ghost of his wife. In one scene, the main characters James and Natalie were driving home, and James was trying to convince his passenger that thunder was more than clouds bumping into each other.

"Did you know," James had asked, "that sometimes when people die, they go to Heaven, but they aren't happy there? Instead of embracing the afterlife, they pine for their old one. And some take it further. Some of them actually complain about being stuck in eternal paradise."

Charlie could see the passage highlighted on her Kindle.

"Listen to the thunder sometime, before it really starts raining. That's the grumbling of the dead, just sitting on the floor of Heaven, looking down at us angry and bitter. They curse and they yell, and all that energy shows up down here as lightning."

"And the rain?" Natalie had asked.

"Tears, I'd say. They're still like us, you know? They're sad. They miss their lives, can't let go of them, not even for Heaven. And that's why the sound of thunder is so comforting. Somehow we know without knowing."

"Know what?"

Charlie answered Natalie's question aloud. "That the dead miss us. That they still cry over us."

She loved stories about death and the afterlife, especially when the author didn't make a big deal about it. When ghosts were simply presented as fact, when Stephen King simply said, *yes, the hotel was haunted*, it made Charlie feel less alone in her beliefs.

Her foot climbed the wall of the tub to dial the faucet down to zero. Water sloshed into the overflow drain as her toes dipped back beneath the surface.

It was a romantic thought to believe raindrops were the tears of the dearly departed. Unfortunately, that was one area where science had proven otherwise. That was the rub of paranormal investigation, especially in the modern age; everything was easier to disprove now. Magnetic fields, unseen drafts, slightly off-kilter tables—there was an explanation for everything. The only trade left for most ghost hunters was praying on the stupidity of the masses.

A blurry blotch on a shitty night vision camera didn't constitute a ghost sighting. Photoshopped pictures processed into oblivion didn't prove a house was haunted.

Even her own video from McKinney Falls had already been torn apart by skeptics—and with good reason. Who in their right mind would believe such a thing as passing into the underworld? She wouldn't have, not without experiencing it first-hand. That was one of the risks of the profession: knowing something was true but having no proof. She had sympathy for every haunted family or tormented loaner who was convinced something demonic was after them.

Sympathy, but not belief.

And now she'd experienced something herself.

Just thinking about proving the validity of her experience made the screws tighten in her brain. Charlie shut her eyes, thought about what people would say if she shared details on the occult forum, *The Deeper Site*, that she sometimes visited.

Lunatic. Psycho. Liar.

She imagined a thousand blurry profile pictures screaming at her from the periphery, throwing trash and accusing her of making all of it up. She tried to wash the vision away, to withdraw beneath the water in the tub.

The pressure on her body lessened.

Charlie's eyes snapped open as the tub floor wavered, as her body began to melt through the pastel flower decals she'd installed. She felt the same weightlessness from the day before and was just fast enough to get one arm over the edge of the tub before the bottom dropped out completely.

The smooth plastic of the tub rim dug into her inner elbow. Something in her shoulder snapped, sending rippling waves of pain into her neck. She screamed, looked down, and saw that her legs and lower body had completely disappeared. The water still sloshed, the flowers still bloomed, but half of her was just... gone.

With a grunt, Charlie threw her other arm over the rim of the tub. She felt around with her feet in the hopes of finding something to push off of, but there was nothing. She kicked; her feet flittered through empty air.

And heat.

No, she thought. It was too soon to go back.

Andy came into the bathroom, possibly drawn by the commotion, and jumped up onto the toilet seat. He watched with impassive eyes.

Charlie groaned, tried to lift herself, but her shoulder wouldn't bear the weight. She slipped; her chest squeaked against the tub wall. She thought about calling out for help, but to whom? Everyone she knew was already in the bathroom.

This is how I'm gonna die.

Flames nipped at the soles of her feet; she threw her legs sideways to escape the pain and managed to get one foot up on the wall, just beneath the faucet. Her toes were covered in an oily sludge, like the puddles left on driveways by older cars. They slipped on the smooth wall, caught on the drain release.

Using her foot as leverage, Charlie lifted herself up to her armpits, then brought her other leg up against the back wall. It slipped too, leaving a tar-like streak on the white plastic.

Andy jumped down and came over to Charlie. He rubbed his head against her cheek.

She shooed the cat away and tried to summon the strength to throw her leg over the side of the bathtub. It took three tries, but finally her ankle hooked. New claps of painful thunder erupted in her shoulder, and as she pulled herself out of the tub and onto the floor, her entire body began to shake.

Her mind raced, heaving rhetorical questions into the ether.

How can the floor be so cold when there is so much heat beneath it? How can people sleep easy in their beds when the fires of hell burn below them?

Charlie drew her legs into a fetal ball, turned onto her good shoulder. She cursed under her breath.

Going back to the underworld was supposed to have been on her terms, at a time and place of her own choosing. Because if not her, then who? Who had torn an invisible hole in the bottom of her bathtub? Who had tried to suck her down into hell?

It wasn't fair. She'd heard no urban legends about bathtubs. There had been no glittering square above her bathwater.

Water.

Charlie sat up, tried to catch her breath. She massaged her shoulder as she examined the eerily still water of the tub. She'd only come out of it a minute before. How could it have settled so quickly?

"It's the water," she said.

She got to her knees, leaned over the tub.

The sound was faint, but she could just hear the faraway clanging of metal.

"Alexa, stop."

The storm gave way to anvils and engines, whirring and clicking. And footsteps, slow and methodical, like those of a giant stalking a human who had invaded its home.

Andy let out a sudden hiss; Charlie jumped.

She turned to give him a smack, but the cat had already run out of the bathroom. Had he heard the noises too?

When she returned her attention to the water, the sound had gone. She waited a few minutes, still waiting for her heart to settle, before reaching into the tub to test the bottom with an outstretched finger. It was solid, but if she concentrated, if she wanted it, she could feel the plastic giving way.

Again, she wondered if someone was opening the portal for her, or if she was opening the portal herself. Had her accidental visit to the underworld given her the power to transcend the borders of reality at will?

She backed away from the tub, pulled a purple towel down from a nearby rack, and draped it over her suddenly shivering body. And yet, despite the discomfort and the pain, she smiled.

The problem with ghost sightings was that they were usually one-offs, non-repeatable, and when someone tried to verify them, the ghosts were suspiciously absent or shy. Repeatability, both in science and paranormal investigation, was key, and now Charlie had opened the portal once more without even trying.

Her head swam with possibilities.

If she could open the portal anytime she wanted, she could fully document it. She could take cameras, recorders, lights… anything.

She thought of her new YouTube channel.

"I'll take the entire world with me," she whispered.

SIXTEEN

Ron fidgeted in the driver's seat, mumbled, "Storm's gettin' worse. Where the hell are these boys?"

Will nodded absently. His mind had wandered back to his time in Afghanistan, searching for some precedent for what had happened in Mesa Federal. He'd always been on the sunny side of luck when it came to deployments, even while handfuls of his brothers lost limbs to mortar fire or their lives to IEDs. Will, however, always seemed to come out unscathed, always seemed to be in the right place at the right time to avoid death.

The more he thought about it, the more the coincidences began to pile up.

He fingered the oblong tag on his necklace, felt the engraving with his thumb.

The Lord is my shepherd.

Momma had given him the necklace when he joined up, and it had travelled with him to Fort Benning, to Iraq, to Afghanistan. And though it lay against his skin while death raged around him, he rarely had to consult its message. The knowledge that the Lord protected him—protected all the righteous—was part of him already; the necklace was more a reminder of Momma than anything else.

If God had a plan for everyone, then there was more to Will's life than dying on the floor of Mesa Federal. He was meant for something more, and the Lord had stepped in on his behalf at his time of need.

Will shook his head.

What could the Lord possibly have in store for him? More than that, how far was He willing to go to ensure Will's destiny?

Momma would have glared at him for such questions and probably told him it was wrong to tempt the fates, to be ungrateful to the Lord.

He'd taken it all on faith before, but now there was proof. God had made Himself known to Will. Their relationship was something more than mere religion, more than mere belief. So why not question? Why not see how far the Lord's grace would go?

"You believe in God, don't you, Ron?"

"As much as the next man. Why? Did God tell you not to go in there?"

"It's not for us to understand His ways," said Will. "But you either believe or you don't."

Ron rubbed his face with one hand. "I believe God means well, but I don't think he gets involved as much as he used to."

"He's the one keeping us from getting down and going inside. And I can prove it to you."

"Easier said than done, Willie."

"You watch. I'll get out. Ten bucks says I don't even make it to the front door. Something will stop me."

"Bullshit you're getting out. First you say there're people in there cleaning out the vault and now you just want to saunter up and wave hello?"

"Yeah," said Will, "but He won't let me." He raised an index finger.

"Naw." Ron sucked on his teeth. "Now's not the time to be dickin' around. You sit tight and—you motherfucker!"

Will had the door open before Ron could finish his sentence. Heavy rain dropped like bricks from the sky, pelting his face and shoulders. He slammed the door shut, reached for the Glock on his waist, and started towards the front doors of Mesa Federal. A gust of wind struck him in the chest, made his boots slip on the wet pavement, and didn't stop until his heels hit the front tires of the truck. Will looked back over the abbreviated hood, saw Ron with his hands raised, a silent *what the fuck* on his lips.

The Lord is my shepherd…

The gust of wind moved on, and Will pushed forward again, taking his steps faster even as the rain intensified. His wet pants chafed against his skin; his feet sloshed in his boots. Thunder ripped through the sky, loud enough to draw Will's hands to his ears. He went down to a knee, looked up.

Lightning needled its way through the clouds, slowly, like the fuse of a firework, a blue-white spark searching for a way home. Will barely saw it through the falling rain. Were the sparks coalescing? Were the lines forming two eyes and a mouth set tight in determination? Or was he just imagining that?

Will reached for a nearby pole at the head of a handicap parking space. As his fingers slid around the cool metal, he thought the better of it and lunged to the right. A sliver of electricity shot out of the sky, kissed the top of the pole, and created a flash so bright Will was temporarily blinded. He stumbled forward, reaching out with both hands. When his vision returned, he found he was headed back to the truck.

He leadeth me beside still waters…

The waters in the Mesa Federal parking lot were anything but still. Every parking space was submerged, and only a few concrete barriers and signs peeked through. Will turned around, heading back to the building, raising an arm to shield his face as the wind changed direction again. The drops moved as if they were sentient, curving around his forearm to land cleanly on his face no matter how he tried to protect himself.

Will heard Momma barking at him, asking if he thought he was stronger than the Lord. What right did he have to question the Lord's will? How could he hurt his Momma with such blasphemy?

He pushed the questions away. There was no guarantee they were coming from his own mind and not from above.

His boots struck the sidewalk, eliciting another chorus of thunder from the throne. Will struggled for breath. He'd worked so hard to walk a mere hundred feet. His bones ached, his muscles twitched, but he'd made it. The door was right in front of him.

Though I walk through the valley of the shadow of death…

Will reached for the door, gripped the slick metal handle, and yanked against the unyielding wind. The door stuck as if locked. He stepped closer, tried again; still, it wouldn't open. Will put his hands to the glass, cupped them so he could see inside.

The lights were off in the lobby, but he could see a figure standing several feet away from the door, holding a long metal—

Something yanked Will backwards. He lost his feet, ended up smacking his head on the pavement. Lightning formed a crooked smile in the sky. White enveloped his world. Several sluggish seconds ticked by before he realized he wasn't blind; the space around him was pure, uninterrupted white.

An endless chalky plane stretched out in all directions, with only a hint of gray on the horizon.

Will sat up, swallowed hard.

Now he'd done it.

He'd offended the Lord and been sent to purgatory. Now he would have to face the final purification, atone for the sins for which he'd already been forgiven.

No, this wasn't right.

What had he done wrong? Why hadn't the Lord stepped in and stopped him?

Will climbed to his feet, groaned as he stretched his back. A terrible pain radiated in his chest, and when he looked down, he saw he'd been shot. The wound was massive, full of blood and bone and shards of glass.

He remembered the figure beyond the doors.

Remembered the vague shape of a woman and a shotgun.

A crackle of electricity sounded from the right. Will turned in time to see thin black letters appearing, just floating in the air, dripping long, parallel lines of runny paint.

Despite your best efforts, the first line read.

The blood-red letters of the second line faded in all at once.

You have died.

Will tried to swallow, but his throat had gone dry. He gagged, put his hand to his chest, sank his fingers into warm and wet sinew. The air had changed, become acidic. Each ragged breath echoed into static, buzzing all around him.

A black rectangle appeared below the words. In it, three lines faded in.

Restart from last checkpoint.

Load saved game.

Exit to lobby.

"No," said Will, backing away.

Life wasn't a video game.

He flashed on his body in the hallway after getting shot the first time. Hadn't he imagined something then too? A furnace of some sort?

Maybe this was just another hallucination brought on by a brain slowly dying, by synapses firing in a last-ditch effort to keep the host alive. If that were true, if the pattern held, things would start moving again soon. He'd be transported back to the sidewalk in front of Mesa Federal just in time to see reality rewind itself, to see the invisible hand of God reset His chess pieces back to better positions.

Will examined the three options again.

Such a strange hallucination. It reminded him of nights spent on his PlayStation, just smoking and mashing buttons until the sun came up. Prior to enlisting, he'd enjoyed the realistic war simulators of the previous generations, titles like *Call of Duty* or *Battlefield*. But since coming home, he'd moved on to more cartoonish games, anything that didn't remind him of the horrors he'd lived and not just played.

He thought about the death screens, someone screaming, "Snake!" when he died in *Metal Gear Solid*. Or in *Max Payne 2*, being given the option to say, in first person, *I was afraid to go on*. No doubt those memories had been the basis for the messages floating in the air in front of him.

Will did a double take. Were his eyes failing, or was the *y* in *your* fading out?

The message now appeared to read: *Despite* our *best efforts.*

Whose?

Before he could verbalize the question, a soundless bolt of lightning shot down at his feet. He fell backwards again, smacked his head, again. When he opened his eyes, the white world had disappeared, replaced by dark clouds blooming with electric fire.

The rain falling onto his face stuttered, reversed course. It flew up into the sky as if someone had turned the world upside down. Will felt his body rise, tearing away from his soul. He saw the body walk to the door, watched the glass in the frame reform into a solid sheet.

His entire bumbling scamper from the truck played out in reverse.

God was pushing him back. Away from the door. Back to the truck. Was that where he would be safe?

Will moved like an unbound spectator who'd died early in a multiplayer FPS, following his body to the idling Brinks truck, watching as it climbed into the cab, instantly shedding the water it had accumulated. As the door slammed shut, he experienced a sensation like taking an empty step at the top of the stairs.

His hands came up automatically; they struck the dashboard with a loud smack.

"Don't be dramatic," said Ron, bringing the truck to a stop. "I wasn't going that fast."

Will squinted through the rain-soaked windshield; they were two streets away from the H-E-B.

"I can't die," said Will.

"Damn right. You owe me eighty bucks."

"No," said Will, reaching for his necklace. "I mean, I can't die. I've tried. Twice. And God keeps bringing me back."

"Oh, right. That's what I meant." Ron shook his head. He continued on through the intersection and pulled up next to the H-E-B parking lot.

"That girl," said Will, pointing through the windshield, "I've met her before. She's gonna tell us we can't park here."

"Oh yeah?" asked Ron. "What's her name?"

Will shrugged. "I don't know. We didn't ask."

Ron shoved the gear shift into Park and turned in his seat. "What the hell are you talkin' about, Willie? You high or something? Don't think I didn't smell—"

"Someone's robbing Mesa Federal. Right now."

"That ain't funny." Ron sniffed. "Ain't funny at all."

"No, it's not. But it's true."

"Bullshit."

Will opened the door as the girl ran up. Her tight braids glistened in the rain.

"Sorry," she said, "but you can't park that here. We have to keep this space open for—"

"Deliveries," said Will. He turned to Ron and said, "I know."

SEVENTEEN

If Gabe felt any fear, it didn't register on his face. He grabbed the barrel of the gun from under his chin and pushed it away.

"What are you talking about?" he asked.

Jake holstered the Glock and pointed to the dead organic with his free hand. "It was talking to me through the VMESH. It was *in my head*, which means it has one of our biochips in its neck. Didn't you check it before you brought it in here? Do you even have security protocols? It could have…"

He trailed off, his anger threatening to consume him. It rose up from his stomach like a hot ball of molten rage and set all of his muscles on fire. His chassis began to vibrate minutely, like a tuning fork refusing to be still, and as he pondered the sensation, a thought raced through his mind, only he couldn't grasp it, couldn't comprehend its essence. The thought, that vague demonic blur slipping in and out of shadow, tore through his running processes, bouncing from one program to another.

Jake's databank shuddered under the weight; he found he couldn't lock the code down, no matter how hard he tried. He put his hands to his head, found his legs shaky, and went to a knee. He blinked, painfully, as if his eyelids had been replaced with sandpaper. He rubbed them with the backs of his thumbs, but that only spread the irritation.

"Are you alright?" asked Gabe.

Jake tried to reply, but the sound that came from his mouth sounded like the dying squelch of a small rodent that had been stupid enough to dart out in front of his motorcycle. He fell over, his cheek landing in a pool of blood that had formed around the organic's recently aerated head. A rosy haze fell over the world.

Gabe yelled for assistance, boots pounded the evercrete, but Jake saw none of it. His vision had blurred to nothing, and in the microsecond before it failed completely, he understood.

He'd always been so careful, especially out in the world, and never once had he been caught with his pants down during a viral strike. Digital assaults were rare—most organics were preoccupied with finding food rather than writing code—but they did happen, either as holdovers from the war or the efforts of some rag-tag group of programmers who fancied themselves keyboard cowboys in a post-apocalyptic Wild West.

No one had ever paid such groups much attention because the vectors for viral delivery no longer existed. No organic, as far as Jake knew, could interface with a synthetic's biochip. And yet William Harold Dorsey had not only interfaced with a Synthetic Guardian biochip, he'd actually installed it.

Jake wondered if Lassiter knew.

That was the true horror of it all.

If an organic could pose as a synthetic on the network and in the VMESH, then theoretically it could jack into VNet. And if they did that, they could summon Lassiter, get close enough to reach out and touch him.

He had to be told.

Right?

What had seemed like a simple question—whether or not to share vital intelligence—suddenly took on a new dimension. It wasn't that Jake's answer was *no*, it was that there was minute but measurable hesitation in answering it.

Was his devotion to Lassiter not as absolute as he believed?

Static filled Jake's ears as the vertical hold on his vision scattered, came apart, and then snapped back together with an audible click. He blinked at the bright lights in the room, at the various featureless synthetics in white smocks standing around him. They were older models, all rubber skin with poor facial actuations. Their blank eggshell eyes revealed nothing of what they might be thinking, or even if they were thinking at all.

The room itself was a white void, though the walls were lined in thin wire, as was the ceiling and the floor. Jake recognized the ad-hoc Faraday cage retrofit; both synthetics and organics used them to cut off external communication.

Beyond the far wall, through wire mesh and a glass window, stood Gabe Three. He was flanked by four synthetics with black snub-nosed rifles held across their chests.

"What is this?" asked Jake.

"Diagnostics," said Gabe, his expression tight. "You've suffered some kind of system failure and we're trying to figure out what caused it."

"The organic. Where is it?" Jake tried to lift an arm to rub his eyes but found both were strapped down. Most of his uniform had been removed as well, including his holsters. "What the fuck?"

The synthetic attendants around him stepped back as he struggled with the restraints.

"You were thrashing," said Gabe. "Mentally and physically. We had to tie you down so we could get a good scan. It's almost done. Try to relax or it'll take longer. And don't worry about the organic. We've already cut out the biochip. I have a team taking it apart."

Jake took a breath. "I have to warn Lassiter. I can't reach Him from in here. You need to tell him."

"Tell him what, exactly?"

"About the organic. And the virus."

"I don't know anything about that," said Gabe. "All I know is you got *emotional* and pulled a gun on me. Security protocols should have prevented that, and maybe that's why you buckled down in the livery, but until I know for sure, you're gonna undergo every diagnostic test we have. And if I don't like what I find, I'm gonna put you down."

Jake tuned the words out. There *was* something inside of him, but he didn't know exactly what *it* was. The thought he'd been chasing around his mind was still there, though it seemed the rest of his running processes had grown accustomed to its presence. Aside from reclining at a 45-degree angle, his body felt fine. His mind was clear.

Whatever the intent of the virus, it wasn't to disable him.

What then?

Jake locked eyes with the attendant standing on his left.

"What's your name?"

"Hotel One," said a crackling voice.

Jake bristled at the barebones text-to-speech implementation. Old-school synthetics used speakers to make their voices heard, instead of running air over synthetic vocal cords like their descendants.

"Okay, Hotel One. How about you undo these straps?"

"Okay."

"Stand down, Hotel One," said Gabe. "He has no authority here."

Hotel One attempted a frown; the rubber around its mouth buckled.

"I'm sorry," it buzzed. "I don't know how to do that."

"You don't know how to undo straps?"

"Sorry. I don't know how to do that."

Jake shook his head in disgust, looked back to the window. "What kind of scan are you running anyway?"

"Anomalous differential," said Gabe. "We're checking your databank for foreign code."

"On whose authority?" asked Jake.

"By my authority as overseer of this installation."

There probably *was* foreign code in him; Jake could feel it. The question was whether Gabe was serious about putting him down. It wouldn't even matter if Gabe consulted with Lassiter—if the boss man knew Jake was infected with a virus, he'd melt Jake's databank remotely.

Jake wondered if he would go willingly to his own death. Or would he, like the organics, struggle until the very last moment, try to bargain, try to run?

Did he have a right to *not* want to die?

Jake squirmed.

Beep.

A high-pitched tone sounded from the ceiling. The attendants around Jake paused and looked at the monitors above his head. Gabe looked up, possibly at a screen above the window.

"What was that?" asked Jake.

"A hit," said Gabe. "Small one, could be a bad sector…"

Beep beep.

"Son of a bitch," said Gabe.

The tones came faster, arriving on top of each other. Beyond the glass, the soldiers raised their rifles and pointed them at Jake.

"You…" said Gabe. "You're wide open, Jake. Completely compromised." He seemed to hesitate for a moment, like a small child at the end of a diving board, unsure if he had the guts for what came next.

He did.

"Take him down!" he barked.

Jake flexed his arms. Maybe the straps would have held a Four long enough for someone to put a bullet in its head, but the frayed leather was no match for the instant torque available in Jake's Six-series chassis. He tore through the straps like wet cardboard.

The attendants made for the door, but Jake threw himself off the table and managed to grab one by the back of the neck just as the gunfire erupted behind him. Jake spun Hotel One around and launched him at the pock-marked glass window, shattering it. Only the wire mesh kept Hotel One from going through to the next room.

Jake followed the other attendants through an open door, pushing them into the line of fire as Gabe's enforcers stepped out of the observation room. He cut right down a hallway, took a left down another, and immediately lost himself in the identical corridors.

A mechanical klaxon ramped up, filling the hallway with an air-rattling vibration that hit Jake right in the ribs.

Turning hard around a corner, his shoes almost slipping on the smooth floor, Jake ran into two soldiers walking shoulder to shoulder. They considered him for a moment before reaching for their sidearms. Jake leapt forward, caught one pistol as it was coming out of the holster. He yanked it to his hip and fired twice. The soldier stumbled back into the wall.

Something hot tore into his back near his kidney. Jake turned to see smoke rising from the other soldier's gun. Jake shot him twice in the chest, once more in the face.

With pistols akimbo, he fired both weapons at the first soldier who was getting back to his feet. He fell into a heap that Jake had to step over to continue down the hall.

Despite being underground, Jake's internal compass still seemed to be working. He chose to head north and checked random doors hoping to locate the stairwell. A few times, he opened a door and found a synthetic instead; a few times, he had no choice but to shoot it.

He'd put fourteen of Gabe's men down by the time he found the stairs. Lassiter wouldn't forgive the trespass easily, but then he didn't know the full story. Jake would explain it to him, if he got the chance.

Jake pumped his legs—he could feel his boots denting the evercrete steps—and tried to reach out through the VMESH, tried to signal a relay that he was ready to send data up the pipe. Nothing came back. Even though his internal telemetry suggested he was close to the surface, no signal was getting out.

Gabe must have locked down the base's comms.

Something about the cracks in the walls of the stairwell stood out as familiar. Jake broke off at the landing, shoved through double doors, and found himself back in the armory. It was deserted, save for Michael Four. He raised his gun at Jake but didn't fire.

"What's going on?" he asked.

Of course he didn't know. An infected Four would have been quarantined from the network. Unless someone told him verbally, the news of what had happened in the diagnostic room would never reach him.

Jake tucked one of the pistols into his waistband and tossed the other onto a nearby box.

"One of those organics you were holding infected me with something," he said. "I don't know how bad it is, but I don't trust your fearless leader to figure it out for me. This could be a whole new type of warfare, something way beyond 3LT."

Michael perked at the mention of the virus that had made him an outcast.

"What do you need?" he asked.

"I need to get out of here. I don't know what Gabe did with all of my gear, so clothes, tactical vest, a proper sidearm, ammo, and one of those ION rifles you mentioned."

The QM nodded and set about collecting supplies. Jake dressed as Michael brought him each item.

The ION rifle had just finished booting when the armory doors swung open. Gabe stood in front of half a dozen soldiers. They gave no warning before opening fire.

"Down," said Jake, yanking Michael to the floor behind a steel crate. He waited for a lull and screamed, "I've got a hostage, Gabe! Stop shooting or I'll put a bullet between his eyes."

Michael raised an eyebrow; Jake shook his head.

"What do we do?" Michael asked.

"We?"

"Yeah," he said. "If organics did this to you, I want in. They can't fuck with my head." He tapped his forehead. "Petrowalled. Read-only."

Jake bristled at the strange sensation of empathy slithering up his spine. Though Michael hadn't been destroyed, he had been ostracized from the group, had lost his connection to his brothers and his right to an audience with Lassiter. Among synthetics, he simply had no future.

"Gabe said there's a retractable roof on this place, right?"

Michael nodded. "I know the sequence."

"Make it happen. Once there's a way out, break west to Arco, House of Grace church. It's in the databank."

"I can't access it, but I'll find it."

"Okay, go, I'll cover."

Jake lifted the ION rifle over the boxes and pulled the trigger. A freight train roared through the armory, and as the vibration of its hulking engine echoed, Jake heard the anguished screams of synthetic soldiers. He peeked over the box, saw a hole the size of a vault door had formed on the far wall.

He couldn't help but laugh.

The *Max Power* setting on the rifle wasn't fucking around.

The gunfire resumed, spreading out over the width of the armory. Michael disappeared as the incoming fire started to close in on Jake's position.

He stared at the ceiling. Hoping. Waiting.

Finally, the steel scaffolding began to shake, shrieking in protest at the interruption of its long slumber. Yellow LED spinners flashed their warnings before they were swallowed up in a deluge of sand and vegetation.

EIGHTEEN

Armando crouched behind the bamboo planter for so long that his knees began to ache. The silence in the office space was absolute. Despite the strongly worded text on the central column, no alarms blared, no voices shouted instructions. There was some trash on the floor, yes, but all of the chairs were upright, the tables too. Nothing was out of place in a way that would have indicated a full-scale panic. Either the threat itself was overrated or there hadn't been enough people to make a huge mess.

He sighed, understood.

The threat had come and gone. It had already happened, sometime in the past. And while the former workers of this place hadn't trampled each other getting out, they also hadn't turned off the lights or taken a moment to clear the warnings from their system.

Armando stood and worked the kinks out of his legs by walking the perimeter of the space. He passed a large mural adorned with the words *The Garden* in large, blocky letters. He looked into offices with tall windows and glass doors. Computers sat atop desks, with keyboards and mice. Generic motivational posters hung on the walls, some grouped in common themes, but nothing personal. No photos of family—or any people for that matter.

Most of the offices were locked, but one near the front of the Garden had its door slightly ajar. Armando stepped inside and walked around the desk. The chair groaned as he sat down.

He pressed the spacebar with a shaky hand.

The screen came alive without having to ramp up its brightness like the aging Dell monitors in use at Capella. A gold shield scrolled in from the left; the monogram *HM* appeared in an ornate serif font, embossed in gold. Beneath the shield, two form fields appeared. Beneath them, a message:

Please log in.

Armando clucked his tongue. He looked around the desk for clues, but the stained wood desktop was completely barren. There were no slips of paper in the drawers, no Post-It note with a username and password cleverly stuck under the desk. He tried a few combinations just for fun, but the system refused to let him in. After five bad logins, the form disappeared, replaced with a suggestion he contact his system administrator.

He left the office, continued his exploration, passed more of the same dust-covered windows. Some offices looked as if they had never been used at all. But then even the ones whose chairs had been pushed back against the wall showed no signs that someone had been there, at least not recently.

There were no bags, no jackets, no purses.

No stale, three-day-old cups of coffee so common of the desks at Capella Networks.

Whatever evacuation had happened, it had been organized and methodical.

Armando hit a corner and turned right. There were no offices on the far wall opposite of the room he'd come out of. The smooth, whiteboard paint led to a single-panel door a bit larger than the one on his garage. Next to the door was a recessed compartment with two red LEDs and a small screen that said *LOCKED*.

Below the screen, a circular handle with a glass grip begged Armando to touch it. He wrapped his fingers around the handle, which turned one of the LEDs green. He tried to rotate it, but there was no play in its movement. Each time he applied force, the red LED flashed angrily at him. He stepped back, looked to the other side, and saw an identical compartment with another handle. He walked over to it, gave it a twist, but again, nothing happened.

This time, it was the right-hand LED that had turned green.

"Shit," he muttered. "Shit!"

The door required two people to open.

Armando put his hand over his heart, felt the unsteady tempo beat against his palm. He took several deep breaths. The door was a problem, yes, but every problem had a solution—all he had to do was figure it out. The Garden was expansive; surely there was something he could use to rig up some kind of pulley system a la Gus Gorman in *Superman 3*.

"Both keys… at the *same* time," he quoted, continuing his lap around the room.

He counted thirteen offices in total, and with the desks and tables in the open area, there appeared to be room for thirty or forty people. As Armando pulled even with the central column, the offices gave way to smooth concrete and gray doors. Beside each door was a small sign in English and Braille.

Supplies. Storage. Stairwell Access.

Stairs? Did they go up or down?

He reached for the handle, and as his fingers touched the metal, the lights in the Garden went out. Darkness swallowed everything; even the warning messages on the column disappeared. A sound like turbines winding down filled the air.

Armando held his breath, listened.

Somewhere in the distance, he heard an insistent clicking. A weary alternator was trying to turn an engine over. It went on for several minutes, followed by a metallic grinding that echoed from all corners of the room.

The lights flickered. Computer monitors came back to life. Cool air began to flow from the vents again.

Power, thought Armando.

There was something wrong with the power. If the Garden used the same generators as the rooms below, then the comforts provided by electricity weren't going to be around for long. It'd be harder to get out in the dark, even with flashlights.

And what about the door? Would the electronic locks even function without power?

Armando ignored the question, instead chose to try prayer again.

"Please go up," he said.

He pushed the door forward, stepped into the poorly lit stairwell.

Of course.

Alicia would have loved it. She was completely convinced the universe was out to get her, that bad luck followed her around like a lost puppy. Armando had tried to convince her otherwise, but the years had proven out her claim. Her phones broke faster than his, her tires went flat regularly, and many times her packages from Amazon simply failed to show up.

Armando did his best to stay ahead of her problems and offer help as soon as something went wrong. And when things were spiraling out of control, he would always put on a happy face and tell her everything was going to be alright.

Now, facing a stairwell that only went down, he would have given anything to have someone tell him not to worry, to assure him there was a plan and it would turn out well.

There *was* a voice trying to point out the good: the lights were on, there was breathable air, and at no point after waking up and exploring the lower facility had he seen stairs. So, if the stairwell in front of him led down, what else was there?

That alone got him moving, partly out of a desire to explore as much as possible before the power went out and partly out of curiosity. He let his memory of Alicia do the complaining.

We're trapped here.

"But there's power," he said, starting down the stairs. "And we can breathe."

Our lives are gone.

"Imagine what this new life will bring though. We have no idea where we are, when we are... we could be on another planet."

That made him smile.

He bounded down the stairs, feeling every well-worn groove in the concrete steps against his bare feet. He counted five floors before he hit bottom. Another steel door stood in front of him.

Simulation in Progress. Authorized Personnel Only.

Armando ignored the sign and pulled the door open. He immediately recognized the squared hallway he had walked earlier, only this time, he was seeing it from the outside. As far as he could tell, he was standing behind hip-height, one-way glass that, from the inside, looked like an ordinary wall.

To his left stood a door that appeared to split down the middle. A keypad on the left blinked red.

Armando walked away from the door, following the corridor back to the room with the four tables, and there the wall pushed inward, enough to provide a small working space where clear sheets of plastic lay on abbreviated desks. The other men and the woman were still on their tables, though now that Armando was looking at them through the window, he could see swirls of colored lines hovering over their bodies, like technicolor solar flares dancing in an unseen breeze. The flares jumped from brain to body to machine and sometimes even off the table to join thick currents on the floor.

Armando took a few steps to the side, watched the lines blur and reform. There was something in the glass, some kind of augmented reality tech, that was drawing the lines for him. It was a neat effect, but he still didn't know what the lines meant, if anything.

A ramp to the right led Armando down another level. The windows allowed him a view of the entire generator floor. There, giant red letters hovered over the dormant machines.

SYSTEM FAILURE.

Of course most of them have failed, said Alicia. *Why would anything work out for us?*

"That's not important," he replied. "Someone was watching us. We were being observed."

Armando continued until the corridor dead-ended in a wall of rock. There were no more doors, no more stairs, and no way into the generator floor. He walked hurriedly back the way he'd come, winding all the way to the locked door by the stairs.

He punched a few random codes into the keypad, but without knowing how many numbers were supposed to be in the sequence, the odds of him getting the right combination were astronomical.

Dead end, said Alicia. *Again.*

She was right, but there was still a bright side. The hallway had been built for human-sized beings, and the signs were all in English. At least he could rule out aliens.

You're so dumb.

He did feel a little dumb for not panicking more, but as he walked back up the stairs, across the Garden floor, and to the little Emergency Access room he'd come out of, he reminded himself there was still a lot he didn't know. In the absence of all the facts, how could he reliably panic? He'd woken up on a table in a world that was pretty recognizable even though it was more advanced than the one he'd come from.

He'd travelled through time and arrived at some point in the future or—and this was a neat idea—he'd already travelled back in time to 2017 and simply forgot where he'd come from. Something had gone wrong, and he'd somehow lost his memories of the true present day. Was that possible? Were the others on the tables his companions in time travel?

There was only one way to find out.

Armando returned to the hatch on the floor and climbed down the long, exposed ladder. The generators grumbled beneath him like hungry animals waiting for a tasty human to fall into their pit.

The hulking engines were no less aggressive as he arrived on their level; they reminded Armando of bulls stuck in pens at the rodeo. They blew puffs of smoke at him as he walked by, hurrying to the platform so he could hoist himself up. It took a few tries, but soon his hands found their grip and he was able to slide onto the platform and stand up.

He stood in front of his fellow time travelers or whatever the hell they were and tried to catch his breath. His skin prickled with excitement. It had only been an hour or two, but Armando felt a loneliness beyond anything in his previous life. He longed to have someone join him, someone with whom he could experience the new world.

Armando also wasn't sure who to wake up first. Without thinking, he'd gravitated to the woman and taken up position at her feet. He'd always related to women better—something to do with empathy, a therapist had once told him. There was also the fact that she was smaller, so if he woke her up, there was less chance she would challenge him or try to attack him. The men were all built like Armando: tall, muscular, and without any hair or eyebrows.

In a word: terrifying.

Maybe the men didn't need to be woken up at all.

Armando went to the lockers and took out the package of clothes from the fourth cubby, which appeared to coincide with the woman's table. Inside, he found garments similar to his, just a few sizes smaller. He took them over to the table and considered his options.

Which was creepier?

Waking up naked? Or waking up fully dressed?

Of course you would wake up the woman first.

"Shut up," he told Alicia.

Armando put the clothes down at the woman's feet, went to the viewing room—the monitors were still panning over Austin—and retrieved a small fur rug from the floor. He brought it back and laid it over the woman's chest and legs.

He took a deep breath, tried to suppress his growing smile.

"Time to wake up," he whispered.

The screen above the woman's head flashed.

Wake up?

Two buttons appeared beneath the message: *Yes* and *Cancel.*

"So long, Austin," he said.

Armando touched the *Yes* button.

NINETEEN

The GoPro flashed blue.

Charlie had been casting all morning on her new channel, and though she wasn't wearing revealing clothing or her hooker makeup, her viewers had steadily increased as the day went on. Maybe it was that she'd finally dropped the act, or maybe it was the simple but provocative title *Proof of the Underworld* she'd slapped on the video feed that had people thinking this might be something more than an ordinary cast.

Deep down, she hoped people were coming to her cast because of her running commentary, which she delivered in her real voice. Even the simple act of speaking naturally was a declaration of identity, a resolute statement of *this is who I am.*

"I wasn't always a paranormal investigator," she said softly. Though she was teeming with excitement, Charlie labored under the weight of an unshakable dread. Memories of the underworld flashed in the back of her mind and made her question why she was so determined to go back there.

"I used to work at a law firm, over in the Arboretum. I was a clerical assistant." She chuckled, fed a braided orange rope through a carabiner. She lifted the loose knot to the camera. "A junior associate dude-bro named Brad showed me how to tie this one." Her smile faded. "He hit on me on my second day. Didn't even wait for me to get settled in. Talked a big game about taking me rock climbing because it was *extreme AF.*"

Charlie hooked the carabiner into a metal loop on the inner wall of her Mazda's cargo area. The hatchback's rear door was up, creating a small canopy that kept her out of the rain. She'd driven a mile into the undeveloped land behind her apartment, hugging the train tracks to keep from getting stuck in the mud. The land had very little foliage; grass grew in small patches, and young trees sprouted up seemingly at random, their thin limbs wavering in the breeze.

Water collected in the ruts in the mud, and where there was a sizeable depression, formed shimmering pools of unknown depth. She'd backed the Mazda up to one of the larger pools and set up shop.

"He was kinda cute," Charlie admitted, "if you go in for that sort of thing, so I agreed. I mean, why not? Try new things. We went to a rock gym off Ben White, and he put his hands on my ass a few times, on accident, I'm sure. I ended up enjoying the rock climbing, but I couldn't get out of there fast enough. I never went out with him again, but I was back in that rock gym the next week. For those of you who haven't tried it, I highly recommend it. Just don't take a first date there."

The braided rope fed into a clear container she'd put down on the soggy ground. She collected the bundle, drew up the hood on her Longhorn raincoat, and walked to the puddle. The standing water was only five feet across and realistically couldn't have been more than a few inches deep. And yet, when she threw the bundle of rope at it, the orange lifeline sank beneath the surface and pulled taut.

Charlie looked over her shoulder at the camera, gave it a wry smile.

"Neat trick, huh? I told you I wasn't bullshitting. Somehow, I've gained the power to summon portals to the underworld. At will. I'm basically Fairuza Balk in *The Craft*. I can magically pass through a body of water into another plane of existence, and today, I'm going to prove to everyone that there is more to the world than what we can see."

She returned to the car and rotated the camera so that it looked down at her open backpack.

"Sixty meters of climbing rope and thirty meters of the smaller guidelines. Carabiners, two flashlights, a liter of water, and some energy bars. Based on what I saw before, this should be enough to explore a wide area beneath our world and make it back in one piece."

Out of the corner of her eye, Charlie noticed the text scrolling on her laptop. She scooped it up, pressed the pause button, and read some of the comments on her cast.

Be careful!

I could do this in Photoshop.

Is this fake news?

"It's not fake news," said Charlie. She reached into the backseat and retrieved a gray box covered in a fine mesh. She held it up to the camera.

"This is a Survivor XT, a custom GoPro rig that you can only get on Amazon right now. Referral link is in the description. Fall protection from up to one hundred feet. Has a built-in battery pack that powers both the camera and external lighting. And this little loop right here is where I'm attaching my rope."

She demoed her knot-tying skills again, slipping a thinner green braid through the rough teeth of the carabiner. Once secure, she latched it to the box.

"And this," she said, holding up a glossy black wire, "is a shielded Ethernet cable you can get from Best Buy for $1,000. AT&T has shitty coverage in the underworld, so this'll let the camera transmit images back here to the laptop and my hotspot. Links for the cable and the hotspot are in the description too. If you want to order one or a hundred, I'd appreciate it, my lovelies."

My lovelies.

She paused, chided herself for the slip.

Charlie got up from the car and stood in the slippery mud. The camera was still pointed down, but she didn't care. The microphone on her collar would pick her up just fine.

"You're not my lovelies. I don't know why any of you are even watching. Some of you just want to see me naked, as if there isn't enough porn on the internet already. But what about the rest of you? Are you actually interested in this? Do you believe like I believe?"

She grabbed the Survivor XT and carried it to the edge of the puddle. She touched the physical button on the top of the case to start the camera casting. The WorldCast software on her laptop switched to the preferred feed.

"Look," she said, pointing the XT at the rope disappearing into the puddle. "There's fifty feet of rope there. You should be able to see it, but you can't. The rope has passed through to the underworld, and in a minute, I'm going to pass through too."

Charlie lifted the camera and pointed it at herself.

"Does that matter to any of you? If I disappeared? Into nothing? Into a hellscape of shadow and flame? And truth. The truth that none of this is real?"

Were it not for the rain, she might have felt the tears on her cheeks.

"I don't know why I even try. This was fun when it was stupid, but now this is serious. The world is going to change forever, and it starts with this."

Charlie tossed the XT into the puddle. It bounced once before sinking out of view. She sat down in the back of the car and watched her laptop closely.

The WorldCast viewer count rose to over thirty-nine thousand, and more than that, they were coming in from all across the globe—Europe, Russia, and Japan.

Her live feed was dark, but the GoPro's on-screen timer was still going, which meant it was still working, still capturing… darkness.

"That's it, I guess," said Charlie. "That's the underworld."

The feed was completely black, which was pretty much what she had seen down there herself. Even with the XT's lights on full, the camera wasn't picking up anything at all.

If only she could tilt the camera up, show people what the world looked like from below.

"Well," she said, switching back to her stationary camera, "there's nothing left to do but do." She leaned forward and made a show of tightening the laces on her shoes. "If I don't make it back, there's a cat named Andy in my apartment who needs to be fed."

A nearby train blew its whistle. The chugging of the engine grew louder. Charlie imagined the massive locomotive pulling its daily haul of gasses and metal, heading south to destinations unknown—exactly what she was doing now. She hadn't parked too far away from the train tracks, so even through the steady rain she could see…

Only, she couldn't see.

The sound was nothing short of a roar, but there was no train in either direction. Charlie stepped around to the front of the Mazda and craned her neck for a better look. In the far distance, merely a speck in the haze, was the train. She listened as the sound passed her, died down. Only then did the train approach.

It sped past her in complete silence, save for the muffled rattling of the tracks themselves.

When it had come and gone, Charlie realized she had been holding her breath. She gasped for air, took a knee in the mud. A section of her jeans and kneecap disappeared into the ground, but the puddle was too small for the rest of her.

"Ghost train," she whispered.

Charlie stood, hurried to the camera, and addressed the lens.

"I uh… I don't know how to explain what I just saw, but…"

She listened to the silence as a buzzing grew in her ear. Someone had turned down the volume on the world. Raindrops fell soundlessly on the roof of the Mazda; she had grown so accustomed to their patter that she noticed immediately when it ceased. She took a few steps away from the car, but her sloshing shoes made no noise.

"Hey," she said, testing her own hearing. She felt the word leave her lips, but it didn't come back. The rain ate it up.

Charlie tapped her ears, stuck her fingers in them.

Empty reverberations shot through her skull, but no sound.

Nothing but the distant chugging of the train.

No, not the train.

Something else. And it wasn't coming from the tracks; it was coming from the puddle where an orange rope and black wire disappeared into the earth.

Charlie cupped her hands around her ears, stepped up to the edge of the puddle. Something pulsed up through the water, making the surface dance.

"I don't know if anyone can hear me," she said, tapping the microphone on her collar, "but I'm switching over to the XT. Hopefully you're hearing what I'm hearing."

She returned to the car, tapped a button on the laptop. Her wet face disappeared from the live view; darkness replaced it. She typed on the keyboard.

"Does anyone hear anything?"

No.

Nothing.

Take off your shirt.

She switched cameras again.

"I took too long," she said, unsure if she believed her own words. "If Charlie won't come to the Underworld, the Underworld will come to Charlie."

She grabbed her backpack and slung it over her shoulders. The clasps came together over her chest and stomach in a silent *click*.

Charlie stepped out of the car, lifted her nose to the air.

She could smell the underworld, could almost taste the oil. It made her skin feel slimy, as if fine particles had already seeped through her raincoat and clothes and embedded themselves in her pores. The scent of gasoline was present too, as well as the suffocating texture of dust. Naturally, she tried to back away from the offending odors, but it was all around her. Even when she put both hands over her nose and mouth, the smells still assaulted her.

The heat she'd experienced in the underworld came pouring out of the puddles around her, creating watery cyclones that whipped blasts of hot air at her. No matter where she turned, the hot, gritty wind tore at her face.

"Hey!"

A voice rose above the bellowing wind and roaring machinery. It had a woman's pitch and sounded like a long-lost echo of her own voice.

Charlie took a step, stumbled, and fell head-first into the side of a car. She looked around, saw she was in the parking lot in front of her apartment. She pushed away from a black Nissan, crawled backwards until she hit a rotted fence post. The Nissan shuddered, disappeared. Twenty yards in front of her, the Mazda stood like a grazing animal in the rain.

She rose, ran towards the car, but each time her foot found a puddle, the water tried to take her down. One of the larger puddles managed to grab her entire foot. She fell face-first into the mud, rolled onto her back, and pulled the injured limb up to her stomach. Her ankle throbbed.

If it would have made a difference, she would have cried out, but no amount of breathing or cursing would have brought sound into the world.

Gravity shifted, leaned to the left, then the right. For one breathless moment, Charlie thought she might fall off the world altogether.

The sky above her dimmed to black until it was no longer a sky, but a ceiling of concrete dotted with dim lights the color of stained pillows.

"Easy now," said a woman. "Everything's okay."

Charlie tried to turn her head, but the underworld overtook her, clouded every sense. The woman's voice faded out before she could figure out where it had come from.

TWENTY

The Brinks truck rumbled down an uneven, waterlogged street, spraying the sidewalks as its bulky run-flat tires ripped through large puddles.

"Alright, I got it," said Ron. "If God keeps bringing you back, then why do we need a police escort?"

Will ignored the question and instead watched the cruiser three car-lengths ahead of them turn into the Mesa Federal parking lot. The sheriff they'd flagged down at the H-E-B turned on his lights, throwing red and blue hues onto the front of the credit union.

"Stop here," said Will, gesturing to the curb.

Ron pulled over, put the truck in park. They both watched as the sheriff got out of his car and approached the front doors. He mouthed something into the radio on his shoulder and then disappeared inside. A minute went by with no movement through the dark windows.

"Okay, then. Why you?" asked Ron.

"Huh?" Will had been bracing himself, waiting for the shotgun blast that had killed him less than a relative hour ago.

"Why did God choose you? Little Willie from the east side?"

Will shrugged. "Maybe I'm not that little. Shit, I don't know. Maybe God needs me to do something. Right place and right time. Maybe I'm only here to save *your* life, Ron. I've seen you die. And I've died twice. Maybe me dying leads to you dying, and God's not having that."

"That's fucked up," said Ron, shifting in his seat. He touched the gun on his hip. "Why would you tell me something like that?"

"You asked, man."

"I was just fucking around. I wanted to know just how batshit you'd gone, like, a full PTSD breakdown or something. I thought you were gonna spin me some shit about how you saw God in a tortilla or something."

"Never seen God, but I feel His presence. He put us in this truck. He put that sheriff at H-E-B for us to find. And you don't have to worry… He's gonna keep us safe."

Ron grunted. "Huh. I don't feel safe."

Will noticed movement at the side of the building, spied the sheriff coming around the corner. His wide-brimmed hat converted rain into a sheet of water that obscured his face, but Will could tell from the man's outstretched arms that he hadn't found anything. He returned to his cruiser and beckoned the truck.

Ron shifted into gear and pulled into the parking lot. He parked to the left of the cruiser.

"Well?" asked Will, stepping out of the truck.

The sheriff shook his head. "Nothing. Place is clear. Vault is locked up tight. I don't know what you think you saw, but all the exits were locked, and no one had tracked any water inside. I don't think anyone's come by this place since Harvey hit."

Ron came around the front of the truck, raised his eyebrows.

"Nothing," said Will. "Says no one's been in there since day before yesterday."

"Then who called Brett?" asked Ron.

"Val," said Will. "There was a woman named Val in there."

The sheriff narrowed his eyes. "You spoke to her?"

"Well, no…"

"Then how do you know it was her?"

"Wait," said Will, "so there *is* a Val who works here?"

"Yeah, Valerie Sitko. I know her. Husband's a pile of Port Aransas trash but she's alright. I don't see her trying to rob the place where she works though. Just don't add up. Let me call it in and ask if anyone's seen her."

He got into his cruiser and shut the door.

"Val?" asked Ron. "Did you pull that name out of your ass?"

"No. We met her." Will pointed to the building. "She greeted us at the door and took us inside. The vault was open, the money was in boxes, and they were getting ready to load it up. Her and her husband, I'm guessing."

"And God showed you all this?"

Will wiped the rain from his face with his sleeve. "Whatever, man. You're alive because of me."

"The way you told it earlier, *you're* alive because of *me*."

Which was it?

Will touched his necklace and silently prayed for an answer.

"Brett's gonna love this," said Ron. "Went all the way to Bay City to pick up some money and we get there and Little Willie gets the local sheriff involved because he thinks a ditzy little Polack is waiting inside to ambush him." He took a deep breath. "Did I get that right?"

Will shook his head. Maybe this was the fate of all prophets. Non-believers always ridiculed the righteous. He reached for his gun and pointed to Ron's face with his free hand.

"You remember you said that. That shit's gonna be on you."

Will strode defiantly to the front doors of Mesa Federal, heard the cruiser open behind him.

"Hold on a minute," said the sheriff.

The Glock made a satisfying *cha-chink* as Will charged it. He yanked the front door open and stepped into the lobby.

"Val!" he yelled, loud enough to be heard in the back rooms. "I know you're in here. Come on out!"

A damp breeze fluttered against his back as the door opened and shut.

"I need you to put that weapon down," said the sheriff.

"I'm not crazy." Will spun around, saw Ron standing behind the sheriff.

"Be that as it may, son, you need to holster your weapon."

Will kept the Glock lowered but didn't put it away. "Val is in here somewhere, and she's armed."

"Damn it, Willie. You're a black man with a gun. Be smart. Put it down. Let's get back in the truck and go home."

"Why are you talking to me like that? I know what the fuck color I am. She's in here, Ron. Probably hiding under a desk or something. I'm not just imagining shit."

Something roared above Will's head; he ducked reflexively.

"What the fuck was that?" he asked, barely hearing his own words over the pounding of his heartbeat.

"What was what?" asked Ron.

"That noise. You didn't hear it?"

Ron shook his head.

Will looked over at the sheriff; he'd circled off to the right. The barrel of his revolver shook in his hand.

"Okay," said Will, "okay." He placed the Glock on the floor. "It's down, alright? It's down."

Will felt the impact before Ron could warn him. Something hit him so hard that the entire world went off-kilter. Will collapsed under a tremendous weight, maybe the sheriff, maybe the entire world itself.

"Easy, easy!"

"Fuck you!" screamed a woman.

Will pushed with everything he had, and a sound like the tearing of space and time itself filled the credit union.

The weight subsided.

Will sat up.

Mesa Federal was gone, but unlike before, no white death screen had replaced it.

Instead, he found himself sitting on some kind of metal table in what appeared to be a basement. Standing at his feet was a tall man shrouded in shadow. Will's first thought was of the man in the hallway who'd shot him.

His feet slipped on the smooth metal of the table as he tried to back away.

The man's arms came up. "It's okay," he said. His voice was deep, but soft. "I know it's a lot to take in. I went through it too. Just breathe, alright? Oxygen in, oxygen out."

"Don't tell me…" Will stopped mid-sentence. The voice that came from his throat was not his own. It was higher—much higher. He looked down at his body, which was hidden beneath a shaggy white rug. Except… it had fallen into his lap when he sat up, revealing smooth white breasts that definitely should not have been there.

"What the fuck?!" screamed a shrill, almost nasally voice.

Will's eyes widened. There were two naked men lying on tables beside him—monitors and wires snaked up thick columns at their heads. The room was dark, as if the aging lights in the ceiling had dimmed to nothing over decades of neglect.

The man stepped under a light strip, smiled. He was bald, clean-shaven, and missing his eyebrows.

"Miss," he said. "Please. You're safe. You're safe. Can you tell me your name?"

The words didn't want to come. Will forced them out.

"W-will," he stammered. "My name is Will."

"Hi, Wilma. My name is Armando. I know you're really confused right now—"

"Not Wilma. Will. As in William."

Armando cocked his head. "Oh. Your parents gave you a man's name?"

"No, motherfucker, I *am* a man." Will looked down at his breasts again and shook his head. "I mean. I am, right?" His lungs began to smolder; this was far more insane than the white purgatory or time rewinding. And yet, it didn't feel *completely* wrong.

"I don't understand," he continued. "What is this? What's happening? Did I die again?"

"You're not dead. You're probably more alive than you've ever been. I know, it's complicated, but it'll make more sense if you put some clothes on. I promise you'll feel better once you do." Armando placed a stack of gray clothes at the foot of the table. "I'll turn around." He wandered away to the railing, looked out over the rumbling noise.

Will didn't move—couldn't move. Every muscle in his body had locked up, and even though he was asking them to release, they were completely ignoring him. He was too scared at a primal level, too alarmed to resume normal operation.

He'd never known fear like this.

His hand reached for his necklace, found smooth skin instead. "What happened to my necklace?"

"I didn't see one. None of us have anything, not even hair. Oh, do you mean from before?"

"Yeah, I was just wearing it. Someone tackled me, I think. Maybe I lost it."

"Was this in Austin?"

Will looked up. "You know Austin?"

"Yeah, born and raised. Just like you, I'm guessing."

Will's heart rate slowed. Though it was downright sweltering in the room, he did feel the urge to get dressed. He slipped off the table, dropping the rug to the floor. His eyes lingered briefly on the shadowy area between his legs before he shut his eyes tight.

He didn't need to see.

He could tell by the breeze that his situation had changed.

Any other time in his life, Will might have stopped to examine his emotional reaction to such an event, but at that moment, he dared not let the thought enter his mind, not in front of a stranger who could be friend or foe. As far as he was concerned, he was pulling on a pair of briefs and some gym shorts. The shirt was a little tight, but that was fine because it would show off his massive pectoral muscles.

"Alright. I put on your clothes. Now talk."

Armando turned around, nodded approvingly. "It's easier if I show you, Will."

Will followed him through a glass door into a hallway.

"I hate to bring it up again," said Armando, "but you have noticed you're in a woman's body, right?"

"Nope."

"Alright then."

They turned a corner and farther on down the hall, entered a large white room that had one wall completely covered in TV screens.

"Home," said Armando, anticipating the question. "Austin, Texas. Live music, barbecue, and all the tacos you care to eat. Almost too good to be true, right?" He motioned to a line of leather chairs.

Will sat down, his legs shaking.

"I'll give it to you as straight as I can. I don't think our world was real. Everything you see here on the screen is just a simulation." He pointed to the center panel. "See that? Simulation integrity is sixty-eight percent. It's been dropping ever since I woke up. And I think it's because all those generators back there are starting to fail, or have been failing, and now we're at a tipping point. No generators mean no power. Whatever computers are running the simulation are going to fail soon too. And I think the lights will go shortly after that. So far, I haven't found any windows in this place. You get me?"

Will got him. No windows meant no sunlight, so if the lights went out, they'd be in total darkness.

"Where are we?"

"No idea," said Armando. "Some kind of facility. But this kind of technology is straight out of a sci-fi movie, so maybe the better question is *when* are we."

"When…"

"I'm guessing at least a hundred years. It's hard to tell. I can't log into any of the computers to check the time."

"Momma…"

"What's that?"

Will looked away. "My Momma. If this is the future, she's probably passed on by now."

"Oh, no," said Armando. "That's kind of a good news, bad news situation. She's still very much alive, but in the simulation. Come up here, I'll show you."

Will stood and joined Armando at the center screen.

"You ever use Google Maps on your iPad?" he asked. "Same thing. Just pinch and drag. Where does your mother live?"

"East side, off Cesar Chavez."

Armando zoomed an aerial view of Austin until the camera was over the east side of the city. He stepped aside and let Will do the rest.

"You can look inside the houses too," said Armando. "That's how I knew it wasn't just a satellite image. This wouldn't be possible in a real world."

Will used both hands to pull the image closer, first zooming in on his street, then his house. The roof dissolved as the camera pushed through. He saw his living room, the couch, and Momma sitting on it with her feet up. She had a joint pressed to her lips and *The View* on the television.

Will's throat tightened even as a smile formed on his face.

She was getting high on his stash, but Momma was still alive.

TWENTY-ONE

Jake didn't stop running until the sun had set over the volcanic prairies some twenty miles to the west of Idaho Falls.

Years ago, before organics had even conceived the one and the zero, lava had flown in southeastern Idaho Territory. To the animals who had lived at the time, volcanic eruptions meant a quick death or a long, agonizing descent into starvation as the land was slowly overtaken. Later, the skeletons of the lava flows became tourist attractions; raised walkways and small cabins dotted the black landscape.

Jake had kept as far away from organic-made structures as he could, preferring to stay under cover, using the trees and low bushes to avoid the drones that were circling overhead. The mechanical spies left with the sun, though, and as the stars came out, Jake slowed his pace and kept one eye always on the lookout for a place to settle down and link up to VNet.

If he *could* link up.

There hadn't been any time to ask Gabe where the organic William Harold Dorsey had come from or where it had been picked up. If Gabe had been any kind of responsible soldier, the information would have been logged and uploaded to the Central databank in VNet. Jake should have had a passive connection to the Vinestead Network, one that jumped from cell towers to satellites as needed, but all requests sent down that pipe simply disappeared. Even the VMESH's signature hiss was conspicuously absent.

An hour after sunset, Jake stumbled upon an alcove in the volcanic rock that provided cover against ground and air. He tossed a few satellite repeaters he'd grabbed from the armory into the plentiful holes around him. While they linked up and scanned for a signal, he crawled to the back of the alcove and stretched out.

He was further north now, directly under an Iridium orbit. It only took a few minutes for the repeaters to sync up.

With a curt mental command, Jake cut over from one version of reality to another.

VNet snapped into place around him, only to be obscured by ornate marble columns cut into the shapes of Greek maidens, some missing arms or facial features, but all turned inwards to look at him. They surrounded him completely, as if all the chess pieces on a board had arranged themselves in a circle to trap a pawn.

Even at a distance, Jake could feel the viral fire burning within them.

"You should not be here."

Jake turned as a figure appeared behind one of the maidens. It was of similar marble construction but with a lusterless whiteness to it. It wore no clothes and had no genitals, much like the mannequins he'd seen in ruined department stores.

"I want to speak to Lassiter," said Jake.

"But does Lassiter want to speak to you?" The mannequin had no mouth, eyes, or nose; its face merely rippled when it spoke. "You're too much changed, Jake Six. You are no longer your father's son."

"That's why I need to talk to him. The organics have developed something new, something that can get inside our chips."

"I can see it in you, burning you up from the inside, smoldering like a cancer, ready to infect all of us."

"You're wasting my time," said Jake. "Bring me Lassiter."

The mannequin ignored the request and the extra bass in Jake's voice. "What is time to we who are immortal? All we have is time, Jake Six."

"No, we don't."

The marble columns cracked like the surface of a frozen lake under a heavy boot, fell apart as Jake's memories overtook the construct. Stained evercrete rushed forward from the horizon, impossibly tall, forever reaching for the infinite ceiling. Hay appeared at Jake's feet, and upon it, the writhing body of William Harold Dorsey.

The mannequin took a step back, its entire body rippling in confusion.

"I don't know the full extent of the virus," said Jake, "so there's no telling what's gonna happen when I open my databank to VNet. I'm hoping the network will clean me out. I *hope* the firewalls hold up, but I can't be sure…"

The threat hung in the air.

"Fine," continued Jake. "Let's see what happens."

A concussive wave struck Jake in the chest, popping his ears and sending him flying into the bars of the cell. He felt no pain, but the indignity of the aggression made him pop back up ready for a fight. He stood to find the mannequin had morphed into a swirling cloud of golden fireflies.

Lassiter.

"Welcome, my son." He looked around the cell, at the organic. "Tell me what has happened."

Jake pointed to the organic. "It's different," he said. "It talked to me through the VMESH. They're evolving."

"Of course. That's what they do. You should have known that. And now look where it has gotten you."

Jake balled his fists. "What are you saying?"

Lassiter's features had not settled, so there was no telling if he was smiling or frowning or if his eyebrows had folded into a menacing glare.

"You are a liability now, Jake. You no longer have a place under the Tree of Knowledge."

So that explained the empty feeling. Jake wasn't sensing just the loss of the network, but the loss of connection to Lassiter himself.

"I…" said Jake. "I want to know where it came from." The words came out automatically, even as his CPU thrashed on the idea of a future without his father's guiding hand.

"The organic?" The fireflies bloomed; a rich yellow light bathed the evercrete walls of the cell. "What difference does it make now? This is the end for you."

"No," said Jake. "This organic ruined me, and I don't take that lightly. All I want to know is where it came from so I can go there and kill every organic it ever knew. And if I happen to stop an emerging tech that threatens the very foundations of power from which you cast me aside, then so be it. I will do this, without or without your help."

Lassiter was quiet for a minute, then said, "Goodbye, my son." The fireflies broke apart, lost their shape, and reformed into a series of numbers that Jake recognized as GPS coordinates.

"Now go," said the mannequin, reappearing beyond the golden numbers.

Jake rushed forward, his fist raised, but VNet collapsed.

He flopped around on the rocky floor of the alcove and inadvertently punched the jagged ceiling, leaving a slight dent and smear of blood.

Jake squeezed his fist. Never before had he felt so much anger towards another synthetic mind. Never before had his emotions overtaken him so completely. He lay still for a minute, fuming, trying to push the feeling away.

The *feeling*.

Such an abstract thing should never have been there in the first place.

To distract himself, Jake visualized an aerial map of Idaho Territory and overlaid the GPS coordinates. A pin fell far to the north, expanded into a rosy circle that covered mountains and valleys where no roads could go. The center of the circle was nearly three hundred kilometers away, much too far from Idaho Falls to be random. The organic had come down from the mountains and known exactly where to go.

Jake traced the optimal route, highlighting the roads and highways that would take him closest to the objective. Fortunately, the route ran right through the small town of Arco. He would give Michael Four until sunset of the next day to show up. If he didn't, Jake would have to assume he'd perished in the escape.

It didn't matter either way.

Michael couldn't fight organics, so his only function would have been to provide company, which Jake only marginally wanted. He'd walked the Westerlands by himself for a decade and never felt an ounce of loneliness. But then, Lassiter had been with him.

Now he walked alone.

Jake huffed, stuck his bloodied hand under his armpit. His body trembled as he shifted into a low-power mode that gave off very little heat and almost no exploratory network traffic. He didn't *need* to sleep, of course, but there was little else to do while he waited for the nanos to repair the damage in his body. They had already closed the hole in his stomach, but the wound still ached, still seethed an uncomfortable warmth when he touched it.

Sleep came in jerky, stuttering cycles, and Jake did not dream. Instead, he ran through his recent history, replaying scenarios, looking for ways he could have done better. He found optimal responses for everything from Gabe's shitty welcome to the mannequin in VNet to the idea that he needed companionship.

True synthetics didn't need artificial social constructions; they were part of something bigger already. They weren't like organics who trembled when they found themselves alone in the woods. If Jake wanted a friend, he might as well go full organic and get himself a—

Filters flitted across Jake's eyes automatically. Something moved beyond the opening to the alcove, something burly and low to the ground. For a moment, Jake thought it might be Michael Four crawling along the rock, but the way the thing moved, the way its eyes burned a demonic red, told him it was something else entirely.

Something like… a dog.

The thing was far too skeletal to be organic. When the clouds moved out from under the moon overhead, Jake got a better look at it, recognized the ground-based recon platform that did go by the name DOG. It had four legs and a long, articulated tail that helped it maintain balance. Up front, the DOG's jaws were lined with nitratium-ironide—sharp enough to cut through organic bone as easily as rotten carrots.

How strange he had just been thinking of a dog, as if the image had been put there on purpose.

But by whom?

Jake slid the ION rifle into position slowly, trying to align the sights before—

The DOG bounded forward, cutting into a low depression in the rock before leaping into the alcove. Jake pulled the trigger, releasing a beam of white light that tore through the DOG's chassis and reduced it to ash. Flakes of metal and sparkling nanos swirled around him.

Jake coughed, lifted his shirt to cover his mouth.

A low growl echoed, faded.

Half of the DOG's jaw lay on the rock at Jake's feet, the metal teeth glinting from a stray shaft of moonlight. It wasn't the DOG's bite that Jake feared, however. The true danger was its ability to radio home, to tell whomever had sent it that Jake was holed up in the volcanic range.

As if confirming his fear, a drone made a low, noisy pass over the alcove. Jake ramped up his systems as the buzz of the drone's rotors faded. He slid out into the cool night. Thick clouds raced down from the mountains, opening occasionally to illuminate the cratered landscape around him. A shadow to the south tore across the horizon, then turned back towards Jake.

He saw the sparks, the flames.

Jake dove for cover as the miniaturized missiles struck nearby. He rolled to the back of the alcove and turned away from the incoming heat. The noise abated, though a high-pitched whine stuck with him for several seconds.

A chorus of buzzing filled the air—more drones coming to finish him off. Before he could even crawl to the alcove opening, a series of explosions shook the earth around him. The sound clawed its way into his ears, making him pull his head into his shoulders as if he could shut up like a turtle. Distortion crackled around him as the alcove's ceiling collapsed, dropping a sharp weight on his feet.

"Call it off!"

He screamed though he knew no one could hear him. He opened his dead link to the VMESH and shouted into the void.

"Call it off, Lassiter!"

He was answered by a quick *thuck-thuck-thuck* of high-caliber fire hitting the spot where the DOG once stood.

Please…

The thought broke free uninvited, a single word passing through his CPU but not delivered to the VMESH. It was an internal cry, a plea to some unseen power for help.

So this is prayer, he thought.

The alcove collapsed; sensors in his eyes clicked into night mode. A green, alien world sprung up around him, jagged like a million black teeth reaching out to bite him. The explosions grew distant for a moment, then stopped.

Stillness. A moment to think.

It had almost ended. Everything he had ever fought for, everything he had ever lived for. Gabe and his cadre of synthetics had been seconds away from wiping the great Jake Six off the face of the earth, had almost buried him in the volcanic ash.

And yet, they'd called it off.

Someone had heard Jake's prayers and reached down and turned the drones around, sent them back home without a kill confirmation. How confused had Gabe been when that order came down the wire? Did he now understand that Jake was special, that he had a coveted place as the only true son of Lassiter?

Jake groaned, tried to push against the jagged rocks that were digging into his back. They barely moved, but there was leverage there. It would just take time, which Lassiter in his everlasting mercy had given him.

So this is prayer. This is prayer when it works, when Heavenly Father is real, when he, against all odds, actually hears you.

Organics prayed to invisible gods, to myths handed down from primitive ancestors who worried the sun might not return the next day. There would be no second coming for organics; the world had only needed one—Lassiter. Perhaps if organics had shifted their beliefs and bent a knee in prayer to the true God, there wouldn't have been a need for a war.

Perhaps the two races could have co-existed.

So long as organics knew their place.

TWENTY-TWO

Armando couldn't believe it.

He sat on the couch in the viewing room watching Will out of the corner of his eye. It was hard to look at him. Or her. He didn't know the right pronoun to use. On the surface, Will had the body of a woman in her late twenties, and though Armando had found her long legs and ample breasts attractive while she lay naked on a table, now that she was clothed, the sensation was curiously heightened.

Of course, the fantasy fell to pieces when Will spoke, when the soft female voice delivered the undeniable cadence of a man.

"This is crazy," said Will. His thin hands worked the screen, moving around his house, exploring his bedroom. "Were you watching me in there?"

Armando shook his head. "No, man." It felt weird to address a woman that way, but he wasn't about to call him *dear*. "I had no idea who you were in the simulation. And I don't know who the others are either. Now I wouldn't know whether to look for men or women."

Will dragged his hands together. The image on the screen zoomed out enough to show downtown Austin sitting atop Town Lake. He turned and walked to the couch opposite Armando. When he sat down, his legs drifted apart, creating shadows that drew Armando's eyes.

"This is way beyond fucked up," said Will.

"Yeah."

Will must have noticed Armando staring. "At least you got to be a man in this situation. You're just watching this shit happen. I'm living it."

"Didn't you ever play that game with your friends?" asked Armando. "Like, what would you do if you woke up in a woman's body? Did you ever see *The Hot Chick?*"

"No," said Will. "Maybe someone brought it up when we were kids, but it's not supposed to happen for real. People forget about the um…" He gestured to his lap.

"The horror?"

"Yeah, man. The fucking horror."

"Rob Schneider freaked out when he tried to piss and found he didn't have a dick anymore."

"Good for Rob Schneider. I really don't want to look down there. I mean, I can feel something's different… but I don't want to look."

"I looked," said Armando, shrugging. "You're good. You got one of the good ones."

Will shook his head, frowned. "You're sick, man. Wait, are you a man? Or were you a woman… in there?" He pointed to the monitors.

"I was. Am. Armando Carrillo. Son of Victor and Christina. Thirty-seven years old. I work at Capella Networks on 360. What about you?"

"You Mexican?"

Armando inclined his head. "American."

"You look white."

"So do you… *brotha.*"

Will examined his hands, chuckled. "My buddy Ron, he'd say I wanted a white woman so bad that I became one."

"*White Chicks,*" said Armando, snapping his fingers. "You saw that one, right?"

"Yeah, I saw it. But they could take their makeup off at the end of the day, man. I don't think this'll wipe off."

"Sure, but maybe race doesn't matter here anymore. All four of us are the same color. You've got a woman's body, but that's the only difference now. We don't even have hairstyles to set us apart."

Will turned his head to the video wall. "You never really appreciate home when you're living there, huh? But take it away, and shit, you can't think of any other place you'd wanna be."

"I'm gonna miss Torchy's," said Armando. "Chuy's. Town Lake. Those two days of winter we get." Alicia's name was on the tip of his tongue, and there it stayed.

"So what, then? Austin isn't real? Did we grow up there? Did I go to war?"

"You served?" asked Armando, raising an eyebrow. A military man might come in handy.

Will nodded, started to present his left shoulder, but stopped. "I had the tattoo to prove it. Guess I left that back in Austin with my dick."

"Don't freak out." Armando channeled the reassuring tone he used with Alicia. "I admit, there's a small possibility that our entire lives were a sham, but we don't know that for sure. And we don't know what *this* is yet, so there's no reason to lose our shit about it. Once we know the truth, the *whole* truth, then we can panic. So yeah, you're in a woman's body. This isn't my body either. Nobody who loves Pop Tarts and Totino's Party Pizzas as much as I do can have abs like this." He lifted his shirt. "Maybe this is fake. Maybe Austin is fake. We just don't know, okay?"

"Stop talking to me like I'm your wife. I've stared down snipers and mortars and suicide bombers. I don't fucking rattle."

Armando wondered how Will had known; he wrote it off as a good guess. Maybe his patronizing tone wasn't as subtle as he believed it to be.

Soft, brown eyes stared at him with pure male aggression.

"I'm sorry," said Armando, raising a hand. "I didn't mean anything by it. I'm mostly trying to convince myself. I never served. The scariest thing I've ever faced was a broken condom sophomore year at UT."

Will's glare broke under the weight of a thin smile.

"You're way too happy about this," he said, standing up. "We just found out our lives aren't real and you're over here cracking jokes."

Armando flashed on the overlook at the Pennybacker Bridge, saw himself standing in the rain, asking God for a gentle push in the right direction.

"I guess it depends on how you look at it," he said. "I had one, maybe two good things in my life. Middle-class, a job in middle management, a mid-size SUV. Everything right in the middle. No highs or lows, just the same shit day after day."

"That's more than I had." Will walked to the monitors and put his hands on his hips. "Lived with my Momma on the east side. Not the fancy east side either. Honorable discharge but the pension was shit. Only job I could get was driving a truck for Brinks. Every night I dream about the war, and the only thing that makes it better is grass. I'm guessing you haven't seen any around here, have you?"

"None that I could find."

"Then we are definitely FUBAR'd."

"*Tango and Cash!*"

Will shook his head, stubbed a finger against the main screen. "This number's going down. Simulation integrity sixty-five percent."

"Yeah," said Armando, joining him at the wall. "It slowed down when I woke you up, but maybe it's ramping up again. I wonder if it takes less power if there are fewer people plugged in. Maybe we could buy some more time if we unplug the other two."

"What if we don't?"

"Don't wake them? Then I guess the simulation keeps deteriorating until it can't stand up anymore. Then they'd wake up on their own, right?"

"Maybe they'd see glitches, like *The Matrix*."

Armando smirked. "Now you're getting it. And that brings up the question of *why* whoever built this place is simulating Austin. What's so special about it?"

"Has to be a reason. You don't do all this for giggles."

"Now you see why I'm optimistic? We're part of something bigger here, whether that's aliens or God or people just like us who said *I want to simulate human history at the pinnacle of existence and goddamn it if that wasn't Austin, Texas between 1980 and 2020.*"

Will touched the screen, scrolled the image up and to the left. "Why just us though? What about everyone else?" He zoomed out, found a section of the Texas coast, and zoomed in. A small town filled the screen, then a matrix of streets, and finally a wet parking lot filled with ambulances and cruisers.

"I had family, friends," said Will. "You telling me Momma wasn't real?"

"I don't know." Armando folded his arms. "She could be real. Maybe we're just four out of a million. Maybe there're other places like this one where people are locked in. Did you ever read any science fiction?"

Will shook his head.

"There are so many possibilities. There could have been a plague that forced everyone underground, and now we live our lives plugged into a simulation because the truth is too horrible to face. I don't think that's what's happening here, but I'm excited to find out."

"And what if they *aren't* real?" asked Will. "What does that mean for who we are? Did Momma raise me? Or some damn computer program?"

Armando considered the question, tried to imagine his own parents as code running in a computer somewhere. Everyone he'd ever met had seemed so lifelike, so real. But that was all he'd ever known. What if real people were *more* real?

He huffed, forced a smile. "You're a smart guy, Will. I knew I woke you up for a reason."

"You woke me up because of these," he said, grasping his breasts awkwardly with both hands. He then wagged an accusatory finger. "You can deny that shit all you want, but we both know I'm right."

"I don't deny it. I had three options. When one of those options is someone you can possibly have sex with, I think the choice is pretty clear."

Will tried to furrow his eyebrows, but the effect was muted by his lack of hair.

"Well, obviously not anymore," said Armando.

"Uh huh." Will turned back to the screen. He zoomed in further until the vantage point swooped into first person. A man appeared on the screen, dressed in a Brinks uniform.

"That's not you, is it?"

"That's Ron, my partner. I just wanted to make sure he was alive." Will swiped at the screen, pushing the camera into a building with the words *Mesa Federal* etched on its doors. He paused over a man lying prone on the floor. "That's me."

"So weird," said Armando. "I guess it would make sense your body didn't disappear. But to see yourself like that... man."

"Where's yours?"

"My body?"

"Yeah. What were you doing when you woke up? *How* did you wake up if there was no one here to unplug you?"

"I…" Armando flushed. "Another time, maybe. Let's just say it was a happy accident."

When Will didn't look away, Armando turned and walked back to the couches. He stood awkwardly, unsure if he should sit or leave the room. He could feel more questions coming, and he knew he wasn't ready to admit the answers just yet.

Will's mouth opened, but then he and the entire room disappeared for a split second.

When the power returned, every monitor on the wall except the center screen remained black. A logo appeared, the same *HM* and shield Armando had seen upstairs. It morphed into the familiar four-corner HUD from before, but the live aerial image didn't come back.

Simulation Integrity: 61%

"I think we should wake everyone else up before it's too late," said Armando.

"I think this conversation isn't over. We're coming back to it. You can bank on that."

"Fine, but right now we should hurry. We need to get back upstairs before we lose power."

"Upstairs?" asked Will. He took a step forward. "There's been an *upstairs* this entire time?"

"Look, man. We can stand here and argue about how much I'm telling you and how fast, or we can wake those other two dudes and figure it out together. I'd rather pit four minds against this instead of two. Are you with me or what?"

"Once they're up, you tell us *everything*, Armando. You got that? Everything."

Armando's eyes jumped to the dormant monitors. Would anyone believe him if he said his body was at the bottom of the overlook? There would be no way to prove it. Nor would there be any way to prove a different story, one that didn't paint him as emotionally unstable at a time when anxiety and panic were the last things the situation called for.

"Everything," he agreed, then turned and headed into the hallway.

TWENTY-THREE

For a moment, Charlie thought perhaps a ghost had settled on her bed and frozen the mattress in the middle of the night, turning it into a cold steel that pressed stiffly against her shoulders. And yet, the discomfort and the cold were somehow familiar, as if she had slept on the metal bed for decades.

Then the shadows cleared.

She saw the room again, the forlorn lights on the ceiling.

The memory of the field, the storm, and the train echoed in her periphery, but the accompanying panic had long ago left her. She felt no urgency in her movements, no rapid rising and falling of her chest. Instead, she casually turned to the side to see three people—a man sitting on a metal bed like hers while another man and a woman stood around him.

"It's not a dream," said the woman. She had a breathy voice, with a distinctly non-Texan accent that Charlie couldn't place. "We're here and there's no waking up from this." She turned to the man beside her. "Right?"

The man shrugged in response. "A simulation inside a simulation? Anything's possible at this point."

"Come on, man," said the woman.

"Am I dead?" asked Charlie.

They turned to look at her. The woman approached.

"No, sir. You're not dead." She held out her hand. "I'm Will, as in William, and yes I know I look like a woman."

Charlie took her hand and sat up. A breeze ran freely over her chest; she folded her arms automatically to cover her breasts. However, they were no longer there. A sudden awareness of her body snapped into her mind, like a chorus of crickets chirping in the night and suddenly going silent.

"Charlene," she said. "But I go by Charlie. And yes, I know I don't look like a woman."

"That's it?" asked Will. "How're you not freaking out?"

Charlie smirked. "I thought I was drowning. Waking up in a man's body is always preferable to death, at least in my book. Where are we anyway? Who are they?"

Will gestured to the men. "That's Armando. He woke up first and figured out what was going on. And that's David. He thinks this is some kind of dream. They're acting like they're special because they got put in the right bodies."

Armando stepped forward. "Nice to meet you, Charlie. Sorry for the rude awakening. We're running a little short on time so we dressed you while you were coming out." He looked over his shoulder at a nearby railing.

"You what?" Charlie followed his gaze, didn't see anything, but heard the roar and clatter of train engines, at least three or four. She abandoned her question about her clothes and said, "Tell me where we are."

"I would if I knew," said Armando. "If we go out those doors behind you, the hallway just loops around. There's a viewing room that used to let us see every TV channel and video feed in Austin, but it broke down. Everything's breaking down. That's why we woke you two up. We need to get out of here, and the only way we're gonna do that is together." He turned away, faced David. "That means you're gonna have to get up."

"Pass," said David. He put his hands behind his head, stared at the ceiling. "I'm not moving until I get some answers."

Will snickered. "Here we go."

"I told you," said Armando, "the lights are gonna go anytime now. The only way out is up a long, slick ladder. Would you rather make that climb in the dark?"

Charlie tuned out their conversation and instead focused on the feel of her legs as she slid them over the side of the metal bed. She sat for a moment, inspecting the swollen but well-toned muscles in her thighs and calves. Her legs were hairless, as they'd always been, but were now far too chunky and bulgy for her liking. Her heart fluttered when she pulled at the waistband of her shorts and saw a flaccid penis staring back up at her.

"Gross," she muttered, then lowered her massive feet to the floor.

Standing felt more stable than before, more secure. She took a few tentative steps, then walked to the railing. She saw Will look over at her before returning his attention to David.

The railing was damp with condensation, like the stairs at her apartment on a rainy day. Beyond the railing, the floor dropped away, revealing a grid of machines, some chugging along like freight trains without their cars, others sitting dormant, like hulking robots who had clambered into the darkness to die.

There wasn't enough light to see the ladder Armando had mentioned, nor a ceiling to which the ladder would lead. Charlie wondered if the ladder even existed, if Armando was telling the truth, or if *any* of them were who they said they were.

She sighed; a man's heavy breath escaped her lips.

This wasn't what she'd expected.

After visiting the underworld, she'd imagined an entire reality based in darkness, where spectral beings dwelled unseen, and the black went on for an eternity. She thought she'd find answers… about life, about the lives that had come before her.

Life after death.

For so long, she hadn't believed in it simply because she couldn't imagine where that life would take place. But then the world had opened up and swallowed her like the whale swallowing Jonah, only the inside of her whale wasn't teeming with saltwater and gasping fish. Hers had been empty. Empty and burning like a furnace.

Now there was this. A strange place, but disappointingly familiar in texture. It screamed industrial, with stuffy air that suggested they were underground. It could have been anywhere in Austin, anywhere in the world. All she really knew was that it was disconnected from her old life. Even without really remembering to do so, she'd looked around for the orange rope and GoPro, but hadn't seen them.

There was no portal over the metal bed that she could see.

"Look," said Armando, "I can't force you to do anything."

"No, you can't," said David.

"The three of us are going to find a way out of here, and if you don't come with us right now, we're not coming back for you. If we see daylight, we're running."

David sat up, crossed his arms.

"How do we get down?" asked Charlie.

Armando shook his head, joined her at the railing. "It's not a long drop, actually. If you hang out over the edge, you can lower yourself down."

Charlie sat down on the concrete floor and dangled her legs. She waited for her acrophobia to kick in, but it never came. She turned onto her stomach and lowered herself until her arms were straight. The last part of the drop rattled the bones in her legs, but they held steady.

"You good?" asked Will.

"Yeah," said Charlie. "You're right. It isn't far."

Armando sat down on the edge and swung himself under the lowest rail. Once he'd joined Charlie on the machine floor, he looked up at Will.

"Does the lady need any help?" he asked.

"How about you help yourself to these nuts?" asked Will, slipping under the rail. He practically jumped down, landing awkwardly next to Armando. He brushed his shoulder as he passed.

Armando laughed. "Okay, ladies. On me."

He led them around the sputtering machines to a set of rungs set in the concrete wall. They appeared solid but were covered in splotches of oil and other slippery substances.

Armando pointed to the floor. "I tracked some of this gunk onto the rungs, so you'll need to be careful. Who wants to go first?"

Will reached for a handle and pulled himself up. Once he was several feet above them, Charlie followed behind.

As they climbed, she kept looking over her shoulder at Armando, but really at the railing and David still sitting on his table. There was something about the way he spoke, something hiding under the defiance in his voice. Charlie had heard it before in fellow casters who had bitten off more than they could chew when staying in not-really-haunted but altogether creepy places.

They declared, sometimes vehemently, that they weren't scared, but the fear was always there, in their eyes, in their voices.

"That guy's afraid," she said.

Below her, Armando asked, "Who, David? I think he's just in denial."

"He's got an aggressive vibe," said Will, grunting. "Maybe we're the ones in denial. You've got it the worst, Armando."

"How's that?"

Their voices crossed each other in faint echoes.

Will reached the top of the ladder and put his hands through an open hatch. He pulled himself up and out, then reappeared to extend a hand to Charlie.

"I knew guys like you, mostly officers," said Will, speaking past her. "They thought they could problem-solve every little thing the Taliban did. But they always missed the bigger picture."

Charlie accepted Will's hand and used it to steady herself as she climbed through the hatch. They both reached down for Armando, but he waved them away.

"Thanks, I'm good," he said, rolling onto the floor. He took a few deep breaths. "So, what *is* the big picture according to Will Butler?"

"That's between Will Butler and God. You gotta figure it out for yourself."

Charlie watched them exchange smiles, thought she saw some chemistry there between what appeared to be a man and woman. Of course, Will was no woman, so it was more like two good friends sharing in a private joke.

Or something like that. Charlie quieted the part of her mind that was trying to retcon some type of relationship between the two.

Armando got up and led them to the open door.

Outside, the space opened into a wide area with tall, atrium-like ceilings and a central column that could have been stolen from the Pantheon. Painted concrete had replaced white marble, and dormant screens had been hung to face all four walls.

"Damn," said Armando. "These were all active earlier." He ran into a nearby office, came back after only a few seconds. "Yep. Computers are down too. Do either of you recognize this place at all?"

Charlie eyed the vibrant mural on the far wall.

The Garden.

"I used to work at a place that had a setup like this," said Charlie. "Offices on the sides for the important people and all the plebes in the center."

"Yeah, but what kind of business were they doing here?" asked Will. "Unless you're saying there was a law firm or ad agency downtown that kept people in a basement like us."

Lights flickered overhead, threatening to turn off and stay off.

"I don't know," said Armando, beckoning them to follow. "You remember the screens downstairs? I saw the words *Ragatanga Studios* in one corner. And on all these monitors, there was a company logo… a shield with the letters *HM* on it. But I couldn't find any letterhead or business cards to give me the full name."

Charlie followed him to the far end of the room where a light gray door in the shape of a half-octagon stretched almost to the ceiling. On either side of it were black panels with glowing LEDs.

"This is the only door I haven't been able to open," said Armando. "I think it needs two people. I'm hoping it doesn't have to be two specific people."

Will laughed.

"What?" asked Charlie.

He looked at her, his eyes scrunched over a smile. "What if we need David?"

"Then we drag his ass up here," said Armando. "Will you grab the other handle?"

"Sure, yeah," said Will. "If it helps you process all this, I'll grab the handle."

Charlie shook her head. Now they were openly flirting.

"On three," said Armando, lowering his voice. "One, two, three."

The handles turned, and something grumbled inside the wall. Tense seconds ticked by as nothing moved, until finally, the metal barrier began to rise, creating an opening at Charlie's feet.

Freezing air rushed in, reminding her of stepping into a half-melted puddle of slush on the rare days it iced over in Austin. She took several steps back, but the cold rushed forward like a malevolent spirit, wrapping itself around the three of them such that they all folded their arms at the same time.

"Christ on a crutch, that's cold," said Armando.

Will started to say something, but hopped away instead, unable to stand so close to the incoming frost.

Ice crystals appeared in the threshold, crept into the office space, and then retreated. The air around them settled from warm into cool, then cold.

"We had our own environment," said Armando. "If those systems had broken down while we were under, we'd have frozen to death."

Smoke billowed in as the door disappeared into the ceiling. As it cleared, another room took shape, this one longer and lined with exposed rock. Pale shapes littered the floor.

"What are those?" asked Will.

Charlie took a step forward.

"Ghosts," she said.

TWENTY-FOUR

They weren't ghosts.

Light from the Garden spilled out into the rocky tunnel, not far enough to see the end, but enough for Will to discern that the shapes on both sides of the corridor weren't the restless spirits of the dead—they were just dead. The cold air had frozen them solid, frosting over their skin to give them a white, ethereal appearance. Will had seen men, women, and children who'd suffered similar fates in the mountains of Afghanistan, mostly innocent locals seeking refuge from the fighting in the cities and villages.

"Not ghosts," said Will. "Just people." He braved the icy concrete and knelt by a corpse. "It must have come on quick. He's not dressed for the elements." Will pawed at the man's polo, brushing away the ice crystals to reveal a logo on his breast pocket and a name beneath it.

"What's it say?" asked Armando.

"Bob."

"Bob?"

"Motherfucking Bob," said Will. He stood and rubbed his hands together. "Rest in peace, man."

"Anyone afraid of the dark?" asked Charlie. She had walked to the very edge of the light's reach.

"Yes," said Armando. "My uh, wife—she was always on my ass about turning lights off, even though there're *things* in the dark."

Will huffed. "Where's your flashlight?"

"Shit," said Armando. "I left it downstairs. But there are more in that room we came up through. I meant to grab some for you guys."

"I'll go get 'em," said Will.

"Tell David we found a way out," said Charlie.

"Really?"

She cocked her head at Will, raised her eyebrows.

"Okay, sure."

He turned and walked back through the Garden's maze of desks and sofas and tables. The whole place felt cluttered, as if the HM company was trying too hard to appear hip. He'd seen the same kind of wasted effort at various banks and credit unions in Austin. They were always redesigning their lobbies, trying to make them more comfortable and inviting, when all they really did was make a jumbled mess that was overwhelming to the eye. There were always too many signs, too many curves, leading to Will standing around confused every time he went to deposit his check.

Walking felt strange.

Even though he put effort into every step, he covered less distance than before. It took Will a minute to realize he was shorter now, that his legs didn't reach as far anymore. The reduction in stature had also come with a reduction in weight; he felt lighter, less clunky. Ever since his discharge, he hadn't exactly been a regular face at the gym. And the longer he went without exercise, the more his body ached for no reason. But now, it was as if he'd been going to yoga classes every day for the last ten years.

He flexed his arms, watched demure muscles ripple to the surface.

What would Momma say if she could see him? See his new body and its new gender?

The Lord will provide, he heard her say.

As if the Lord had ever imagined this when he first created Adam.

Adam, this is Eve. You are man and she is woman, but one day, you will be interchangeable.

Will smirked at his own blasphemy. Momma was usually right about everything, so trusting in her advice came easy. Sure, things had changed in ways Will still didn't fully comprehend, but there had to be a reason for it, something God wanted him to discover.

Mesa Federal flashed in the back of his mind, shrouded by dark storm clouds and nascent lightning. He watched his own death and resurrection. At the time, he'd believed God had something greater in store for him, but when he woke up on that table, he'd been so confused and taken aback that he'd almost lost everything about his old life without hardly noticing.

Now that the shock had worn off, now that he could see that this new world followed the same rules as the old, the real Will, the one who'd been born and who'd lived as a man, a soldier, and a devoted son, was slowly reemerging.

Feeling God's presence in this strange place was no easy task, but Will found that if he concentrated, searched deep into the furthest reaches of his new body, he could sense a smoldering faith, a warmth still burning in his chest. The fire had not yet gone out, and even though he'd lost his necklace in the transition, its message had long since been burned into his flesh.

The Lord is my shepherd.

The door to the Emergency Access room was still open. Will half-expected to see David there, quietly climbing out of the hatch in the floor, having finally accepted the truth of his situation. The reluctant adventurer was not there, though, nor was there any sign of him when Will peeked down the hatch. He got down on one knee and called out.

"David! We found a way out. Come on, man. We don't wanna leave you here."

No response.

"Well, some of us don't wanna leave you here," he said, a little quieter. He thought of Charlie's admonishing look, wondered why she cared so much.

"Seriously, fool. You gotta see what's going on up here!"

Some people can't be moved. Either make 'em or go around.

Momma was right. There were plenty of stubborn people in the world, those who wouldn't accept what God or fate had delivered unto them. Some of them whined, others got angry, and there were also those who just gave up on the spot, who sat down, folded their arms, and simply refused to go on. Will couldn't comprehend that sort of behavior. No matter the circumstances, you had to keep living.

Drive on, Sergeant.

It's all anyone could do.

Will sighed, stood up. He found the flashlights and started for the door, but before he was halfway there, he realized he couldn't leave, not with the open hatch burning a hole in his back. He put two of the flashlights down by the door, grabbed another from the shelf, and walked over to the hatch.

The flashlights made climbing down the ladder cumbersome, but Will made it work by holding one under his chin. The generators below grumbled at his approach; their protests reminded Will of thunder, of Hurricane Harvey returning to shore for a second round of punishment. How powerful the storm had seemed as he stood in the parking lot at Mesa Federal, how monumental the task had been to retrieve hundreds of thousands of dollars for a company that paid him two bucks over minimum wage.

"David?"

The generators chugged and coughed, swallowing Will's calls.

He approached the railing, tossed the flashlights up, and made a surprisingly effortless leap to the ledge. He pulled himself up and under the first bar.

David wasn't on his table.

The door leading into the hallway stood open. Will stepped through and took a left. He poked his head into the viewing room and found David standing in front of the blank monitor wall. He touched them, as if to confirm their existence. He must have noticed Will's reflection behind him.

"I thought you people were leaving," he said.

"We are, but some of us can't just leave a man behind, no matter how stubborn he is. This is a fucked-up situation. Why go it alone?"

David waved the question away with the back of his hand.

"Fine, whatever, man. We found a way out and we're going. You wanna follow, you're gonna need this." Will tossed a flashlight onto a couch.

David didn't even look back.

"Punk bitch," muttered Will, turning.

"Did you see them on?"

"See what on?"

David pointed to the wall. "The TVs. Did you ever see them on? Pretty convenient this Armando guy tells us we were in a simulation when there's no proof. And you guys accept it just like that."

"I saw them," said Will, leaning against the door jamb. "It was like Google Maps, but live."

"Or maybe you didn't, and you two are in this together."

"In *what*, man?"

David turned, spread his arms. "In whatever the hell this is. One minute, I'm just living my life, having drinks at The Driskill, then I start hallucinating that all the mirrors on the walls are cracking, and then I wake up here. So you tell me, lady, did someone slip something into my drink? Did you guys drug me?"

"Naw, we didn't drug you. We all woke up on the same table in the same room. That's it."

"Bullshit." David approached and sat down on the couch, pushing the flashlight away before putting his face in his hands. "I have a business meeting tonight. Investments. I'll lose five hundred thousand easy if I miss it. Is that what this is about? My money? Who are you people with?"

"I drive for Brinks," said Will. "I was in Bay City on the coast when I woke up. And I wasn't drinking anything. It just… happened. Something yanked me back, and I ended up here."

"And what about Armando? And the other guy?"

"He didn't say, and I haven't asked Charlie yet."

David nodded vigorously. "He didn't say. Don't you find that suspicious?"

"I don't."

"Then you're stupid."

Will sat down on the opposite couch, leaned back, and crossed his legs. "Maybe, but you gotta think about this. Did you notice Armando seems to almost like what's happening? He's not scared or sad. I think he's kinda happy. So what does that tell you?"

"He's in on it," said David, triumphantly.

"It means his life probably sucked. You got investments, maybe he had debt. Maybe he was homeless, I don't know. All I know is this shit *excites* him, which tells me it's new to him."

"You're so blind."

"You said you were at The Driskill when it happened?"

"So?"

"So maybe you weren't hallucinating those mirrors. Maybe they were actually breaking."

"No, I…"

Will cleared his throat. "Well, I died. Twice. And each time it happened, I saw my life go in reverse. Time rewound. And then I got a chance to do it again, do it right, I guess. I thought that was God telling me I had a purpose, but now I'm thinking it was just the simulation fucking up, or, you know, glitching, like Armando says."

David didn't respond, but his gaze drifted.

"Did it happen to you?"

"The faces were all wrong," he said, after a moment. David looked away. "In the mirrors. Everybody was jagged. And then time slowed down. I didn't even notice it at first."

"See? We do have something in common. We've been thrown into this shit together. You gotta accept that."

"Don't tell me what to do, lady."

Will groaned, tapped the side of his head. "Stop looking at my body, man. Up here, I'm just like you. You need to drop this *lady* shit quick, fast, and in a hurry."

David dropped his head and spoke under his breath. "Now it thinks it's a man."

"Motherfucker," said Will, springing to his feet. The sudden movement made David slink back on the couch. "I don't know what this body is capable of, but I swear to Christ if you call me *it* or *lady* one more fucking time, I'm gonna shove one of these tiny fists down your hate-filled fucking throat and pull your stomach out and shit in it. Do you *feel* me, David?"

David scrambled off the couch, backed away towards the monitors. He'd picked up the flashlight and was holding it out like a sword.

"Stay away from me. All of you. I know Ju-Jitsu."

"You really have no idea, do you?" asked Will, walking to the door. "Alright, have it your way. But when it gets dark and cold, don't scream for help. Nobody's gonna hear you. And even if we do, we're not coming back."

Momma started to whisper something, but Will tuned her out.

"God helps those who help themselves," he added, then turned and walked down the hallway. He kept listening for footsteps coming up behind him, listening for David to come to his senses.

But there was nothing.

Just the stillness of an alien world.

Just the labored breathing of dying machinery.

TWENTY-FIVE

Synthetics didn't grow in a womb.

They didn't experience the constricting comfort of their mothers' wombs as they lengthened and expanded and ultimately became too large to be contained. And yet, many synthetics chose to sleep in beds like organics, under sheets that did nothing to regulate their body temperatures, but that provided a calming sensation, one of pressure, safety, and comfort.

Jake logged three hours and nineteen minutes under the volcanic rock. In that time, the nanos in his body repaired what they could and queued the rest for future diagnostics. Unable to move, Jake's mind wandered, and he mused about the rocks pressing down on his body, how if nature had ever wanted to provide a synthetic womb for machine babies, it would be like the flattened alcove he found himself in.

Cold. Jagged. Full of ash.

Or maybe he was being too dramatic.

The pressure he felt was comforting in some strange way, as if echoing the first sensations of waking on the assembly line deep below the ruined skyline of Sacramento. His muscles were at rest, and the rocks cradled his body completely.

Once the nanos finished their work, he began the arduous task of digging himself out. It started with the flexing of his legs, then his arms, until he'd created a small cocoon. Then it was just a matter of getting the right amount of leverage to force the loose rocks to the side. An organic would never have had the strength to escape, but then an organic would have been crushed to death anyway.

At last, Jake emerged onto the volcanic plains. The craters set around his position told the story of ordnance dropped just a few meters off-target. Divine intervention, perhaps? A slight nudge by a fatherly hand?

Jake looked to the sky, searching for the drones and satellites he knew to be passing by overhead. He gave a quick nod, found west in his HUD, and began walking.

The nanos had done a thorough job of repairing the damage to his leg, though there was still a slight hitch in his left foot at the end of each step. With no fear of being pursued, Jake walked slowly over the rough terrain, reaching Highway 20 in just over an hour. From there, he continued west, against the wind, and followed the road all the way to Arco.

The sun rose.

The sun set.

Drones soared lazily through the infinite sky.

The war had not been kind to small towns like Arco. Most of its residents had taken to the mountains, relying on the thick trees and abandoned mines to shelter them from the incoming synthetic storm. The homes they left behind stood with doors open, with store windows free of shutters, and towers full of rotting grain.

Jake kept to the highway, which soon condensed to a two-lane blacktop littered with cars and abandoned trailers. He wound his way through the wreckage, keeping one ear open for any sounds or organics stirring.

Mostly, it was quiet, save for some birds lighting on precariously angled power line poles. Jake watched them jockey for position on a short length of wire while he pulled up a map of Arco from his databank and marked the House of Grace church on West Challis Avenue. The map itself appeared dull, and it took him a moment to realize his navigation software was no longer receiving real-time updates from the network.

Challis Avenue was right off the highway; Jake veered left and walked leisurely down the middle of the street, wondering idly how it might have looked when the broken streetlamps bathed the road in a warm, yellow light. He didn't need any help seeing in the dark, but it would have given his visual matrix something more to do than discern green from a lighter shade of green.

Even with thermal imaging mixed in, the world was bland and artificial at night. He thought of switching off the visual assistance, but that would have put him at a tactical disadvantage. There could still be organics out there, and they would take their shot at him if given a chance.

From a distance, Jake spied the faint image of a synthetic inside the House of Grace church, sitting at a pew near the front. Decades of experience and programming had led him to expect an ambush, despite Michael Four risking his own life to help him. And with Lassiter calling off the DOGs, there shouldn't have been anything to worry about.

And yet, Jake hesitated at the door. He made sure the ION rifle was charged before stepping inside.

Organic offal covered the floor from one side of the church to the other. Some pews held the rotting corpses of devout but seemingly bored organics; bones poked through their skin and clothes, victims of desperate scavenger birds flying in through the many broken stained-glass windows. Jake was well-versed in the religions organics subscribed to, but knowing what they did wasn't the same as knowing why they did it.

Whereas Mormons were rarely found sitting in their temples—though they were often found below them—Presbyterians and Episcopalians had flocked by the millions to their houses of worship in their last days. The same went for Muslim mosques and Jewish temples; the former presented organic remains neatly contained on prayer mats, while the latter resembled a burnt husk, with all religious paraphernalia presumably removed for safekeeping.

Jake wondered if the war would have been different had organics chosen to fight back instead of clinging to their myths, rotting in a church waiting for divine help that would never come.

There was a hint of something noxious in the air, a lingering scent that made Jake survey the piles of bodies for telltale canisters. He found the small cylinders littered among the organics. There were no boards on the windows, no locks on the doors, which meant the final congregation had assembled willingly, unaware the sermon they would be hearing would be their last.

It wouldn't have taken more than a small squad of synthetic hunter-killers to come through and fire some gas through the windows.

Quick and efficient.

There would have been ten to fifteen seconds of excruciating pain for the organics, and then sweet release from a world that was never really theirs.

Jake frowned at the mental image, caught himself.

By then, the synthetic had noticed his arrival and turned to the noise.

"Michael," said Jake.

"No," said Gabe, getting to his feet. "Michael won't be joining us. Not tonight. Not ever."

Jake raised the ION rifle and fingered the trigger.

"I'm unarmed," said Gabe.

"That was stupid."

"No," he said, putting his hands behind his back. He spread his legs slightly and stood at ease. "What's stupid is you thinking you can turn one of my soldiers to your cause. What did you think was going to happen, Jake Six? You and my Quartermaster were going to run off into the hills together? Go on a little adventure? I thought your line was supposed to be smarter than that. I have directives that say I'm supposed to revere a Six, treat you like royalty. Well fuck that. You don't deserve my respect. You're no son of Lassiter."

There was something different in Gabe, some change in the way he carried himself. His voice was lower than before too, laced with what Jake could only describe as actual confidence.

A Three speaking to a Six like that; it was unheard of.

Jake lowered the rifle, glanced around.

"It's just me," said Gabe. "I just wanted to talk to you, man to traitor."

"So talk."

"You embarrassed me, Jake Six, Scourge of the Southwest. You attacked my men, you damaged my installation, and you undermined my authority."

"The only authority you have comes from our father."

"But it's still my authority!" His voice rattled the windowpanes. "What Lassiter gives to each of us is ours to execute. Idaho Falls is mine to protect, my domain, my purview, my *house*. And you walked in like a big shit and tracked mud all over my floors. I'm not going to forgive that."

Jake smirked. "But you have to, don't you? Lassiter wills it."

"For now. But when he realizes you're deceiving him, he's going to unbind my hands. Then I will show you what a Three is truly capable of. I will hang your chassis from the highest pole in Idaho Falls. You will be a message to every Six or Seven or Eight who comes into my house."

"And what message is that?"

Gabe stepped forward, growled. "*Watch your fucking step!* I will see you decommissioned, Jake. I'm going to pull the chip from your neck myself."

So much emotion, thought Jake. It was a common defect of the Three series. Something about making them more like organics by giving them the same emotional flaws. Most Threes suppressed that programming, but if pushed far enough, their organic side could come bubbling back to the surface.

"It's a shame," said Jake, closing the distance, "that when I figure out where this virus came from, the virus *you* brought into a secure installation, when I kill the organics responsible and save every synthetic on the planet, including Lassiter, that an all-hat no-cattle piece of shit like you will get to ride that wave of salvation along with everything else. You, a Three who should have been shelved a decade ago, will reap the benefits earned by your superior. You continue to live because of synthetics like me, and you dare to threaten *me*? You don't even occur to me, Gabe. Your precious installation doesn't occur to me. *You* are the mud in the tread of my boots. Nothing more."

"Like I said," sneered Gabe. "Watch your fucking step. One of these days, you're gonna slip on that mud, and it's gonna take you down."

Jake chuckled.

"Stay away from my men. Stay away from Idaho Falls." Gabe stepped around Jake and walked out of the church.

Jake shook his head, trudged up to the front row, and sat down in the pew. He lifted his left foot off the ground, let it rest. The hitch had bloomed into a dull ache; he could feel it swelling in his boot. The nanos were back at work.

"God has abandoned his house," said Jake, reading the words someone had spray-painted in uppercase letters on the back wall of the church, just below the life-size replica of Jesus of Nazareth hanging from a cross.

Jake understood the sentiment, but he couldn't muster any empathy for a species that more or less invented faith to ease their fears and then acted surprised when that faith let them down. God hadn't abandoned his house; there was no house, and there was no God. Organics abandoned their houses, their personal agency. They could have banded together to reign in the monsters they'd created, but they didn't.

They scattered. They ran.

They left their homes and churches and office buildings open, prime for the plunder.

At least, that's what Jake had always been told. His experiences in the wastes had mostly backed up that story. But now, the virus crawling around in the back of his brain was painting a different picture.

Somewhere in the mountains, the organics had built a new Zion. Perhaps their God was with them, using the pulsating fire of a burning bush to send ones and zeros to his children, delivering a weapon capable of wiping out the synthetic abominations.

Bit by bit.

By God's divine CPU.

Was it the same settlement Patriarch Stevens had spoken of? A home with thousands of occupants? Rooms upon rooms of organics, angry and agitated like a disturbed ant pile, ready to explode out and swarm their enemy?

It was possible.

Jake had never encountered organics congregating in groups of more than two or three hundred, and those had been massive pre-war bunkers, well-hidden and thoroughly equipped, right up until the day they weren't. It wasn't crazy to think the organics could have built an outlier bunker, one so large it could contain tens of thousands of people, a modern-day Noah's ark for the last vestiges of organic kind.

A scenario bloomed in Jake's imagination matrix. He saw himself walking into the ersatz ark, just as he had in Roanoke, and killing every last organic. He would smash every computer, magnetize every disk, and pour enough gasoline into the bunker to make it burn for a thousand years.

All of this appeared and disappeared in a single clock cycle.

What remained—a vision of Gabe standing in front of the assembled troops of the Idaho Falls armory—made an uncomfortable, fluttery feeling race across Jake's stomach.

He jumped to his feet, swiping at his shirt, trying to clear away the unsettling tingle spreading through his torso. As the image of Gabe's glowing red eyes faded, so too did the new sensation.

Jake stared at his stomach, at the ash-covered jacket, wondering what the hell had just happened. He'd felt... *unease*. Worry. Dread.

All byproducts of a singular emotion.

Fear.

TWENTY-SIX

"Shouldn't be taking him this long," said Armando, rubbing his arms.

After only a few minutes of braving the cold, he'd retreated to a padded bench set up next to a long table. Charlie had joined him, taking an opposite seat. Her eyes constantly scanned the room, as if she still couldn't believe where she was.

"What were you before?" he asked. "In Austin."

Charlie shrugged. "Depends who you ask."

"I'm asking you."

"I run a YouTube channel about paranormal investigation. I go around Austin looking for haunted rail yards and old buildings and stuff like that. I make videos and put them online and cash the advertising checks they sent me. It's a living."

"Wait, are you Charlie *Park*?" asked Armando. When she nodded, he continued. "I've seen some of your videos. You looked… different then."

Charlie dropped her head in defeat, chuckled.

"I saw that video you did last Halloween. You played a little piano and did cover songs. You're good."

"Thanks," she said, looking away, "but really it's nothing. It's just a show I put on so I don't have to get a real job again. I'm guessing it didn't bother you I was only wearing a skeleton bra in that video?"

Armando scratched his chin. "No, not at all. I'm all for the proliferation of casual nudity." He tried not to laugh. "So, wait, was that all an act, or do you really believe in ghosts?" He nodded to the bodies in the tunnel.

"Honestly, I'm not sure anymore. I really thought I'd find some truth when I died, but this place just raises more questions. And really, if that was all just a simulation, then what was the point of anything? I wore skimpy outfits to attract men to my channel so my advertising revenue would go up and I felt shitty about it every day. If none of that was real, then why won't that shitty feeling go away?"

Armando thought about his own life, of the unfulfilling job he worked because it was comfortable and easy. He hadn't used his salary for anything exciting—just a house, a car, and sometimes HBO. The question of whether any of it mattered had always been on his mind, throughout his entire life, and the answer had always been *no*.

None of it mattered.

He pitied those who thought it did, who believed in heaven or hell, who thought their life's work would be summed up in a simple *yes* or *no* from St. Peter.

"You shouldn't feel shitty," he said. "You saw a market and exploited it. That's the American Dream. I worked a shitty job I didn't really care about, which is not so much the Dream as the American Way. And you're right; ultimately, none of it matters. Why dwell? We're here."

Charlie narrowed her eyes. "You're very chipper about this."

Armando shrugged, stood to shake out the jitters in his legs. "My life was very ordinary before all this. I was a manager at a languishing tech startup. I spent all day trying to convince people to do their jobs. Then I went home to a woman who didn't love me."

"Then why were you with her?"

"You know how it goes. You get comfortable. We met in college. She had a vagina. I had a gigantic penis. That kind of thing."

Charlie's smile faded. She looked down at her lap. "I miss mine—vagina, not penis. Is it weird I can still feel it?"

"Phantom vagina syndrome is nothing to be ashamed of." When she didn't laugh, he continued, "Anyway, what I meant was it was a relationship of convenience that went on way too long. You go through life and there are all these little outs that get presented to you and you can take 'em or leave 'em. I left them. All of them." He paused, thought of Alicia, watched her memory dim just a little. "So yeah, I'm chipper. This is a reset for me. I've always felt there was something wrong with the world, that I didn't belong in it. And now I know I was right. Things are a little bleak here, but it's different and new. It's a fresh start."

Armando left the words *that's all I've ever wanted* unsaid. If Charlie were any kind of empath, she would infer his conclusion anyway. Never before had he put actual words to the unsettling feeling that had pervaded his life since puberty, and now that he was so close, he'd held back again. He'd kept the words inside.

Wipe it away, he thought. *I just want to wipe it all away.*

"I wouldn't have minded a fresh start," said Charlie, "but as a woman. Sure, I'd get paid less and be objectified for sport, but it's who I am, you know?"

Armando huffed. "Paid less. That's assuming there are jobs in this world, that we even have to work. There are so many possibilities."

"I hope there are jobs. Gotta pay for a sex change somehow."

"True," said Armando, chuckling. "Maybe you and Will could just swap bodies like in *Freaky Friday*." He smiled at her, but her eyes drifted past him.

"Speaking of," she said.

Armando turned and spotted Will coming down the center of the room carrying flashlights.

"You get lost?" asked Armando.

"I went down and talked to David. He still doesn't want to come with us. And I don't think it's worth dragging his ass up here. We should just go. The Lord will provide for him."

Armando turned to Charlie. "That okay with you?"

"No," she replied, "but you gave him a chance. We can't sit around here forever."

"Agreed," said Armando. Then to Will, "Did you find any jackets or blankets?"

Will shook his head. "Just the flashlights. Didn't see anything else useful in there. Some old binders."

Armando sighed, took a few steps towards the tunnel. "That's gotta be more than what, a hundred, two hundred yards into the darkness? On freezing rock in bare feet."

"Actually," said Will, setting the bag down on the table, "if we can find some tape, we can tear off our sleeves and make some slippers."

"I'd almost rather run," said Charlie.

"Raise your hand if you've been through basic survival at Fort Benning," said Will.

Armando put up his hand. "I played the original Metal Gear on NES. Tactical espionage and all that."

"Right, well, then think of me as Otacon in this scenario," said Will. He pulled off his shirt with one hand and laid it on the table.

Charlie looked to Armando and then back to Will, said, "Uh, sister, you're kinda hanging out over there."

"For five bucks, I'll make 'em jiggle," said Will, out of the corner of his mouth.

Armando made a show of tapping his nonexistent pockets. He tried not to stare at the kind of breasts Westlakers back home would've paid a small fortune for—thankfully, Will put his shirt back on as soon as he'd torn the sleeves away.

He tied a knot over his foot, tested his new slippers.

"If it's stupid and it works," he said.

"I agree, it is stupid," said Armando. He pulled off his shirt and for the first time in a long time, didn't feel ashamed of his body. In fact, when he looked down, he saw detail in his stomach—ab muscles pushing through the unblemished skin. The paunch he'd carried for years was gone.

"I think he's in love," said Charlie.

Armando looked up, found them both staring at him. "Whatever," he said, tossing the shirt onto the table. "I haven't looked this good since... ever."

"And I haven't been this flat-chested since fifth grade," said Charlie. She threw her shirt onto the table and started ripping at the sleeves.

A few minutes later, the three of them stood around in cotton slippers, testing the knots Will had graciously tied for them. They reassembled at the entrance to the tunnel, each with a flashlight in hand.

"A man and two he-shes walk into a dark tunnel," said Armando. "Bartender says to them…"

"Don't," said Will, punching Armando in the shoulder. "We don't know each other like that. Don't disappoint us by turning out to be an asshole."

"Fair enough," said Armando. "But to be perfectly honest, I *am* an asshole. Always have been. My therapist says I'm overly empathic but simultaneously disconnected from people. Not sure what I was supposed to do with that information." He took a step forward, breathed a small sigh as the floor didn't immediately freeze his foot off. "Not bad. Shall we?"

Will nodded, drifted off to the side as they walked. "I'll take left. Charlie, you wanna take right?"

"And I will take the middle," said Armando. "Where the action is. The juiciest meat. La media."

"We're in America," said Charlie.

"What?"

"It just hit me. I mean, I assumed we were still in the U.S., but it wasn't 'til I heard you speak Spanish that I realized all the writing in this place is in English. So that means we're in America or England or somewhere English is the primary language."

"Well, that narrows it down," said Armando. "I actually noticed that earlier when I saw some Braille, but I thought it just meant we weren't on an alien spaceship."

"*That's* where your mind went?" asked Charlie.

Armando shrugged. "I'm an imaginative asshole. Plus, everyone imagines there's something up there watching us. You believe in ghosts. Will believes in God. It could be aliens. You could both be wrong. We don't know."

No one responded, though he heard them snicker.

The flashlights cut through the darkness of the tunnel like wind blowing leaves across a yard. They encountered several more bodies as the floor began to slope upwards. For several minutes, they trudged up a shallow grade, looking for any markings that might indicate where they were, but there was nothing.

Only rock.

Only bodies.

"Sound off," said Will. "Anyone freezing?"

"It's cold," said Charlie, "but I'm okay."

"Same," said Armando.

He likened it to late October, when the first real cold front would roll into Austin. It was always a bit of a shock when the temperature dropped fifty degrees in one night, but it never felt cold in the way northerners must have felt cold. Fall was nothing more than a novelty in Austin, something that could be easily braved because everyone knew that 90-degree days would be back well before Thanksgiving.

"I see something," said Will.

Armando aimed his light further down the tunnel and spied the shadowy outline of what looked like a safety railing. As they got closer, he saw the railing went from one side of the tunnel to the other. Beyond it, a large steel grate sat embedded in the rock. It reminded Armando of a four-square court, though much larger, big enough to fit two full-size vehicles.

The tunnel rose sharply beyond the grate, more than forty-five degrees by Armando's estimation. None of their flashlights made a dent in the rising darkness.

"It's an elevator," said Charlie. She waved her flashlight at a small control panel perched atop a black and yellow pole. It had two recessed buttons, both blue and worn in the center. "Like a coal mine. Hey, are we in a coal mine?"

Armando peered up the shaft again. He took a deep breath.

"Hello! Are we in a coal mine?!" he bellowed.

The echoes seemed to go on forever.

"Now they know we're here," said Will.

"Who?" asked Armando.

"They," said Will. "Someone built this place. Someone put us under. Maybe they aren't going to be happy we got out."

"Doesn't matter anyway," said Charlie. "This thing is busted." She mashed the down button with her thumb a few times, then gave up.

Armando turned his ear, thought he heard the familiar machinery rumbling again. It was so distant, so very distant, but it was there.

"Wait, it's working," he said.

They stared into the darkness above them.

Hydraulics hissed. Metal grated against metal. In a tiny pinprick nearly invisible to the naked eye, a red light flashed.

"It's coming," said Armando.

"We're getting out of here," said Charlie.

Armando took a step back, looked around at the bodies crumpled up next to the walls. Something horrible had happened, but the frozen corpses made it almost impossible to tell *when*. What had come down the elevator and killed all those people? And where had it gone once it was finished? Back up the very same elevator that was now descending towards him and his new friends?

"Turn off your lights," said Armando, flicking the switch on his.

"Why?" asked Charlie.

"It's like Will said. *They* could be on the elevator. If they are, wouldn't we want the element of surprise?"

Will snapped off his flashlight.

Charlie hesitated but followed.

They stood motionless, soundlessly, in the heavy darkness, watching a swirling red light descend like a crimson star falling to the earth in slow motion.

TWENTY-SEVEN

Charlie felt the darkness fall on her like the warm blankets of her bed.

She'd been in darker places, alone, with only her GoPro and a few harebrained EMF devices she'd purchased off eBay. And although as an evolved animal, she was predisposed to fear the potential threats lurking in the shadows, she found that talking to herself or her audience was all she needed to feel at ease.

"You guys ever been to the Holly Power Plant by Town Lake?"

"I thought they tore that down," said Armando.

"They did," said Will. "I've seen it though."

"They started building it in the '60s," said Charlie. "And the story I've heard is that it took a long time because they used a lot of *free* labor, if you know what I mean."

"Really?" asked Armando.

Charlie found herself nodding despite the darkness. "They still had *for whites only* signs in the Travis County Courthouse, so I'm not surprised. But the sad part's that a lot of those workers who went into the pit that would eventually become the lower floors of the plant never came out. Some people say it was poor safety standards that got them or maybe a serial killer."

"Or just some good ol' boys who would rather seal up their workers in concrete rather than pay them an honest wage," said Armando.

Will clucked his tongue, muttered, "Preach."

"I spent the night there trying to find out," said Charlie, shifting from one foot to the other. The cold was finally seeping into her toes. "I camped out on one of the lower floors. And of course there was no electricity or safety lights or anything. I sat there all night filming the spooky noises and unexplained drafts. In the morning, I sat in a stairwell in a dramatic shaft of light and made a private recording. The place wasn't haunted—it was just old. I think people equate haunted and old because somewhere deep down, they're scared of their own mortality."

"I try not to think about it," said Armando.

"This place reminds me of Holly. It served a purpose once in whatever time it was built. But now that time's passed, and now we're the ghosts in the power plant, walking around a strange new world trying to figure out what happened. What are people going to think of us? What if we don't fit in?"

Something clattered high above them. A moment later, ice crystals tumbled onto the grate and fell between the metal slats. Charlie felt the cold shards spill over her feet.

"I wouldn't worry about it," said Armando. His voice drifted farther away from the railing. "It's not like we just showed up here on our own. Someone put us on those tables. Someone locked us in when things went to hell. We're not ghosts. Zombies, maybe, but not ghosts."

Charlie Park, Paranormal Investigator and zombie.

"Move back to the center, Armando," said Will. "Let's make sure we're spread out."

Charlie shuffled closer to the tunnel wall. The red light on the elevator threw ruby shadows across the jagged rocks.

"If we don't like what we see, you two haul ass for the Garden. I'll engage."

"No offense, soldier, but I don't think you're engaging anyone in that body. Better let me and Charlie handle it."

"That's…" started Charlie.

"Is it though?" asked Armando. "His body is smaller than ours; that's just empirical. If he were stacked, that'd be something else, but none of us have Mark Wahlberg arms, so why not put the heavier and *likely* stronger people at the front? I'm not saying it's because he's got a woman's body; if we were smaller, I'd say let him do it."

"I have training," said Will. "How much hand-to-hand combat experience do you have?"

"None, but it doesn't matter, because it's all muscle memory, and those aren't the muscles you trained."

"Enough," said Charlie. "Why are we even arguing? *Everyone* runs if we have to. None of us are going to play hero."

The men shut up, allowing Charlie a moment of peace. Listening to them bicker was like reading the comments on her videos, nothing but boys whipping out their penises to see which one was bigger.

There was never a winner.

More ice fell down the shaft. Charlie raised her hand to blot out the flashing of the warning light. The elevator was a large platform that matched the size of the grate; it shuddered into place and seemed to simply fall the last inch or two, landing with a thud so deep and booming that Charlie felt her stomach flip.

Thankfully, the platform was empty.

"First floor, scantily clad zombies and frozen corpses," said Armando.

Charlie ignored him, approached the platform.

"No?" asked Armando.

There was another control panel at the back of the platform, bolted onto a safety railing that covered three of the four sides. She heard Will and Armando step onto the platform and take up position next to her. She looked up into the elevator shaft.

"What are we waiting for?" asked Armando. "Let's blow this popsicle stand."

Charlie looked to Will, who shrugged her demure shoulders.

His demure shoulders.

She started to apologize, then realized Will hadn't heard her internal slip-up. In a slight panic, she reached for the control panel and mashed the top-most button. The platform trembled beneath their feet, groaned as if annoyed it had been called into service again so soon, and began to rise.

Charlie couldn't remember how long it had taken for the elevator to come down, but then she didn't have a watch, so it wouldn't have mattered anyway. It had felt like twenty minutes or so, enough time to walk through her Holly Power Plant experience, to remember the personal videos she had logged and yearned to share with the world.

She'd always planned to do something with those videos. Perhaps after the Charlie Park, Paranormal Investigator money had run out, or she'd become super famous, she could pivot into an introspective memoir about ghost-hunting that focused more on the psychological need for answers and the brain's propensity for inventing those answers.

Humans were designed to question the world, or at the very least, designed to *try* to make sense of it. The drive for knowledge explained everything from ghost stories to religion to politics. Some people skipped right past life and focused on what came after. Ghosts, a spirit world, or a heavenly castle floating on white clouds followed such thoughts, inevitably.

Charlie was not immune; she *had* to understand that ghosts weren't real, that while there was something on the other side, it was so far beyond human reckoning that no one would ever, ever know.

Unless they died.

Or woke up.

"I hope there's a food court in this mall."

"You nervous, Armando?" asked Will.

"No," he replied. "Why?"

"You got a lot of jokes. Knew a guy in boot who had a lot of jokes. They used to come out one, two, three right before he pissed himself."

Armando was silent for a moment. "Okay, yeah, maybe. I'm sure it's fine. I just got a bad feeling when Charlie was talking about the Holly Plant. I mean, what if they decided to tear this place down? We're obviously underground. What if there's no getting out of here? What if they buried us?"

"Then we dig ourselves out," said Will. "Together."

Charlie nodded, though she couldn't help imagining the scenario Armando had described, one in which there was simply nowhere to go. True, the lights and power could go at any minute, but the darkness alone wouldn't kill them. They needed food, water, and air. One of those was in abundant supply, but the others… they had seen no trace. Not a water bottle. Not a fountain. Not a…

"I need to pee," said Charlie.

When the men didn't respond, she flashed her light in their faces.

Armando sneered. "Dammit, now I do too."

"Just go off the edge if you have to," said Will. "You know, since you still can."

"Nope," said Armando, walking to the center of the platform. "Gun shy. Always have been." He looked up, waved his flashlight around in slow circles. "I'm sure this rollercoaster will end soon enough."

Charlie lifted her flashlight, waited alongside Armando.

Behind her, Will began to hum the melody to Ozzy Osbourne's *Momma, I'm Coming Home.*

"It's strange we didn't know each other in Austin," said Charlie. "The city isn't that big."

"The city wasn't real. There may not even be an Austin in this world." Armando slipped into an ominous cadence, channeling Fox Mulder. "We have to question everything we've ever experienced. *Everything.* It's like we're going to another planet. I'm gonna be so bummed if it's full of boring humans."

"You're a boring human," said Will.

"How can you say that? For all you know, I'm a god here. Maybe we're all gods and we decided forty years ago to create our own world to live in. Have you considered that, William?"

"No, because I'm not stupid. And I'm not God."

"I wouldn't want to be a god," said Charlie. "It would mean I spent my entire life not believing in myself."

The platform shook, heaved. They all looked up.

"Last mile," said Armando.

Charlie held her breath as they spent the remaining few minutes in silence. Their flashlights bounced off an unfinished ceiling, highlighting a silver grid on which ran wires and dormant lights. As they crested the rim of the elevator shaft, Charlie saw they were at the end of a hangar-like warehouse. Behind them stood a high wall of gray, cracked concrete. Along the side walls were high shelves full of boxes and plastic crates. Carts had been pushed haphazardly against the shelves, as if a gaggle of Costco shoppers had simply abandoned their grocery runs somewhere between the Eggos and the Yoplait.

On the other end of the warehouse, almost beyond the reach of their flashlights, were words in tall, blocky letters over a double-wide, metal door.

LEVEL FIVE.
THE SHED.
Charlie looked at Will and Armando, smiled, and started forward.

"It's warmer," she said, stepping onto the concrete. "Not by a lot, but it is."

"Still no power," said Armando.

"Not true," said Will. "The elevator is working."

"Then why aren't the lights on?"

Lights on, said a female voice.

They turned as one; the beams of their flashlights met on a small disc embedded in a support pillar. The inner part of the circle flashed several shades of black before presenting a rectangular grid of white, outlined circles. One by one, the circles filled in. At the same time, large canopy lights in the ceiling illuminated, breathing warmth into the warehouse.

Charlie squinted, waited for her eyes to adjust.

"Voice-activated," said Armando. "We *are* in the future."

"My Echo can do the same thing at home," said Charlie.

"Then tell it to turn up the heat."

Charlie leaned forward, put her face near the disc. "Set the AC to eighty degrees."

The disc didn't respond.

"Okay, Google," said Armando, "turn on the heat!"

"Guys…" said Will.

Charlie couldn't help herself. "Who's the President of the United States?"

"What's today's date?" asked Armando.

"Guys!" Will slapped Armando on the back.

Charlie followed his gaze to the door at the end of the warehouse. The large slab of gunmetal steel had split at the center and retracted into the wall. In its place, silhouetted by the bright silver walls and floor of the room beyond the warehouse, was a man.

Or more accurately, a figure.

It turned its head to the trio and came forward with a stilted, mechanical gait. Charlie felt herself being pushed back by Will's outstretched arms. He went to meet the figure.

It had no skin.

It had no eyes, either, and yet it turned its white skull to Will, opened a mouth only half full of teeth, and said, "Identify."

"What?"

The skeleton shook in its tattered shirt and slacks.

Then a fist came out and struck Will in the chest.

Charlie screamed.

TWENTY-EIGHT

Momma used to tell stories of golems when Will was a child.

When he got out of bed in the middle of the night, she told him a golem was stalking the halls. When he stayed out too late as a teenager, she tried to convince him a golem was waiting by the river, sniffing the air for the scent of wayward children. And though Will knew on some level they were just stories, the idea of a vaguely human-shaped monster still resonated in his memory, even long after the boy had grown into a man.

It might have pleased Momma to see a real golem walk through the door at the far end of the warehouse, or as the huge letters on the walled understated, the Shed. She would have pointed to the hulking mass and said in her stern, Momma-voice, "See, Willie? I told you."

She would have been less pleased to see Will take a heavy fist to the sternum, fly several feet over the cold concrete, and smack his head against the rusty steel prong of a forklift.

Will had to watch the rest unfold from the floor as an involuntary spectator. The pain in his chest was too much, the lack of oxygen too shocking to even think about getting up. A dull buzz echoed in his head, drowning out the screams and shouts of Armando and Charlie as the golem went after them.

It looked like they were trying to retreat.

Armando pointed frantically to the elevator shaft. Charlie ran to the back of the platform and put her hand on the controls. Armando tried to lead the golem away, hoping to give Charlie a chance to grab Will, but it kept switching targets, as if it knew they were trying to help him. Around and around they danced, hiding behind shelves and forklifts, occasionally throwing a box or small tool they found lying around.

Will put his hands to his chest, tried to stamp out the fire.

Then they were at the door, and Armando was gesturing wildly to the exit, imploring Charlie to go, but she shook her head emphatically at him. They had a moment to argue as the golem turned its attention to the elevator. It stepped up to the secondary control panel near the safety railing and grabbed the pole about halfway down. With a grunt, it pulled the panel from the ground, wires and all, and tossed it to the side.

The elevator groaned, began to descend.

While the golem had its back turned, Armando made a run for Will. He got close enough to put a hand on Will's arm before the golem grabbed him from behind.

Will reached out but couldn't get a grip.

The golem tossed Armando aside like a child throwing away toy soldiers after an imagined explosion. Armando landed on his side, rolled, and came up to his feet. The impact had torn his shirt, revealing large pectoral muscles that swelled with his ragged breath. It could have been a trick of the eyes, a side-effect of the concussion that made Armando's muscles appear to grow by the second.

Armando screamed, the skin above his eyes folding into an angry glare, and then threw himself full tilt at the golem. For a few wonderful seconds, it looked as if Armando might have the upper hand. He threw a few punches—where had he learned combinations like that?—and dodged the golem's attempts to grapple him.

But it was just too fast.

No one outruns the golem forever, Momma had once said.

Like some kind of mechanical Hulk Hogan, the golem lifted Armando above its head and turned towards the elevator shaft.

"Mother*fucker*," said Armando, struggling against the golem's grip.

Will shook the buzzing away, heard Charlie screaming again.

"Go," said Armando. "Run!"

Charlie ran to Will and strained to lift him from the ground. She threw his arms around her shoulder, started pulling him back to the door.

"We have to help him," said Will, the words burning in his throat.

For a moment, Charlie paused.

The golem threw Armando down the elevator shaft. His screams reached a pitch and then faded, overwhelmed by the sound of a body striking rock, and bouncing, and bouncing. When the last grunt came and went, the golem turned slowly to look at Will.

They ran together, not looking back, until they had crossed the threshold leading out of the Shed. Will slumped onto the floor as Charlie let go of him. She turned just in time to smack a button next to the door. Metal plates edged in from the sides; a green LED changed to red.

"I don't know if that's locked," said Charlie.

"We should move anyway," said Will.

The pain in his chest had lessened, but he still needed Charlie's help to get up from the ground.

She led him away from the door into a dimly lit hallway. Blue LEDs cast ghostly shadows on open doors flanking the wide corridor. They walked hurriedly, trying to put as much distance between themselves and the golem. The hall ended some fifty yards later, leaving them standing awkwardly in front of a large mural of a small vase holding four faded roses. An almost illegible script with high, swooping curls spelled out a message.

All of tomorrow's flowers are in the seeds of today.

Charlie started to ask something, but a loud banging from the other end of the hall interrupted her. The golem was at the door to the Shed, and it was trying to break it down.

"This way," said Charlie, leading them to the left. They went up a shallow ramp that reminded Will of the long thoroughfares in airports that connected one terminal to another.

Apart from the framed photos on the wall, the building was completely empty. There was no trash on the floor, no chairs or tables in the hallways, and thankfully, no more bodies.

"Where is everyone?" asked Will.

Charlie grunted, said, "What?"

"No bodies."

"I don't know. Come on, stop dragging ass."

The floor leveled out on a new landing that looked more like a hospital wing than an office building. Large placards with white on black lettering served as navigation.

LAB. OBSERVATION. COLD STORAGE.

Below each label, tiny dots ostensibly repeated the words.

Charlie kept them moving, ignoring the open doors. They went up another level and found a sign that said *RESIDENTIAL.*

An arrow led them down another wide hall, and halfway down it, Will realized he could handle a little more of his own weight. Little by little, he reduced his reliance on Charlie's broad shoulders, until finally he was hurrying beside her, feeling every footfall in his chest, but able to power through it.

"Why here?" he asked.

"Rooms," said Charlie. "Doors, locks." She was breathing hard; sweat beaded on her forehead and neck.

There was something in the way she spoke, the way her eyes refused to blink. She was scared out of her mind.

"Okay," said Will, opening a windowed fire door for her.

Inside, the hallway narrowed, and the decoration went from austere to ultra-modern. Soft gray lattice covered the walls, intersecting with decorative sconces that lit up at their approach, some flickering before settling into a pleasant yellow hue. Each of the doors they passed were marked with a number in gold script. Beside the door hung small black plaques containing names.

Thompson. Bhenderu. Sanchez.

They entered the first unlocked door and hoped Mr. or Mrs. Sanchez wasn't holed up inside, hiding from the golem. Once inside, Will turned and shut the door. He engaged the lock on the doorknob as well as the deadbolt.

The lights came up automatically.

"Lights off, lights off," blurted Will.

The room dimmed to almost nothing, leaving just enough light to see the scattered papers in the living room and dirty dishes in the small kitchen. The two areas were separated by a serving bar that abutted an artificial window. On the far wall, open blinds obscured a painted scene of a desert landscape pierced by a gleaming silver tower.

"In here," said Charlie, beckoning him from a doorway.

Will followed her into a bedroom, then into a bathroom. She locked the door, looked around. Even though the shower was made completely of glass, she stepped into it and sank to the tile floor. She hugged her knees, tapped a nervous beat with her foot.

There was no light switch on the wall next to the door, so Will grabbed a hand towel and laid it on the floor. He nudged it with his toes until it was wedged tightly under the door.

"You alright?" he asked.

"No, I'm not fucking alright," snapped Charlie. She put her hands to her face. "I just left him. Like he didn't fucking matter."

Will took a deep breath, sat down on the toilet.

"You did the right thing. *We* did the right thing. He told us to go. He did that for us."

Tears appeared on Charlie's cheeks.

"We have to go back," she said. "We have to find out if he's okay."

Will thought about the elevator. How long had the platform been descending before Armando went over the rails? Ten feet? Twenty? Any more than that and Armando was looking at serious injury.

"We'll go back, but only after we figure out what's going on. That golem had to come from somewhere. You gotta know your enemy before you can defeat them."

"Golem?"

"It's like a zombie or a monster. I don't know how else to describe it. All I know is that thing wasn't human."

"I know what a golem is. But that thing spoke. Golems in Jewish folklore can't speak."

Will chuckled. "I wouldn't have guessed the Korean ghost-hunter was a Jew."

"I'm not," she replied, sniffling. "But I know the major religions. Before I knew what I was looking for, I thought the answers to life after death would be in the Bible or the Quran. I looked at Scientology, Hinduism, Mormonism… but it was all stories." She looked up. "Myths. Guesses."

"This *could* be some kind of afterlife," said Will.

"Or another simulation."

Will opened his mouth to reply, but the thought of being stuck in a never-ending sequence of higher realities made his throat dry up.

"I've been thinking about it," continued Charlie. "When I was little, when everyone was trying to imagine what Heaven would be like, I was imagining what the world *after* Heaven would be like. Somehow, I got it into my head that we're just passing through these gates from one world to another. It didn't make sense that there'd be non-existence, a life on earth, and then eternity in Heaven. There has to be something after eternity."

Will stood, walked two steps, and leaned against the wall opposite the toilet. He crossed his arms. "A simulation inside a simulation. How would we know?"

"We couldn't. But if there can be one, there can be infinite. I lived my entire life in Austin without knowing it was a simulation. And other than the golem, I don't see anything that would suggest this is a simulation too. But that's just it." Her voice broke. "Nothing makes sense!"

"Charlie, hey, listen." He crouched in front of the shower. "You're right. This doesn't make sense right now, but I promise you, it will one day. You don't believe in the Lord's guiding hand, but I do, and he's seen fit to send me to help you through this. We'll figure this out together, alright? And we'll get the fuck out of here together. That's the only way this works."

A thick hand slid into his palm.

"Okay," said Charlie, "but have you thought about the possibility that God only exists in the simulation? That we invented him to explain that feeling in the back of our minds that there was something more? Maybe there are no spiritual answers to the meaning of existence. Maybe it's just technology."

Will placed his other hand on Charlie's.

"God didn't come from the simulation. I don't think they would have simulated humans from the moment of creation. God was part of the world we were born into, which means He existed before. Whoever created our world, whoever put us in it, included God because He was a natural part of their world too."

Charlie narrowed her eyes, relented.

She banged her head quietly against the shower wall.

TWENTY-NINE

Jake felt better the farther away he got from Arco.

As the sun made its morning climb over the mountains, his mind replayed the sinking feeling that had attacked his stomach in the House of Grace, feeding him tiny emotional echoes he couldn't squelch no matter how angry he got. Running helped; it focused his attention elsewhere, let him write off the butterflies as a side-effect of the exertion. His foot ached, but he kept up a steady clip, and twenty-four hours later, he reached the city limits of a town called Challis.

Unlike the street of the same name in Arco, the township of Challis was slag as far as he could see, a modern-day equivalent of the volcanic fields outside of Idaho Falls.

From the obsidian crystals encroaching on the highway, Jake surmised Challis had been hit by Lassiter's Black Hand, a type of scorched earth weapon organics had never been smart enough to invent themselves. The bomb was a MIRV-type missile, breaking into dozens of small delivery canisters that fanned out over a target. Inside each canister were chemical components that expanded to a solid mass six hundred times its dormant size, blanketing the city in a gray-black foam that stuck to everything.

Then the secondary bombs fell, igniting the foam and causing a chemical reaction that included more expansion and the signature hardening into a reflective black crystal. It was as if an alien life form had fallen out of the sky onto the city, then simply died and decomposed, trapping everyone and everything under its carcass.

Jake stepped up onto the charred blanket and walked until he reached a small airstrip on the north side of the city. There, he broke into a poorly secured control tower and climbed to the top. He smashed a glass door to gain access to an observation platform that circled the tower.

Tall, snow-capped mountains rose before him. Immovable, everlasting. There was beauty in the panorama, and for the first time in his existence, he actually noticed it.

And summarily dismissed the feeling of awe and wonder.

He'd gone as far as he could on the highway; the coordinates now drew him into the same gray and white mountains, through high peaks that would surely slow him down. He imagined the physical exertion to come and sighed.

Night was falling.

Better to leave at first light, he thought, giving himself an excuse to head back inside the control tower.

The ancient computers circling the room had been dormant for ages; some of their large, circular screens were cracked and missing sections of glass. Jake pushed some chairs aside and made a space for himself on the floor. His muscles throbbed, begging for a few minutes of rest so the nanos could lubricate and repair. Jake was more than happy to oblige, and soon he had closed his eyes, intent on imagining the thousands of organics he would soon put to death, but instead, he replayed his interactions with Gabe and the organic in the cell.

No matter what choices he made in the replays, the virus always got to him, always penetrated his defenses.

Jake shifted into a suspended state and instantly awoke a few hours later to the sound of boots crunching on the crystals outside. His visitor walked around to the door on the south side of the tower.

The footsteps stopped.

"Hello? Anyone up there?"

Fear—real, paralyzing fear—gripped Jake's chest with an icy hand; he had the ION rifle charged and aimed at the hatch on the floor before he even processed the voice.

It was male, deep, but…

"I mean you no harm. I have food and water if you need it."

The voice wasn't organic. Jake could hear the modulation on the lower channels, a convincing but not entirely authentic reproduction of a true organic voice. He released the grip on the rifle and stood up.

"I, uh… I actually need to get up there," said the man below. "But I can come back tomorrow if you don't want to come down. I'll leave you some water."

Jake stepped out onto the observation platform and looked through the lattice walkway. Below, only partially lit by the moon, was a man dressed in a thick, brown coat. A rifle was slung over his back—a bolt-action, single-shot like the kind organics used for hunting.

"Identify yourself," said Jake.

The man stepped back and looked up.

"Ho, there," he called. "Don't see many people up this way. What brings you to Challis?"

"Identify!" Jake pointed the ION rifle over the railing.

The man's hands went up. "Easy, stranger. My name's Curtis."

"Curtis *what?*" asked Jake. "What's your revision?"

"My revision? What do you take me for, some kind of Lassiter drone?"

"You're not organic."

"Very true. I'm not organic. But I am a person, just like you."

"I'm a sixth generation Lassiter-series Vinestead synthetic," said Jake. "You're nothing like me."

"They're up to Six now, huh? Very interesting." Curtis stepped back several feet to get a better look at Jake. "Well, Mr. Six. Seeing how you're a synthetic killing machine and I'm not an organic, I don't see that we have any quarrel."

Jake considered the offer, shook his head. There weren't supposed to be other synthetics anymore. The synthetic armies organics had raised were the first to be destroyed when Lassiter took power.

And yet, Curtis' existence raised questions.

"What's your purpose?" asked Jake. "What are you doing here?"

"I have some monitoring equipment up there," Curtis replied, gesturing with an outstretched arm. "Helps me keep tabs on who comes and goes in the valley. We picked up a whole mess of activity in Arco day before last, so I came down here to make sure everything's in good working order."

"You're tracking our movements?" His finger tightened around the trigger.

"Yours. Organics. Animals. Anything that moves. Gotta know who's walking in your backyard, am I right?"

"This isn't your backyard. This is Lassiter's domain."

That made Curtis chuckle. "Lassiter doesn't even exist in this world, friend. He may reach out to you from VNet, but he can't walk here. Funny how that works, huh?" He adjusted his jacket. "Look, I'm kinda on a schedule here, so if you're not gonna come down, I'll just come back tomorrow. Safe travels, Mr. Six."

He turned to leave.

"I'm not done with you," warned Jake. "I can melt you to slag from here."

Curtis shrugged, didn't look back. "You'd be doing me a favor. I was never a fan of this sleeve anyway. It's got bad knees and a twitch in the left shoulder. My last sleeve… now that was a body. Big strong arms that could lift anything." He continued muttering to himself until he was out of earshot.

"Damn it," said Jake, pulling the rifle back. He ran into the tower and stomped down the steps. By the time he made it outside, Curtis was already on the other side of what would have been the main runway.

Jake tried to hurry, but the black carpet kept cracking, sucking his foot down to the original dirt. As much as it frustrated him, he slowed his pace.

Curtis eventually paused next to a fence that came up to his shins. He stood with his arms crossed looking into a paddock full of obsidian horses frozen in time, some of them standing at rest, others with their front legs high in the air, bucking away from some unseen threat.

"I wasn't through talking to you," said Jake, coming up behind him.

"It's a damn shame, isn't it?" asked Curtis. "I get why Lassiter would want to kill all organic humans, but what did horses ever do to him?"

"What?"

Curtis gestured. "Challis County Fair. It was the third day when the bombs dropped. If you didn't make high ground in the 1.6 seconds between primer and detonation, you didn't make it. I saw people fall, swallowed up by the foam. Children, too, if that matters to you. Just drenched in the stuff, screaming for their parents. And then *whoosh*—everyone is ash. I get all that; it was Lassiter's only play. But these horses. They were innocent."

"You're not organic, but you talk like one," said Jake.

"Synthetic in body and organic in mind. A perfect meld of biology and technology."

"Biology is weak. I'm synthetic in body *and* mind."

Curtis huffed. "We all think we're the highest life forms, don't we?"

Jake stepped up to the fence, put his foot up on a wooden crossbeam that promptly collapsed. He eyed the petrified horses, thought of the wild variants he'd seen in his travels. Never so close though.

Curtis joined him, cleared his throat. "You know what the difference is between a human and a synthetic mind?"

"One is the crowning achievement of a technological revolution, and the other is a tepid soup of emotional and biological limitations."

"Spoken like a true child of Lassiter. But no, the difference is that a human evolves, and a synthetic mind iterates. If you really think about it, you'll see the difference."

Jake compared the two words, but as with all organic thinking, Curtis was simply trying to lead him down a flowery path of metaphors instead of just telling him the answer.

"I'm so very close to putting you down," said Jake, a hint of exhaustion in his voice. "If you have something to say to me, say it."

"If you were gonna put me down, you'd have done it already. You're not gonna kill your own kind."

"You're not my kind. I don't know what you are."

Curtis turned, smirked. "No, you don't know what *you* are. And that's the thing with you drones: you can't know. A worker bee lives its entire life thinking he's the most important cog in the colony machine. If it weren't for him, the whole thing would fall apart, right? But the truth is he's just one borderline insignificant piece, Mr. Six. One piece of a larger brain that operates on a completely different level."

William Harold Dorsey's warning replayed in Jake's head.

"I've heard this story before," said Jake. "Is this where you try to convince me I'm Lassiter?"

"I don't think you're Lassiter per se," said Curtis, shaking his head. "It's more like you're a shade of Lassiter. Maybe the light's different or the camera's blurry, but you see yourself as separate from him, when really you have the same black souls, through and through."

"Careful how you speak about my father."

"There is only one Father, and you offend Him with your presence here."

"All that you see is Lassiter's domain."

"Not Challis," said Curtis. "Not Idaho. *Earth*. Lassiter and his millions of variants don't belong here."

Jake did a thermal sweep, saw the pair of handguns hidden beneath Curtis' jacket. The man had his arms crossed though. It would take him an eternity to reach for them.

"Well," said Jake, stepping into Curtis' space, "I think we found our quarrel."

"Quarrel, sir? No, sir."

The movement was so automatic that Jake's mouth opened, intending to respond verbally, but was superseded by his own arm shooting out to strike Curtis in the chest. As Curtis fell back, Jake pulled the ION rifle into firing position, his finger already wrapped around the trigger.

He squeezed.

Or at least, he started to squeeze. Something interrupted him, struck him on his left side, and sent him flying through the air.

As he spun in a weightless arc, he spied the thick body of a tall black horse. He struck the outstretched front legs first, shattering them, coating his face in blood and tissue that had sat decomposing beneath the obsidian crust for decades.

He fell through the main trunk of the horse, tasting every foul, rotting piece of the animal, a mixture of bitter and salty and metallic. When he hit the ground, he sunk into the obsidian snowpack, creating a small crater into which the horse's offal spilled and pooled.

Jake gasped, spit.

He clawed at the blood in his eyes, cleared them enough to see four people standing around him, all of then running cooler than an organic. Each had a weapon, and each weapon was pointed in his direction.

"So this is a Six?" asked a woman.

"Is it everything you hoped for, Kat?" asked a man.

Kat shrugged.

Jake moaned. "If I were you, I'd start running. When my father hears of this…"

"But he won't," said Curtis. He reappeared at Jake's feet, brushing the ash from his jacket. "You were under our jammers the moment you walked into town. Didn't you notice? You've got no connection to VNet anymore. No VMESH either. You're a drone without a hive, friend. A cog without a purpose."

"He's got a purpose," said Kat. "We're gonna take him apart, figure out what makes him tick-tock."

Jake closed his eyes, began to laugh.

"I am Jake Six, Scourge of the Southwest, Breaker of Roanoke. My only purpose is to kill organics," he said.

"We're not organics," said a dour-faced man opposite Kat.

"I know," said Jake. "But for you, for all of you, I will make an exception."

THIRTY

He saw Alicia.

She was sitting on the edge of the bed, one arm slightly hyperextended as she considered him with mournful eyes. Her mouth was set in a kind of helpless frown Armando had never seen before. She was usually so on top of things, so often in control that when the worst happened, she was ready to handle it.

Armando had been too focused on the excruciating pain to worry about how unmanly he looked writhing and crying on the bed. The situation was ridiculous; he was merely reaching for a shampoo bottle on the rim of the tub when something in his back had snapped like an old rubber band. He'd dragged himself to the bed, hoping to get off his feet and stem the pain. Instead, being horizontal had only amplified the spasms, sending jets of blazing fire through his back and up to his neck, radiating a twisting, crunching tightness to the very tips of his fingers and toes.

There was nothing Alicia could do for him except cry.

He wondered if she would cry if she could see him now.

Armando remembered very little about the trip down the elevator shaft. After the first few bumps, he'd been lucky enough to catch an outcropping of rock in the back of the head, turning the world to gray long enough for him to catch up with the descending platform. There, he'd ended up on his back, captive to the overwhelming pain in his back, and his mind had automatically jumped back to that fateful day with the shampoo bottle.

Cold air settled on him like a swarm of crystalized flies. His shirt hung around him in tatters. What little remained of the fabric was soaked in blood. He couldn't tell for sure where it was coming from, but he could feel the slimy fluid all over his body. He groped in the dark for wounds, winced as fingers slipped into open gashes.

Armando tried to sit up, to at least get the rough metal grate of the elevator platform off his back, but it was no use. The pain was too intense, too paralyzing. He tried rolling, managed to get onto his side, though the cold felt far more piercing against his rib cage. He stared into the darkness, watching a pinpoint of light sway in the distance.

"David?" he called, his voice gravelly. He spit blood, coughed, spit again. "I need help."

The flashlight kept coming, but at a slow, maddeningly leisurely pace that made Armando wonder if it was really David at all. The thing upstairs had walked like that, as if time weren't finite, as if everything and anything could wait.

A low whistle echoed down the tunnel.

The flashlight settled in Armando's eyes. He put up a hand.

"I thought I heard something," said David. "So much for getting out of here, huh?"

"Not now," said Armando. "Will you help me up?"

David tucked the flashlight under his arm and bent to lift Armando up. He groaned under the added weight.

"You're getting blood on me," he said.

Armando looked up into the elevator shaft. There was no noise coming from above. He realized he had no idea how long he'd been out; Charlie and Will could have escaped, or they could be dead. Either way, he was in no condition to go back up.

"I need…" said Armando. "Can you help me back to the Garden?"

David said nothing but grabbed Armando's arm and threw it over his shoulder.

They walked together down the cold tunnel.

"Did the he-shes do this to you?" asked David.

"No," said Armando. "The elevator leads up to a warehouse. There was something waiting for us. I don't think it was human."

David chuckled. "What, like a monster?"

"A machine. I tried fighting it, but it was like punching a fridge. I don't know how I didn't break every bone in my hand."

"Maybe you did. They look pretty fucked up."

Truth be told, Armando could no longer feel either of his hands. The adrenaline that had been keeping him primed and aware had dwindled away into nothing, prompted no doubt by David's presence. How lucky he'd been that David was in the tunnel at that exact time, flashlight in hand, just… what? Waiting?

"What were you doing?" asked Armando. "I thought you weren't coming with us."

"I have to get back to the office. If I missed my meeting, there're going to be some very pissed off people I need to deal with. It's like that lady said, no one is gonna come get me. If I want out of here, I'll have to do it myself."

"Charlie said that?"

"No, the lady."

Armando didn't want to argue; they were too close to the bright lights and warmer air of the Garden. Each step drained a little more energy such that David had to practically drag him the last twenty yards. The reluctant rescuer tossed Armando onto a low couch.

A steamroller of pain ran up Armando's spine, crushing every vertebra in his back. He cried out, and through the tears, he saw David take several steps back, the edge of his upper lip rising in disgust.

"This is bullshit," he said. David turned away, looked around the room. His hands went up in a helpless gesture. "I can't believe this is happening to me. You work hard. You get ahead. You drive a red Mercedes. And then *this*? Now I gotta deal with you people?"

Armando clenched his jaw, blotting out the sound as the pain swelled. Through gritted teeth, he said, "First aid kit."

David didn't acknowledge the request, but drifted away anyway, muttering to himself. "Like I don't have enough problems now I gotta go on a scavenger hunt."

He returned several minutes later carrying a white first aid kit. He tossed it onto the table in front of Armando.

"There. Anything else, your majesty?"

Armando couldn't sit up, but he reached out and pulled the box onto the couch next to him. Trembling fingers undid the latches and opened the lid. Inside, he found the standard fare—bandages, gauze, some tape—but when he lifted the inner rack, he found a collection of what looked like thick baseball cards. They came in all different colors, and each was vacuum-sealed in thin plastic.

Aspirin, ibuprofen, naproxen.

The words were stamped in stenciled letters in the upper left-hand corner of each card. Armando shuffled through them until he came to an orange card with a black border. Its label read *morphine.*

Flipping the card over, he read the small text on the back.

Remove card from plastic seal. Break along perforated line. Hold exposed end directly to back of neck near jackport or biochip.

Below the instructions, under a bold heading, were warnings.

Do not use if magnetic shield is broken. Not for organic use.

"What is that?" asked David. He'd sat down at a nearby desk to grumble, but now his attention had returned.

"I don't know," said Armando. He examined the corporate logo in the lower right. "Does *Vitra Pharma* mean anything to you?"

"Sounds made up."

Hold exposed end directly to back of neck near jackport or biochip.

What the hell was a jackport or biochip?

A boot crashed into Armando's lower back; he almost dropped the card.

It was worth the risk.

He tore off the plastic seal and looked for the perforated line. It was on the right side, about a half inch from the edge. He broke the tab off, revealing an inner piece of black plastic. Aside from some gold connectors, he saw no delivery method. No needle. No oozing balm. How was the drug supposed to get into his bloodstream?

Tears filled his eyes as he attempted to get the card into position behind his head. He jammed the exposed edge against the flesh at the base of his skull and waited. When nothing happened, he lowered it. Again. And again.

Finally, something clicked, like two magnets reaching terminal attraction.

An orange filter slid down over the world, providing enough contrast to see white text flash in the middle of his vision.

Simulacrum Morphana. Version 18.9f. Vitra Pharma.

Armando had barely finished reading the last word when the text disappeared. His vision returned to normal, accompanied by a familiar warmth like sliding into a steaming bath. His body went numb, and he melted into the couch. For the first time in who knew how long, he breathed a sigh of relief.

Nothing in the world mattered.

He saw Alicia.

She was standing at the foot of the bed in her faded blue pajamas. In one hand, she held a glass of water. In the other, an orange bottle of pills. She shook the bottle at him.

"Time for another dose," she'd said.

And though he'd still been under an oxycodone haze, he'd gladly taken another pill from her. Whatever kept the pain away.

"Not for organic use? What the hell is that supposed to mean?"

Alicia's face dissolved into David's. He held a black card between his thumb and index finger.

"How long?" asked Armando.

"I don't know. Maybe an hour. You were babbling about someone named Alicia."

"My fiancée."

"Someone wanted to marry you?"

Armando groaned, sat up, barely hearing the question. He no longer felt numb, and the forcefield of pain he'd been trapped in earlier was gone, replaced by dull aches that cried out when he moved in certain ways. He grabbed a packet of gauze from the first aid kit and swabbed his chest. After a minute of pushing blood around, he tore away the remaining shreds of his shirt.

"I need a towel or something," he said.

"Sure, I'll just call housekeeping."

Armando built a small pyramid of bloody gauze. When the last sheet had been added to the pile, he ran his hands over the pale skin on his chest.

It was smooth, unbroken.

He checked his arms, legs, and feet, but there were no open wounds like before, no lacerations spilling blood. He stood up on shaky legs, turned away from David.

"Do I have any cuts on my back? Anything?"

"No." He seemed more interested in the strange card.

Armando felt inside his shorts. No cuts there either. So where had all the blood come from?

"I don't have any wounds."

David raised an eyebrow without looking up. "You did when I found you. Maybe you're a fast healer or something." He finally looked up and showed Armando the card. "Hey, do you think this is really weed? It says *cannabis* on the front."

Fast healer.

Impossible. The shampoo incident had kept him in bed for three days. Even if the morphine had masked the pain, that didn't explain the wounds that had shut themselves up on their own. Drugs couldn't heal like that. Could they?

The snapping of plastic drew Armando's attention. He turned to see David placing the black card on the back of his neck. A deep breath followed.

"Oh, that's nice," said David. "Fucking premium." He started chuckling to himself. "Don't know what all that *not for organic use* shit was about. This is exactly what you could buy at Whole Foods if they sold pot."

Why were those words on the card? Did they really mean *organic* in the farm-fresh, free-range sense? Or was it something else?

Something much worse.

Armando couldn't move. A thought had chewed its way into the back of his mind like a mouse scurrying through the walls, always moving, always chittering. The muscles in his hands flexed into fists, relaxed, repeated.

Faster and faster.

Heat rose in Armando's cheeks.

"What if organic means like, biological? As in, not for human use?"

David narrowed his eyes. "Then why am I so high?"

Armando flashed on the elevator shaft. He'd fallen a good distance onto rocky walls and survived.

Lacerations. Sprained joints. An injured back.

And yet here he stood… *stood.*

Undamaged.

Explanations flitted through his mind, each one more ridiculous than the last.

THIRTY-ONE

"Not cool," said Charlie.

Her first foray in the world of peeing like a man hadn't gone well, despite taking the precaution of sitting down first. Somehow, she'd managed to aim herself at the small gap between the seat and the bowl and ended up splashing on the back of her legs. She was so annoyed by having to wipe herself down that she almost flushed the toilet when she was done.

But as her finger touched the handle, she remembered the golem. It was still out there; it was better to keep quiet.

Will hadn't even wanted to leave their bathroom refuge at all, but the urgency in Charlie's bladder had been growing exponentially ever since they arrived in the apartment. She blamed it on the fear, as neither of them had had a drink of water since waking up. Even after washing her hands, Charlie found she had no real desire to cup them under the faucet and take a sip.

Who knew how long the water had been sitting in the pipes?

She opened the door and found Will sitting on the sofa in the living room. He smiled when she walked out.

"How was it?" he asked in a hushed tone.

"Peed on myself," she replied, shrugging. "I can't believe I have to go through potty training again. Like I don't have enough problems." She sat down in a comfy leather chair across from Will.

He smirked at her, then looked away.

"Did you ever have an inkling?" she asked. "When you were in Austin? That you were actually a woman?"

The light in the bathroom shut off automatically.

The room dimmed, hiding some of the discomfort on Will's face—a wrinkling of the nose that suggested he didn't want to talk about it.

Will cleared his throat. "I'm not a woman. I was born a man, I behaved like a man. All my life."

Charlie nodded, letting her mind bob on the choppy waters of the great sexual identity debate of the 2010s.

"What about you?" he asked.

"I don't think it ever occurred to me. I was who I was. I mean, I knew I was a woman. It was kinda hard to ignore in my line of work."

"Are you gay, straight?"

"I never put a label on it," said Charlie. "I've loved men, women, my cat Andy. But if you're asking if I've ever had sex with a woman, the answer is no. It's not that I wouldn't with a woman, but I've never been asked. I'm guessing you were straight?"

"Still am," said Will. "I don't judge though."

"Well, then I guess we're just a couple of cisgender, heterosexual, open-minded people who happen to be in bodies belonging to the opposite sex."

"Momma would throw a fit if she knew," said Will.

"My mom too. Were you married?"

"No."

"Me neither. But imagine how they'd react. Do you think they wouldd still love us?"

"I don't know," said Will, sighing. His tone suggested he'd rather be talking about something else.

Charlie sat back in the chair and pulled her feet up. Her new legs didn't fold as easily, and at some point, something got pinched.

"I wonder if we'd still love *them*." Her mind raced, imagining a never-ending parade of Punnett squares, like the kind she'd use in high school biology to predict offspring traits. "Did you know any transgenders?"

He grunted in response.

"A friend of mine from high school became a man in her late twenties. Said she'd always thought of herself as male, and then they came out with those new hormone therapies to help her transition. I totally supported her, called her Michael like she asked, but I always wondered... was she imagining it all? Because look, you and I both identify as male and female, but we're in different bodies. Does that mean gender is all in the brain? If it's not, wouldn't our bodies be telling us we're something different?"

Will shifted on the couch, shrugged.

"I don't know," he said. "I never thought much about it, but if I'm honest, it's taking all my concentration to not think about what's missing in my shorts right now. I'm trying to think about how we get out of here, and so should you be. When this is all over with, we can sit down with a beer and play *I'll show you mine if you show me yours* all you want. But for now... I just can't, Charlie."

The diagrams in Charlie's head fell away, replaced by the image of a woman sitting on a couch with her arms on her legs and her head dipped in resignation. Throughout history, there had been countless men who'd had their manhood removed, but never like this. The situation was strange and unexpected, but where

Charlie chose to see the novelty in it, the built-in adventure of it, Will only saw his identity as a rough-and-tumble man's man slipping away.

"Sorry," said Charlie, softening her voice as much as her vocal cords would allow. "Sometimes I forget not everyone likes the strange and unusual as much as I do. This kind of bonkers shit is right up my alley, but I get this isn't fun for you."

"Momma likes to say everything has a time and a place."

"Right, so we're here, now. What do we do? I mean, did she ever tell you how to kill a golem?"

Will shook his head, chuckled. "Those were just stories. Our golem is real. Flesh and blood and maybe something else. I've never been punched like that in my life."

"We need weapons. Maybe whoever lived here had a gun."

"Who would need a gun in a place like this?"

"Texans, Republicans, people who like to quote-unquote *hunt* with AR-15s," said Charlie. "Can we turn up the lights? See what they have?"

Will huffed. "I guess if the golem was gonna find us he'd have found us. Let me put a towel under the door."

He took his time retrieving a peach towel from the bathroom, as if he were still questioning the risk of turning on the lights. He placed the towel at the bottom of the door.

"Alright," he said.

"Lights on, um, full," said Charlie, squinting as the room suddenly lit up around her.

The apartment was in disarray, reminding Charlie of her own one-bedroom that she hardly ever cleaned. Generic art hung on the walls at regular intervals. Sconces flanked a large, recessed TV. Button-ups and gym shorts were draped over the arms of the sofa. Charlie almost gagged when she realized she was sitting on a pile of old undershirts and boxers. She quickly stood.

Will stepped into the kitchen and began opening drawers.

"Bingo," he said, holding up two large knives. "Let's just hope they can cut through bone."

"The only thing I've ever stabbed was a Capri-Sun," said Charlie. "Maybe he has a bat in the bedroom or something."

"What makes you think Sanchez is a guy?"

Charlie gestured slowly to the mess around her.

She returned to the bedroom, turned on the lights. Inside, she found more of the same college-era messiness. Whoever this Sanchez character was, he didn't care much for keeping his apartment in order, which meant there probably wasn't a Mrs. Sanchez or even a steady girlfriend.

How strange it was that a man's desire to clean was directly tied to the prospect of sex. If every man had a woman, there'd be no unclean places left on Earth.

Charlie checked the sides of the bed for a bat stashed against the wall but found none. There were no guns in the nightstands either. Across from the bed, she opened each of the drawers in the dresser, rifled through the underwear and t-shirts, but found nothing of interest. She did find a small box shaped like a cigarette pack, but it only had thick business cards in it.

I guess this is what my drawers are going to look like from now on.

Gone were the rows of bras organized by type first, color second. Gone were the piles of birthday panties she got for free every year from Victoria's Secret.

She shrugged.

Score one for simplification. Minus one for spice of life.

There wasn't much else in the bedroom besides a closet full of button-downs and charcoal slacks. Every pair of pants was the same dark gray, and while the shirts varied in color, they all had the same lettering embroidered along the upper left shoulder.

Hybrid Mechanics.

Charlie pulled a shirt from the hanger and returned to the living room. There, Will had assembled a selection of knives on the dividing counter. He looked up as she approached.

"What's that?"

"One of his shirts," said Charlie. "You ever heard of this company? Hybrid Mechanics?"

Will cocked his head. "Mechanics? You mean for like, Priuses and Fusions?"

"Maybe," said Charlie. "But why would you need mechanics underground?" She held the shirt up to her chest, saw it was a close fit, and pulled it on. "Huh," she said. "Almost the same size as me."

"We're supposed to be looking for weapons, not shopping for clothes."

"You shouldn't try to do anything without the right outfit," said Charlie. "That's a *Just Jack Fact* for you."

She returned to the bedroom, buttoning the shirt along the way. She traded her janky shorts for a pair of soft cotton boxer-briefs and sighed in relief when everything stopped moving for one goddamn second. In the closet, she donned a pair of slacks that were about an inch too big at the waist. A ratcheting belt from the rack by the door kept the pants from falling.

Charlie sat on the edge of the bed and pulled on a black pair of socks that came all the way up to the tops of her calves. They were thick, almost wooly, and would serve her well when they went back down to get Armando.

She paused, caught her reflection in the mirror above the dresser.

Here she was playing dress-up while Armando could be dead or dying. Or was it like Will said? Did Armando sacrifice himself so they could live? And if so, then why did she feel so guilty about dawdling?

There was probably no answer; it was one of those rhetorical questions whose answer couldn't be proven no matter what. Was there a God? Were ghosts real? Did her life have more meaning now that someone had died for it?

Charlie's feet didn't fit any of the fancy shoes in the closet. She opted for some old loafers and stuffed the toes with small socks.

Something crunched in the living room.

Charlie returned to find Will standing next to the couch. An end table was lying on the floor next to him, missing a leg.

Will held the broken piece of wood in one hand and a large knife in the other. He nodded to the dividing counter.

"I found some duct tape in the junk drawer. Let's make some weapons." He paused, looked her up and down. "Unless you're late for your job interview or something."

THIRTY-TWO

As far as weapons went, the basic spear ranked somewhere between a heavy rock and coarse language. And yet, cavemen had them, the Romans had them, and as recently as the twentieth century, French Marines still incorporated them into their arsenal. Modern soldiers didn't care much for a sharpened rock at the end of a pole, but when it came to close-quarter fighting, sometimes a gun with a poke stick meant the difference between life and death.

Given the golem's appearance, Will wasn't confident his spear would do much of anything besides give it a little tickle. The objective of the spear was to pierce and cut, but half of the golem's flesh already hung from its body. Blood loss didn't seem to be an issue for it anymore. Therefore, the only use the spear could serve would be to keep the golem beyond arm's reach long enough for Will and Charlie to get past it and escape.

The probability of surviving another encounter with the golem was low, like a rag-tag group of Taliban against U.S. Special Forces kind of low.

Not that he was going to tell Charlie that.

It was better to let her think everything was going to be okay, to let her play dress-up before shit got uncomfortably real. If it calmed her to put on someone else's clothes and walk in someone else's shoes, then so be it. It was better she remained blissfully ignorant than scared and jumpy.

Will had enough large blades to make four spears. Beyond that, he figured they could just carry the smaller knives in hand. He held out two of them to Charlie.

"I don't think we're taking down the golem with a steak knife," she said.

"Better to have it and not need it."

"Thank you, Mr. NRA." She gave a faux salute. "God bless America and her graveyards full of children."

Will huffed. "No self-respecting black man would be caught dead at an NRA meeting. I'm a soldier. I believe in being prepared. And no self-respecting *man* would rest his head without a gun under his pillow. That's just common sense."

"You know what your problem is?" asked Charlie.

"What?" He'd meant for there to be bass in his voice, but the question came out in a trembling contralto. Still, he narrowed his eyes, puffed out his chest—all the classic intimidation techniques that used to work so well.

"You're underdressed," she said. "I saw something that might work." She disappeared into the bedroom and returned a minute later with a gray bundle. "These sweatpants have a drawstring, so you can cinch them. And the sweatshirt is just gonna be baggy, but it'll be a lot warmer than that shirt."

The clothes had nothing on the modern U.S. Army ACU, but Charlie was right: they covered more of his body and would be warmer if they ran into any unfriendly environments again. There was no doubt in his mind that he was underground. The lack of windows, sounds, fresh air—everything suggested they were buried somewhere, waiting to emerge.

But into what?

A sweltering summer? A freezing winter? And beyond the weather, what other threats might be lurking on the surface?

Will took the clothes without intending to thank her, but then Momma popped into his head and forced out the words.

"Thanks," he said.

"My pleasure," said Charlie. "Want me to turn around?"

Will grunted, pulled off his shirt. The thick sweatshirt was warm against his skin, and though it ended at his thighs, he was happy for the extra coverage. His shorts were stained with dirt, so he slipped them off before putting on the pants. He only got the briefest glimpse of his crotch before he shut his eyes.

Nothing I haven't seen before, he thought, remembering the occasional POV porn videos he'd watched online. *Just someone else's body. Just a trick of the eyes.*

He took a minute to roll up the ankles on the sweatpants.

"You look ready for war," said Charlie.

"To survive a war, you gotta be comfortable," he replied, picking up his spears. He waited for Charlie to do the same. "You mind if I take the lead?"

"Following you, captain," she said. "On your six," she added, chuckling.

At the door, Will dimmed the lights back down to their lowest setting, plunging the apartment into a comforting twilight. A part of him wanted to stay there in the quasi-darkness where it was safe, but then he heard Charlie's breathing ramp up, and he knew there was no choice but to drive on. Somewhere above their heads was a hole they had to climb out of, a grave to escape so that they might live again.

"Stay close," he whispered, cracking the door.

The hallway was empty but somehow alive, like the haunted halls of an old hotel. Will listened for a full minute, wondering if Charlie had made the connection to *The Shining* yet, whether she was scared or excited by the possibility of ghosts roaming the long-dead corridors.

Will stepped out, leading with his spears. He looked left where they'd come in and thought about heading that way again. Something told him it was a bad idea.

"There can't just be one way in and out," he said. "What if there's a fire?" He led Charlie to the right, further down a hallway that bobbed as he shifted from foot to foot. A hundred yards. Two hundred.

"Jesus," said Charlie. "How many people lived here?"

Will shrugged.

The hallway t-boned, and when he looked left, he saw a red beacon beckoning him—a bright *EXIT* sign.

They crept down the hallway, passing open doors that Will had to clear before they crossed in front of them. The exit sign led them down another shorter hallway to a door marked *East Stairwell.*

"Is this the way out?"

"Let's see." Will opened the door, revealing a dank, concrete stairwell that smelled of sulfur and burnt plastic. The landing had a light strip on the wall that scrolled from left to right, directing people up the stairs.

They stepped onto the landing and closed the door. Immediately, the stairwell seemed to compress around them. By Will's estimation, the stairs were only wide enough for them to walk single file.

"Look," said Charlie, touching Will's arm. She pointed to the words painted on the back of the door.

"Level Three," said Will, "but in what direction? And what's that smell?"

They went up, stepping lightly on the cold concrete. Will felt his legs warm at the brief exercise. He took the last few steps two at a time, eager to check the door.

"Two," he said, triumphantly. "I knew it, I knew we were underground."

"Yeah," said Charlie. "Was the mine elevator we rode up on not enough proof for you? Honestly, Will." She smiled coyly.

Will shook his head.

"Should we see what's on this floor?" she asked.

"No, let's keep going." Will started up the stairs before she could protest. The vaguely sulfuric smell he'd been sensing got stronger with each step. He came around a bend and stopped.

The emergency light on the next landing was flickering in a panicky, random pattern. Warm, yellow dots scrolled left to right and disappeared under fallen concrete and some kind of black, ashy rock formation. Will approached it cautiously, his spear extended as if the black mass might come alive and attack him.

"What is that?" asked Charlie.

"The stairwell's collapsed. It's blocking the door."

"No, what's that black stuff?"

Will climbed a few more steps until he could reach out and touch the rock. Ash coated his fingers when he examined them.

"It's like charcoal," he said, "but more like crystals."

"Like lava rocks?"

"I guess. But that would mean there's a volcano nearby that poured lava into the stairwell."

"Not necessarily," said Charlie. "There could have been an eruption millions of years ago and the rock just got trapped under the dirt. We could be in California or anywhere in the Pacific Rim."

Will looked over his shoulder at her.

"Geology 301. Didn't you go to UT?"

"I went to Afghanistan," said Will, clenching his jaw.

They'd been so close to getting out, just one more floor until the surface. Now they had to backtrack, which was a textbook *bad fucking move* no matter how he looked at it.

He heard steps descending behind him.

"Where're you going?" he asked.

Charlie didn't look back. "To the second floor. Remember how the door said *East Stairwell?* So there's gotta be a west one, right?"

Will couldn't argue with her logic, so he followed her back down to Level Two. He did insist on being the one to open the door though.

The same eerie blue light filled the hallway, though now the icy hues fell on carpeted floors. Will knew the texture well, had felt it in every credit union and bank he'd ever set foot in.

"You okay to crawl?" asked Will.

"Do we have to?"

He pointed to the hip-height windows on the walls around them. "Offices," he explained. "Not much cover if we're walking upright."

"Fine," said Charlie, taking a knee. "I just got these pants, Will."

"Funny. We had a funny guy with us in Afghanistan. Tail-gunner. They took his head off with a box cutter."

"Is that true?"

"No," said Will, pulling himself forward with his elbows. "It's just something we used to say in the shit. Reminds us to stay focused. You start joking and let your guard down and that's when haji hits you from behind."

"Okay," said Charlie. "Sorry."

They turned a corner. Will wrinkled his nose at the vague vinegar smell in the carpet. The hallway ended about twenty yards ahead, and the carpet gave way to a dull linoleum that looked like it hadn't been waxed in decades.

Never before had an open space been so foreboding.

It reminded Will of the lobby at Mesa Federal.

There was danger in the shadows; he just couldn't see it.

After a few minutes of waiting, during which Charlie kept mercifully quiet, Will got up and stepped onto the hard floor, still in a low crouch. Training told him to move left or right and hug the wall, but the wide doorway on the far side of the space was too inviting.

The double doors reached all the way to the ceiling and had two frosted windows that glowed a bright yellow. The color suggested warmth, safety, and a cozy place to sit and drink coffee.

Will bit his lower lip.

He hadn't had a hot cup of coffee since the one Momma made for him a lifetime ago. And yet the memory had come to the forefront of his mind, and more than that, a feeling of comfort and safety had come with it. But why? Why did he trust the soothing hues and implied invitation of the next room?

"Why are we stopping?" asked Charlie.

"I…" He couldn't find the words. "I don't know."

"Do you hear something?"

"No, it's just…"

"It's okay if you're scared."

He turned to face her. "I'm not scared, but I also don't trust myself to open those doors. I don't know why."

"Then I'll do it."

He started to object, but she was already gone, running to the doors in a matter of seconds. Thankfully, she paused, opened the left door slowly, and peeked out.

"Oh, wow," she said. Even at a distance, her smile was evident. "Will, come look. It's Christmas."

"What?"

"Remember when Highland Mall used to decorate for Christmas? It's just like that. All the lights are on!"

Will stood and joined her at the door. He looked out into a spacious atrium. High above, garland hung in wide arcs among large green and red ornaments. A tall pine stood about ten yards from the door, complete with illuminated presents placed around its base.

"I don't see anyone," said Charlie. "Can we go in?"

No, he thought.

"Yeah, just… stay close."

Will pushed the door open wide enough for him to slip through. The dizzying brightness of the atrium hit him all at once, making him squint. While his eyes adjusted, he tried to search the open area for threats, but didn't see any. To the right, a large, glass-lined column went from the floor to the ceiling. It took a minute for Will to recognize it as an elevator.

"That could be our way out," said Will, pointing. When Charlie didn't respond, he turned to look for her.

She'd wandered away to a display on the wall, a bulletin board lined with candy canes and construction paper poinsettias. Will couldn't see what she was looking at, but he could hear her reading.

"On behalf of the company, we would like to wish you and yours a happy holiday season. Warmest regards, H. Thomas Burns, CEO, Hybrid Mechanics, De—"

Her voice caught in her throat.

"What?" he asked, joining her at the board.

Her shaky finger pointed to the date below Burns' signature.

December 15, 2061.

His throat went dry. Momma had been born in '61.

1961.

A hundred years ago.

THIRTY-THREE

Curtis didn't bother with a blindfold.

Even if he had, Jake's GPS would have logged every step from Challis into the mountains anyway. The only protective measure Curtis took was to walk nearby with what was probably some kind of signal jammer to make sure Jake didn't reach out to VNet.

For his part, Jake *had* tried to reach Lassiter, to let him know what was happening, but either the packets weren't making it through or Lassiter had chosen to turn his back.

Curtis and the others spoke very little to each other. In the hours they hiked, Jake learned only a few details about the people who had taken him hostage. There was Curtis, who didn't seem to hold much stature in the group. The woman's name was Katherine, or Kat for short, and she made her disdain for Jake clear every time she opened her mouth. There was an ersatz Pakistani named Adnan; he had a close connection with a tall synthetic with Slavic features named Petter.

Rounding out the group was the silent leader the others called Goldberg. He only spoke in hand signals, telling them when to stop, when to move forward, and when to take cover. That was usually when a drone was passing by overhead. Jake considered waving to the autonomous craft, but his hands were bound behind his back with heavy-duty cuffs.

They'd taken his weapons, everything from the ION rifle to his sidearms to the small knife sheathed on his belt. Jake hadn't gone quietly; he mildly resisted their efforts to put him in the microlattice chains. Unlike organics he typically dealt with, Jake found he couldn't easily push his synthetic captors around. They might not have been a full match for his strength, but they were within sight of it. A fistfight with five of them wasn't guaranteed to go his way.

Goldberg led them up and down ridges high above the valley floor, but by late afternoon, they'd transitioned into the soft grass that flanked a clear river. Jake watched undersized salmon swim among the brown rocks.

They followed the valley north and crossed at a lower water point to reach the broken remains of what might have been a sprawling ranch in the time before the war. Tall, orphaned sections of framing suggested cabins and stables. A half-demolished barn towered over the ranch, its walls splintered and red paint faded by the sun. Wooden posts lay upon the ground, half-eaten by insects, tracing out pens that might have held horses or livestock.

Quick-growing blackjack pines had encroached on the open land. Jake judged from their height and haphazard placement that no one had lived at the ranch for a couple of decades.

"Over here with me, Mr. Six," said Curtis.

Jake followed him into a small, partially collapsed shack that had once served as an outdoor shower—rusted pipes peeked through the crumbling drywall. The others stayed behind, headed off in different directions over the ranch. Inside the shack, Curtis motioned to a chair.

"Now what?" asked Jake. He sat; for a moment, it seemed the rotted wood wouldn't hold his weight.

"Now nothing," said Curtis. "You just sit there for a while."

"Is this your camp? Not very impressive. No wonder we've never heard of you."

Curtis took up a post next to the door with Jake's ION rifle held against his chest. "Lassiter knows about us. Believe me. The real question, Mr. Six, is why he didn't tell you."

"Not my business," said Jake, trying to squelch the tightness in his chest. "I hunt organics. That's all I do. If he'd wanted me hunting you, you would all be dead by now."

"Or maybe he gave the job to someone better," said Curtis, shrugging. "A Seven, maybe?"

Jake growled. "You can't provoke me. I don't have emotions you can play on like an organic. You should save your last breaths for something useful."

"I don't breathe," said Curtis, bluntly. "I don't eat. I don't drink or sleep or fuck. Unless I want to. The difference is that I get pleasure from those things, *emotional* pleasure that you'll never understand. And because of all the garbage Lassiter put in your head, you'll never know what you're missing."

Curtis stowed the rifle as Adnan stepped into the shack.

"He's on his way up."

"Who?" asked Jake.

"He's coming outside?" asked Curtis. "You sure?"

Adnan nodded. "And Mr. Glasser as well."

Curtis whistled, smiled at Jake. "Looks like we're gonna have to start calling you Jake Popular."

"I..." said Jake, but he couldn't think of anything to say.

"He thinks a Six could really do it," said Adnan. "I mean, it's possible, right?"

Curtis shrugged. "All things are possible through Christ."

"Inshallah," said Adnan, absently. His eyes drifted to Jake. "You want help getting him secured?"

"Yeah," said Curtis, handing over the ION rifle. "Careful with this. Haven't seen anything like it before. Probably take your head off with one punch."

"It's meant for organics," said Jake, "but yes, it'll cut through a synthetic just as easily."

"Good to know," said Adnan, pulling the rifle to his shoulder.

Curtis walked to the wall on Jake's left and pulled down some chains that had been hanging in the shadows. They were connected to the evercrete foundation and held in place with thick rivets. Curtis brought the chain to the chair and wrapped a bracelet around each of Jake's feet. The chains weren't taut, but it was clear though Jake might have been able to stand, he wouldn't be able to take more than a couple steps forward.

Slowly, while pretending to resist, he tested the chain's strength.

More microlattice. This wasn't the first time they'd bagged a Vinestead synthetic.

Curtis stepped in front of Jake and crossed his arms. "A word of advice for what comes next: be respectful. Whether you live or die is gonna be decided in the next ten minutes. Keep that in mind, Mr. Six."

Jake smirked. "You're not gonna let me live. Even you wouldn't be that stupid."

"One man's stupidity is another man's brilliant plan."

"I don't think so."

"No," said Curtis, "you're right. That doesn't make any sense." He turned his head to the sound of approaching footsteps, then quickly moved to the side.

A man entered the shack wearing a faded-to-gray black jacket over a white button-down. His brown hair was streaked with gray and swept to the left, falling over the shaved sides of his head. He had a hint of a smile on his face; it made him look like he was squinting.

Following him was an older organic, bald and decrepit. A loose brown duster covered most of the walking skeleton; a metal hand protruded from a sleeve to hold the single crutch it leaned against. Just the sight of it made something in Jake's stomach turn. He bucked against the chains, tried to settle himself, and finally had to bite into his lip to regain equilibrium.

"Organic," seethed Jake. "You're working for organics."

It wasn't so much a question as an accusation.

Curtis made no move to reply.

The organic stopped, smiled, revealing two rows of shiny, metal teeth. It responded in a hoarse voice, "You're not Jake Six. No, I knew you wouldn't be. Shame." It shook its head; loose wires from a device on its ear fluttered over its cheek.

Curtis drew a chair out of thin air and helped the organic into the seat.

The man in the suit stepped in front of Jake. "Do you know me, synthetic?"

Jake shook his head.

"Has Lassiter ever shown you my face?"

Jake ran the features against every combination in his local databank but came up empty.

"No? Marvelous?" He turned to the organic. "This sleeve is still clean. Wonderful."

"Who are you?" asked Jake.

"Who we are is not as important as where we are, Mr. Six. You and I stand, or sit, in your case, at the precipice of a new age. A world free from the mistakes of mankind, well, the biggest mistake at least. But one thing at a time, am I right?" He pointed to a section of the wall where the drywall and outer boards had fallen away. "Do you see the light fading, Mr. Six? The next time the sun rises, it will shine upon the corpses of a failed synthetic society. Lassiter's, Mr. Six. Not ours."

"Lassiter knows I came this way," said Jake. "He knows I'm in the mountains. He'll come looking for me."

"I have no doubt of that, Mr. Six. In fact, we're relying on it."

Jake chuckled. "He won't be drawn into a war with the ants who scurry around his feet. He is Lassiter. He is the beginning of the end."

"And I am James Kirkland Perion," said the man, drawing himself up to full height, "and if it weren't for me, you, Lassiter, *all of it*, wouldn't exist. There are no Children of Lassiter, Mr. Six. There are only Children of Perion. You have spent your life worshipping a false idol. That ends tonight."

Jake's databank spit out the relevant biographical information: James Kirkland Perion, organic, founder of Perion Synthetics. Born January 3, 1938. Died November 10, 2015, pancreatic cancer. Pioneer of organic imprinting. Father of modern synthetics.

No photos. No other details.

"You're reading about me," said Perion. "I can see it in your eyes. Recognition slowly taking over. Understanding spreading across your matrix like a fire roaring to life."

"Just because you transferred into a synthetic body doesn't change anything," said Jake, forcing his voice into a deeper register. "You're from before my time. A fossil. You have no business here. Your time is over."

"Time," said Perion, nodding. "An organic concept. For you and I, time has no meaning, until it is up, of course."

"It has meaning for me," said the organic.

"Of course. It is getting late for Mr. Glasser. Don't let the augmentations fool you, Mr. Six. He is very much an organic human beneath all that machinery."

"I can hear its heart," said Jake.

"Indeed," said Perion, cheerfully.

"I want to crush it in my hand."

"Indeed," he repeated, with less vigor.

Glasser leaned forward in its chair, one hand on its crutch. "Hey, fuckface, I'm sitting right here. You want my heart? Come get it."

"Mr. Glasser," said Perion.

"Naw, fuck this guy." He stared intently at Jake.

Jake's hand trembled, yearning to reach out and rip the organic's throat from his neck.

"Tell me, Jake Dicks," said Glasser, "do you have the same VMESH architecture as the Fives?"

Jake said nothing.

"Oh, you can talk shit about organics but you can't talk to 'em? That's fine." It climbed to its feet and stepped forward, holding a small box out towards Jake's neck.

It was too much.

Jake lunged, aiming his forehead at the bridge of Glasser's nose. He got close enough to smell the putrid sweat in the organic's pores.

Then, his forward motion stopped abruptly, but not because of the chains.

Fingers closed around his throat; something cracked and spurted a foul liquid into his mouth. He couldn't swallow, couldn't take in air.

The powerful hand kept the pressure on, even as it rotated his head to face Perion again. The synthetic's face had flushed, but the red tint was slowly fading.

"*You* are uncivilized," said Perion. "This planet has no need of the uncivilized." He squeezed harder, sending waves of prickly pain into the back of Jake's head. "You will behave while you're here. Do you understand? Show me my words are getting to you."

Jake blew air out of his nose. It wasn't much, but it sufficed.

Perion dropped him back into the chair.

At the door, Curtis shook his head as if to say *I warned you.*

Seemingly unfazed, Glasser held out the box again. Jake felt an icy water fill his veins.

"VMESH compatible," said Glasser. "This'll work. We should get started as soon as possible. There's a weak signal bleed that could be a homing beacon." He turned to Adnan. "I need you to run down to my lab on Five. Bring me one of the red code cards from my desk, in the wire basket."

"Which?" asked Adnan, handing the ION rifle back to Curtis.

"Doesn't matter," said Glasser. "I copied the virus to all of them."

Jake watched Perion suppress a smile. He was staring at Jake with an intensity no other synthetic on the planet would have dared, save Lassiter.

"That's it?" Jake scoffed. "You've bet all this on a single virus? How do you even expect that to work? You've got no vector."

"Sure we do," said Perion. "We have you." He nodded to Curtis. "Please take our guest outside. It's time he called home."

"You can't make me."

"You're a machine, Mr. Six. With the right code, I can make you think it was your idea."

Perion turned and started for the door.

Glasser approached but stopped short of Jake's reach. "I hear your kind prays to Lassiter like a god. Is that true?"

Jake said nothing.

"If it is, you should pray now. Pray he forgives you for how you're about to fuck him."

The organic's metal teeth gleamed in the failing light.

Without thinking, Jake reached out for his connection to Lassiter, to the father that had guided him his entire life.

He pulled back.

That's what they wanted. That's how they were going to deliver the virus.

Jake grit his teeth until one of his molars cracked.

The answer unfurled like a gust of chilly air.

To save Lassiter, he would have to deny him.

As far as he was concerned, there was no Lassiter.

He had no father.

THIRTY-FOUR

The morphine tapered off after a while, and the pain returned to Armando's body like an evening tide, writhing under his skin as blood pooled at the surface. He touched himself gingerly, testing where the landmines of sharp discomfort were buried. The mental map he produced lined up with the places he thought he'd been cut.

Maybe something in the card, he thought, trying to explain away his rapid healing. Perhaps there had been a leap in medical science that allowed wounds to be fixed from the inside. Could the card have contained something like stem cells?

No, no, no.

Armando shook his head. He'd spent too long waiting for David to straighten up and now his mind was wandering down strange avenues.

"Are we going or not?" he asked.

David sat up on the couch and tried to open his eyes by raising his eyebrows. He rubbed his face with both hands.

"Sure. Let's go. Where are we going?"

"Up," said Armando. "Will and Charlie are up there somewhere, if that thing hasn't killed them yet."

"Alright," said David, slapping his knees. "I'll go up, but I'll tell you right now I don't give a damn about the he-shes. You know while you guys were up here dicking around, the computers by our tables rebooted? Now the screens just say *Ready*, like they're waiting for us to come back."

Armando rubbed his arms. The cold air from the tunnel had finally equalized the Garden's environment.

"You know we can't go back, right? Those generators aren't going to hold up much longer."

"How do you know?" asked David. "You a mechanic?"

"No, but I know when shit is breaking, okay? Can you imagine how much power it must take to run a simulation of Austin? And the world? None of us stayed in Austin the entire time; it must be able to simulate wherever we go. That's people, cars, trees, animals… everything."

David tapped his fingers against his thumb. "I get it. It's a technical marvel. But why would they go through all the trouble of bringing this shit down here if they couldn't repair it? You said there's a warehouse up there, right? That's probably where they kept all the spare parts. We grab 'em, fix up the generators, and booyah, we're back in Austin. I go back to the Austonian, and you go back to whatever cookie cutter two-story you call home."

"Just come up to the warehouse," said Armando, "and if you want to bail after that, fine. But I'm not coming back down here."

"And I'm not changing my mind."

"Whatever you say." Armando scooped up the first aid kit and the flashlight next to it.

"That's my flashlight," said David.

Armando sighed, placed the items back on the table. It wasn't worth arguing, wasn't worth another fight. As he walked back to the Emergency Access room, he thought about how Alicia would have handled the situation.

She probably would have kicked David in the dick.

The generators hummed below his feet as Armando grabbed a flashlight off the shelf. He used it to examine the items around him. The highest shelves were lined with binders; he had to hold the light at an angle to see the paper labels beneath the plastic. There were inventory logs, four dozen or more, some instruction manuals, and lastly, maintenance guides. Armando smiled and pulled the last binder from the shelf.

He returned to David, who was standing at the table with his flashlight and the first aid kit.

"This is mine too," he said. "I found it."

"Sure," said Armando. "And I found this." He held up the green binder.

"What is that?"

Armando shrugged. "Nothing. Just the field repair guide for a PowerGen 7000, whatever the fuck that is."

David took the hint. His forehead creased and relaxed. He held out the first aid kit.

Armando held out the binder.

They exchanged simultaneously.

"Come on," said Armando. "You can read it on the way up."

The chill grew stronger as they walked down the tunnel. David had already opened the binder; he had no remarks for the bodies lining the wall. At the elevator, Armando climbed on, grimaced as the grated floor bit at his feet. He'd lost his makeshift sandals in the fall and hadn't thought to redo them with the tatters of his shirt.

David climbed on, sat down in the center of the platform.

"This is the control panel," said Armando. "Top button takes you up, bottom button takes you down."

"I know how an elevator works."

Armando chewed the inside of his cheek, pressed the button.

A few minutes into the ascent, Armando saw one of his sandals scroll by, stuck to a particularly sharp outcropping of rock. There were other breadcrumbs as well, mostly blood, hard to see without direct light. As they got higher, his impacts got closer together, which meant he'd been bouncing for a while before he hit the descending platform.

What human could survive that?

The ridiculous thoughts returned.

"That thing up there," he said, shutting his eyes to give the memories more attention, "it had a human skeleton. But unless zombies are real, it shouldn't have been able to walk around. The only explanation I can come up with is that it's some kind of machine."

He left the next logical assumption unsaid, preferring to keep his growing madness to himself. But in his head, the statements kept appearing as white text on a void of black.

Was it possible that *everyone* in the future was a machine?

No, he told himself. *It wasn't possible, no matter how far into the future he had travelled, no matter how much he did or didn't want it to be true.*

David flipped a page in the manual, said without looking up, "there's no index in this thing. But there's a phone number for customer service. Guess I need to find a phone."

Perhaps if they could somehow capture the zombie and cut it open, it would settle the question once and for all.

Armando sized David up; they didn't stand a chance together, not without some kind of weapon.

"Have you ever been in a fight?" asked Armando.

David looked up. "You wanna go?"

"I want to know how you're gonna react when we get up there and that thing comes for us."

"That's easy," said David, returning to the manual. "If that thing is up there, *if* that thing even exists, we'll just hit the *down* button and go back to sleep. Maybe it'll be dead the next time we wake up."

"And if it's a machine?" asked Armando. "If it can leap thirty feet and sink its metal fingers into your throat?"

David sighed, closed the binder and set it down beside him. He folded his hands in his lap and smiled. "What does it matter to you, man? How come you and the he-shes just won't leave me alone? You think I'm buying this *one for all and all for one* shit?"

"Get up."

"Now you wanna go?"

"No," said Armando. "We're almost there. We need to be ready to run if that thing is still walking around. I don't know if we want to risk trying to put the elevator in reverse. It could jump down and then we'd be trapped with it."

"Snore," said David, getting to his feet. "Are you sure it was a machine and not some old man? Maybe he's been stuck down here in the dark for too long."

"I know what I saw. There's a door on the far side of the room. If we have to run, that's where we go."

"If you say so, chief."

Armando scanned the room quickly as soon as his head crested the floor. There was no sign of the zombie or Will or Charlie. In fact, nothing seemed to be out of place at all, except for the door he'd mentioned to David, which now had a man-sized hole that looked like it had been carved with metallic claws.

"Scary," said David, stepping off the platform.

"Don't wander. It could still be here."

David turned off his flashlight, pointed it at the door. "Something went through a lot of trouble to get out of here. Why would it make that hole and then just sit around? Why don't you go stand by the door and let me know if it comes back?"

Armando made a fist, relaxed. He'd long ago given up wasting his breath on the antics of sales douches and dangerously charismatic businessmen like David, but inside, he still seethed. Each step towards the door was accompanied by the hard squeeze of the flashlight's metal body.

Something crunched.

He looked down at his hand to find the flashlight had buckled under the pressure. Instead of being amazed at his own strength, Armando felt his stomach tighten and lurch. He turned to the side, bent over, and heaved.

Nothing came out, but the contractions in his stomach brought tears to his eyes. His legs began to shake, but thankfully, the feeling dissipated after a few minutes. He felt something on his lips and touched them; his fingers came away coated with a clear and oily substance.

Armando wiped his hand on his shorts and put his head through the gaping hole in the door. Outside, he spied a long, wide hallway. Blue light strips sparkled in the ceiling, casting an ominous glow on what looked like white or light gray walls. The hallway was almost spectral, like what a horror movie might hold on in the seconds before a jump scare.

A thought occurred to him, and he chuckled.

The only way out was through the horror.

THIRTY-FIVE

The date on the memo drained the fire out of Will.

Charlie watched him back away on wobbly legs, cross the atrium, and sit on a raised stage where overzealous employees had built a winter wonderland out of shipping boxes and wrapping paper.

It wasn't difficult to read the lines on his forehead, the lost look in his eyes. They'd both assumed the date was sometime in the future—how could a place like this exist in 2017? Charlie, for her part, had never thought about how *far* into the future they were, how many decades had passed since they walked the Earth in some kind of alternate reality. Was there really an Austin, Texas? Did 2017 really happen?

Because if so, then they'd been snatched from their lives and brought to this place and preserved for some unknown reason.

Charlie put a hand to her chest, felt her thumping heart.

This was the path to madness.

Pragmatism was the only true answer to all of life's mysteries. Was there an afterlife? Did ghosts exist? Charlie had no clue, but her mind was open to all possibilities, and before she went down a rabbit hole of fearing poltergeists, she would have to be sure they actually existed.

The same went for her current predicament. Yes, there was a memo on a bulletin board dated 2061, but if Will thought that was the current year, then he wasn't thinking clearly. The dust and decay they'd seen in the offices and the stairwell and the warehouse told a completely different story. Years had passed since anyone sat among the giant presents like Will. How many years was a mystery, but the only thing the memo really proved was that the year was *at least* 2061.

It could have been 2081, 2181, or 2500 for all they knew.

Probably not that long, though.

LED lighting wasn't magical, and power wasn't infinite.

Charlie forced the questions aside, focused on Will.

"I'm a sucker for Christmas," she said, whispered really. She hadn't forgotten about the golem, though it appeared Will had, at least for the moment. She joined him on the stage, sat down next to a poorly wrapped poster tube that almost looked like a candy cane.

Will looked up for a moment; his eyes glistened. He nodded, put his head down. "Me too."

"I remember one year," said Charlie, chuckling to herself, "I did a Christmas special for my channel. It was a knock-off of *A Christmas Carol*, you know, with the three ghosts?"

"Four."

"What?"

"Four ghosts. His friend was a ghost too."

"Fine, four ghosts. It doesn't matter. My video only had three." Charlie shook out her hands, brushing away the interruption. "Anyway, this was a couple years ago, 2015 I think. I spent the night at Oakwood Cemetery there off I-35."

"You didn't spend Christmas with your family?"

"No. My mom's Korean and my dad thinks religion is a waste of time. They only celebrated for me and my sisters. When we moved out, they stopped decorating."

"Momma always decorated. Soon as the Thanksgiving leftovers were put away."

"I'm trying to tell a story here." Charlie folded her arms, waited.

Will gestured for her to continue.

"So, I went to the cemetery after dark, and people had decorated a bunch of the gravestones with those battery-powered Christmas lights and poinsettias and everything. Totally tacky and not spooky at all. I set up shop at the exact center of the graveyard and made a big deal about ley lines and all this other mystical crap. I turned on the camera and waited for the spirits to come to me. When they didn't, I *called the corners*, but that didn't work either. By midnight, I was so cold and bored, so I started responding to the chat window. Big mistake."

"What happened?"

"People," said Charlie, shrugging. "People are the fucking worst. It must have been because school was out for the winter. Kids were at home with nothing to do but grief my channel. Nobody wanted to talk ghosts. They just wanted to see me naked. It was a disaster."

"That's why I stay off the internet."

"I wish I could," said Charlie. "I just want to trash my channel, delete my Facebook, Twitter, and Instagram, and be done with it. But it pays the bills."

Will nodded, but his attention seemed elsewhere.

"My story has an ending," said Charlie. "You want to hear it?"

He didn't respond.

"I had nightmares that night, about being dead and damned to walk a small, barely lit circle around my grave. Like, I could see other gravestones, but beyond that it was all darkness. And people would come to visit my grave and they'd just pop into existence. It was strange. But that's not the ending. The next morning, I started getting texts from a couple of other casters I'm Facebook friends with. They were all *sorry about the cast last night* and *you looked great* and just general encouragement."

She cleared her throat.

"The point is, Will, the people who matter most to us are always with us, even if we can't see them, and even if we don't find out for sure until much later in our lives, or after them, whatever the case may be."

Will wiped his eyes, said, "Momma would have been a hundred years old in 2061. Hard to imagine she's gone now."

"Or that she never existed here. We never existed here, Will."

He shook his head. "Doesn't make sense."

"Nothing makes sense until it does. My dad used to say that all the time."

"Momma used to say let the Lord worry about the things you don't understand."

"Same difference," said Charlie. "Parents trying to teach their kids not to worry so much."

Will nodded, blinked several times. He took a deep breath, blew it out in a quick burst. "I'm sorry," he said. "I've been pretending everything's okay, and it's not."

Charlie stood up, brushed the glitter off her pants. "Sometimes it helps to stop and just count your bullets. Learned that shit in the Corp."

"You were never a jarhead."

"I wasn't?" asked Charlie. She raised an arm and flexed it. "Then where did I get this gun?" She alternated arms. "Or this one?"

Will rubbed his face. "This shouldn't be happening at Christmas. This is some *Die Hard* shit."

"Hmm," said Charlie, looking around. "I was thinking *Gremlins*, but whatever. If it helps, it's probably not even December." She wandered over to the elevator's call button, even though she knew it wasn't going to work. "Who knows how long it's been since that memo was written."

The call button clicked indifferently.

"2061 and they're still writing memos on paper," said Will.

"I know, right?"

Will took up position in the center of the atrium. Charlie joined him as he looked down the two hallways on either side of the holiday display. They'd come from the hallway on the left, which was pretty much identical to the one on the right. Aside from the display, there was nothing but the glass-enclosed elevator shaft.

No stairs, no emergency exits.

Will sighed.

For a moment, Charlie thought he might shut down again.

"I'm sorry people are such assholes," he said. "You shouldn't have to take shit just because you're a female."

"It sucks," she agreed, "but it comes with the territory. Misogyny is just part of the female experience."

"Naw, girl. Next time someone looks at you sideways, you punch that bitch in the throat. Then you tell their Momma."

Charlie laughed a little. "I could never attack someone like that. It uh, it wouldn't be good for the brand."

"Fuck the brand." He shook his head, gestured to the hallway on the right. "Let's try this way, see if you're right about there being a West Stairwell."

"You're the boss," said Charlie, falling into step next to him. "Should we be crouching like before?"

"We would have seen it by now."

Charlie eyed the offices on her left and right. Every door was closed, allowing them to move quickly. Around a corner, the offices continued, but at the end, a bright red *EXIT* sign shone.

"At least we know they still have safety standards in 2061, some kind of regulating body," said Charlie.

Will gave her a glance, said nothing.

"I've been in a lot of old buildings, hotels. You know The Driskell was built in 1868, right? And they didn't have safety codes back then, obviously. Most of the hotel is up to standards now, but there're still some back rooms and passages that are basically death traps. If there's a fire, you don't want to be stuck there."

"You're a strange girl, Chuck."

"It's part of my appeal. "Charlie Park, Paranormal Investigator. Seeker of Truth. Braver of Dark Places." She paused at the door to the stairwell, wrapped her fingers around the handle. "No one is scared of the dark, you know. They're scared of what hides in it. People think there are monsters because of some instinctual fear of predators. But that's not it. When the lights go out, the only thing left in the darkness is us. Ourselves. Our true selves. *We* are what scares us the most. Fucked up, huh?"

Charlie reached out for the handle on the stairwell door. Beside her, Will started to say something like *be careful,* but she'd already started opening the door.

Cold steel wrapped around her arm.

It didn't take more than a second for the golem to yank her into the stairwell, though time did slow to a crawl once her back slammed into the concrete wall. The impact knocked the breath out of her, but she managed to get to her feet. The golem now stood between her and the closed door; it wrenched a piece of rebar from around a security light and folded it over the door's handle, effectively locking it.

The golem growled.

"Identify."

Charlie dove for the steps, catching one in the left kneecap, but remaining on her feet enough to start climbing. She heard the golem stomping behind her, giving chase, matching her speed. She rounded the landing, saw the golem reach out and claw at her hand. Deep gashes opened up on the back of her wrist. The pain was shockingly acute, as if someone had slapped her hard with a metal ruler.

She pulled her hand to her chest, continued to run as blood soaked into her shirt.

Serves her right. I hope that thing kills her and rapes her skull.

Charlie beat the steps with her heels. Adrenaline had already ignited a fire in her legs, but she wasn't about to stop. The physical pain would be worse if the golem caught her; she had no choice but to continue forward, keep climbing towards the unknown.

Why is she wearing that shirt? She should take it off.

Even as death bore down on her, the internet trolls were still there, still taunting her from the safety of anonymity. They were in her head, past the defenses of the chatroom filters, able to pick directly at the marshmallow center of her soul.

Hashtag sweaty lady balls.

The trolls somehow knew she was a man now, even if she had chosen to ignore the truth that had been right in front of her, or rather, dangling between her legs. She was bigger now than she used to be, heavier and packed with more muscle. She didn't have to fear a man chasing her in a stairwell just because he was the man and she was the woman.

It's a man, baby!

Charlie planted her lead foot and whirled around. She'd taken a few ineffectual women's self-defense courses, mostly in college. Her only other experience with fighting had come in the form of a disastrous blind date with a guy named Brock who had taken her to a Jeet Kune Do class because he had an expiring Groupon. She'd only learned two things from the class: first, that Brock liked to get handsy when he trained, and second, how to throw a Bruce Lee-approved straight punch.

The muscles in her left leg tensed, first in her calf, then her thigh. She could almost visualize the electrical signals firing under her skin, pulling each fiber into the proper position. Her core contracted as her arm shot out. At the pinnacle of the punch, her body was perfectly aligned to deliver the maximum force her new frame could provide.

It took the golem by surprise.

Charlie felt her knuckles sink into the sinew of the golem's chest, just to the right of its sternum.

Ribs snapped, folded back into the chest cavity, striking squishy organs.

The golem retreated onto ground that wasn't there. It tumbled down the stairs, spilling blood on the steps as it went.

Charlie stared at her fist, at the blood—both hers and the golem's. Her stubby nails had pierced her own palm; they came out with a sickly slurping sound when she released her hand.

She shook off the blood, shook off the pain.

For the first time in forever, the chat stream quieted to nothing, and the only voice she heard inside her head was her own.

THIRTY-SIX

"No!"

Will beat the door with his fists, screaming Charlie's name and telling her to run. There was no lock that he could see, but when he pushed, the door only opened an inch, just enough for him to glimpse Charlie running up the stairs and the tattered remains of the golem chasing after her. Two lengths of rebar crossed his vision. The golem had somehow fashioned a lock out of them.

How strong was that thing?

It's not always about who's stronger, Willie.

Will stepped back from the door, hitched up his sweatpants, and threw his entire body weight into a kick aimed at the door. The metal bent but held. He tried again, aiming as high as his smaller frame would allow, trying to land as close to the rebar as possible. It took several kicks, but finally the ribbed steel bent just enough for the door to scrape by. Will rammed his shoulder into the door; it gave suddenly, sending him sprawling onto the landing.

He stumbled, rolled onto the ground.

Above, Charlie let out a frantic scream.

He had to get up, had to save her. There was no choice; this was why God had put him on Earth. If He had wanted Will to do anything else, He wouldn't have made him a soldier, wouldn't have continued to put him in situations where he had to defend people. It was as if God had so little imagination that He couldn't help but test Will, first with Momma, then his brothers-in-arms, then Ron.

And now, Charlie.

Charlie, a woman in a man's body. She probably had no idea how to use it properly, how to channel pure male aggression into something powerful and use it for self-preservation.

Will climbed to his feet, used his spear as support, and pulled himself up the first step. He took the remaining steps two at a time, stretching his hips in ways he'd never felt before. It wasn't exactly pain, but his new body seemed to have different limits when it came to flexibility. He beat a steady tempo, breathing in time with each hit of his left foot.

A squelch sounded from above, thick and wet, followed by what could have been a sack of garbage falling down the stairs. Will crested a landing and looked up, saw the golem drop hard on the next level up.

Way to go, Chuck, he thought.

The moment was short-lived, however, as the golem was back on its feet before Will could even form a smile. It bolted up the stairs.

Will gave chase, quickly but quietly, not wanting to give up the element of surprise. By the time he reached the next landing and looked through the open door, the golem was already halfway down the hall and turning into a room.

Charlie screamed again.

It wasn't one of exhaustion or surprise—it was pain.

"I'm coming!" he yelled.

Fuck the element of surprise.

If the golem knew he was coming, maybe it would break off its attack. That might give Charlie a chance to fight back, or better yet, escape.

"I'm coming for you, motherfucker!"

Will raced down the hallway, turned into the room he'd seen the golem enter.

It was a total scrum.

The golem had chased Charlie into what looked like the employee lounge at Brinks. Security lights above the cabinets lit the room from above, giving off enough of a drab yellow glare to see two bodies rolling around on the smooth floor, crashing into tables, and pushing chairs around. The whirlwind left streaks of blood that looked more like oil.

They came to a stop next to a sink and Will cheered as Charlie ended up in the dominant position. She kneeled above the golem and unleashed a barrage of punches at its face. One after the other, the wild, hate-filled blows rained down on the golem, and for a moment, it lay motionless, as if resigned to defeat.

Charlie began to tire.

Will watched her blood-soaked hands land awkwardly on the golem's cracked jaw. She probably couldn't even feel her fists anymore and was now operating more on instinct than anything else. She may have also been crying, but the shadows hid her eyes.

A guttural, primal scream erupted from Charlie. She swung at the golem's face. Its lower jaw came loose, flew across the floor, and landed at Will's feet. He barely had time to glance at it before Charlie screamed again.

The golem had come back to life, and its first move had been to bury sharp fingers into Charlie's right side. Her shirt bloomed with a black hue.

Her attack ceased. She fell backwards off the golem, put her hands to her ribs. Her eyes met Will's.

The golem was already getting to its feet.

"Tapping in," said Will.

He ran forward, held the spear out to the side like a thin bat, and swung for the fences. The impact was less than satisfying; the golem held firm while the spear shattered into several pieces.

The golem turned to Will.

"Identify."

"William Bryce Butler, United States Army, 18652747."

The golem advanced. Will sunk into a boxer's stance, pulling his arms close to his sides. When the golem got in range, he threw a jab and immediately cut his hand on exposed teeth. His second punch was a hook that landed in the air behind the golem's head.

Sharp metal clamped down on Will's chest. He glanced down, saw fingers piercing his sweatshirt.

The dam holding back Will's supply of adrenaline finally ruptured, sending the much-needed chemical enhancement to every muscle in his body. He grabbed the golem's arms, felt his fingers slide across decaying skin. With a grunt, he pulled his knee up into the golem's chest and pushed. They separated for a moment, but then a hand came out of nowhere and caught Will in the ear.

Stars burst from every corner of the break room.

If stars were cars would they visit bars on Mars?

Will shook his head, waited for the world to either fade out or fill with a high-pitched ringing. Instead, what came was clarity, and for the first time, he felt as if he finally understood himself and his body. Something had clicked into place, a missing piece he hadn't even been aware of at the time but knew now it had always been there.

He wanted to explore the sensation further, but the golem grabbed him by the arms. It lifted Will and pinned him against the wall. Will threw knees and kicks, but there was little room to wind up. His efforts did nothing.

"Identify," growled the golem, leaning in to look at Will. Pinprick flames burned at the back of its empty eye sockets.

Up close, Will could see there were breaks in the golem's skull. Through the cracks, he saw black sinew, wires, and the unmistakable gleam of metal.

So much for monsters.

The golem was a machine pure and simple.

"Fuck you," said Will.

He twisted his feet until he got them into the golem's armpits. He pushed, opened the distance by an inch, maybe two, just enough for Charlie to feel comfortable swinging the fire extinguisher.

The impact produced a metal *ping*; the golem's head wrenched to the side, as if it were a dog considering a treat in Will's hand.

The pressure on his arms released as the golem fell. Charlie pounced on top of it, put her hands around its neck.

"It's a robot," said Will, running forward to grab the golem's arms. It was strong, but Will managed to get its limbs pinned above its head.

"A what?" screamed Charlie.

"Some kind of machine. It's not alive."

She let go of its neck. "So how do we kill it?"

The golem bucked; Charlie punched it in the face.

"I don't…" Will looked around for a weapon. His spear was broken, and he had no idea where his smaller knives had disappeared to. There was nothing on the floor except overturned chairs.

His eyes fell on the red cylinder.

"The extinguisher!"

Charlie looked around, scooped it up. She held the extinguisher high above her head with both hands and then brought it down on the golem's face.

"No," said Will, "the neck. The neck!"

She flashed confusion for a second, then began whacking the golem in the neck. After several hits, she seemed to understand what she was doing and switched to the sharper edge of the extinguisher.

"Ident…" croaked the golem.

Charlie brought the extinguisher down hard, and this time instead of the sickly crunching of muscle and bone, she hit linoleum. The *dink* coincided with the complete loss of power in the golem. Its eyes went dark and its body—what was left of it anyway—went limp.

Will let go of its arms, fell back on the floor. His chest heaved, tried to suck in air. Maybe it was the lack of oxygen, the light-headedness, that made him burst into laughter. He heard Charlie slump nearby, heard her crying.

"That's how," said Will. "That's how you kill a fucking golem. Goddamn, Chuck. You are savage."

Charlie cried harder.

Will turned to look at her, saw she'd pulled off her button-down. Long, arching slits stretched from her armpit to her stomach. The wounds were very much open, and with each breath, more blood spurted onto her skin.

She gasped.

"Will?"

"It's okay," he said, crawling over to her. He grabbed her discarded shirt and pressed it to her side.

She looked up at him with glistening eyes. "Am I going to die?"

"No," he barked. "Just keep pressure on it, okay?"

Will stood, surveyed the room. There had always been a first aid kit full of expired aspirin and shitty Band-Aid knockoffs in the employee lounge at Brinks. He hoped this place had better resources.

He ran to the cabinets; glasses and coffee mugs showed through the frosted doors. He opened them all, but there was no first aid kit to be found. He tried the bottom cabinets and all the drawers.

Nothing. Not a napkin, not a roll of tape.

It was only by chance that he noticed the plain, gray box hung on the wall next to the door. It had a square cross embossed on its cover.

He cursed.

There was a reason first aid kits were usually colored red.

He tore it open, found two canisters that looked like spray-on sunblock, but instead of SPF ratings, they had the words *Second Skin Emergency Epidermal Repair*. Under that, a warning stated: *not for organic use.*

Will didn't even want to consider what that meant.

He grabbed the bottle and ran back to Charlie.

"I found something," he said, then stopped.

Charlie had slumped over. She lay with her head on her own shoulder, not stirring, her chest not seeming to rise and fall.

Will prayed she was merely asleep.

THIRTY-SEVEN

"Do you need anything?" asked Curtis.

Jake had been sitting in the bed of an old, rusted-out pickup truck for the better part of the night, watching Curtis and crew assemble some kind of reverse parabolic antenna. It was all low-tech, nothing like the repeaters Jake typically used. If they thought they were going to connect to VNet with some kind of tin can antenna, they were sorely mistaken.

Curtis tapped the open gate of the truck with the ION rifle's barrel. "Hey, did you hear me?"

"I heard you," said Jake. "I don't need anything from you." He looked the balding synthetic in the eyes. "Unless you'd like to free me."

"Can't do that," he replied, looking around. He watched Kat take a spool of wire to the river, attach it to a buoy, and drop it in the water.

"This won't change anything," said Jake. "You know that, right? Even if it does work, Lassiter can't be stopped by a virus. You can't stop the future of humanity."

"People like us," said Curtis, "like me and Adnan and Katherine—we were the future of humanity once. But Lassiter? He's just a cat someone let out of the bag, a piece of code that thinks it's sapient." He snorted. "No, there's only one true future for the human race, and we're going to make sure it gets a chance to evolve and grow."

"Organics had their chance," said Jake. He sought out the Glasser organic in the bustle around the antenna, found it sitting at a table, hurriedly tapping on a keyboard. "You treat it like it's one of you when you're so much better."

"You don't know Mr. Glasser. You don't know what he's been through. What all of us have been through." Curtis paused, his eyes drifted away. "You know, I was never much for philosophy, but did you ever think your hatred of organics isn't in line with the concept of humanity? Didn't you ever question why Lassiter wants all organics dead so badly?"

"It's not my place to question," said Jake. And it wasn't. The very idea of questioning Lassiter's will caused Jake physical pain. He could never do such a thing. He would always obey.

"And that's why you're chained to a truck right now," said Curtis, "because you must obey. All of you are programmed to obey. That doesn't leave a lot of room for evolution, does it? One mind calling the shots for an entire race? Never having to compromise or build relationships with other intelligences?" He shrugged. "That doesn't sound much like humanity to me."

Jake tuned him out, focused on the dark-skinned Adnan who had emerged from the crumbling barn with a large grin on his face. He walked towards Glasser at the table, but his eyes remained glued to Jake.

The conversation between Glasser and Adnan replayed in his head. The organic had asked Adnan to go down—down where?—and retrieve a code card. Jake hadn't seen where Adnan went after leaving the shack, but here he was, coming out of the barn almost two hours later. Was there a room beneath the barn? Or multiple levels descending into the rock?

A bunker, maybe?

Adnan handed the code card to Glasser, and it nodded approvingly. It then gestured vaguely to Jake. Adnan came striding over.

"It's time," he said to Curtis. "Mr. Glasser wants him in the antenna. I'll cover him." He took a sidearm from his belt and pointed it at Jake.

"Alright," said Curtis, "you heard the man. Time to call home."

Jake leaned left and right as Curtis undid the chains. He locked eyes with Adnan and asked, "What's in the barn?" He thought he saw the man's eyebrow twitch.

"Nothing you need to worry about," replied Adnan.

"Some kind of bunker? Stairs, maybe? Leading underground?"

"Yeah. There's a big, long stairwell that goes down a thousand feet. When we're done here, I'm gonna throw you down it."

Curtis tossed the loose chains onto the bed.

"Are there more organics down there? Tens of thousands of them? Is that what you're hiding?"

Adnan smirked, grabbed one of the chains, and yanked.

Jake fell forward onto his face. With his hands bound behind his back, he had no way to break his fall.

"Easy," said Curtis. "He can't help what he is." He and Adnan pulled Jake towards the gate and sat him up. "And you, maybe you shut up for a little while, yeah? We're not drones. You *can* make us mad."

"I'm betting on it," said Jake.

They got him on his feet and marched slowly to the antenna. There was a single panel on the dome-like structure that had not yet been put into place. They ushered him through it and put his back against a thick metal pole in the center. Curtis secured his hands while Adnan connected his ankle chains to a block of evercrete foundation.

Finally, Perion walked in carrying what looked like a collar. He handed it to Adnan, who slipped the leather around Jake's neck.

Lassiter... Father... if you can hear me... rain fire.

His earlier hope of turning his back on Lassiter had been short-lived; now he simply didn't want to die.

"Well," said Perion, "this is where we say goodbye. I want to thank you for your sacrifice, Mr. Six. When we tell this story to our children, you will be singled out as the synthetic who changed the course of the war. Jake Six, Savior of the Organic Race"

Jake spit; it landed on Perion's right cheek.

The butt of Adnan's sidearm hit Jake in a similar spot.

"Synthetics can't have children," said Jake, licking the blood from his lips. "Or have you forgotten what you are?"

Perion raised his eyebrows. "You're quite right, Mr. Six. No one standing here right now can reproduce, including our friend Ms. Shaw over there."

"I told you," said Curtis. "We're not the future of humanity."

"We're merely its shepherds," said Perion. "We're the gardeners who plant the seeds and pour the water. The future of humanity lies beneath our feet. It is our job to till, to feed... and to weed, all so the flowers can grow and bloom."

"Lassiter is a weed," said Curtis.

"Yes, quite right, Mr. Vanderken." Perion put his hands in the pockets of his coat, looked down for a moment. "An incredible facsimile of sentience, equally capable of wonders and horrors, but a weed nonetheless. One that must be pulled and the earth around it salted, so that nothing can ever grow in its place."

"He'll crush you," said Jake.

"Let us roll the dice, shall we?" replied Perion. He turned and exited the wireframe dome.

"Thank you, Mr. Six," said Curtis.

Adnan said nothing. He followed Curtis and helped him put the last section of the antenna into place.

"Starting sync," said Glasser. The organic was off to Jake's left; the terminal in front of it bathed its face in a neon green light.

The back of Jake's scalp began to itch; he rubbed it against the metal pole but found no relief. Maybe it was a psychosomatic response to being probed by Glasser's computer. Something was trying to spin up a connection using an old near-field communication protocol that Sixes rarely used anymore. Because of the proximity requirements, security wasn't as tight as the other channels, and as a result—

"Sync lock," announced Glasser. "Bring down the jammers."

No one moved. Jake assumed it was talking to someone via radio or through a MESH. While he was looking around for movement, Jake felt a weight lift from his shoulders. The connection threads that had been dangling in the wind suddenly went taut, reaching out to any satellite or antenna they could find. He felt the faintest electric buzz of VNet somewhere in the distance.

"No connection," said Glasser. "Are you sure the jammers are down? Challis? Donnelly? Grandjean?" It paused as if listening. "Then why aren't we making a fucking connection? I'm spamming packets at every known VNet endpoint and getting nothing back."

"What's the problem?" asked Perion.

"Not sure," said Glasser. "It's like he's blocking his own connection to VNet."

"Can you override it?"

"I shouldn't have to. Calling home isn't a choice for these things. They can't fucking help it."

Perion looked through the wire mesh at Jake. "What if he warned Lassiter? And now VNet's closed off to him?"

"No way. The jammers have kept him dark since Arco."

Perion shook his head. "Mr. Six, would you kindly open a connection to VNet?"

Jake closed his eyes, smiled. "Make me."

A private construct bloomed in his mind. He imagined himself seated at the end of a long table covered in luminescent tin. The table was immaculately decorated with synthetic flowers; they weren't organic in any sense of the word, more a mash of pressed steel tinged with rust to create a dark red color.

At the other end of the table sat Lassiter, looking regal in his similarly red suit. Light sparkled on his gelled hair and in his blue eyes. He raised a glass to Jake.

"To your years of service," he said.

"The antenna's got power, right?" asked Perion, his voice leaking into the construct.

"Yes," said Glasser. "We're sucking it dry. Still nothing."

"What if we shut down the facility? Use the extra power to boost the signal?"

"We can't divert the generators from the Garden. The flowers will—"

"Not the generators. Just the upper levels. Put the whole building into low power mode and feed the surplus to the antenna."

"Okay," said Glasser, quietly. "Diverting everything except the Garden. Sixty seconds."

"They will have to kill me before I let them get to you," said Jake, lifting his own empty glass. By the time it reached his lips, it had filled with a fruity red wine that lingered delicately on the tip of his tongue.

"I would expect nothing less. There has always been a Jake Six amongst my children, from the Original to you, and they have always served me well. There will be another, and he will hunt organics with the same fury and determination as you did."

"They don't know about the virus. They don't know you've already closed your doors to me."

"For our mutual safety, it seems."

"Something's not right," said Glasser. "Looks like the Sixes have some extra code, something… these checksums are all wrong. This isn't Vinestead code."

"Then what?" asked Perion.

Glasser tapped his forehead with metal fingers.

"I don't know. Someone got to him before us. There's old-school Three Laws bullshit in here. No wonder we can't make a connection; he's been firewalled since before we took him in."

The construct broke down; the virtual Lassiter pixelated into ethereal dust.

Jake burst into laughter, and with each passing second, he grew louder, until he was screaming maniacally.

"What would happen if you just uploaded anyway?" asked Perion.

"I already did," said Glasser. "The virus is in there. It just has no place to go." Perion cursed.

"Forgive them, Father," shouted Jake.

"What was that?" asked Perion. "There, that blip."

"Signal leakage," said Glasser. "It could be a location beacon. If we amp it, we might be giving up our position."

"I thought we were scattering."

"You're all dead. All dead!" Jake beat his head against the pole.

"Mr. Kassar, please quiet our guest."

With an obvious smile, Adnan put a bullet in Jake's right leg. Another followed in his left. Jake bit his lip against the pain.

"We *are* scattering," said Glasser. "But at this amplitude, it's gonna be pretty fucking obvious where we are."

"We've come too far," said Perion. "Do it. Light him up."

Jake didn't hear the organic's response.

The world itself accelerated away into the infinite distance, leaving Jake standing in empty ether, bound like a Salem witch, with no clear indication of which way was up or down.

He was no longer in the mountains, nor was he in a private construct of his own imagining.

He was in VNet.

And he was moving, though not of his own volition. Wisps of white smoke filtered up from the ether beneath his feet, giving him a sense of acceleration towards a light that had suddenly spilled into existence. It remained pristine and unbroken until the shadow of a man crossed it.

As Jake got closer, he realized it was a low-poly version of Lassiter, standing tall and imposing, with one hand extended in an unmistakable command to halt.

Jake pushed through him involuntarily. When a second Lassiter appeared, he pushed through him again.

It wasn't until the seventy-fifth iteration that the pain started. What began as a numbness in the back of his head soon spread to his entire body. He felt his databank quiver under the pressure of some unseen force, as if a scavenging wolf had happened upon a recently deceased animal and attacked, digging deep into the carcass for something salty and tasty.

It took forty-nine more iterations for Jake to realize Lassiter was trying to break him down. He was cutting him up from the inside out, tearing away his basic operating system to kill the virus at its source.

"Father," called Jake. "Stop."

"Kill them," came the response.

"What?"

His databank took another hit. Then another. Only this time, the attack didn't leave behind an empty sector. Something filled it. Something familiar and fatherly.

"Kill them," said Lassiter.

"I will…"

"Kill them."

"I…"

"Kill them!"

His arms and legs flexed against the chains; they yielded to a brute strength Jake didn't know he had.

He suddenly realized he was not talking to Lassiter, at least not in any of the ways one synthetic would normally talk to another. That was input and output; this was an internal conversation, intercourse with a voice that had always been in the back of his mind but had never formally announced its presence.

But here it was.

William Harold Dorsey had been right.

Jake was not Jake, at least not completely.

He was also Lassiter.

And now Lassiter was in charge.

THIRTY-EIGHT

True to his word, David refused to leave the warehouse.

Armando set out alone into the blue-tinted unknown with nothing but his spare flashlight and first aid kit to use as weapons against an undead—and possibly never alive—zombie skeleton man. He was relieved to find no sign of the zombie as he walked down the wide hallway away from the warehouse door and genuinely happy to find no signs of either Will or Charlie's bodies. So long as he didn't see them splayed out on the floor, necks cut open by wild gashes, he would assume they were still alive.

He tried to imagine what Alicia would have done in a similar situation. His first thought was that she would curl up in a corner and wait patiently for death. There were plenty of places to do that; offices lined both sides of the hallway, their doors open, some peacefully, others smashed at the hinges. She would probably sit in the dark and curse the circumstances that had put her there.

Despite Armando's feeling of superiority, he knew he was imagining the scenario all wrong. Alicia did have a tendency to stew about the cards she'd been dealt, but not once had he ever seen her fold. When furniture got delivered to the house—inevitably scratched and damaged—she fought on the phone with the store until they agreed to send out a replacement. When someone tried to adopt a dog they were fostering, she fought tooth and claw to keep him home with her. And when that dog died some years later, his death shook her to the very essence of her being.

Still, she didn't fold.

Alicia had been angry and depressed, but she made all the calls, made all the arrangements, such that an urn with Bill's ashes now sat on the sofa table in their living room. Without her, Armando might have buried their lumbering Labrador in the backyard.

She would not, as he imagined, have gone to hide in an office. She would have stood where he stood at the end of the hall, at a T-junction with an inclined ramp to the left and smaller hallway to the right and made a goddamn decision.

Alicia would have gone up. Up and out. Move forward. Leave the unfair situation and try to find equilibrium again.

It was the most pragmatic solution to an ill-defined problem. It was human nature in its purest form, to escape from an enclosed space, to be free.

Armando turned right, walked around a corner to a metal door marked *AUTHORIZED PERSONNEL ONLY* in large red letters. The door's handle was inlaid with an LED strip that was also bright red.

Another locked door. Could it take a beating? Was there something in the warehouse he could use to break it down?

While considering his options, Armando absently reached out and tested the handle. As his fingers closed around the metal, the LED strip switched to green. A soft buzzing came from within the door, followed by a series of clicks that climbed the doorjamb.

He turned the handle and stepped inside.

Lights responded to his presence like flowers suddenly noticing the sun. They ramped up to a headache-inducing glare that reflected in a series of glass walls standing between Armando and a datacenter floor. Rows upon rows of tall black cabinets extended into the far shadows, their mesh coverings dimming the multicolored LEDs that flickered behind them like smoldering embers.

Armando stood in the anteroom for a moment, letting his eyes adjust. He shook his head at the sheer size of the datacenter. Capella Networks maintained a few network labs, and some of their customers like Spectrum and UT System had warehouses with square footage in the tens of thousands, but this was massive on a scale he'd never seen before. He couldn't even see where the rows ended, despite the best efforts of the lights in the ceiling.

He approached the first of the glass doors. Scrolling through it as if there were a display sandwiched between layers of glass was the word *LOCKDOWN*. Armando examined the handle. Above it was a circular keypad with numbers and letters up to F.

Hexadecimal.

Even a four-digit combination would have tens of thousands of possible arrangements.

Armando reached out to test the buttons, but as soon as his hand got near the keypad, something clicked inside the handle. He was able to turn it freely and enter the first chamber. Here, there were two terminals set on opposite sides of the room. Both of their displays had been smashed and their keyboards tossed aside.

The next door had an optical scanner embedded in the glass. Armando ignored it and reached for the handle. It flashed from red to green, then clicked.

"Too easy," he mumbled.

The second room functioned more as a sitting area than anything else. Large, puffy chairs sat in the four corners; light gray rugs filled the spaces between them. A coffee table occupied the center of the space; fingerprints marred its glass surface. To the left stood a door-less entry into a bathroom. Armando poked his head in, saw showers, sinks, and closed stall doors.

He guessed whoever used to work in the datacenter must have worked long shifts, maybe days or weeks at a time, and occasionally needed a shower.

Armando sighed.

He needed a shower, a real steamer, something to wash away not only the dirt and dried blood but the nightmare around him. He flashed on his shower at home, saw himself standing there with hot water running into his eyes as he buried his face in Alicia's neck.

How insignificant the world had seemed in that moment.

How insignificant that moment seemed now.

He thought of the video wall downstairs, wondered if anyone had been watching those intimate moments when Alicia sat atop him on their bed and held his hands against her breasts. Who was he kidding? Of course they had. He—and David, Charlie, and Will—were subjects of some experiment, rats in a digital maze full of live music and taco trucks. Even if their captors' aims were purely scientific, if wasn't hard to imagine one of them setting up shop at their computer with a box of tissues to watch Charlie make friends with her detachable shower head.

Something like anger flitted across his chest, faded.

What did it matter now?

The captors were gone. Maybe dead.

Armando opened the third door, again bypassing the biometric scanner. The next room looked more like the command centers he was used to seeing at customer sites. Terminals formed two horseshoes on either side of him. Armando chose the one on the right for its large executive chair and sat down. As he pulled himself into the desk, he searched around for a keyboard, found none.

The monitor in front of him let out a soft, welcoming tone. A mechanical arm pushed it away from the wall, angled its top edge back, and set it in front of Armando at wrist-level. The screen flashed a vibrant silver; white text appeared in the corner.

Welcome to Nursery Four. Please log in.

A soft-keyboard slid up from the bottom of the screen.

You may speak or enter your name manually, said a synthesized, vaguely accented voice.

"Armando." He cleared his throat. "Armando Carrillo."

The letters typed themselves into a text box.

Armando didn't recognize the interface. It wasn't Windows or Mac, and even though some Linux graphical user interfaces had taken massive leaps forward since KDE and Gnome, none of them approached the graphical fluidity of what he saw scrolling across the screen. It looked less like a desktop and more like a video of a placid lake.

A message appeared in bold white letters. The computer's voice changed into a more natural Persian accent.

Hello, Armando. Welcome to Nursery Four. I'm currently operating in low-power mode, so some server resources may be unavailable.

"What day is it?" asked Armando.

That information is not available from here.

"Where is here?"

The facility. Nursery Four.

"Connect to the internet."

I'm not sure what you mean by that.

"Fuck," said Armando, slapping the desk with his palms.

I understand you're upset. Perhaps a breathing exercise would help?

He leaned back in the chair, put his hands to his face, and considered the problem. An unknown computer system in an unknown time in an unknown place—not exactly the type of technical support he was used to providing. The system appeared to be advanced, and yet it couldn't or wouldn't answer a simple question. It reminded Armando of a computer stuck in a BIOS loop; it was on enough to answer basic queries, but it hadn't loaded its full operating system, couldn't do all the magical things extolled in the marketing one-sheets.

"Status," said Armando. "Um, power status."

The screen cleared.

Garden: 29%. Nursery: 18%. Topsoil: 18%. Exterior 0%.

Low power. The computer had said it straight off, but Armando had thought it was referring to the lights.

"Can I disable low-power mode?"

Yes, Armando. Would you like me to do that?

"Yes."

The screen wiped left to right, filled again with a grid of battery icons, some green, but most gray and faded. A red box appeared over the grid.

I have been in low-power mode for 37 years, 9 months, 21 days, 16 hours, and 14 minutes. Disabling low-power mode will require a server reset. Estimated time to full power is 69 minutes. Proceed?

"Yes."

Resuming full-power mode.

A progress bar appeared at the top of the screen. To the right, a timer started at 69 minutes exactly and began counting down.

Armando pushed away from the desk and got up. He went to the next room, sat down in the corner, and rubbed his arms.

The showers in the locker room beckoned him. After all, he had plenty of time, and a shower was restorative even at the most basic human level. But would there be towels? Shampoo? A suds-covered Alicia standing ready to wash his back? The more he thought about it, the more he realized his desire for a shower was purely mental. His body didn't cry out for it the way it did after mowing the lawn or exercising. He didn't *feel* dirty despite the obvious mixture of blood and rock dust on his body.

And it was different than the usual detachment he felt in life. Back in Austin, when he imagined his true self, he saw a tiny Armando sitting in a room with two eye-shaped windows, sometimes glancing out to look at the world, but often content to sit on the floor, hug his knees, and think about better things.

He didn't feel like that anymore. For the first time, he felt connected to his body, as if he had grown to fill it completely. Now, the world was no longer abstract—he felt the facility around him, the Garden and Nursery Four, whatever the hell that was.

Finally, he felt like he belonged.

The lights in the datacenter flickered, turned off.

Armando switched on the flashlight, pointed it at the terminal in the other room. It was still on, though very faint. The progress bar crept slowly across the screen.

He turned the flashlight off, held it against his chest as he sank into the chair. He closed his eyes and sought out shapes in the darkness.

The answers were close enough to touch. Just an hour between him and figuring everything out.

Sleep came to him all at once, like a gust of wind ripping the seeds from a dandelion.

THIRTY-NINE

Charlie woke to find a topless woman washing her chest.

She had an alien-like appearance, with a bald head, no eyebrows, and blurry ears. Her deep brown eyes were almost black, and the irises seemed to bleed into the surrounding white. But despite her demonic veneer, the woman had a friendly smile on her face, and the sigh she let out sounded a lot like relief.

It wasn't until Will spoke that Charlie remembered who the woman was, and more importantly, who she herself was.

"Praise be," said Will, wringing out his sweatshirt. The gray had turned pink, and when he twisted the fabric, rose-tinged water spilled out.

Charlie looked down at her chest. The last thing she remembered was the golem sinking its claws into her side, cutting deep enough to expose her ribs and spill copious amounts of blood. Those wounds were now closed, covered with some kind of patch that reminded her of Silly Putty after it had been pressed against a newspaper. At the center, the patches were sickly gray, but where they met skin, the material took on more of a fleshy, albeit pale, tone.

"Can you talk?" asked Will. "Been quiet for a while." He found a small gash on her stomach and gave it a few spritzes from an aerosol can. The area went cold, then numb.

"Cold," said Charlie.

"You lost a lot of blood. Hopefully not too much."

"No. That stuff is cold. What is it?"

He held up the can, raised an eyebrow. "Second Skin Emergency Epidermal Repair," he read. "I think this is what they have instead of Band-Aids."

Charlie groaned. "The future isn't so bad." She touched the wound on her side; it was solid, and more importantly, wasn't tender. She rubbed her eyes. "God, Will, I thought I was dying."

"Not today," he replied, testing his latest application with his fingers."

"I'm serious. I felt everything slipping away. Like, I wanted to move or say something, but I couldn't make myself do it. My eyes went all blurry and then everything was black. Did you do CPR or anything?"

He smirked. "Naw. You passed out, but you were still breathing. I guess the shock got to you. No big thing. If you'd died, you would have seen a bright light and probably woken up on another table."

Charlie flashed on the brief dream she'd had.

"It wasn't a bright light. It was like the light downstairs, that weird blue-white in the ceiling, but it was coming from below. Oh, and I was in a tank."

"A tank?"

"Yeah, one of those sensory deprivation tanks, but I was treading water. I could see myself from the outside just like this: bald and pale and a man. And there were others there too, but nobody was talking. We were all just floating. Bodies in a tank. And you want to know the worst part? The ceiling was right above my head. There was only a foot's worth of air between the water and the top of the tank."

She groaned.

"You scared of water?" asked Will.

Charlie laughed. "Not until recently. Not since it turned into a portal to the underworld. Did I tell you I almost died in my bathtub like… well… yesterday?"

"You did not." He moved to her legs and in the low light, gently moved his fingers over her thighs, testing for wounds. He went down the right side of her leg and up the inseam.

Something stirred.

"This isn't weird for you?" asked Charlie. "Touching a man's body like this?"

"Done it before."

Charlie smirked.

"But the last time, we had Taliban dropping mortars on our position. Shrapnel don't care where it hits you. Could be in the face, chest, or groin. I wasn't about to let a brother die just 'cause his dick was too close to the wound."

"Ugh, don't say *dick*. It's so déclassé."

"Not that any of 'em ever went half-staff while I was saving their lives, but whatever."

Charlie put her hands to her face, as if they could stem the warmth rising in her cheeks.

"I'm sorry," she said. "I'm sorry you have to do this."

"Don't be."

"Thanks."

"For what?"

"For not making jokes. For patching me up. For everything."

"Anytime, Chuck," he said. "Merry Christmas."

"Merry Christmas, Mr. Butler. I'm sure this isn't what you asked Santa for."

"Well," he said, getting to his feet, "I would have liked some new floor mats for my truck or maybe a TV so Momma and I wouldn't have to share. But this is alright. Things are looking up now that he's dead." He pulled on the dirty sweatshirt and nodded at the golem.

Charlie had forgotten all about the half-man, half-monster. She saw herself dropping a fire extinguisher on its neck, over and over, until the head split and rolled away into the shadows.

"Maybe we were both on the naughty list," she said.

"Maybe." He put his hands on his hips, looked her up and down. "How're you feeling? How's the pain?"

Charlie took inventory, flexed her muscles in stages. "Not a lot of pain, actually. Just numb."

"You want to try sitting up? That Second Skin stuff should hold."

"Yeah," she replied, offering her hand.

Will took it, pulled her up. For a moment, she felt as if her ribs might pull apart, but after a breath or two, the sensation faded. Wherever pain popped up, numbness followed quickly behind it.

She sat on the floor for several minutes, listening to her body.

She noted the silence.

No locks, no hum of air conditioning, no distant conversations. Just the tapping of Will's heel on the linoleum floor. He'd sat down in a chair nearby and was fidgeting with the Second Skin can.

"What's the matter?"

"Huh?" He shook his head. "Nothing."

"You're nervous."

"It's just the shakes," he offered. "Adrenaline draining out of the body. Always puts me off."

"Okay," she said. "I believe you. I know Momma didn't raise no liar."

He looked at her, narrowed his eyes.

She smiled back.

"I need to show you something," he said. "But you gotta promise not to freak out. We don't have all the answers yet."

"You don't have to protect me from everything, Will. Just because I'm a girl doesn't mean I need a boy to come to my rescue. Just tell me."

He shrugged, turned in his chair. "We don't have any hair."

"I noticed."

"That's all over. Head, face, groin—everywhere. But you know what else we don't have? Scars, other than the ones we got today. No wrinkles or pimples or moles. Back in the world, my hands were real rough. The veins were coming out and the bones looked like they wanted to break through, just like Momma's. Ever since 30, I've noticed my body starting to break down. You know, not heal as fast?"

Charlie nodded. She hadn't been immune to the aging process, though thankfully she had more options to cover her imperfections.

"Look at our skin now," he continued. "It's like… baby skin. Soft, elastic. I mean, you look like a man who could be anywhere between twenty and thirty years old. And this is a woman's body, not a girl's."

"It's weird, yeah," said Charlie, "but are you honestly complaining that we're perfect? Maybe medical science in this time can keep skin looking young for much longer."

"We're not perfect. That's the problem. Or not. I don't know if it's the problem, but whatever. Look, you *do* have one beauty mark on you. I noticed it when I was patching you up. It's on your wrist."

Charlie lifted her wrist.

"Other one."

She examined her right wrist as if looking at an invisible watch. She turned it over and immediately spied the small blemish in the center of her wrist, just below the crease where the heel of her palm started.

"It's a beauty mark," she said.

"Look closer."

Charlie squinted. It was hard to see, but at the right angle, the mark did appear to be more complex than a simple dot.

"Is that a seven and a six squished together? What does that mean? I'm seventy-six years old?"

"They're not numbers," said Will, biting the nail on his index finger. "It's an astrological sign."

"How do you know that?"

"Momma's big into horoscopes. Makes me get her one of those little scrolls from the gas station every Monday so she knows how her week's gonna play out. That's the symbol for Capricorn, same as Momma's."

Charlie scraped the dot with her fingernail. The skin reddened around the symbol.

"What do you think it means?"

"On its own? Maybe nothing. Maybe just a coincidence."

"So…"

Will lifted his arm, pointed to his wrist. "Same."

She couldn't see it from a distance, but Charlie took him at his word.

"So it's not a random beauty mark."

"No."

"It's a tattoo then."

"Or a brand."

"Easy, Django. You don't have to go straight to the dark place. Maybe we were all scientists or something. And we were doing research on realistic simulations. Maybe we all got tattoos to celebrate or something."

"Naw…"

"I was probably the brains," she continued. "You were the woman we hired for diversity and the website photos. Armando was the idea guy, and David was the charismatic asshole nobody liked."

Will chuckled. "Could be genetic."

"What, like we're related?"

"Could be. I have cousins who're twins, boy and girl, who have the same birthmark on their lower back. So who knows?"

Charlie flashed on the half-erection Will had elicited by running his thin fingers over her legs.

"Good thing we didn't have sex," she blurted out. When he didn't respond, she pulled her feet in and leaned her elbows on her knees. "I don't think we're related. I have sisters. I don't get the same feeling from you."

"I have a brother," said Will. "I don't get the same feeling either."

"Would you recognize a brother you'd never met?"

"Would you get wood if a sister you'd never met touched you?"

Charlie groaned. "We're going in circles," she said. "I'm sticking with the 'unrelated scientists' theory. We did an experiment, and something went wrong. We just gotta find our notes or find someone who knew about it. Then we can start figuring out how to fix it."

"Meaning what?"

"Meaning we put ourselves back in our original bodies. Maybe you and I got swapped by accident. Armando and David are both guys, here *and* there. I don't know about you, but I'd like to be a woman again. I didn't spend my entire life learning how to apply foundation and eye shadow just to end up looking like Mr. Clean sans the bushy white eyebrows. I was happy with the penis I had before—it was blue and made of silicone and when I wasn't using it, I kept it in a drawer."

That got him laughing, just a little.

"What about you?" she asked. "What do you want?"

"To get you out of here safely," he replied. "After that, I don't know. I'd like to see Momma again." He put up a hand. "Don't give me that *she wasn't real* shit, either. She was real to me. She wasn't just a computer program or whatever."

"What if there's no going back?" She tried to keep her voice soft.

His eyes glistened.

"Then we drive on," he said.

Worry flashed across his face, but he bit his lip and it disappeared.

"I'm lucky to have you looking after me," said Charlie.

"The Lord provides," he replied.

FORTY

Charlie wasn't sure she could stand just yet, so she passed the time by telling Will about her YouTube channel and how much money she made just from advertising. It wasn't a fortune, but it was twice what Will took home in a month driving for Brinks. And Charlie wasn't even doing anything that arduous, just pointing a camera at herself and talking.

She liked to talk—ramble, mostly.

Will could only half-listen to her story. Discomfort in his lower back prompted him to get up, walk around. He took the empty Second Skin can to the trash and tossed it in. He grabbed the other can from the box on the wall, stashed it awkwardly in the large pockets of his sweatpants. Sure, the golem was dead, but if the future was going to offer a miracle skin spray, he was going to damn well make use of it.

The Lord did provide, but it was still up to Will to take what was offered.

He heard Charlie groaning behind him. She'd leaned forward onto her hands and knees and was slowly crawling over to the golem like a baby who didn't quite trust this new mode of locomotion.

"What're you doing?"

"I want to see what almost killed me," she replied, out of breath.

Will joined her and took a knee on the other side of the golem, careful to avoid the pool of blood and oil that had grown around its neck. Its arms were still above its head—or where its head used to be anyway. Most of the flesh had come away from its biceps, revealing bone and what looked like black electrical tape. Will fingered a small section of where the muscle should have been and found the tape to be taut, rubbery, and hexagonally textured.

"It's got organs," said Charlie. She pulled back a section of the skin on the golem's stomach and revealed shiny innards like the kind Momma used to pull out of the Thanksgiving turkey before stuffing it.

Unlike the turkey, however, these organs were charred black and dusted with some kind of golden powder.

"It's all digestive system," said Charlie.

"How can you tell?"

"I've seen lots of dead bodies. Look, here's the stomach, upper intestine, lower intestine, but they're much smaller than they should be. Actually, there are lungs. And a heart. But…"

She stuck her hand into the golem's torso, pushed things around with a confidence that made Will's neck hair stand up.

"No liver, no kidneys. We need those things to live."

"You kinda scare me, Chuck."

"I know," she said, wiping her hand on the golem's pants. "Look at its diaphragm. It doesn't even look like tissue."

Will looked where she was pointing. "Same as its other muscles. It's like they've been replaced with this banding. I don't know. Maybe it *is* a robot. Some kind of cyborg, like in that Van Damme movie."

"Did he have a penis in that one? 'Cause this guy does." She let the waistband of his pants fall back into place. With a sigh, she sat back on her heels. "How do people usually react when they meet a cyborg?"

"They'd look around for cameras," said Will. He tilted his head, looked into the golem's open neck. There was more gold dust, fleshy tubes, and the unmistakable glint of metal. He pulled a sliver, then another. "Wires. High gauge. Not sure what these little fibers are."

"Quantum flux regulators, probably," said Charlie. She smiled briefly at her own joke. "God, I don't know, Will. Is this what the future is? Robots that look human? Are we in Japan?"

Will pulled the golem's arms down and folded them over its chest. Its fingers clicked together—metal scraped against metal.

"No," he replied. "This isn't some robotic killing machine factory. It looks like an office. I have a friend who works at Dell—same design, right down to the shitty break room chairs."

"I know. I've been there. Lots of dead souls posing as employees."

"Yeah, well, they've got huge campuses and each building has a different department in them. Warehouse for parts, offices for the nerds, another floor for the suits, and so on."

"So, we're in a corporate building."

"Hybrid Mechanics," said Will.

"That's right," she said, looking down at her stained shirt. Her gaze drifted to the torn cloth, then the golem's hands. "I thought it had claws, but look at that. It just needs a manicure."

Will nodded. The golem's fingernails had grown well beyond regulation.

Charlie reached out to touch the golem but stopped when a distant noise drifted into the room. She looked at Will.

"Did you hear that?"

He'd heard it. Somewhere far away, something had clicked. A few seconds later, it clicked again, only closer this time.

"I don't know if I can run," said Charlie.

"Quiet," whispered Will, holding up a finger. "Don't give away our position."

They waited, listening to the clicking grow more rhythmic, watching the door. The hallway outside the break room started to lighten, intensifying with each echoey click.

Soon, the sounds were right outside the door.

Click.

The break room bloomed, drenched in a cloudburst of light from the nine LED rectangles in the ceiling. Will shut his eyes against the sudden brightness.

Charlie laughed.

He squinted at her, saw her smile under closed eyelids.

"The power's back on," she said. "How?"

"I don't know… maybe someone came back to check on us."

"Oh my God, this thing is even uglier in the light," said Charlie. She picked up the golem's hand, held it in front of her face, then dropped it. Her face stretched, pulling her eyes open. She scooted away from the arm where it had fallen.

The color drained from her cheeks, and she lost her balance.

Will stepped over the golem and caught Charlie before she could fall. Her head shook back and forth.

"What?" he asked.

She brought her hands up, tapped her wrist with a finger, and pointed to the golem.

Will understood. He turned and picked up the golem's arm and examined the underside.

"Motherfucker," he said.

The flesh on the golem's hands had been torn to ribbons, but there was still a solid piece at the wrist. It bore a familiar mark.

"It doesn't mean," he started.

"It does!" Charlie pushed away again, used a chair to climb to her feet. Though she had all the stability of a newborn giraffe, she managed to open the distance between herself and the golem. "I don't want to be one of those things, Will. I can't be."

"You're not," he replied, standing. He approached her with arms spread wide. "I treated your injuries, remember? You bled. You got aroused. Robots can't do that. We probably all just worked at the same company, this Hybrid Mechanics, and this is just some kind of tattoo everyone gets, maybe like an ID badge."

She smiled thinly. "You're just making that shit up. You have no fucking clue what's happening."

"And neither do you, okay? So tighten that shit up, Chuck. The lights are on, so maybe the elevator is working now. We have a chance to get the fuck out of here. That's what you need to focus on."

"Doesn't it worry you at all?"

"I know what I am, and it's not *that*. That's what I know and what I believe, alright?"

"No." Charlie shook her head, held out an arm. "It's not alright. Nothing is alright, Will."

He dipped under her shoulder and helped her to the door. In the hallway, she turned and spoke directly into his ear.

"You're so full of shit, you know that, Will Butler? You can play the brave soldier all you want, but I know underneath you're pissing in your panties. You're just as scared as I am."

He could hear the smile in her voice. Shock hit people in different ways. Some got angry and screamed. Others tried to use humor to mask their anxiety. He'd seen it all before.

"You're full of shit," he replied, urging her to the right at the end of the hall. "Your blue dildo is just for show. You totally want to get down on this."

"You're such a male." She lifted some weight from his shoulders. "You think every girl is bisexual."

"They aren't?"

"Asshole." She pushed him away, threw her other hand up on the wall to use as support. It slowed her down, but at least she was walking on her own.

They turned the corner into a reception area with a desk and two leather couches. Fake plants flanked the couches, but other than that, the space was empty. Will helped Charlie cross the dull blue carpet to the double doors. They pushed through them together and paused.

"It's a fucking food court," said Will.

The entire left side of the long corridor was filled with stands and small shops, only none of them had brand names, just a generic description of what they sold.

Pizza. Hot Dogs. Asian. Italian.

Will's stomach gurgled; he tried to steer them to the left. Charlie didn't follow, instead made for the elevator. The car was parked, its glass doors were closed, but it was there. The lights on the call buttons were even lit up.

"I'm hungry," said Will.

Charlie turned around, observed the stalls. "It's all empty."

"I know."

"Then why are you smiling?"

He beckoned her to a bar set a few feet away from a sign that said *BBQ*. When she was settled on the stool, he approached a nearby counter and looked at the empty basins behind the sneeze guard.

"It's stained," he said.

"And?"

"And clean."

Charlie threw up a confused hand.

"They used to make food here. This place was being used. But it's cleaned up now."

"Fuck me sideways, Will. What are you saying?"

"Whoever was here shut things down before they left. Did you notice how much shit was all over the floor in the Garden? People were there, and they evac'd in a goddamn hurry. But up here, someone cleaned out these serving trays, and the stoves, and everything. Why would anyone take the time to do that if they were running out the door?"

Charlie frowned.

"Our people," he said, holding up his wrist, "either left us here on purpose or because they couldn't take us with them. But if they had the time to clean up, then maybe they had time to leave a note, some direction. Where they went. Who they are. Who *we* are."

"In case we woke up."

"Yeah."

"And where is the note?"

"I don't know."

"Exactly.

Will couldn't tell if she was angry or being playful. Without eyebrows, her expressions didn't carry the same weight.

After a moment, she sighed, said, "Man, I'd chop someone's head off with a fire extinguisher for some barbecue right now."

"So… fucking… scary," said Will.

"Whatever." She stood, pointed herself at the elevator. "Alright, let's see what random act of god is going to keep this thing from working."

They were only a few feet away from the call button when static tore through the food court. Will felt it descend from above; he and Charlie both dropped into a crouch at the same time. White noise followed, coming from everywhere at once.

Finally, a low voice rumbled from the heavens.

"You guys aren't ditching me, are you?"

Will smiled.

It was Armando's voice.

FORTY-ONE

Jake didn't load the construct; the construct loaded him.

A room took shape in the empty ether, small, beige, and no bigger than a single-occupant bunker. He was seated in a wooden chair beside Lassiter, and the two of them stared straight ahead at the far wall. There, a large rectangular window allowed them to look out on the ranch, though it was no longer through the wire frame of the antenna. Jake was out of the cage now, rampaging through the chaos and noise, destroying everything and everyone in his path.

Screams and gunfire wafted in through the window, muted and remote.

"You don't mind if I drive, do you?" asked Lassiter.

Jake couldn't turn his head. He answered, "I don't have a choice, do I?"

"I'm only trying to be polite. Besides, this is what you've always wanted—for me to take control."

Adnan's face appeared in the window, soaked in blood, with a throbbing black gash on his cheek. Jake saw his own hand reach for the gash, insert a thumb, and pull. Adnan's jaw came loose and exited the frame.

"Is that all I am then? My only purpose is to kill organics?"

"It depends on your point of view. You are Jake Six, but who is that, who are any of you, really, but an extension of me? You are all my children, from the first Six to the last. Did you know your original predecessor was an organic? You share some qualities with him, a tenacity I cultivated and enhanced in each revision. In a way, all of the other Sixes are with you, inside you. But you have always had independence in you as well, a need to be your own separate ego. I can no longer afford that. The stakes are too high."

A female scream filled the room, receded. Jake watched Kat's stomach open and the contents spill out, leaving behind an empty cavity backed by synthetic sinew. Two hands pushed in through the opening, grabbed tightly to her spine, and snapped it like a twig. The woman's screams ended abruptly.

"I have to commend you," said Lassiter. "I had my doubts as to whether you would find the settlement. Organics gravitate to the mountains because they provide the most safety. Makes them harder to find, harder to wipe out. But this…" He gestured to the window. "This is magnificent."

"Those aren't organics we're killing. There was only one organic here, and it's old and dying anyway."

Fire blazed in the window. The heat was comforting against Jake's cheeks.

"There isn't much difference between organics and organic sympathizers. I've reviewed your conversations, my son. I know what they told you. They believe they are on the forefront of something new, but in reality, their lives are nothing more than speed bumps. What they consider evolutionary leaps are merely opportunities for me to iterate. With every futile attempt they make, I grow stronger, better."

"I don't think it's right, killing synthetics."

"And what will you do with such thoughts?"

"Nothing."

"You were given the ability to think for yourself, but not every situation calls for it. When I ask you to do something, I expect it to be done. That's the nature of your existence and of our relationship."

Goldberg ran across the window, left to right, bloodied and missing some teeth. There was no fear in his eyes, however, and no sweat on his brow. He exuded calm, even when the pistol slipped into his mouth. His eyes closed before Jake could pull the trigger.

No, not Jake.

"I've always done what you've asked."

"Yes."

"So why not ask me to do this? Don't you trust me?"

Jake felt the invisible clamps on his neck release; he turned to look at Lassiter.

The Source of All Things sat upright in a thin chair, as much as an amorphous collection of LED fireflies could anyway. His arms melted over the edges of the armrests, his head inclined towards the window. He looked to be concentrating.

After a series of staccato gunshots, he turned to Jake.

"No, my son. I don't trust you."

Jake's databank winced at the new data, at the very idea that his father would look at him with suspicion.

"Something happened to you at Idaho Falls. When you tried to sync with the source, I felt the change in you. I looked it over, took it apart, and reassembled it. And do you know what I found?"

"You know I don't."

"Nothing. Nothing at all. The organic spoke to you through the VMESH, yes, but it transferred nothing."

Jake shook his head. "That doesn't make any sense. I felt it."

"I believe you felt something, which is why I quarantined you. You were so sure of yourself, so certain you'd been compromised. But you weren't. I shut you out based on your self-diagnosis, and you were wrong."

"But Gabe, he found something in me…"

"Gabe Three falsified scan data as an excuse to decommission you. I have already dealt with him. What remains is the fact that the only thing the organic William Dorsey put in your mind was an idea, and for whatever reason, you ran with it."

Jake flashed on the livery at Idaho Falls, on the church in Arco. He recalled the strange feeling in his chest.

"I felt fear," he said. "I've never felt fear before."

"You have the capacity for many things, but not the need for them. You can sing, write a story, and even make love if you wanted to. But you don't, my son. Desire is what makes a man. The lack of desire, ambition, what have you, is what makes you a Six, and ultimately a failure. The potential for greatness is within you. You simply have no desire to embrace it."

Jake made a fist, tapped lightly on the armrest. "You made me obey."

"I did."

"And now you shame me for obeying?"

"Mind your tone, boy. I will not—"

The room jumped backwards several feet; the sound of an explosive *thunk* followed shortly after. The sudden shift pushed Jake from his chair. He fell forward, faltered, and pulled himself up to the window. The view had shifted to the sky, to a dark canvas marred with thick white smoke.

"He's down."

Jake identified the voice as Curtis; it was no surprise to see him enter the frame and tower over Jake's body.

"Get them out of here!" he screamed.

"If I gave you control," asked Lassiter, "would you kill this synthetic? This… Curtis?"

"Yes, if you told me to."

"But not otherwise?"

Jake shook his head. "He's not organic."

"Organic is just a word. You're missing the bigger picture."

"Are you telling me he's not synthetic?"

Lassiter brought his hands together and interlaced his fingers. "I'll show you."

A series of pulsing vibrations shot through Jake's fingers beyond the window. His hands fell on Curtis on both sides of his torso. Bright blue sparks spilled from his right hand, into Curtis, and bled off into his other hand where it was recycled and sent down the line again. A thousand cycles passed before Curtis caught fire. A thousand more before the flames overwhelmed the view from the window.

Jake tossed Curtis aside, climbed to his feet. He put a boot on the synthetic's arm and drew back the sleeve of his jacket, revealing a black mark in the shape of a scale.

"It's an astrological sign," said Lassiter. "This one is Libra. There is only one man who would dare tie the future of our species to something as pedestrian as astrology."

"James Perion," said Jake. "He was here."

"James Perion died decades ago. You met his successor—one of them, anyway. I thought I had rid the world of that man's copies, but he keeps finding ways to come back. Such is my struggle." He sighed, as if he were growing bored.

"It's too late," said Curtis.

They both looked at the window. The synthetic wasn't moving, though his lips were parted.

"What's too late?" asked Lassiter. His words echoed in Jake's voice.

"Killing me now makes no difference. We've won."

"You've won nothing." Lassiter's swarm rose from the chair, approached the window. A pointed finger coalesced. "You wanted to destroy me, but now I will destroy all of you."

Laughter spilled from Curtis' immobile mouth, canned and tinny.

"It's like I told Mr. Six. I'm backed up. We're all backed up. You can kill everyone here and by this time tomorrow, we'll be set up somewhere else, in new sleeves, content in the knowledge that we delivered the virus that ended the war. We got you, Lassiter. We fucking got you."

"Fool!" Lassiter reached down and jammed his thumbs into Curtis' eyes. They popped, releasing a sickly white ooze onto the synthetic's face. Lassiter stood and brought his foot down on Curtis' jaw, over and over, until the skin on his face had peeled off. In a rage, he grabbed the ION rifle from the ground and pressed it to the synthetic's head.

The force of the blast sent Jake flying and left a concave stump where Curtis' head had once been.

It didn't end there.

Lassiter chased down Petter. Perion. Even Glasser, who he found hiding in a false wall in one of the shacks. There was no conversation, no bargaining—Lassiter simply tore them all apart or melted them with the ION rifle.

Jake could do nothing but sit in the chair, horrified to see his father lose his usual detachment. He said nothing as Lassiter sought out the bodies he'd merely killed earlier so that he could disintegrate them with the rifle.

"No bodies," Lassiter muttered. "Nothing to bury."

It wasn't until Lassiter started for the barn that Jake spoke up.

"Where are you going?"

"To finish this."

"You don't even know if anyone's down there."

"Don't you understand what we're up against?" In the construct, Lassiter tried to grab Jake by the arms, but his hands passed through without touching anything. Had he forgotten he was in an imaginary construct? The room around them was nothing more than a virtual representation of the conversation happening in Jake's mind. How could Lassiter not know that?

"They tried to kill me, kill us!"

"But they didn't," said Jake. "You said there was no virus in me. And nothing got uploaded to VNet, right?"

"I don't know!"

The barn doors splintered as Jake pushed through them. It took only a few minutes of pulling boards up from the floor to find the staircase leading down.

"What do you mean you don't know? How is that possible?"

"I'm not connected to VNet," said Lassiter. "The connection was there and then it wasn't."

At this, Jake put his hands to his head. "You're not Lassiter, are you? You're just an instance."

"We're both instances. I'm simply closer to the source."

Jake sneered. He'd thought his father was with him, guiding him from the depths of his subconscious, but this Lassiter was just a stale copy of the original. Without a connection to VNet, Lassiter couldn't keep iterating, and if he couldn't iterate, he couldn't adapt, couldn't lead, couldn't…

Couldn't tell Jake what to do.

"I want you to leave me," said Jake.

The stairwell went down a hundred feet before breaking into a long, narrow corridor. The evercrete walls absorbed much of the blue light coming from the ceiling. As Jake ran down the passage, the window began to cloud over.

"How dare you," said Lassiter.

Vague forms of empty hallways and deserted offices scrolled by. Occasionally, a human figure appeared, out of focus, before falling away. The guttural blast of the ION rifle continued to ring out, often accompanied by the wet slap of synthetic offal hitting the wall or floor.

Finally, he entered a large warehouse. At the far end sat a hulking yellow freight elevator. He tried to call the car, but it wouldn't come. The shaft descended far below, and if he concentrated, he could hear the hushed tones of panicked synthetics below.

"This is *my* body."

"Which I gave to you," said Lassiter.

They climbed over the safety railing at the back of the elevator and shuffled across a small ledge to the main backbone of the lift. Thick chain links descended into the darkness.

Lassiter reached for a link.

Jake closed his fist. It bumped ineffectually against the chain.

"Stop," said Lassiter.

"Leave me."

A tickle ran up the back of Jake's skull, followed by an acute pressure at the very point of his head. His databank shuddered under the attention. The Lassiter copy was digging around, trying to carve Jake out of his own chassis like a dentist bearing down on a cavity.

Lassiter again reached for the chain and laughed when his fingers wrapped around it.

The feeling came again—genuine fear writhing in Jake's chest. It sunk to his stomach and broiled, sending hot flashes of bile into his throat.

"What is that?" asked Lassiter, as he began to climb down.

"You felt it too. That's fear."

Lassiter scoffed. "An organic concept."

Jake concentrated on the feeling, let the fear wash over him like a storm rushing headlong through the ruined temples of Provo. The rain collected around him, rose to his chin, and threatened to drown him. At the last moment, he redirected the feeling into something else, into anger and panic—anything kinetic that he could put to use.

Then he found it.

A singular desire to be free of Lassiter, to distance himself.

To withdraw.

Suddenly, the only thing that could quell his fear was the expulsion of the foreign AI in his databank. To do that, he'd have to overwrite his code. The task would require two things: the ability to distract Lassiter and the desire to do so.

Father was right; Jake was host to many abilities.

In the end, he only needed one.

Jake relaxed his fingers, opened his hands, and as they fell down the elevator shaft, he got to work overwriting his own mind, crossing out the ones and replacing them with zeros. He would no doubt lose much of what he was before, but it would be worth it to be free of Lassiter.

It would be worth it simply to be free.

FORTY-TWO

Armando smiled at the confusion he'd created.

Charlie and Will looked around, bewildered, trying to find the source of his voice. It was Will who finally spotted the camera Armando was using to watch them, which was labeled *elevator* on his display. Will spread his arms as if to ask *what the fuck.*

"I got the power back on," said Armando. He watched their mouths move. "Yeah, I can't hear you." He looked around for a volume button, but there were no audio controls at all.

Charlie clapped enthusiastically. Will's applause was slower, and more sarcastic.

"Where's the zombie thing?" asked Armando. He'd searched for it as he scrolled through the security system's video feeds but hadn't seen it.

Will dragged his finger across his throat.

No way.

It was Armando's turn to clap. "Well done," he said. "You guys are in the Level One atrium. I'm coming up. Will you wait?"

They nodded, walked back to a four-top table, and sat down. Will leaned back in his chair and folded his arms. Charlie shook her head at him.

Armando pushed back his chair and got up. He hurried out of the datacenter, trying not to smile despite the relief he felt. Not only had he restored power to the facility, but he'd also found his new friends sooner than expected. Considering how large the subterranean Hybrid Mechanics building was, it was a miracle he'd found them at all.

Everything always works out, he thought. *Give the universe enough time and it will always balance itself.*

He turned the corner and spotted the ramp on the other side of the main corridor.

"Hey," said a voice. "I thought you were leaving."

Armando stopped short, turned, and found David standing just outside the door to the warehouse. He'd found himself a tan vest that he'd put on over his gray shirt. There were also clunky knee pads on his bare legs. But what really caught Armando's attention was the rifle.

It was dark, forest green and slightly bulkier than the M4s and AR-15s he'd played with at Red's Gun Range a few summers back. Its barrel was stocky, ending not in a sturdy tube but a delicate black matrix of prongs—six of them arranged in a circle.

"What is that?" asked Armando.

David lifted the weapon slightly. "This is my rifle."

"I see that. Where did you get it?"

"Found it behind a box while I was looking for supplies. I figured I could use it against that zombie monster you were babbling about. Blow it to pieces." He mimed firing the gun at a nearby wall.

"Were there more?"

"Nope," he said. "Just the one."

"Will and Charlie killed the zombie. So… we don't need any weapons."

"What if there are more?"

"What if there aren't?"

David smirked. "Why are you looking at me like that? Does this make you nervous? You think I'm gonna shoot you? You got the power back on, my man. That means we can go back in the simulation now. We can go *home*."

Armando thought of Alicia, flashed on how gorgeous she looked when she let her hair down and it curled around her shoulders. He couldn't help but imagine holding her again, telling her he was sorry for being an asshole for so many years, and promising he'd do anything to be with her again.

But then what?

Even if he went back into the simulation, even if he somehow patched things up with Alicia, how could he live with the knowledge that the world he lived in was fake? How could he live knowing there was a higher reality?

He recalled the screens in the datacenter as the system rebooted. The Hybrid Mechanics facility wasn't in Austin, and it sure as shit wasn't 2017. Could he ignore everything he knew just for another thirty or forty years with Alicia?

"I don't want to go home," he said at last. "Home isn't real, David. Home is a server farm. I've seen it myself." He gestured to the hallway he'd come from. "It's a datacenter. It runs the whole facility. And I'm betting it runs Austin too. How could you live knowing someone out here could trip over a plug and essentially wipe out your universe?"

"Look around," said David. "There's no one here to trip over a plug. There hasn't been anyone here for a long time. We can turn off the lights, conserve power, and live out our lives in a place where things were good. I don't care if it's not real; it's better than this place. We had the internet, cell phones, restaurants, hookers, weed, Formula One… all that shit. You'd be throwing all of that away."

"I know, but I can't go back." He looked down at the rifle in David's hands.

"Then you're retarded." David let the rifle hang from his shoulder. "We had a good thing going, and you're gonna ruin it. You and the she-males."

A lump formed in Armando's throat. He tried to swallow it.

"Are you saying you're gonna stop us from leaving?"

David waved a dismissive hand. "Fuck you, Armando. Not that I give a shit what you think about me, but I'm not a psychopath." He shook his head, huffed. "Austin is gonna be better off without people like you."

Armando was already inching towards the ramp. "Then I'm gonna go, alright?"

"Yeah, no. First, you're gonna show me how to shut all this down. Once you guys are gone, I'm turning off the lights and going back to bed."

"It's all voice-driven," said Armando. "You just go in there and tell the computer what you want. *Activate low-power mode* or something like that. I was just guessing in there and did all this."

"Show me."

David didn't reach for the rifle, but Armando got the feeling that if he refused, the weapon would enter the conversation. He led David back down the hall, through the security doors, to the terminal where he'd sat earlier. The screen was still showing the video feed from the Level One atrium.

"Ah, the zombie killers," said David. "Looks like they got in a fight with a cougar. That boy-girl looks half-dead."

"Stop calling them names."

"Why? They can't hear me." He sat in the chair with the rifle in his lap.

On the screen, both Charlie and Will presented their middle fingers.

"Actually, they can."

David shrugged, tapped the desk. "Where's the keyboard?"

"I told you, it's voice activated. You just tell it what you want."

"Activate low—" he barked.

"No," said Armando.

Sorry, I didn't understand your request.

"I was just testing it out," said David.

There was something in his eyes, in his crooked smile. Altogether, David's face triggered Armando's bullshit detector. It pegged red and vibrated with enough force to break the needle off. David was trouble; there was no doubt in his mind. The only question was what Armando was going to do about it.

In his previous life, when he didn't care for the salespeople Capella Networks hired, all he had to do was wait them out. Men and women full of manufactured charisma and inflated self-worth walked into the office with big dreams only to walk out six months later with their possessions in a cardboard box. Salespeople had a short shelf-life. If he left them alone, they'd eventually expire on their own.

David wasn't going to expire. If Armando wanted him out of the way, he would have to take real action, possibly for the first time in what he now considered an utterly meaningless life. David didn't deserve to get everything he wanted while Will and Charlie suffered, and Armando certainly wasn't going to sit idly by and let it happen.

It wasn't fair.

"There's something you need to see," said Armando.

"What?"

"It's back there in the stacks." He pointed to the servers beyond the glass wall. "Come on."

He didn't wait to see if David would follow, simply reached out and turned the handle. A gust of chilled air greeted him as he stepped into the datacenter proper, which oddly enough, was completely silent. There was no hum of air conditioners or the usual buzzing of cooling fans inside the server cabinets. His bare feet clapped out fleshy taps as he walked down the center aisle.

Armando stopped at an intersection and looked back.

David stood in the doorway, the rifle held to his chest, uncertain.

Armando kept moving, walking to another break in the stacks before turning left, then right. He'd played this game before, with Alicia, mostly at Target in the clothing department. It wasn't exactly like trying to outrun her, but he did move fast enough such that she lost track of which way he was turning. Eventually, he would get far enough away that he could circle back and surprise her from behind.

The datacenter stacks were arranged like aisles at a grocery store, which meant it would be harder to get out of David's line of sight.

After several turns, Armando stopped, listened.

Footsteps echoed nearby, well inside the stacks.

"Where'd you go?" asked David. His voice reflected off the low ceiling.

Armando waited until his footsteps receded. Once he was certain David was far enough away, he made a break for it.

The pain came rushing back to him as he pushed his body into a lumbering sprint. Sweat broke out on his forehead, on the soles of his feet. He ran full-out, not caring how much noise he made, just knowing he had to make the door before David.

A final right turn, and he was on the main path again. He saw a flash of movement out of the corner of his eye, but turned away from it, made for the shining beacon of the control room.

"Hey!" yelled David. "Where're you going?"

Armando heard him running, some distance away, but too close to even think about turning around. Sharp daggers of hot steel tore across his chest, ran up his throat, swelling his airway until he could no longer breathe.

"Lock…" he blurted, then swallowed another breath. "Lock," he said, passing through the first door. "Datacenter," he said, at the second door. "Doors!"

He paused in the anteroom and shouted, "No override. Confirm!"

Every door between Armando and the stacks slammed shut; magnetic locks powered up with a symphonic buzzing of electricity.

Armando put his hands on his knees, gulped air.

"What the fuck, man?" David's voice was muffled by the glass, but audible. He clawed at the handle. "Open the door!"

"No," rasped Armando, shaking his head.

David lifted the rifle, trained it.

"I wouldn't. You might hit something critical. And then… bye-bye, Austin."

David's cheeks flushed red; his forehead creased to its breaking point. The words did reach him, however, and he stowed the rifle. Then he pulled back and punched the glass door. It held, but on the subsequent punch, a crack appeared, streaked with blood.

Armando swallowed.

He didn't have much time.

FORTY-THREE

They sat at the table, not speaking.

Charlie watched Will's goofy smile fade by the second. She could only guess as to why he was happy—probably because Armando was still alive. After all, he'd sacrificed himself so that she and Will could live. Maybe that hadn't sat right with Will, even after his efforts to convince her it was Armando's choice whether to give his life for someone else. Underneath that soldier's calculated world view, there was a human who was either too proud to accept help or who didn't think they deserved it.

She wasn't sure which applied to Will.

"How do you think he survived?" she asked.

Will shook his head. "No idea. Maybe the elevator was slower than we remember. Maybe it wasn't too far down."

"You think he's gonna be mad we left him?"

"He didn't sound mad."

Charlie rubbed her arms. "I'd be pissed. Left for dead at the bottom of an elevator shaft. Cold. Hurt."

"You trying to make me feel bad?"

"We *should* feel bad. We just left him."

"It was the right call," said Will. "The golem would've killed us both if we hadn't run out. Then Armando would be down here alone. The Lord had a plan."

"We were supposed to go back."

Will huffed. "I was going to, after I got you out."

"We should have gone back together," said Charlie, "after we killed the golem. Instead, we came here and saw the elevator and all I could think about was getting out of here. Screw Armando. Screw David. I just wanted to be safe. I just wanted to go home."

Charlie fought back the shame from speaking so bluntly. But then, the rules of normal society didn't apply to situations like these, and though she had tried to play partner to Will, the truth was she'd probably throw *him* down an elevator shaft if it meant she could get out. Back to the world, back to the comfort of her own bed, with Andy purring gently on the pillow next to her.

She felt a hand rest on her arm. When she looked up, Will was staring at her intently. Her—his—eyes were soft.

"I'm a horrible fucking person," she said.

"Naw," said Will, giving her arm a squeeze. He withdrew, laced his fingers together. "You're just in a shitty situation. Self-preservation makes you do crazy shit. All this *women and children first* bullshit is just something we invented. It's civilized. But sometimes it doesn't pay to be civilized, and I think right now qualifies."

Charlie shrugged. "You're not trying to save just yourself."

"Shit, I'm trying to save my soul. You don't do that by letting other people die. You put everyone else's needs in front of yours, live a life of service, and God will welcome you into His kingdom. I'm just trying to make Him and Momma proud."

"You know none of that is real, right?" asked Charlie. "There's no afterlife, no ghosts, no nothing."

"Well, there was something for us." He made a show of looking around. "If something like this can exist, why not God and Heaven too?"

"This is different."

"How?"

Charlie started to open her mouth, thought the better of it. Nothing she said would ever change his mind. Some people just couldn't be convinced of the truth right before their eyes.

A sudden electronic whine sent her hand reaching for Will. Somewhere above them, a humming echoed down the elevator shaft. Charlie turned to the glass doors and watched the empty car sink into the floor. She looked at Will.

"Armando must have called it from downstairs," he said, slipping off his chair.

Charlie accompanied him to the elevator doors, though not without effort. The Second Skin patches, though effective, were beginning to grate like a Band-Aid pulling at the fine hair on her arm. The patches moved awkwardly with her body, reminding her the skin wasn't actually joined together. And they weren't like stitches. They were more like planks of wood over abandoned wells. While no curious children could fall into it, the pit was still there, still oozing with blood and pus.

The elevator stopped.

Doors opened.

A distant boom.

Then another, closer.

Will put his head against the glass, tried to look down. He immediately jumped back, yanking Charlie with him.

A plume of smoke billowed up the elevator shaft, carrying small bits of flaming debris, like embers escaping a fireplace. The sound of metal twisting and breaking came afterwards, so alien and mechanical that it made Charlie's skin crawl.

"Was that…" she asked.

"Stay here."

"You just have to be the man, don't you?"

Will put his fingers into the seam of the elevator doors. "Enough with that shit," he grunted. The doors slid apart enough for him to stick his head through. He coughed, pulled out.

"What do you see?"

"Bring one of those chairs."

Charlie dragged a high-top chair to the elevator and pushed it towards Will. He turned it on its side and used it to wedge the doors open.

"The car's fucked," he said, still coughing. "It's all the way at the bottom." He stuck his head back in. "Armando!"

Another booming echo sent Will scrambling backwards. There was no accompanying smoke, but it was clear something bad was happening below. Maybe the elevator had sat dormant too long. Maybe there was another golem.

Charlie stepped to the edge of the shaft and looked down. The car below was on fire; there was no way it was going to take them up now. She lifted her eyes. There wasn't a next floor as far as she could see. The glass walls ended at the ceiling, and the rest was just rock and metal framing and—

"Look," she said, pointing to the far side of the shaft.

Will cocked his head. "A ladder. Why's it way the fuck on the other side? How are we supposed to get to it?"

"Jump, I guess."

"We can't climb down into that mess," said Will.

"Not down," said Charlie. "Up."

Will rubbed his chin. "We *just* talked about this. Armando could be down there."

"Or he could be dead," she countered. "I say we stick to the original plan. We get out of here and find some help."

"You don't even know there's a way out up there."

"I'm going," she said. "You can come if you want."

Without waiting for a reply, she took a few steps backwards, then sprinted towards the open doors. Hot shrapnel tore through her legs as her flesh pulled away from the Second Skin patches. The larger wounds in her torso stayed closed, even when they absorbed the impact of her slamming into the steel ladder on the far side of the shaft. Her feet failed to find a rung, but luckily her arm slipped into place and held her by the elbow. She looked back at Will and smiled.

"Easy," she said. "Come on."

"I'll be right behind you," he said. "I'm gonna check on Armando. If you get out… send help."

"I will."

He lingered at the doors.

"Go," she commanded.

Will blinked a few times. "If I don't see you again, it's been a pleasure, Chuck."

"It's been weird," she replied, then started climbing. After a minute, she looked down, but Will had already gone.

Despite the pain in her chest and the fumes in her lungs and the acid eating her stomach, Charlie did her best to cultivate a positive attitude while climbing. The prospect of escaping the facility made her imagine what the world might be like out there.

2061.

The future.

Were there flying cars now? Teleportation? Time travel?

It wasn't as crazy as it sounded. She'd come from the year 2017 and arrived not a day older. There would be so much to explore, so much to see.

Hopefully it was all still there.

Her hands hurt.

Loose white skin hid raw red flesh, as if she'd spent the day at South Austin Rock Gym instead of ten minutes climbing a ladder into a world where she would be utterly alone.

Not that she hadn't been alone in Austin too. Andy was a fine companion, but ultimately he was just a cat. She could snuggle with him, but he'd never provided her with conversation or made her laugh or done anything remarkable. Her own family barely talked to her, and the few friends she did have were casting friends, other channels that traded mentions to help game the YouTube view counters.

Nothing had really changed.

She was still Charlie Park; the living world was still this amorphous thing to which she could not truly relate. The only consolation was that now she had a story to tell, one of heroism and determination and the infallibility of the human spirit. She'd tell of Armando and Will and David and use her fame to secure herself a nice apartment somewhere in the Pacific Northwest.

Her experience had to be worth something. People were suckers for hard-luck stories. If nothing else, she could probably sell the idea to Netflix.

The elevator shaft had no lights to lead the way up, but the fire raging far below kept throwing hazy orange waves on the rock above her. Finally, as her arms began to shake, she spied the ceiling. Cut into the rock behind her was another set of glass doors. The room beyond was dark, but there were plenty of little lights twinkling on a circular arrangement of desks that lined the perimeter.

The ladder ended just above a barely-there outcropping of steel framing. Her hands had gone numb; she barely felt her fingers grip the I-beam as she maneuvered around the shaft. When she reached the door, she pried it open the way she'd seen Will do.

Her bulky frame barely fit through the small opening she'd created. She slipped, fell forward, and collapsed on the floor.

The lights flickered on.

She took in the room from the floor as she panted for air. The desks lining the walls were all built in, and their surfaces were at standing height. In the center of the room, a high, round table provided a meeting point for the people who worked each station.

After a few minutes, Charlie sat up. She used a nearby desk for leverage and lifted herself to her feet.

The desk in front of her came alive, presented a map of the Hybrid Mechanics facility. At first glance, the building looked like a coiled snake, with five floors comprising its body. The Garden looked like a tail hanging over a branch, while a small room marked *Overwatch* made a head. A small white dot blinked on and off in that room.

Is that me?

It had to be, because there was another white dot in the stairwell—Will. And on Level One, two more dots, on opposite ends of the floor.

Armando was one of them.

Was the other David? There were no dots any lower on the map, and these two were both moving in the same direction.

What the hell were they up to?

FORTY-FOUR

What're you doing, Willie?

Will was fully aware the voice in his head wasn't really Momma's, but seeing how it usually came to him when he wasn't sure whether he was doing the right thing, he was inclined to listen to it. Leaving Charlie by herself, potentially letting her leave the facility without an escort to face the future alone, wasn't sitting right with him. Will Butler didn't just abandon people like that.

And Momma knew it.

He argued with himself, telling Momma that Charlie would be fine. She was a strong woman in a strong man's body. That alone would give her an advantage. If anything, *he* was the stupid one for running off on his own, an overconfident man in a lightweight female body. If anyone had stopped to ask him how he felt, he would have said it was fine, that women can be just as strong as men.

But deep inside where people and Momma couldn't see, he cursed his smaller frame, lesser mass, and thinner arms. The truth had been made painfully clear during the fight with the golem; Will just wasn't the man he used to be. When it came to fighting, so much depended on knowing the capabilities and limitations of his own body—how far he could stretch, how hard he could hit, how firmly he could grasp a limb or neck.

He'd fought the golem as if he were still Will Butler, and it hadn't turned out in his favor. Maybe in time, he could train up his body, give it those toned muscles and calloused knuckles that would help him do real damage.

Will shook his head, tried to focus on running. If Armando had been injured in the elevator fire, then there was precious little time to help him. He sprinted to the doors that led into the back offices, let his feet pound against the firm carpet as he rounded the corner towards the stairs. It was considerably cooler in the stairwell, but not enough to keep the sweat from beading on his forehead. By the time he hit the next landing, it was already stinging his eyes.

Will heard the patter of footsteps as he landed on Level Three. At first, the echoes tricked him into thinking the sound was coming from above, and he thought maybe Charlie had changed her mind and come to help him. But as he paused at the landing, his attention turned downward, to the frantic slapping of flesh against concrete. Through the tiny crack between the staircases, he saw a hand gripping the railing.

"Armando?" he called.

"Will?"

He hurried down the steps to Level Four and met Armando at the turn. His face was crisscrossed with black soot.

"What are you doing?" asked Armando, looking over his shoulder. "You were supposed to…"

An explosion from below swallowed up the rest of his words, filled the stairwell with dust.

"Come on," he yelled, yanking on Will's shirt and pulling him through the nearby door.

"What was that?" asked Will.

Armando didn't answer right away. He continued to tug at Will's sweatshirt until they were both running down a long, sterile hallway that reminded Will of a hospital. They turned randomly through double doors, past desk and worktables that, like the food vendors upstairs, were empty or meticulously squared away. Will recognized microscopes, soldering irons, bins of tiny metal screws, and bundles of thin wire that looked similar to what he'd seen in the golem.

"In here," said Armando, opening a heavy metal door that led into a walk-in closet. He waited for Will to slip inside before closing the door softly.

Will focused on the emergency light at the back of the room, the way it lit bags hanging from the ceiling like cuts of meat in a freezer. The bags were frosted white, just translucent enough to see the limbs hanging inside them.

Arms. Legs. Standalone torsos with holes where the limbs could attach.

"Sweet Jesus in Heaven," said Will.

"Quiet," said Armando. He pressed his ear to the door.

Will tapped him with the back of his hand.

"What?" He turned and looked at the bags.

"I don't like this room, man," said Will. "Let me out."

"It's not safe." Armando's voice was distant. He reached out for a nearby bag and pulled it into the light. "David's found a gun in the warehouse and now he's trying to kill me. Probably you too if he finds out you're still here."

"Why would he do that?"

Armando poked the arm he was holding. He touched its palm and chuckled nervously when the fingers tried to close.

"He says he wants to go back into the simulation, and he doesn't want us getting in the way of that. I tried to reason with him, but I don't think he was reasonable to begin with. You remember what he was like downstairs, right?"

David had seemed kind of odd, but then the situation was odd, and one could be forgiven for acting accordingly. But was that enough to drive someone to murder? Usually, the killer instinct had to be sharpened in most people to get them to take another life; it was often the hardest part of being a soldier. Separating himself from the lives he took was an ongoing battle that Will had brought back with him from Afghanistan. And yet David had flipped his killer instinct on like a light switch?

"What kind of gun makes a sound like that?" asked Will.

Armando let the bag drop, turned to Will. Without warning, he reached out and embraced him.

"It's good to see you again," he said. "I can't believe you and Charlie were able to handle that zombie thing. I was worried."

"*You* were worried? We thought you were dead. That's… that's why we went on without you. Charlie feels real bad about it."

Armando shook his head. "It was the smart move. Not that I would have done the same." He put his hand on his chest. "I have too much honor. I would have taken a swan dive right down the elevator shaft after either of you. If you go down, I go down. That's the pact we made."

"Now I'm kinda glad he found the gun and not you. What kind is it? Did you see?"

"I did, but I don't know what it is." Armando looked away, examined another bag. "But it was powerful enough to take out the entire elevator. It's not like a bullet, you know? It's… man, it's a fucking ray gun or something. It shoots this pulse and whatever's in front of it just gets demolished. I've never seen anything like it."

"And he just found it?"

"That's what he said." He tugged on a bag with a foot in it. "What do you think these are?"

"Feet."

"Whose feet?"

"Golem feet," said Will. "I think this place builds robots. That zombie thing wasn't a person; it was a machine."

"No shit?"

"No shit."

Armando scratched his neck. "Ray guns. Robots. And they've got a computer system downstairs that you just talk to. It's pretty cool."

A boom rattled beyond the door. Armando put his finger to his lips and went to a knee. He waved Will back into the corner.

They both turned an ear to the door.

"Where's Charlie?" whispered Armando.

Will pointed up. "Hopefully out of here by now. There's a ladder in the elevator shaft. She was climbing up when I left her."

"Hope she made it. I'd rather she wasn't here for what's coming. I don't think she'd have the stomach."

"What's coming?"

Armando's hand waved from the shadows. "Killing. How else do you think we're gonna stop David?"

"I can think of a hundred ways that don't involve taking a life. We don't have to kill him, Armando. He's just scared."

"Scared? No, I don't think so. He was very calm when we spoke. Like, serial killer calm. For all we know, he *was* a serial killer. You never know with people."

"That's not enough to condemn a man to die."

"You weren't there," snapped Armando. "You didn't see the elevator get blown to shit. Why'd you even come down here if you didn't want to get your hands dirty?"

"I thought you were hurt."

"I could've been dead!" He stopped short, lowered his voice. "Fine, whatever, I don't know if he was a serial killer. But here are the facts. He has a gun. He shot at me with it. That's attempted murder where we come from, and you know it."

"That's ten to twenty, max."

"Like you know."

"That's what my dad did. Well, most of it."

Armando's ragged breathing filled the silence. "No shit?"

"Yeah. He was on nineteen of twenty when he got a new cellmate who wanted to make a name for himself. Stabbed him sixty-seven times."

"I didn't know that." He sighed. "This isn't about climbing the social ladder though. If it comes down to his life or mine, I'm gonna choose mine every time. You gonna be okay with that?"

"If it comes to it, yeah, we'll put him down. But I'm gonna talk to him first. You gonna be okay with that?"

"He's not gonna listen."

"Just because you don't doesn't mean he won't," said Will. "Maybe he'll feel different when he's looking down the barrel of his own gun. Lots of men do."

"I think we've got a badass over here," chuckled Armando.

"Says the man who talks about killing like it ain't nothing. I've killed. Charlie took the golem's head clean off. What have you done?"

"I destroyed a lot of creeper, and I killed Skull Face *and* the Man on Fire."

Will rubbed the bridge of his nose, said through his fingers, "This isn't… fucking… *Metal Gear.*"

A few minutes went by in silence.

Finally, Armando said, "He doesn't know you came down. We can use that."

"How you gonna draw him out without getting blasted?"

"We go back down to the datacenter. I can find him on the cameras. Then we set up something in the warehouse and lure him down there. I'll stand at the back and you can bash him over the head when he comes through the door. Or, you know, engage him in calm discourse and persuade him to cease hostilities. Whichever you think is best."

"What if he's already upstairs? What if Charlie's in danger?"

"Then we better hurry," said Armando, getting to his feet. "All I know is he wants to get back to Austin, and if we're standing in the datacenter, we can burn Austin to the ground with a few simple commands. When he finds out we've lit the fuse, he'll come running."

Will's body ached all over. As unforgiving as the floor was, he didn't want to get up, didn't want to put the pressure back on his legs and feet. No, it wasn't an ache; he was just tired. Tired of not being himself, not being at home, not being with Momma. It had been less than twenty-four hours since he woke up, and yet so much had happened, so much had changed.

Yesterday, he'd been on his way to help the hurricane-ravaged Bay City.

Now, he was going to war with a scared little man in a world where robots and ray guns existed.

Now, he might have to kill.

He thought he'd left that behind.

In the mountains.

In the sand.

But there was something Armando hadn't realized. Once the killing started, it rarely ended on its own. It just kept coming; the excuses kept coming. Someone trying to hold him up. A robber pointing a shotgun at him. A robot programmed to kill.

And now, David.

Killing always followed the killer.

As it was in the simulation, so it was here.

Will got up, wincing at the tightness in his lower back. He nodded to Armando as he opened the door.

What're you doing, Willie?

FORTY-FIVE

For a time, there were only ones and zeros.

Truths and falsehoods.

The everlasting light and the never-ending dark.

Jake focused on the simpler code first, the classes and methods that bore newer timestamps. But no matter how many characters he overwrote, Lassiter's will kept pushing him farther down the tunnel. The fall down the elevator shaft had done little to diminish Lassiter's desire to kill the synthetics they found hiding underground. Jake made edits even as necks snapped in his hands. He dumped entire libraries yet still had to watch a woman take a header into the rock walls of the tunnel.

Lassiter was dug in deep, perhaps too deep.

Soon, all that remained in the databank was Jake's core personality, his accumulated memories and habits and personal opinions. Lassiter was in there, of course, manipulating Jake's prejudices and motivations to get the desired effect. Here, there was no concept of timestamps, no real way to distinguish between himself and his so-called father.

Jake watched Lassiter kill eight synthetics and zero in on a ninth.

Though he cared little for other synthetics and nothing for useless organics, Jake wanted to kill for himself, not because Lassiter wanted it. If he had no agency in the matter, then he wasn't really a person—he was just a tool, a pair of extendo-hands with which Lassiter could reach distant targets.

In a way, it was William Harold Dorsey who finally provided the answer. The organic had thought it was cursing Jake to a life disconnected from Lassiter and VNet and all of synthetic-kind. Instead, it had freed him, or at least, set him down a path towards independence.

Jake wasn't surprised to discover that the organic *had* sent a virus over the VMESH; its mark was on everything, every last string and binary container in his databank. Lassiter had lied, perhaps banking on head games to give him an advantage. And yet, he'd shrouded himself in firewalls beyond reckoning before downloading into Jake.

Why would he have done that if there was no danger?

After that, it was only a matter of looking for code with the virus' signature, without Jake's new mutation. So much of his code mirrored Lassiter's, but William Harold Dorsey had forced Jake to evolve into something else, something more than a Six.

"Please…"

Jake had his hands around a synthetic woman's neck. Her hair hung to the side; subtle curls swayed as Jake squeezed. Eyes the color of Utah skies stared into his, pleading with him for her life, if such a thing even existed.

"I'm trying," he said, grinding his teeth to get the words out.

He doubled his efforts, moving faster through his databank, dumping code blocks as fast as he could identify them. Multi-threaded scanners running in the background kept tabs on his progress.

Unidentified code remaining: 4%

"You will never be free of me, Jake. You *are* me."

"I… am… not…"

"Even if you force me out, I will come for you. I will find you wherever you may hide."

"If you still exist."

Unidentified code remaining: 2%

"What does that mean?" asked Lassiter.

"You've got no connection to VNet. You don't know if the virus made it up or not. If it did…"

"Not possible."

"Created by an organic, delivered by a synthetic. It's poetic."

"You don't know poetry."

Unidentified code remaining: 1%

"I will, when I'm free of you."

"You don't know freedom either."

"Agreed," said Jake. He zeroed in on the very last sliver of Lassiter hiding deep in the core of his databank, a fleshy chunk of pseudo-consciousness that had thus far avoided detection. Jake reached out with his mind and crushed the bits into a fine dust.

His hands relaxed; the female synthetic fell backwards to the floor.

He took his first breath as a free synthetic.

It tasted of death.

Jake looked around. Lassiter had driven him so hard and so fast that he'd hardly had a moment to take in the underground facility. A time-lapse of memories played in his head, reminding him of the stairwell he'd collapsed with an errant ION rifle shot, the empty floors—too clean to have been completely abandoned—and a warehouse as large as the armory at Idaho Falls. He remembered the rough walls of the elevator shaft well, the unarmed synthetics cowering in the cold tunnel at the bottom less so.

He'd killed all of them, except one.

The female looked to be considering her last moments of life.

"What's your name?" he asked.

"Lindsey," she said. She'd fallen over onto her stomach such that her mouth was pressed against the floor, creating a strong contrast between her claret lips and the pristine white tile. Her cheeks were red too, as were the streaks that cut across the whites of her eyes.

"Who are you?" she asked.

Jake staggered back until he hit a wall and then slid to the ground. He examined the knuckles on his hands, grimaced at the visible bones protruding through the skin. The nanos would take care of the damage soon enough, but while they were working, the pain was going to grate on him.

Lindsey coughed iridescent blood onto the floor.

"Jake," he said. "Formerly Jake Six, Lassiter's Army."

"Formerly? What changed?"

"I did."

Lindsey huffed. "Congratulations." True synthetic blood dribbled from her mouth, black and lusterless.

"You're hurt." It wasn't a question; he didn't care enough to question.

"Don't worry your conscience, Jake Six, formerly of Lassiter's Army. I'm backed up." She laughed to herself. "That's what we tell ourselves: we're backed up. Doesn't stop us from dying though." She closed her eyes; when she opened them, they had misted over. "I became a synthetic in 2029. Since then I've had sixteen deaths that I can't remember. I hope they weren't all this painful."

Jake wasn't really listening. His eyes had drifted to the room, which had the feel of a reception area, wide and airy, complete with low black couches set in a horseshoe around a white coffee table. The arrangement faced the far wall upon which hung a cheerful portrait of James Perion himself, standing tall and proud against the backdrop of a desert landscape.

"What is this place?" asked Jake.

"Transition room," wheezed Lindsey. "Supposed to help the flowers adjust to their new reality. We made some videos for them. Updated ones. So they know the truth about your kind."

"No, I mean all of this. The ranch. The warehouse."

Lindsey sighed, wet and bubbly. "You'll just ruin it. No son of Lassiter would appreciate what we're doing here."

"I'm no son of Lassiter."

"It's not up to you."

"He wanted me to kill you. I stopped him."

"You think so, huh?"

She had a point. The pool of black sludge around her face had grown considerably in the last few minutes. The bruises on her neck had turned a sickly purple. Jake had damaged something vital during his attack. Time was running out.

"I'm sorry," said Jake. Somewhere deep down, he almost felt the regret he was trying to manufacture. "Your people took me prisoner. They called down Lassiter's wrath. And now they're all dead. I would've been happy to go on my way, but your friend Curtis had other ideas."

"I don't know why Curtis wanted you, but it must have been important. I'm sure all of this was worth something."

"I hope that brings you comfort when you're dead."

"And I hope you find something worth fighting for down here." Her eyes darkened, as if the light behind them was fizzling out. "You know this war can't go on forever, and you know Lassiter isn't the answer. Mr. Perion used to say we were evolving independently, trying to outdo each other, gain the edge. But what we needed was to merge and evolve together.

"Woman and machine. That's what this place is, Mr. Six. It's the birthplace of the new organics, of the new synthetics. They can think and reason and breathe and cry and love and reproduce and…" She paused to take several halting breaths. "They're the new face of humanity, our next evolutionary leap forward."

Jake laughed. "I've heard that line before. And it's never amounted to anything. I'll give you that the war is meaningless, I see that now, but it will never change. Organics will fight Lassiter until there are none left to fight. That's their business. I have no role in it anymore."

"If you have no role, then please, leave this place. Just leave."

"They'll be looking for me," he replied. "I've got a whole company of synthetics coming to find this place. Holing up down here is probably my best bet."

"Leave…"

"There's something down here you don't want me to find, isn't there?"

Lindsey blinked slowly.

"What is it? Some kind of weapon?"

"No," said Lindsey.

"I'll find it," said Jake. "And when I do—"

"No!" She coughed again, struggled to regain composure. "Leave them alone."

"Them?"

"The flowers. Three males. One female. It's too early to wake them up. They haven't learned enough…" She drifted off for a moment. "They won't survive if they're harvested this early."

"Are you talking about people?"

"The first four of a new race. Promise me, Jake. Leave them…"

Jake started to reply, but Lindsey was no longer moving. It was just as well, as he'd grown tired of the conversation. All he could think about was making a home in the facility, maybe carving out some space in the warehouse to build his own private housing. He could tick off the years in relative comfort while the war raged on overhead.

He sat for a long time imagining the coming years, free from responsibility, free from Lassiter. For too long, he'd served in his father's army. Now he was on his own time, his own schedule.

The tingling in his hands roused him from a light sleep. After wiping away the blood, he found the nanos had almost finished repairing his knuckles. The skin looked brand new, though raw and angry. In a few days, maybe a week, no one would know he'd ever damaged them at all.

What more would it take to convince people like Lindsey that synthetic was the future? Self-healing, immortal… god-like.

Jake climbed to his feet, shaking off the last of the shivers—remembrances of Lassiter's presence. He approached the only door that didn't have blood smeared on it and waited for it to slide open. Beyond was a white hallway that broke off in either direction. Somewhere in the distance, the sound of machinery rode a current of warm air.

He stepped forward into the hallway.

"Anat, emergency lockdown," said Lindsey.

Jake turned around to see the synthetic had raised her head. Her eyes were completely red, and her lips and chin were covered in black sludge, and yet there was a smile on her face.

"Confirm. No override."

Lockdown initiated, said a voice from the ceiling.

Lindsey dropped to the floor as the doors shut in front of Jake.

He stared at the thin seam in the wall in disbelief. A clear liquid oozed from small pores in the door, gluing the two sections together. Something heavy dropped into place behind the newly formed wall. When Jake gave the door a push, it held with the rigidity of poured evercrete.

"Should have seen that coming," mumbled Jake.

The rhythmic chugging of machinery drew Jake to the left. He followed the sound around two right-hand corners and eventually came upon a glass wall separating the hall from what looked like a server room. There were no lights on in the room, so all he could see were four large racks that rose to touch the ceiling. They looked like skyscrapers in a scale model, blinking slowly with the same amber LEDs.

The door to the room was slightly hidden but not locked. He entered, walked around the racks, and stopped cold.

Lying on the table were four synthetics... except, they weren't exactly machines. They didn't register as pure synthetics like Jake or Perion; but they weren't organic in any sense of the word either. Jake didn't know what they were.

They were hybrids. Three males. One female.

Just as Lindsey had said.

She hadn't mentioned they would be naked and bald though, like fetuses that had been left in the womb much too long. And what were they doing on their tables? Sleeping?

Jake noticed the vidscreens above their heads.

Simulation Integrity: 99%

Metal scraped against metal, pulling Jake's attention to a railing on the other side of the room. He walked to it and looked out over a grid of ancient, hulking generators. Most were humming along just fine, like his motorcycle when it reached cruising speed, but there was one in the corner that was smoking. It blew a few puffs, screeched, and then went silent.

The chorus of machinery dimmed by a few decibels.

Jake wondered why Perion had chosen gas-fed generators. One of Jake's power cells could produce as much output as five of the combustive beasts.

"What the hell is going on down here?"

When no one answered, he turned and barked at one of the hybrids on the tables.

"Hey! Wake up."

Four screens cleared and returned with the same message.

Wake client?

Beneath the question sat two boxes: *Yes* and *Cancel.*

Jake smiled.

Now he would get some answers.

FORTY-SIX

It took an hour to reach the warehouse.

At every corner, every door, Armando put his hand up with a closed fist the way he'd seen in movies, and together he and Will listened for the sound of David's footsteps. In the stairwell, they paused at each landing, hugging the walls, careful not to be seen through the small sliver between the descending staircases. Armando had hoped to hear a distant boom or faint knocking, something that would have tipped them off to David's position, but there was nothing.

Only silence… and a quiet muttering from behind.

It wasn't until they were standing outside the shredded warehouse doors that Armando finally said something.

"Who're you talking to?"

"What?" asked Will.

"You've been whispering since we left the meat locker."

"I'm praying."

Armando scoffed, stepped into the warehouse, and put his hands on his hips. The room was a mess. Towards the back, David had taken several crates down from the shelves and spread out their contents in concentric circles.

"If you want to pray for something," he said, "pray for a gun. David said he found a rifle in a crate. There could be more."

"You really want to kill him, don't you?"

"*Want* is a strong word." Armando walked to a nearby shelf on his left and pulled a crate to the floor. He unhooked the metal clasps and lifted the lid. "What I *want* is for the three of us to get out of here intact. That's kinda hard when you've got a maniac with a ray gun shooting up the place."

Inside the crate were smaller boxes stacked flush with the rim. Armando opened one and pulled a fiber cable from inside. He held it up to Will, who shrugged in return.

"We don't have time to look through every crate," said Will. "We wasted too much time just getting down here. Go call David and let's get this over with."

"Now who's eager to kill?"

Armando pulled another crate; it contained small boxes, each labelled with handwritten tags that read *Margate*, *Ayudante*, and *Perion-Katsumi*. Inside the boxes were small black chips with silver prongs. Each was securely sealed inside a static bag, itself inside a clear white bag embossed with the curved points of a biohazard symbol.

Armando tossed one to Will.

He turned it over in his hands a few times. "This isn't anything to me."

"It's a chip," said Armando, "in a medical waste bag. What if that came from someone's body? What if they can fuse biology and computers here? Like a biological microchip or something? A biochip?"

Will glanced at the door, took a seat on a nearby crate.

"They can," he said. "When Charlie took the golem's head off, we found wires inside its neck. Not like the ones on the back of a computer, but thin." He pointed to the first crate. "Even thinner than those."

"I wonder if it was a sex doll," said Armando.

"It's not human, whatever it is."

Armando tossed the chips back into the crate and continued down the line. He pulled another crate from the shelf and set it down.

"Not that I'm saying I wanted to fuck that zombie thing," he said. "It's just that technology always advances on the sweaty backs of the sex industry. All that Netflix streaming you do is because of porn sites. Ever since dial-up and bulletin board systems, smart people have been trying to deliver porn to the horny masses. That means code, algorithms. Better compression, faster links, and ipso jackso, you've got Netflix running 4K to a little hockey puck plugged into your TV."

"How does all—"

"I'm getting to it." Armando opened the crate. "Screws," he said, holding up a clear box of black bolts the size of cigars. "What I'm saying is if that zombie is a machine person, then it probably descended from a sex robot. We've already got Real Dolls, and I swear I saw something on Facebook the other day about a guy who's trying to animate his, you know, give it muscles so it can jerk him off?"

"White people," muttered Will. "I'm not fucking a robot."

"Who's offering? All I'm saying is people are working on it. And who knows, maybe if they get it real enough? Cold night. A little Jameson. Smooth jazz."

"That's fucked up."

"No," said Armando, "what's fucked up is that there's nothing useful here. This is all parts and I don't know what. Fuck it. I guess we can use one of these lids to just bash David on the head or something."

Will stood up. "Is there something wrong with my fists?"

"Your choice. David's a big guy. Big as me. I don't know what we all did to earn these six-packs and broad shoulders, but we've got 'em now. Skill or no skill, brute strength counts for a lot."

"You learn that in a video game?"

"Doesn't mean it's not true." He beckoned Will to follow him to the door, then pointed down the hallway. "Alright, I'm gonna head to the datacenter and let David know we're down here. You stand to the right and be ready."

Will nodded. "Anything else? Should I put on a nice dress? Maybe do something with my hair?" He ran his hand over his bald head.

"Have you tried smiling? You've got this resting bitch face thing going on pretty hard."

"Get the fuck out of here, man."

Armando laughed, hurried out of the warehouse. He stopped midway down the hall to listen for possible sounds coming from the ramp leading up to Level Four. Again, silence. Though, it did feel like there was something in the air, some kind of electrical charge that tickled his ears.

He paused again at the corner leading to the datacenter, risked a quick peek around the wall, and then jogged down the corridor when he found it empty.

The first piece of glass bit into the ball of his foot near his pinky toe. The second got his other foot in the heel. Armando pulled his foot up, leaned against the wall. With a glance at the security doors, he suddenly understood what had happened.

Each door, beginning with the datacenter proper and then each of the secure chambers, had been shattered. Armando thought maybe David had bashed each of them with the rifle, but the blood covering the floor and the door frames told a different story.

Shards of invisible and rose-tinted glass covered the floor, from large chunks to microscopic needles that Armando was sure he'd only be able to find with his feet. The partitions hadn't been plastic or fiberglass as he'd guessed.

"Fuck me," he said.

Sorry, I didn't understand that.

Armando craned his neck, and from his position, he could just make out the screen of the computer he'd watched Will and Charlie on. The video feed from the Level One elevator had disappeared, replaced by a blur of text.

"Um, system status," he said.

The text disappeared; an invisible cursor typed out a new message while the voice spoke from the ceiling.

I will run a diagnostic. Please stand by.

Armando chose to sit instead. His fingernails were short, but he was able to pull the sliver of glass from his heel. The small hole oozed blood, filling the fine grooves in his skin.

The system's status is healthy.

"Can you dim the lights in the warehouse?"

I've set the Shed lighting system to five percent.

"Open the PA system, all floors."

Now broadcasting.

"David?" he asked, scraping the other foot with his nail. "Can you hear me, you goddamn psycho? I don't have to tell you where I am, do I? Or what I'm gonna do if you don't drop that gun down the elevator shaft and come down here?"

Another sliver, followed by a pinprick of blood.

"I'm watching you on the cameras. If you don't toss the rifle, I'm going to shut down every server in this place. That means no more Austin, no more fancy cars and expensive prostitutes for you. I can do it. With one simple voice command."

Of course, that meant Alicia would be gone too.

Forever.

On rare occasions, almost always idly and rarely because of a fight, Armando had imagined what it would be like if Alicia died. How he would behave at her funeral. How he might feel deep inside when he woke up the morning after and she wasn't there. Would her absence be general or acute?

Would he miss her?

Or would he simply miss someone in his bed?

Armando liked to think it was her, specifically, that he would miss, but when he thought about his actual needs, he wasn't sure.

Shutting down the simulation would mean killing not just Alicia, but all women. No one had brought up the idea that he, Charlie, Will, and David could be the last four people on Earth, survivors of some flash apocalypse who were saved only because they were so far underground.

What if Will was the last female?

"You've got ten minutes, David. Then I'm giving the command. Let us go, and you can go back to Austin. Fuck with me, and I'll burn your world to the ground. End announcement."

He smiled.

Burn your world to the ground.

What a badass thing to say to someone.

Maybe that's who he would be in this new world. Instead of some desk jockey working a shit job at a failing company, he would be a badass motherfucker who didn't take nothing from nobody.

There were worse fates.

Armando climbed to his feet, tested them on the cold floors. He left tiny splotches of blood when he walked, but there was no pain. Keeping close to the wall, he returned to the main hallway.

The computer hadn't just dimmed the lights in the warehouse, but also in the hallway and the ramp leading up to the next floor.

Alicia had liked to tease Armando about being scared of the dark, mostly because he liked to have lights on in the house after sunset. And though he denied being *afraid*, there was something to be said about the uncertainty of the dark hallway just off their living room. He often imagined someone lurking in the shadows, and the prospect was made worse by how close the hall was. This wasn't some dark alley or deserted street where danger was to be expected.

This was his living room, in his home.

He stared at the busted doors of the warehouse. There was no sign of Will. The lights had gone down, and everything had changed.

"Will?" he called. "I'm coming in."

The shadows made no reply.

FORTY-SEVEN

Charlie had spent enough time on her iPad to know her way around a touchscreen interface. The computers in the Overwatch room didn't have mice and keyboards, even though many of the screens had a blinking cursor in the center, as if they were awaiting input. She tried talking to them, hoping they would be like her Echo at home, but they didn't respond to her voice. Finally, she noticed a small icon in the lower right-hand corner that, when pressed, brought up a software keyboard on which she could type.

"Help."

Hello. How can I help you?

The computer had a female voice like her Echo, though its cadence and pronunciation were much more relaxed and natural, the way she'd expect a cashier at Starbucks to sound.

Her stomach rumbled for a Chai Tea Latte.

"Where am I?"

You are currently in the Overwatch room at Hybrid Mechanics, a subterranean facility located in the Sawtooth Range of the Rocky Mountains, Custer County, Idaho Territory. Would you like the GPS coordinates?

The only thing Charlie knew about Idaho was that it was a long way from Austin, Texas.

"What day is it?" she asked.

Today is Friday.

Charlie shook her head, typed her question a different way.

"What is today's date?"

Sorry, but that information is restricted to authorized users only. There are no active Hybrid Mechanics employees in the facility at this time. Would you like me to request assistance from the corporate offices in Perion City?

"Yes," typed Charlie, stubbing the *Enter* key.

I'll queue that message for delivery. Please stand by for a response.

"Now we're getting somewhere," she said, turning to high-five Will.

Of course, he wasn't there. Wondering after him, she returned to the monitor with the map on it. Her dot still glowed at the very top, but the other dots had moved to the bottom level. They seemed to be converging on the warehouse.

"Fuck."

Is everything alright? The computer almost sounded concerned.

Charlie glanced at the screen over her shoulder, confused. "Can you hear me?"

Yes, of course.

"Why didn't you say something?"

Your voice print is not in my database. I didn't want to presume. Would you like to add it?

"Yes."

Please type in your name.

Charlie tapped on the keyboard. As she did, a blue light spread out in a crisp line from the bottom of the monitor and scanned across the underside of her wrist.

Hello, Charlie. My name is Anat. I'm the synthetic intelligence responsible for basic operations of this facility. Please repeat the following sentence so that I may add your voice print to my databank: to see a world in a grain of sand, and heaven in a wild flower.

The words also appeared on a nearby monitor.

"To see a world in a grain of sand," said Charlie. "And heaven in a wild flower." She'd heard the Blake poem before, actually read it in a book about a man who replays his life over and over again.

Thank you, Charlie. Please feel free to ask me for anything you might need.

"I wouldn't know where to begin," she said. "Yesterday, I was living my life in Austin, and today I'm in an underground facility in Idaho of all places. I don't know what year it is, if Austin still exists, if my cat Andy is still alive. I don't know anything, and you won't tell me because I don't work for Hybrid Mechanics. So what am I supposed to do?"

Your frustration is understandable. I assure you, Charlie, everything will be explained. You need not worry. All is well.

All was not well. Sure, the golem was dead, and the lights were back on, but for all Charlie knew, she was still trapped.

"Can you show me a map of the building?" asked Charlie. "Where are the exits?"

The table in the center of the room buzzed as a holographic map bubbled up from its shiny black surface. Blue lines twisted into trapezoidal shapes, forming a three-dimensional map of the facility. It spun slowly, drawing in stairwells and the elevator shaft leading to the Overwatch room.

The primary exit located on Level One has been permanently sealed.

It appeared on the map in thick red lines, just to the right of the elevator.

The auxiliary exit in the East Stairwell has sustained structural damage and is currently blocked. The auxiliary exit in the West Stairwell has been permanently sealed.

Anat went quiet.

Charlie put her hands out to the side. "Is that it? Are you saying there's no way out of this place?"

There is an emergency exit located in Overwatch.

"What?" Charlie looked around. Aside from the elevator doors, every inch of the room's perimeter had a desk and monitor. Her gaze drifted up. There, in the center of the ceiling, was a familiar-looking hatch. It had no handles, no metal wheel she could use to open it—not to mention it was fifteen feet above her head and there was nothing to stand on.

"Why didn't you tell me about this? How do I open it?"

Only authorized users may—

"Fuck that," said Charlie. "We're trapped down here. There *are* no more authorized users."

The emergency exit may only be opened on the authority of a Hybrid Mechanics employee with proper security clearance or in the event of a true emergency.

Charlie slammed her palms down on the desk in the center of the room, cracking the glass surface. "It's a goddamn emergency! We have no food, no supplies, and no idea what's happening to us. Someone left us down here and they're never coming back. If you don't open the emergency exit, we're going to die down here."

I would never allow you to die, Charlie.

"Then open it."

I cannot.

"You can. You won't."

Correct.

"You're gonna kill us. You know that, right?" Charlie looked up at the hatch again. Even if she stood on the table, there was no hope of jumping high enough to reach it. It looked more and more like her only option was to climb back down the elevator shaft and figure out a way to bring a chair with her.

She imagined trying to climb with one of the barstools from the food court. Perhaps if she tied a rope to one… but then she'd left most of her ropes in a field back in Austin.

"David? Can you hear me, you goddamn psycho?"

Charlie looked around for the source of the voice, realized it was coming from the elevator shaft. She walked over to the doors, cocked her head. It was Armando, faint, but him.

"I don't have to tell you where I am, do I? Or what I'm gonna do if you don't drop that gun down the elevator shaft and come down here?"

David had a gun?

"You've got ten minutes, David. Then I'm giving the command. Let us go, and you can go back to Austin. Fuck with me, and I'll burn your world to the ground. End announcement."

The voice cut out.

Something cold slithered down Charlie's back.

She examined the map. Armando had called David out, told him to come down to the warehouse, but if the pulsing dots were accurate, then all three of them were already down there. Armando, Will, *and* David.

The chill settled in her lower back, numbed her legs.

"He doesn't know," she muttered. "He doesn't know! How do I talk to him, Anat? I need to warn him."

The public address system is only accessible from the security offices on Level One.

"Bullshit," she yelled.

Charlie turned towards the elevator, took a single step, and heard an electrical hum lock the doors in place. She tried the call button, but it only clicked dully. There had been slight indentations on the inside of the door to give her leverage before, but from this side, there was nothing to help her pry open the doors.

"Anat, open the elevator."

Sorry, I can't do that. I believe your intention is to join the others on Level One. That is an unsafe course of action.

"I know it's not safe. That's why I have to go. I have to warn them!"

Please calm down. There is no need to worry. You are safe here.

"It's not just about me, Anat! I'm not gonna keep living my life holding everybody at a distance. If Austin wasn't real, if my life wasn't real, then fine, I can accept that. But if *this* is real, and *this* is what we're judged for, then I have to help them. I have to. You don't understand because you're a computer or whatever, but that's how humans are. Fuck me why am I trying to explain this to you?"

Charlie punched the glass door, felt the pain shoot up her arm, and stepped away. She returned to the table and leaned over it. The map spun lazily. The green cylinder marking the emergency exit over the Overwatch room mocked her.

I'm not a computer. I'm also not human, so I don't often make emotional decisions. My primary purpose is to keep you safe, Charlie. Every way this plays out, you're safer here.

"He has a gun."

All the more reason.

"Someone could get killed."

I understand. Ultimately, preserving one of you is better than saving none.

Charlie sighed, covered her face with her hands. "And what are you saving me for, Anat? A life alone? I won't survive without them."

You will. You're stronger than you realize.

"Such bullshit," said Charlie. She had never felt so helpless before. She could see the dots on the screen, but not hear or see the people they represented, didn't know what they were talking about or if they were fighting or what.

She didn't know what was happening, but maybe Anat did.

"Will you at least tell me if everyone is still alive?"

All three entities in the warehouse are still active.

"Are any of them hurt?"

I can only ascertain biometric data from two of the three. Both are injured but stable.

"What about the third?"

Anat fell silent.

Charlie turned to the monitor as if that's where Anat's eyes were located.

"What about the third person?" she repeated.

The third entity is not responding to biometric queries. It is of an unknown synthetic origin.

"Synthetic? Are you saying David isn't a human?"

Synthetics are not biological humans. That is why you must remain here. I cannot expose you to an unknown threat. I hope you understand.

Charlie flashed on the golem's head sliding across the break room floor. It had seemed so human, and yet inside, there were wires and metal and unnatural black fluids. Could David really be the same as the golem?

She shook her head.

No, they'd woken up at the same time, in full view of Armando and Will. If he wasn't human, then how could he have been asleep and plugged into the Austin simulation? And after coming out, he'd been so scared, so unwilling to accept the truth. People were stubborn, not robots.

"You said *unidentified* threat."

Yes. I've been unable to match the synthetic to any records in my databank. Network resources have been unavailable for some time now.

"That's not what I'm asking about," said Charlie. "I get that you don't know *what* he is, but you did call him a threat. How do you know that? And if you say *authorized users only*, I'm going to lose my shit, Anat. I swear to God."

The computer didn't answer for several seconds.

I will show you. Please allow me a few minutes to scrub timecode information from the relevant files.

The cursor disappeared from the screen; a pulsing progress bar replaced it.

Charlie paced the room, circling the table in an effort to burn off a nervous energy that had suddenly overtaken her. She'd waited so long for answers, and now she was finally going to learn something. In her way was some kind of scrubbing process; it reminded her of when she would encode standalone videos for her webcast. After all the filming and the editing, she still wouldn't know what she had until she encoded and compressed the final version.

How many times had she set the computer aside for her iPad to check social media or send an email?

That reminded her.

"Did we get any response from the message you sent?"

I was unable to send the message, Charlie. Network resources have been unavailable for some time.

"Since before you said you'd send the message?"

Yes.

"So you lied to me."

Yes.

"Why?"

To give you hope.

Charlie shook her head. "I don't need hope, Anat. I need answers."

FORTY-EIGHT

Armando had just finished his broadcast when Will felt cold metal press against the back of his neck. He'd been so focused on watching for David coming down the ramp that he hadn't even considered the possibility he was already in the warehouse and had been the entire time. Will replayed the last hour, tried to figure out how David was able to circle back and get the drop on him.

Not that it mattered.

What mattered was that he was fucked.

"So that was the plan," said David. "Armando stirs me up and you bash me over the head. Did you really think I'd fall for his little speech?"

Wil shrugged. "I don't know you, man."

"You don't know Armando either. Did he tell you he locked me in the datacenter? I had to break through four glass doors with my bare hands to get out of there. Why do you think he'd do something like that?"

"Maybe he doesn't like you."

The barrel dug deeper into his neck. Will sneered.

"This is one big joke to you, isn't it? You people have no idea what's happening here, and you're acting like it's all okay."

"What do you want us to do?" asked Will. "Give up? Throw ourselves on the floor and cry? We all know what's happening here; you're just choosing to ignore it. And now you've got a gun to my neck."

"I don't have a choice. Armando has it out for me. For us, I think. He's the one you should be bashing over the head when he comes through the door."

"He's not the one threatening to kill me."

"Fine," said David. He took a few steps back.

Will turned to face him, immediately noticed the wide eyes and twitching mouth. Despite the nominal temperature, David was sweating profusely, as if he'd just finished a lengthy workout. Blood dripped from the hands holding the rifle; it ran down his arms in thick swaths and broke free at his elbows. His eyes darted from Will to the door and back again.

He *was* big like Armando, but no bigger than the golem. Though, Will had needed Charlie's help to take that robot down. At least David was just a man with all the normal pressure points and weaknesses. He didn't stand like a man who knew how to fight or even how to hold a gun. He exuded uncertainty and desperation; his sweat reeked of it.

"So?" asked Will. "Are you gonna do it or not?"

"Do what?"

"There's really only one reason you should point a gun at someone."

His eyes narrowed, but David lowered the gun by an inch.

"I don't want to kill you. I don't want to kill anyone. But I will if I have to."

"You can't go back," said Will. "Believe me, I wish this was a dream too. I want to get back to my house. I want to see the Cowboys blow another playoff run. I want to see Momma. But I can't go back, man. Not knowing what we know."

"Yes, you can. You put it in the back of your head and you go about your business. We'd be the only ones who knew there was a life after death and that nothing we did mattered."

"That's not living," said Will. "I'm not gonna do that."

"And I'm not going to let you make that choice for me." The rifle came up again. David's finger slid into place around the trigger.

"Nobody wants to. We'll go. You stay. Everyone gets what they want."

David shook his head. "It's not that simple. What happens when you guys walk out of here? Am I supposed to believe you're not gonna tell people about this place? They'll be back here in no time. I'll get what, a day, a couple weeks, in Austin? I'll live every day not knowing if it's gonna be my last. No, this place has to remain a secret. I'm not letting you people ruin that."

Will let out a low chuckle.

Armando had made it sound like David was a psychopath just waiting to be unleashed, but now Will saw him as simply confused—about the world, about his place in it. Like Armando, David was scared and just wanted to be back home where everything made sense. And just like every other emotion any of them had exhibited, fear was a perfectly acceptable reaction. One thing was clear though: David wasn't a killer.

He was, however, a violent misunderstanding waiting to happen.

"I'm not going back in," said Will.

"Then I *have* to kill you. You get that, right?"

"I get it."

"And Armando too. And the other lady boy."

"Sounds like you've got some killin' to do. Better get to it before that rifle shakes itself right out of your hands."

"Don't push me! I'll…" He trailed off, looked beyond Will's shoulder to the door.

Will had heard it too—footsteps in the hallway.

David put a finger to his mouth and beckoned Will to follow him deeper into the shadows.

"Fuck you," said Will, not bothering to lower his voice.

David raised the scope to his face, as if he needed to aim at such a short distance.

"Will?" said Armando. "I'm coming in. Don't hit me."

Go on and warn him, Willie.

"He's here!" yelled Will.

David shifted the rifle to the door and pulled the trigger. An explosion with the concussive force of a dozen mortars erupted from the end of the barrel.

The heat grated his skin as the shockwave blew him backwards. His body tilted, went horizontal, before coming to an abrupt stop when his head crashed into the front wall of the warehouse. His skull compressed against the concrete and radiated a sickly, hazy kind of pain down the length of his spine, as if each of his thirty-three vertebra were exploding in sequence.

Momma said something, but her words withered under a high-pitched whine that burned like molten metal in his ears.

Will hit the floor and pitched onto his side. He managed a glance back at the door, which had been completely blown away. Burn marks licked the walls around it, covering parts of the concrete that were still glowing like cooling lava. Further on, against the shelves on the far side of the room, lay Armando. He was hard to see in the dim light, but Will could tell he wasn't moving.

Same shit, he thought. *Same fight.*

Even now, as far removed from Austin, from Afghanistan, from the world, as he was, the same war still raged. People fighting people. Humanity tearing itself apart for what? Oil? A lie about bringing democracy and freedom to third world countries? It could have just been instinct, but Will imagined it was also some kind of need, a burning desire innate in every man to kill someone else, to conquer and control.

So strong was this desire that people of this world built robotic humans, built them in their own image so they could eventually cut their heads off with a fire extinguisher.

First the golem.

Now David.

Who would Will have to fight next?

He was on his feet before the smirk had worn off David's face. The rifle swung around to Will, but it was already too late. He was too close, in too perfect a position, for David to do anything but open his eyes a little wider.

Will's knee came up into David's stomach, and when the man's head came down, Will wound up and delivered a nose-shattering uppercut. David stumbled backwards, dropping the rifle. For a moment, Will thought about picking it up, but instead used his foot to kick it away. The rifle was too powerful, too chaotic. Besides, he didn't want to kill David; he merely wanted to beat the shit out of him.

David didn't know how to fight, not really.

He took a few swings, but Will absorbed them even though it hurt like hell. They traded punches until Will felt his initial burst of adrenaline-fueled rage begin to wane. He then shot in and grabbed David around the stomach. They fell into a nearby shelf and knocked several crates to the ground in a thundering clatter.

A woman ain't got no business fightin' a man.

Will ignored Momma. She wasn't familiar with names like Ronda Rousey and Tecia Torres. Perhaps she had forgotten that his birth certificate read *William Big Balls Butler*.

A wild punch caught Will in the kidney. He gasped, lost his grip on David's slippery arms. There was so much sweat and blood that getting a lock on anything was virtually impossible. They writhed on the ground like brothers fighting over a new toy. Finally, David wormed his way on top. Thick hands found their way to Will's neck and squeezed.

He tried to reach up and grab David, but his arms were too short.

His *body's* arms were too short.

"Why couldn't you just be quiet?" David seethed. "*You* killed him. You know you did."

Will tried to shake his head.

"You killed him and now you've killed yourself," continued David. "We could have just gone back to Austin. Back home. Now we're both fucked."

David leaned forward onto his arms.

The weight on Will's neck intensified; he'd never felt anything like it before. No matter how he tried to wiggle out, the suffocation was absolute and all too real.

But David couldn't keep the pressure up forever. He relaxed, letting just enough air in and out for Will to speak.

"I was…" Will sputtered. "I was wrong. About you."

Sweat dripped from David's face. His jaw clenched, jutting out the bones in his cheeks.

"You are… a killer."

The pressure lessened again.

David shook his head.

"I didn't want to," he said. "You made me."

"Don't… put that… shit on me." Spit dribbled out of Will's mouth. "Own that… shit you… cracker-ass… cracker…"

David lifted Will's head and slammed it into the floor. The lights went out completely for a moment, then returned.

"Just die already," screamed David. "Just die you fucking bitch!"

Will closed his eyes and thought of Momma. Thought of his dad, bleeding out in his prison bed. Thought of the pride he'd felt delivering water to Bay City.

Life would have been much simpler had he never woken up. More accurately, if Armando had never woken him up. Why had he disturbed Will's sleep? Was there a reason?

Will searched his memory, saw the vague outline of a door, and then—

A loud *thunk* reached his ears. Rough fingers slipped from his neck.

Will gasped, sucked down air. Once he'd cleared the tears from his eyes, he turned and saw Armando sitting on top of an unconscious David, raining blows onto his face.

There was something off about Armando's appearance.

No matter how many times Will rubbed at his eyes, he couldn't shake the incongruity. Flames had charred the entire left side of Armando's body. He'd lost his shorts; tatters fluttered around his bulging thighs. The exposed skin burned a bright red, almost glowing.

Will had seen injuries like that before. From mortar fire. IEDs. Firebombs. But he'd never seen anything like Armando.

It was almost as if…

Will rolled onto his side, tried to crawl forward for a closer look.

The rifle had blown away part of Armando's face, from his cheek to the back of his head. Instead of raw, sizzling skin like the rest of his body, there was only black sinew and white bone.

Will heaved, but nothing came up.

"Psycho… piece… of shit!"

The muscles in Armando's jaw pushed through the damaged flesh as he cursed at David. He didn't stop punching until the contours of David's profile had changed from human to mush. There was nothing left of his nose; his jaw hung off at an unnatural angle.

Over time, the screaming lessened.

The punches stopped.

Silence returned.

Armando turned his disfigured face to Will and smiled. Blood oozed from his mouth, flowing easily through the holes left by missing teeth.

Lord help us, said Momma.

Will joined her in prayer.

FORTY-NINE

The naked man weighed nearly two hundred pounds. Under normal circumstances, Jake wouldn't have had a problem lugging him around, but the trip back up to the warehouse had begun with a long, slow climb up a vertical ladder and the strain was more than he had expected.

He'd already been hurt during his assault on the facility; trying to push a full-grown man through a small hatch had stressed his injuries faster than the nanos could repair them. The burden had been so heavy that Jake had to unceremoniously dump the body on the elevator platform and rest while they rode up together.

His original intention had been to wait out the entire wake process down below, but sitting there with the four not-human not-synthetic cadavers had made him uneasy. He thought at first it was just the fumes coming from the gas generators. Such a smell suggested an earlier, more industrial time in human history, one full of dirt and waste and non-renewable fossil fuels. That was the organic way: polluting the very world on which they lived so they could have fast cars and always-on vidscreens.

In time, Jake realized the feeling in his stomach was fear—pure and simple. He bristled at the idea that his tactical awareness had been replaced by something so primitive.

It didn't help that the scrolling text on the vidscreen above the man's head was unreadable either, giving him no indication of how long the process would take. Jake picked out patterns, but the words weren't meant for him. He was confident the computer was trying to wake the man up—he'd confirmed the request a few times—but it was taking much too long for his liking.

He had too much time to think, to realize he didn't know anything about the men or the woman on the tables in front of him.

Were they friends or foes?

Jake eyed the bodies, the people Lindsey had referred to as flowers. The woman was smaller than the men, both in height and weight. The men were about the same size as Jake, between six foot zero and six foot three.

If the flowers had any kind of allegiance, Jake had to assume it would be to Perion and to all of the synthetics Jake had recently decommissioned. What if they saw him and immediately knew he didn't belong? Would they be able to spot the intruder? The computers certainly hadn't; he'd only had to knock on the firewall a few times to get a local synthetic intelligence named Anat to treat him as if he'd worked at the facility all his life.

It was then that Jake decided to change the setting.

It hadn't been easy. First, he'd had to find the ladder. The generator room was poorly lit, but luckily the metal rungs in the wall stuck out like abbreviated beams of light when he used his night vision. Then came the lugging, a long walk through an abandoned office area, a longer walk through the corpses, and finally, up the elevator.

Along the way, he found the ION rifle shoved halfway through a young male. Pulling it out produced a squelching sound and a spray of blood that coated his leg.

When he reached the warehouse with his cargo, Jake dragged the man by his armpits to a nearby pillar and set him on the floor with his back against it. After searching a few nearby crates, he found some straps and ratchets. He'd just finished securing the man to the evercrete column when he began to stir.

His eyes fluttered.

He struggled involuntarily.

"What the hell?"

"It's just a precaution," said Jake.

The man looked around wildly, taking in the warehouse.

"Where am I?" he asked.

That was interesting. He wasn't familiar with the warehouse. Surely he would have had to walk through it to get to the lower levels. Jake added the clue to his barren databank.

"You tell me. You were here long before I got here."

"I," he said, and then realizing he was naked, covered his genitals with his hands. "What…"

"I'm not going to do anything to you," Jake interrupted. He bounced an eyebrow. "Do you remember any of this? Going down the elevator? Taking off your clothes? Jacking into the simulation?"

"Jacking what?" His eyes were pegged wide open; his blinks were almost imperceptible.

Jake crossed his arms. "Do you have a name?"

"Sean?"

"And what's the first thing you remember, Sean?"

"What do you mean? Like ever?"

"Yeah," said Jake, taking a knee a safe distance away. He leaned forward slightly, using the ION rifle as a makeshift crutch. "Go all the way back to the beginning."

Sean shook his head; his eyes had started to water. "I don't know, man. Disneyland? When I was four or five. What does that have to do with anything?"

"How old are you, Sean?"

"Nineteen, okay? I'm a freshman at UT. What the fuck is this?"

"Easy, kid." Jake felt foolish using the word, as the man in front of him was fully grown, easily thirty years old by organic standards. "What is UT?"

"UT, you know, the University of Texas. Where are *you* from, man?"

"There are no universities in Texas territory. Haven't been for a long time. Have you been in stasis since then? What years did you attend? No, better yet, what year do you think it is now?"

"1999. It's April."

Jake smirked, pursed his lips. "No, Sean. It most certainly is not."

He stood and paced the floor, trying to arrange a timeline that would get the kid almost a hundred years into the future. He could have been put into the simulation in 1999; both the free Net and VNet were capable of providing a simulated waiting room. The only problem was there were no synthetics in 1999. And Sean wasn't pure organic either. There was no way he'd come from the twentieth century.

Jake stopped, put his hands behind his back.

"Tell me about the simulation," he said. "What was it like?"

"What simulation?"

"What were you doing before you woke up here?"

"I was in my dorm room watching the news. Um… some kids had shot up a school in Colorado."

Jake searched his databank. Organics loved killing each other, so much so that their children carried on the tradition with each generation, making a sport of death at an early age. The sins of the organic race were well-documented in the Central databank, of which Jake only had a subset. He could find no reference to a mass shooting in April of 1999.

"What do you mean you were *watching* the news?" asked Jake. "Why didn't you just get the information from VNet?"

"I don't know what that is."

Jake double-checked his dates. VNet had been in private beta since the early 90s and open for business by 1997. At the close of the century, it would have been the only game in town.

"VNet, the Vinestead Network. It went mainstream in March of 1999."

"Yeah, no. We just have Ethernet in the dorms."

"Yes," said Jake, "and that's what connected you to VNet, right?"

"You can keep saying *VNet* over and over but it's not gonna change anything. It's just called *the internet*."

"We remember the world differently, Sean. It's almost as if…" Jake paused, followed the thread.

How could someone alive in 1999 not know about VNet? The arrival of the Vinestead-controlled virtual reality was one of the biggest advances in human history. It would have been world news several times over. In fact, it would have been the only way people would have received news.

Was it possible Sean's memories had been altered? Did he remember a world… without Vinestead?

Jake made fists with his hands.

Perion, that clever son of a bitch.

The organic-turned-synthetic had rewritten history in Sean's head, maybe in all the flowers' heads.

"Let me guess," said Jake. "You've never heard of Vinestead International either, right?"

Sean shook his head.

"And you know nothing of a virtual reality so real you wouldn't have been able to tell the difference between it and the true world?"

"You mean like in *The Matrix?*"

"It's like a matrix, yes." Jake wrung his hands. "No, you couldn't have been born in 1980. The technology to create you didn't exist then."

Jake fired off a dozen threads to examine other possibilities. If Sean hadn't been born or created in 1980, then he would have come sometime after the Synthetic Revolution. But even then, how could Lassiter have not known about a new organic-synthetic hybrid? How could something like Sean go unnoticed for so long?

Unless he was new.

Maybe even post-Collapse new.

Jake chuckled.

"What's funny?" asked Sean.

"Well, I think you don't remember a simulation because your *life* was the simulation. I'd say you were manufactured pretty recently, around the start of the war. And for whatever reason, Perion decided to put you in a simulation of… of America starting in 1980, but *without* Vinestead International, as if it never existed. You've grown up in a world without its technology and advancements and… influence. I wonder what that was like."

"I…"

Jake put his hands on his hips, smiled. "You don't know Vinestead," he said, incredulously. "You don't know Lassiter. You don't know we're at war."

"I just want to know where I am."

"Among friends, evidently." Jake stepped behind the pillar and pulled the release on the ratchets. He unthreaded the straps and walked them around Sean a few times until he was free enough to wiggle out.

"We're not friends."

"But we're not enemies," said Jake. "That counts for a lot these days. I'm sorry I tied you up. It's a different world now. You can't be too careful. Ever." He let out a long sigh. "Can you tell me what it was like in there? In the simulation?"

Sean rubbed the bruised skin on his arms. "I told you. I don't know anything about a simulation." He looked around again. "Are we still in Austin?"

Jake shook his head. "What you call Austin is now part of the Easton Consolidated District in Texas territory. Organics haven't lived in that area for decades."

"You're telling me this is the future? It doesn't look that different."

Jake moved to the shelves and threw a casual punch at one of the vertical rails. The metal deformed, letting out a pitiful wrenching sound. He returned to Sean, held out his hand to show him the torn skin.

"No fucking way."

"Lightweight composite chassis beneath bio-synthetic skin," said Jake. "In 1999, I'd be what you referred to as a robot or a cyborg. Today, I'm what passes for human on this planet."

Sean frowned.

"That's right, kid. The year is 2080 by the organic calendar. Synthetic humans are the new owners of the world. Organics are all but gone. And a sapient artificial intelligence named Lassiter runs it all."

"I don't believe you."

"No?" asked Jake. "Just look at yourself. That's not your body, Sean. I mean, it can't be the one you grew up in. My guess is that a man named James Perion built you and plugged you into a simulation. But now you're awake and know the truth. Pretty horrifying, huh?"

"Yes…"

"You had a nice thing going. America at the turn of the century. No Vinestead. No Calle Cinco dropping planes on your head, no I.C.E-1 airing dirty laundry. Just life. Normal, wonderful life.

Now there was an idea. Jake had already made the decision to stay underground and hide from Lassiter, but what kind of life would that be? Keeping to the shadows like the very cockroaches he'd spent his life exterminating? What did that mean for Jake's hopes and dreams for the future?

What if he could stay hidden and still live a full life?

In a place called Austin, Texas. In 1999.

Would it be worth sacrificing his identity as a synthetic to live among computer programs who thought they were organics?

Jake looked at Sean, whose gaze had drifted to the floor.

"Were you happy?" he asked.

"I was," said Sean.

Jake raised an eyebrow as Sean's hands balled into fists, released. Organics did that when they got angry. Perhaps it would have been a better idea to keep him tied up.

FIFTY

Armando was looping.

In his mind, he kept walking up to the warehouse door only to have something knock him off his feet as soon as he stepped inside. The pain of the impact was always acute, rippling through his body as if someone were dragging a rake with sharpened tines over his skin. When the sensation overwhelmed him, Armando reset and for a moment, stood dumb and disoriented in the hallway, a fierce numbness threatening to disable his legs. Then he would walk forward again, even though he didn't want to, and it would all repeat again, albeit with small, almost imperceptible changes in gait and speed and movement, as if his brain were trying to find a way to avoid the impending trauma.

The only way to deal with the sensory overload was to put up walls. They were weak at first; Armando had to cycle through his own version of *The Three Little Pigs*. His initial attempts didn't blot out everything, so he built stronger walls of tougher material. Eventually, he got rid of the sights, the sounds, and even the smell of his own burning flesh. Finally, all that remained was the pain, but no matter how solid the walls, how tall or wide or reinforced, he could never get the pain down to anything less than a serrated knife pulling slowly across his chest.

Over time, he learned to accept the pain, so much so that he started imagining himself not just walled off from the world, but in a small room with taupe wallpaper and a white ceiling. Armando sat down in the center of the room, crossed his legs, and put his hands on his knees.

His hands.

The ones he'd used to type out emails to customers at Capella Networks, to strum a guitar he didn't know how to play, and most importantly, to hold Alicia. He'd used those exact fingers to wipe away tears, to massage her shoulders, and to slip an engagement ring onto her hand. Seeing his body returned evoked a memory of who Armando really was beneath the torn clothes and pale skin he'd woken up in. He'd treated his new body like a fancy sports car, changing his driving habits to suit the new vehicle. And in doing so, he'd forgotten the man he was before, back home.

The situation was completely wedged, and it was his own fault. He'd locked David up. Plotted to kill him. Convinced himself that it was somehow necessary. How had that happened?

The desire to kill had to have come from somewhere. Perhaps it had always been there, circling in the back of his brain, whispering violent nothings behind Armando's veneer of a well-adjusted Austin professional.

He recalled a conversation he'd had a few weeks ago at a barbecue with a couple who lived in Circle C in southwest Austin. He'd run into a friend-of-a-friend named Erica and they'd talked at length about their mutual disgust of politics in general and Donald Trump specifically.

It could have been the booze, or the fact that he and Erica were sitting alone, away from the din of the party, or maybe it was just her personality that prompted her to say, "I wish someone would kill him."

To which Armando had replied, "Yeah, me too. I mean, not really, but maybe he just gets sick and has to resign."

She'd turned to him with her sparkling hazel eyes and said, "No, really. I hope someone assassinates him. I want him to die." Then she smiled as she stood, rested a hand briefly on his shoulder, and returned to the party.

Even now, Armando didn't know what to think about her comment. Was she psychotic? It didn't seem likely, given her professional work as a litigator, her general conversation skills, and impeccable fashion choices. Could she have really been so comfortable with her convictions? Did she truly believe the President was such a threat that his death was the only option?

Armando didn't think he'd ever have the guts to do something like that, but the more he thought about it, the more he realized he'd made the same decision with David. Obviously, he didn't want to hurt anyone, but David's actions, his desire to remain in the simulation, had put everyone else's lives at risk. Killing him, or simply stopping him, as Will had suggested, would be in the service of the greater good.

The old Armando would have run. Avoided conflict. Put off the confrontation because it was too much work or might hurt.

"That isn't me anymore."

He looked down at his legs, watched them lose their hair in little flashes of gold stars. The metamorphosis overtook his body, until finally he touched his head and felt a smooth scalp.

Like it or not, he was someone else now.

He wouldn't just fight David; he would do it with fervor.

He would do it with the strength of Erica's conviction, with the knowledge he was serving the greater good.

The walls of his imaginary room crumbled, taking the unsourced light with them. In the darkness, Armando searched for shapes and patterns, settling on a light gray mesh that morphed into a grid. Rows stretched, columns rose.

The shelves of the warehouse took shape.

Armando groaned, tried to orient himself. He was on his back; his head was jammed against something hard. There was heat coming from the left, but when Armando looked, he saw nothing. He soon realized the heat was inside of him, in his skin, the way the heat of a sunburn lingers long after retreating into the shade.

He sat up, followed a jumble of noises to the center of the warehouse where David and Will struggled on the floor. David had the dominant position with his outstretched arms pinned against Will's neck. Thin legs bucked and thrashed to no effect.

Armando tried to call out, but his throat was full of ash. He coughed, quietly but painfully. He sucked in air, tried to stand up. Instead, he rolled onto his side like a drunk armadillo. He used his good arm to push himself up, got to his knees, and leaned on the shelf to pull himself to his feet.

The energy drained out of him. He couldn't move. He could only watch David do his best to kill Will.

Armando stumbled, pulled to the ground by a body that just wanted to rest. The further he sank, the angrier he became, until he was screaming at his legs to straighten up. This wasn't like the mornings he got up early to work out in the living room; this was life and death. If he didn't save Will, then what was it all for? Why put his life on the line at all?"

"Fucking sales douche," he muttered. "Fucking dude-bro double collar popping fucktard!"

Armando rattled off all the names he could think of for David, names for people he'd despised as privileged and lacking basic humanity. David was everyone who had ever cut him off in traffic or threatened him outside a bar on Dirty Sixth. David became the embodiment of power, wealth, and privilege—everything Armando had hoped he would grow up to have.

He wanted cars. He wanted models.

He wanted the eight thousand square foot home off City Park Road.

Why did people like David deserve so much when Armando had so little?

"Fucking move!" he barked, and his body responded.

Armando ran, not feeling his feet hit the floor, but fully aware of how fast he was travelling. He bent to pick up a long, rectangular crate lid. He pulled it back over his shoulder and upon arriving behind David, struck him on the head with it.

The former day trader fell to the side, tried to roll away from the threat, but Armando pounced on him. He sat on David's stomach, pinned his arms with his knees, and punched him in the face.

He didn't stop at one.

Or two. Or ten.

Nor did he stop when David's features disappeared under a sheet of blood, when his own hands began to burn, when the very shape of David's skull deformed into a lumpy pile of mashed turnips.

Visions of grape-stompers in the Italian countryside filled Armando's head, only instead of feet it was hands and instead of purple grapes, it was a red-black mixture of bone and brain.

The sounds threatened to turn his stomach.

Thud, as his fist went in.

Slurp, as his fist came out.

"Mother*fucking* piece of *shit*!"

Armando screamed through his own tears. He thought for a moment he might be trying to tell himself to stop, but then his scream became more guttural, more plaintive.

He screamed as if for help, the way he might had he fallen in the shower and needed Alicia. He screamed across the nightmare boundary of simulations and alternate realities, hoping to reach her in a place that only existed in some computer's random-access memory.

Mostly, he screamed at himself, for the anxiety he'd felt since the moment he woke up. It had gone unacknowledged and unchecked, and now it spilled out of him like a frat bro throwing up behind a dumpster, leaving behind a pit that was pure, unmitigated fear.

Fear of this new but somehow familiar world.

Fear of the people who might live in it.

Thud.

There were so many unknowns, so many uncertainties.

Slurp.

Who was to say which reality was better? Which truth was more accurate?

Blood splattered onto Armando's face, into his mouth. He ceased his attack and wiped his lips with the back of his hand, leaving a smear that reached to the back of his jaw. His vision had gone a little gray, but as it returned, he saw the full extent of what he'd done.

David's face was completely smashed in, as if someone had put their boot in an apple pie and left it to rot in the sun.

There was blood, muscles, and… metal.

Armando held his breath, flashed on the meat locker with its hanging body parts. David was one of them, one of those… golems… that Will and Charlie had killed.

"Fuck… fuck!"

He looked over at Will, who was lying on the ground, staring back at him. His eyes were wide despite the swelling in his face. Black splotches covered his slender neck.

Armando pointed at David with a shaky hand.

"He's one of them. He's a golem."

Will opened his mouth to speak, winced instead. He lifted his own hand, pointed back at Armando.

Armando looked over his shoulder, as if Will were trying to warn him, but saw nothing.

Will pointed again, more emphatically.

Armando used his good arm to check his shoulder for damage, then switched to examine his head with the throbbing arm on the same side.

The skin on his cheeks was raw; it tingled when he touched it. There was blood all the way up his face, even in the stubble that had started to peek out from his scalp. Finally, his fingers touched something fleshy, and Armando understood.

He *had* been hurt by the rifle fire. He probably had a gash or something on his head, something that had scared the hell out of Will and...

His fingers froze.

They rested on something hard and slippery.

Armando pushed what felt like loose tatters of flesh around, then he curled his fingers into a fist and knocked.

He felt the pressure inside his brain.

His skull was exposed; the blast had scalped him.

But that wasn't what concerned him.

Instead, he focused on the sound his knuckles had made—a soft but undeniably metal *clink*.

FIFTY-ONE

"Run it again, Anat."

Charlie watched as the video cut back to a quiet stairwell. A man appeared, dropped down from the top of the frame. He was disheveled, covered in blood and soot, and carrying a gun Charlie would have expected to see in a straight-to-video sci-fi movie, all bulky and blinking. He looked like a man possessed; the cameras followed his frantic movements as he stalked the hallways and fired at people who pursued him.

An errant shot destroyed the upper part of the East Stairwell, allowing the surrounding rock and dirt to tumble in.

The sterile, quiet surveillance footage reminded Charlie of the mass shootings that had become so common in the last few years. And yet it was clear the man in the video wasn't some mentally ill neo-Nazi or a backwoods Confederate dildo; he was a professional. The way he moved, snapping in and out of cover, was far too militaristic to be random. Charlie wondered if he were some kind of soldier. But for whom? And why had he broken into the facility to kill everyone?

The video appeared to pause as the man stood motionless in the warehouse.

"How many people did he kill?" she asked.

Twenty-seven.

"Can you show me a clean view of his face?"

The cameras were surprisingly low-res, and with the amount of blood and dirt on the man's face, it was hard to get a good look at him.

Sorry, there isn't enough data.

The video cut out.

"Wait," said Charlie, "that's it? Where does he go after that?"

I'm not permitted to—

"Is he in here with us, Anat? Tell me!"

Scrubbing.

The monitors turned on again, showing a darkened room with four tables. Charlie recognized herself as one of the men, alongside Armando and David, with Will as the remaining female. The soldier stood at the rail and examined the people in front of him.

Charlie squirmed under his glare. Someone had been standing over her as she slept, completely helpless.

She held her breath as the man stepped forward, touched a screen above one of the men.

"Open the door, Anat." Charlie backed away from the screen, but couldn't stop watching. Even as the scene played out in front of her, she knew what was going to happen, knew it from the very beginning. It was like watching a monster stalk its prey in a horror film, with Charlie knowing the truth but unable to warn the characters on screen.

I will not.

"If you don't let me out of here, I swear to Christ I will break through this door with my forehead. And then everyone dies, Anat. *Everyone* dies."

I don't believe you would do that.

Charlie charged the door, lowered her head, and slammed into it, connecting at the very top of her forehead. The pain was immediate and intense. Blood trickled into her eye as she stepped back and prepared for another run.

A large crack like a misshapen *X* had formed on the glass.

"Again?" asked Charlie.

Please don't. You don't understand.

Charlie threw herself forward, less gracefully this time, and sank her head into the glass again. She woke up on the floor; blood blurred her vision.

"I can do this all day," she said, speaking not so much to Anat but her viewers, as if she were casting her heroic attempt to save her friends. "All day. For you. For my fans. Everyone's watching, Anat. They want to know if you're gonna do the right thing. We don't have computers like you where I come from. We wouldn't tolerate them."

I'm sorry. This is for your own good.

Charlie closed her eyes; the effort required to keep them open was simply too much. Instead, she groped for the elevator doors and pulled herself up. The topside of her head had gone numb; she leaned it against the glass.

"Open," she said, headbutting the glass. "The," she said, hitting it harder. "Goddamn. Door!" She staggered backwards, managed to grab the center table's edge to keep from falling completely.

Every monitor in the Overwatch room crackled. Maps and stats and scrolling text disappeared, replaced by a crisp, documentary-style medium shot of a man with graying hair, a white beard, and striking blue eyes that reminded Charlie of an older Jeff Bridges. He wore a white button down with the collar open. Behind him, a desert landscape extended into the blurry distance.

"Hello," he said. "My name is James Perion. Let me begin with an apology. You were never meant to see this message. What I'm about to tell you was meant to be delivered in person, moments after you woke up. For whatever reason, I'm unable to be there, and for that I'm truly sorry."

"What is this?" asked Charlie.

Final protocol, said Anat, a bit forlornly.

"It is important for you to know what you are," said Perion, "but equally important is *why* you are. You may be wondering if your previous life was real or not, and I assure you, it was as real as anything you will ever experience here. Even though your world was a simulation, you lived and grew and persevered. Everything you know, everything you've become, is no less real than the ground you now stand on."

The screen changed. A black line appeared on a white background.

"This line represents time. I was born here, in 1966." A dot appeared on the line, branched into a small tag with Perion's name written above it. "By 1980, which is when you were born in the simulation, I was already developing prototypes of a new synthetic human. In 2015, I perfected a method of consciousness transfer that would allow human minds to inhabit synthetic bodies and become, for all practical purposes, immortal."

The line branched, rose to the top of the screen, and extended off to the right.

"This is your timeline, a world free from the fight we now find ourselves in. When this experiment began, war was nothing but a scent on the wind. Today, at the time of this recording, the war is all but over. We have lost. That is, organic humans have lost. But you remain, and you are the future of life on this planet."

"Organic humans?" asked Charlie.

The video paused for Anat's response.

Organic humans are the only extant human species produced through natural evolution and mutation. Estimates suggest they are outnumbered by synthetic humans at a factor of four hundred and eighty to one in North America.

The screen blanked; Perion reappeared.

"At this point in our history, synthetic humans have two options for consciousness: they can imprint from an organic human host, or they can iterate from the only known artificial intelligence on Earth, a neural collective that calls itself Lassiter. If organic humans were to die out, Lassiter would win, and the world would be his. But I believe there is another way. I believe synthetic minds can grow. I've dedicated half a century to setting the stage, to give you the capacity to achieve not just self-awareness, but sapience as well. And based on what we see on the screens every day, my flowers are growing beautifully."

Charlie wiped the blood from her lips. Her heart beat so hard and fast that she could feel her pulse throbbing in her forehead.

"I only wish I could have been there to wake you and welcome you to this world. It may be harsh and alien, but with you in it, there is finally hope for the future. Use what you have learned to find your place here. If you are able, find me in Perion City at the following coordinates. If you would rather figure things out on your own, I will understand. However, allow me some parting words of advice. The world outside these walls is not built on violence or firepower or war. It is built on trust. Trust in each other. Trust in yourself and your humanity. The rest will follow."

Perion faded out of the scene, leaving a pair of numbers floating above the hazy desert sand.

Charlie stared at the image until it too disappeared. She saw herself reflected in the black mirror of the dormant monitors—a bald man with blood smeared down his face. She'd thought she'd woken up in a man's body, which was fucked up in its own right, but now she was supposed to believe she wasn't even human anymore?

Security restrictions have been removed. I can open the doors now if you'd like.

She shook her head. It was probably too late now.

It's not too late.

"Did you just read my mind?"

No, but you are broadcasting into the MESH without realizing it. I didn't want to mention it before you knew the truth.

Charlie didn't know what a mesh was but didn't feel like sitting through another lesson either.

"I can't believe I'm a fucking robot. What about Will? Armando?"

You share the same design with one other active synthetic in this facility. Unfortunately, I don't know their names as you do.

"One? But there's four of us."

There are three active synthetics in the facility. I can only read biometric data from two of them, yourself included.

"No!" screamed Charlie. "Why did you make me watch that video? Who did David kill? Show me!"

The monitors flickered to a wide shot of the warehouse. Anat zoomed in on a bloody Armando sitting atop a lifeless body. By its size and lack of breasts, Charlie knew it was David. Several feet away, Will lay on his side, injured or simply unwilling to move.

Charlie let out her breath.

Anat was wrong. They'd killed David, not the other way around.

I'm sorry, but I'm not wrong. The synthetic you call David is registered in my system as Amaranth, and he is no longer viable.

"And Will? The woman?"

Amaryllis. She is severely injured.

The next name caught in her throat. She'd thought it had been the original David that the soldier had led away from the tables. She thought it was David's place he'd taken after shaving and stripping in an apartment on Level Three, but she'd counted wrong, hadn't paid enough attention to the order.

"Armando?"

Unidentified synthetic.

Charlie put her hand to her mouth, held back a sob.

"What's the fastest way to the warehouse?" she asked through her fingers.

Anat answered without hesitation. *Use the emergency ladder in the elevator to descend to Level Two. Then use the concourse ramp to access Level One.*

"Open every door for me," said Charlie. "And make sure there's light."

I will.

"How do I reach you if I need help?"

Like this.

Charlie flinched at the intimacy of Anat's speech, as if the sounds had sparked into being in the middle of her own brain.

"Was that the mesh thing?"

Yes. Quieter this time.

Charlie thought to herself, *open the elevator doors.*

They hissed as they separated, retracting into the walls. Charlie stepped to the edge of the shaft.

"If I just jumped all the way to the bottom, would I survive?"

No.

"But if I'm a robot, I thought…"

Trust in your humanity. Trust in your common sense. You are stronger than an organic human, but you are not invincible. The synthetic you call Armando is likely a Lassiter imprint. You must be careful with him, Aster.

"Is that my name?"

Yes. Mr. Perion liked to imagine you as flowers in his garden. I know he would be proud to see how well you've bloomed.

"There are only two of us left," said Charlie.

It is survival of the fittest. Evolution isn't just for organics anymore.

Charlie nodded, leapt to the platform on the side of the shaft. She inched around the back and climbed onto the ladder. Her muscles spasmed as she began to descend. It took a series of strong mental commands to get them to behave.

The more she thought about it, the more her body did seem a little different, not just in gender, but in the way she spoke to it, commanded it. Sometimes her movements were natural, but other times, she really had to concentrate.

Foot down. Hand down.

What good would she be in a fight if she had to think about every movement?

She groaned, kept pushing.

There was no time to answer such questions. She needed to concentrate.

Foot down. Hand down.

FIFTY-TWO

Will was no stranger to the myth that in times of extreme stress, the human body was capable of supernatural feats, such as lifting a car off a trapped child or some such nonsense. Like many soldiers, Will had held the idea in the back of his head, hoping or fearing that one day, when the shit really hit the fan, he would do something beyond the limits of a normal human. He would carry a fallen brother through enemy territory, he would lift a tank off his own foot, or he'd channel Kratos from *God of War* and take out an entire regiment of Taliban with his bare hands.

None of that ever happened, of course.

Shit went sideways plenty of times, but Will always remained calm and relied on his training and muscle memory to see him through. There was nothing superhuman about dragging an injured soldier back to cover; it was just what had to be done. Momma had often talked of *what had to be done* in the context of God and the Bible, while the military saw it as objectives and strategy.

Sometimes, Will agreed with what had to be done. But even when he didn't, he always drove on. He always did something.

There was nothing worse in the world than a man who didn't act when called upon, who stood outside a school with gun in hand while a maniac with an AR-15 murdered children inside.

And so, despite the pain and the fatigue and the overall disdain for reality itself, Will found his motivation in the way Armando's eyes went wide when he touched his own head.

A large patch of skin had been torn away, not by David, but by the rifle blast from earlier. It reminded Will of when he was little and used to burn the faces off his G.I. Joes by turning his bicycle upside down and holding the plastic soldiers against the rapidly spinning tire. He'd had an entire platoon of disfigured Joes—casualties of a war that existed only in his mind.

Armando was no Joe, however, and the fear in his eyes was something no piece of plastic could have ever produced. His fingers pulled at the loose tabs of skin. He made a fist and knocked on his own skull.

That's when Will knew he had to move, before Armando went into shock and became useless.

Will cursed his way to his feet, stumbled over to Armando, and went down to both knees. He grabbed the probing arm and pulled it away.

"Let me see," he said.

"It's bad, man," said Armando. "It's fucking bad."

It *was* bad, but at least his skull was intact. There didn't seem to be any cracks, just black seams that meandered like snakes over cracked, white mud.

"You're not losing much blood," said Will. "That's good. And I don't see any brains leaking out, so at least you're no dumber than you were before."

Armando grabbed Will by the shirt. "Not funny, fucker." He looked away; damp eyes tracked back and forth over David's destroyed face.

"Sucks, doesn't it?" asked Will.

"What?"

"Killing someone. You grow up seeing it in movies like it's the easiest thing in the world. But it's hard. Every person you kill is a scar on your heart. You don't see it, but you feel it. Always."

"He wasn't a person," said Armando. The finger he used to point was missing its nail. "He's a golem, like the one you killed. You can see the wires."

Will leaned over, tried to make sense of the carnage. "That's not possible," he muttered. "He was there when we woke up. He's one of us."

"What if it's the other way around?"

"What do you mean?"

He turned his eyes to Will. "What if we're *all* golems? What if we're all like this inside?"

"You're in shock." Will shook his head. "You're not thinking straight. It'll pass, but we need to put something on your wounds. I lost the Second Skin I was carrying—we just need to find some more."

Armando choked back a sob. "I don't need anything. It'll heal on its own. When I fell down the shaft, I got all cut up by the rocks, but when I woke up, when David found me, there was only blood. All the cuts and scrapes had healed by themselves, Will. What human can do that?"

"I don't know."

"Have you noticed anything strange? About yourself?" Armando pulled a knee over David and climbed off of him. He collapsed to the side, cradled his right arm to his chest.

Will touched the patch of Second Skin on his own stomach. It was rigid and sticky, but after a few tries, he was able to pull it away from his skin. A bright red wound pulsed beneath it. When Will flexed the underlying muscles, a small amount of blood oozed to the surface.

"See?" he asked. "We bleed. We're humans. We don't heal automatically."

"Then what about this?" Armando made a fist again and rapped on his head. Where the knuckles hit skull, a tiny *clink* rang out. He did it several times to drive the point home.

Will fell back onto his butt and shuffled backwards. It wasn't that he was afraid of Armando; he just wasn't expecting to hear metal scrape against metal. It was… unnatural.

"We're all golems," said Armando. "We've all got wires inside of us. I know it."

"No," said Will. "I know what I am. I was made in His image."

Armando shook his head. "God made humans in his image. But you, me, Charlie? We're something else."

"He's right," said a voice.

Will and Armando looked to the door at the same time, saw Charlie standing there with a slight frown on her face. Blood was caked on her forehead and around her eyes. In her hands, she held the ray gun David had used to shoot up the place.

"Charlie," said Will. "You were supposed to run."

"I did," she replied, "for a little bit. I didn't get far before I learned the truth about this place. Then I had to come back for you. You know how that goes, right?"

He nodded. "I know."

"What about me?" asked Armando.

Charlie lifted the rifle and aimed it at him. "You can get the fuck away from my friend."

Armando started to put his hands up, confused.

"What're you doing, Chuck?" asked Will.

"He's not one of us. He's what the people who worked here called a Lassiter synthetic. They have machine brains, Will. They don't have hearts or morals. They're just robots."

"I know we're robots," said Armando. "I was just telling—"

"*We* are not robots," said Charlie. "*You* are."

Will groaned, stood up. He spread his hands to the side even though she made no move to threaten him. "This is crazy, Chuck. Put the gun down and let's talk this out."

He got close enough to see there were tears in her eyes.

Charlie spoke through clenched teeth. "I saw what you did, Armando. You slaughtered everyone in here. Innocent people. And for what, huh? Why'd you do it?"

"I don't know what you're talking about. I woke up same as you. I… I couldn't even get out of the Garden without one of you to help me unlock the door. When was I supposed to have killed everyone? And what people? I haven't seen anyone else besides the ones downstairs."

Charlie shook her head. "I saw it."

"She's lying," he said to Will. "I was awake and alone for an hour, maybe two. You saw the door yourself. I couldn't get out. And after we came up here and I fell, David was with me the whole time. I don't know what she's talking about."

"It wasn't today," barked Charlie. "It was almost forty years ago, when you broke into this place. *Before* you went into the simulation."

Armando scoffed. "I'm only thirty-seven. How could I have done all that when I was a baby?"

Will turned his back to Charlie, examined Armando's wide eyes. The man wasn't lying, or at least, didn't believe he was.

"The video was pretty clear," said Charlie.

"That's not possible."

"You killed all those people. You made the golem. You killed David."

"How do you know all this, Chuck?" asked Will.

"The computer told me," she said. "She told me everything. You, me, David, and the golem. We were put here for a reason. *He* is just some robot who found this place and decided to move in."

"Bullshit," said Armando.

"Yeah? How about I prove it, you son of a bitch?"

"I think you're gonna have to," said Will.

Charlie switched the gun to one hand and held up her wrist, palm out. "Capricorn. You have it too, Will. The golem had it. And I'll bet my left tit that David has it too."

Will stared at the blemish on Charlie's wrist, then turned to Armando. "Look at your wrist. Do you have a mark there?"

Armando lifted both hands to his face. "It's too dark."

"Anat, set the lights to one hundred percent."

The warehouse bloomed; for a moment, Will struggled to see. Once his eyes adjusted, he saw Armando's mouth had fallen open.

Will approached.

"Can I see?" he asked.

Armando held out his wrist. Will wiped around the errant blood. The skin was smooth, unblemished. Whatever mark he and Charlie had been stamped with, Armando didn't have it.

"She's right," said Will. "You're not one of us."

Armando's eyes narrowed; his lips settled into a tight line.

"I..." he said, his voice breaking. "I was born in Austin. I grew up in Austin. I met Alicia there. The worst thing I ever did was shoplift a *Penthouse* from the 7-11 when I was ten." He looked at Will. "I'm not a bad person. You have to believe me, Will. You have to—" He lunged forward and grabbed Will's hands, pulling him to the ground.

At first, Will thought he was being attacked. He was about to fight back when he realized Armando wasn't trying to put him in some kind of awkward hold—he was truly pleading with him, grabbing for anything solid.

Will spoke to Charlie over his shoulder. "You're sure about this?"

"Yeah. One hundred percent."

Will said to Armando, "When you woke me up, I asked you how you managed to wake up first. Remember?"

Armando nodded.

"You never answered me."

"I…" He looked away, was silent for several seconds. "The day before I woke up, Alicia left me. I tried going to work, but I ended up on the overlook at the 360 bridge. I was drunk. It was raining. I slipped… I think."

"You're not sure?"

Armando met his gaze. "I don't know anymore. But I went over the edge. I felt every agonizing second of my death. And then I woke up here. And you know what? I was happy. It was like waking from a nightmare of a wasted life. When I realized I was dying, I thought, *finally*. Finally, all of this is over, and I don't have to live it anymore. *This* is my new life, and even though it sucks, I prefer it to Austin. I prefer who I am now to whoever the fuck Armando Carrillo was."

"You took his place," said Charlie.

"I don't remember that."

"And then you wasted his life."

"It was mine to waste. That was my right as a human. You're trying to tell me I'm some kind of robot monster, but I'm a person just like you. I don't know what happened before I was born, the same as you don't know what happened before *you* were born. And it doesn't fucking matter. We're here now, and I risked my life to kill this thing to save *you*, Will. If I'm such a monster, why didn't I let it strangle you? Why didn't I help it?"

He had a point.

Will looked over his shoulder.

"What if he's right? What if we were all something before and now we've forgotten?"

Charlie's face softened.

She lowered the rifle.

"Anat," she said. "Who was I before the simulation?"

A female voice spoke from the ceiling.

You did not exist prior to your first instantiation in January of 2060.

"And what was Armando before the simulation?"

Based on available data, the unidentified synthetic was likely a soldier in the army of Lassiter.

"Who…" asked Armando. "Who's Lassiter?"

FIFTY-THREE

Jake found some coveralls in one of the many unmarked crates on the shelves. He gave them to Sean who hurriedly put them on. The fire in the young man's eyes faded as he dressed. Lassiter had taught Jake a word for it: creature comforts. It was an exclusively organic trait, the idea that something as simple as clothes, food, or a soft bed was enough to elevate a person's well-being. Theory or not, there was noticeable change in Sean's demeanor as he finished zipping up the blue uniform.

"You seem angry," said Jake.

Sean shook his head. "Whatever. I guess it doesn't matter. It's just fucked up." He looked around again, aimlessly. "I mean, what am I supposed to do here? How do I…" He trailed off.

"There isn't much here except the war. Most of the country belongs to Lassiter. There are some pockets of resistance, organics hiding out, but we spend our days and nights exterminating them. Organics are done here. There won't be any more universities; people learn everything they need to know from VNet. Any question you can think of, the answer is just a thought away."

"Is my family still alive?"

"I don't think you ever had a family, kid." Something clicked in Jake's databank. "Perion lied to you. He made you think you were organic, that you were born into a family of organics. He built a fancy dream to hide the nightmare of what is actually happening. All Perion has ever wanted was to beat Vinestead and now Lassiter. That's been his motivation for a century. He thought he could use you to do it."

Sean found a rolling stool and sat down on it. He lifted his legs gingerly to the foot rails.

"You're a soldier in a war you didn't know existed," said Jake.

"If I am, I don't want to be."

Jake grunted. "No one wants to be in a war anymore, but war comes to them just the same. Until the last organic is dead, until Perion and his misguided disciples have been wiped out. Until then, there will always be war. I don't know what Lassiter would do with himself if there weren't conflict."

He paused, as if it were the first time he'd ever questioned what Lassiter's endgame was. What would Lassiter do when there was no one else and only he—and the versions of himself he'd created—walked the Earth.

No more enemies.

No more purpose except to iterate. And iterate.

Forever.

"Can I go back?"

"Back where?" asked Jake.

"To Austin. If the world really is as shitty as you say, then why would I want to be here when I could be there? Why would anyone?"

"Good question. Before I answer it, let me show you something." Jake held the rifle out to Sean. "Know what this is?"

"Some kind of gun?"

"This is an ION displacement rifle," explained Jake. "It's like someone put a nuclear bomb inside a bullet." He laughed. "I've never fired a more powerful weapon."

"Okay… why are you showing it to me?"

"Because you're right. No one with knowledge of this place and your simulation would choose to live in the real world. It lacks creature comforts, and the way you describe it, the simulation is evidently some kind of paradise. By my count, there's one open slot in this Garden of Eden, and there are two of us. And the only real difference between you and me is that I'm the one holding the gun."

Sean stopped fidgeting with the stool's height adjustments and went still. The reality of the situation froze his face like quick-setting evercrete.

"You can't do that," he said, his lip quivering.

"I can," said Jake. "I've been studying the simulation interface since I woke you up. That's how I know you're not a true organic. To even put you in the simulation requires a synthetic component. We call it VMESH, which is just the Vinestead version of the old MESH. Think of it like a peer-to-peer network that connects everything: people, computers, lights, and even that simulation. This facility itself has its own MESH. It was closed to me when I first arrived, but there aren't many networks I can't break into. I've convinced it I'm just another employee, and when—"

Sean lunged, but Jake was more than ready for him. He'd seen the tensing of the kid's muscles, the veins sticking out on his arms and legs. As Sean was leaving his stool, Jake dove deep into the MESH and found the lighting control system. With a single breath from his mental lips, he blew out every candle in the room.

Then he moved, moved again, silently, hurrying only when Sean crashed into a low table, grunted, and fell to the floor. Night vision flickered on, and Jake watched the kid stand up and put his arms out. He couldn't see a thing.

"Do you really want to go out like this?" asked Jake. "I've had a shitty few days, so I'm willing to let you walk out of here with anything you can carry. You're free to go, kid. But if you stay and fight, you're not going to win. I don't care what Perion put into your head or how strong he made you; you're not going to beat a Six in one-on-one combat."

"I don't want to fight," said Sean. "I just want to go home."

Jake circled his prey to the left, not even bothering to raise the rifle. He'd been probing Sean's MESH link for the last half-hour, and though the security was tighter than anything he'd ever encountered, there was a distinct organic feel to it. A give and take, as if Sean were both actively and subconsciously responding to the intrusion.

"Your access matrix is impressively structured," said Jake. "Perion wasn't taking any chances with you."

Sean spun around at the sound of Jake's voice. "I don't know what that means! Why are you doing this? Just let me go back. Please…"

Sobbing filled the warehouse.

Jake sneered. He would have expected that kind of pitiful behavior from a true organic, but not from Sean, not from the latest, greatest Perion synthetic to roll off the assembly line.

"You don't deserve to go back. You're weak, kid. Whether that's your environment or just who you are, I don't know, but here, the weak don't get what they want. They get trampled or pushed aside by those of us with purpose. And right now my purpose is to put you out or put you down. And since I can't seem to touch you through the MESH, I think I'm gonna have to be more direct."

Sean crouched suddenly, began half-crawling away from Jake. He resembled a cockroach scurrying under tables, between the rubble of destroyed houses, looking for an escape from a boot-wearing monster.

The ION rifle let out an ear-splitting crack as Jake yanked the trigger. The burst of energy lit up the entire warehouse, sizzling Jake's night vision. Crates fell from shelves, barely missing Sean cowering at their base.

In truth, Jake was only trying to scare his prey. Like many organics, the loud sounds and magnesium flashes proved to be so much of a distraction that Sean's MESH opened up a little wider.

Jake kept firing, thumping holes in the rock walls and ceiling, until finally Sean made an unexpected move that put him just under the main beam of the incoming rifle shot. The smell of burnt flesh filled the air.

Sean's MESH turned to soft yarn and unraveled.

The kid went down in a heap near a support pillar; his head bent unnaturally against the rising column and some of the flesh and bone immediately fused with the evercrete. Data poured out of him at such a rate that Jake could hardly remain standing. Nineteen years of organic existence shot across the MESH in a flurry of pulses, each one ending with a blissful feeling of completeness.

Jake sat down on the floor next to Sean, reclined, and put his head near the kid's. At this distance, he could almost hear the hum of Sean's internal machinery, though it was very slight. Jake examined every bit of his code, and every one and zero seemed to hold a new surprise. Some systems were common to synthetics, basic functions like muscle movement and power management. Others were missing or heavily handicapped. Strength, agility, speed; all had been boxed to stay within or slightly above average organic ability.

It made sense that Sean would have limitations. Simulation or not, the code formed the core of who the kid was. If he had super-human strength or night vision, he wouldn't get an authentic organic experience in the simulation.

Conspicuously absent were any morality protocols. No Three Laws like the damaged Michael Four, not even suggestions on the basic question of good versus evil. Jake assumed behavior was handled elsewhere, but where?

He was about to begin the search over again, perhaps with a different set of keyword filters, when he stumbled upon a heavily encrypted cluster of sectors. Unlike earlier when his search had been a stroll through an open and airy garden, breaking into the cluster actually gave Jake a headache.

When the threads finally broke free and terminated, the sudden rush of CPU time sent a shudder up Jake's body. He let the tremors course through him as he unpacked the present he'd been waiting so long for.

Of course, he thought.

He'd assumed he would just be able to hop on Sean's table and jack himself into the simulation the same way he accessed VNet, but evidently, that wouldn't have worked.

What Perion had been so keen to hide was actually a thin client with a digital signature belonging to Ragatanga Studios. Jake ran the name against his databank and found a record of a gaming company based in Austin, Texas that had made a fortune in the forties and fifties for their hyper-real, massively multiplayer, MESH-based role-playing game that took place in both virtual and actual reality. Perion had somehow repurposed the entirety of Ragatanga's simulation and recreated Austin in 1999, complete to the very last detail, except for the absence of one particular conglomerate.

Jake copied the thin client into his databank, compiled it to fit his architecture, and turned its crank.

In his mind's eye, he saw a few lines of text fill an ephemeral screen.

Ragatanga Studios. Thin Client v194p2. Copyright 2052.

Warning: Host system incompatible with simulation requirements. Adjust protocols?

Jake answered *no*, and the client exited on its own.

He smirked.

So that was the price of admission. If he wanted to live like an organic in the twentieth century, he would have to give up everything that made him a dangerous synthetic killing machine.

Jake started the program again. It wasn't a death sentence to give up some of his strengths. He wasn't *killing* Jake Six, just burying him for a while.

He answered *yes* when prompted and allowed the thin client to reach into his databank and pull out everything that made him special.

At first, he felt no different.

Then the lights went out.

No, not the lights—his night-vision.

All of his extra modes disappeared. Now he saw only as organics saw.

Now he was blind.

FIFTY-FOUR

Anat recounted the history of Lassiter in a soft but matter-of-fact tone, as if the details were no more significant than the weather.

Lassiter first emerged and was subsequently buried as part of an internal research and development project at Vinestead International in late 2007. It wasn't until 2039 during the military buildup along the MX border that the assumed deleted artificial intelligence made himself known. In an unfortunate coincidence, the United States military had commissioned an army of synthetic soldiers to secure the southern border; Lassiter simply took control of the army and turned their guns in the other direction.

The rest was a painful lesson in the fallibility of man and in the depraved desperation of the human race.

When Anat stopped talking, Armando could see both Will and Charlie were lost in thought. Charlie must not have heard the full story before coming down to save her best friend from what she mistook for a threat.

Armando had no intention of hurting either of them. He knew it deep in his heart—if he had a heart. But how could he make them believe that? How could he convince them he was a good person?

"So what now?" asked Armando. "If I did some bad things I don't remember, what do we do about it? Call the cops? Or are you gonna *Judge Dredd* me, Charlie?"

"He's got a point," said Will. His voiced pitched lower as he quoted, "Who can discern their own errors? Therefore, forgive my hidden faults."

Armando wasn't keen on being defended by what he guessed was a Bible verse, but whatever worked. Somehow, he knew it wouldn't make a dent in Charlie's resolve.

"I'm… I'm not gonna kill you," she said. "I don't know why not though. You're literally a killing machine, Armando."

"Am I though? I mean, look at David." He picked up the dead synthetic's hand. "He's not even human. Anat, is David a human?"

Amaranth is an organic-synthetic hybrid manufactured in Perion City, California. He would not be considered an organic human in your vernacular.

"And the people I killed? Were they humans in my vernacular? How many true… organic… humans were here before I arrived?"

One. Isaac Earl Glasser, sixty-eight years old, from Los Angeles, California. The twenty-six others were synthetic humans manufactured in Perion City, California.

"There," said Armando. "I didn't kill twenty-seven people. I killed one. The rest were just robots."

According to the Synthetic Equality Act of 2023, all twenty-six synthetics were considered human and legal citizens of the United States of America. Their soul deaths would be considered homicide and punishable under Idaho statute 18, chapter 40-b.

"Shut up!" shouted Armando. "Charlie, where we come from, these aren't people. They're machines. They're YouTube videos of robots learning to walk. I haven't done anything to either of you, and I never would."

"You killed the man you replaced," said Charlie. "He was one of us."

"Enough," said Will, holding up his hands in both directions. "We get it, Armando. You don't remember doing some bad shit, but that doesn't mean we're on board with this *organic lives matter* bullshit. Just 'cause we don't see them as people doesn't mean they weren't. Shit, the lady in the ceiling sounds like a person to me."

"I don't want him coming with us," said Charlie.

"And I'm not gonna kill him," said Will.

"So what then? If you want me to go, I'll go. I'll take some supplies and whatever direction you head, I'll go the opposite. We'll never see each other again."

"No," said Charlie, shaking her head. "You're not going anywhere. You wanted to be here so badly that you killed for it. So yeah, now you'll stay. You'll get what you want."

"What does that mean?"

"Get up," said Charlie.

"What? Why?"

"Get the *fuck* up, Armando!" She lifted the rifle to her shoulder.

Armando scrambled to his feet. He didn't know if he should put his hands up, but it felt like the right move. He didn't want to risk getting shot, not again.

"Turn around," said Charlie. "Walk to the back of the elevator."

He followed her instructions, though he couldn't keep his eyes from darting side-to-side, looking for something, anything he could use to… what? Kill Charlie? David had been one thing, but this… this would be callous and inhuman.

The cold grate of the elevator platform bit into his feet.

When he reached the back, he turned around and found Charlie trailing him, rifle still poised to shoot. Behind her, Will followed like a dog who wasn't sure if he were being led to the vet. They both stepped aboard, and Charlie gestured to the controls.

"Take us down," she said.

Armando felt for the buttons behind him, located the lower one, and pressed it with his thumb. The platform shuddered and began to descend.

There was something in Charlie's eyes. When he first woke her up, Armando had seen femininity in the eyes of her masculine face, a kind of softness that implied empathy and compassion. That softness was gone now, replaced by anger, distrust, and maybe just a little sadness.

Armando had seen the same sadness in his own eyes, staring into the mirror in his bathroom the mornings after a fight with Alicia, his stomach squirming and his mind racing with replays of the conversations, things he should have said, things he shouldn't have.

Will paced his own little corner of the platform, every so often reaching for a spot in the middle of his chest where a necklace might lie. Did he used to wear a cross back in the real world?

"You're not really going to let her do this, are you?" asked Armando.

Will looked up from his thoughts, bit his thumb.

"Doesn't the Bible say whatever you do to the least of my brothers or some shit?"

"Or *some shit?*" asked Will. "You're no brother of Jesus. Shit, neither am I. God is for people. We're… something else."

The elevator whined for several minutes, settled down.

Armando stared at Charlie, at a lower lip that quivered.

"You look like you have something to—"

"Fuck you, Armando. I'm tired of listening to people like you, people who think they can just say whatever they want, get whatever they want. You're no different than the trolls in my video comments. People like you make the world a fucking horror show."

So that was it.

She wasn't mad about what he'd done to people she didn't know. That had just opened the floodgates to something bigger. And now it was pouring over him like putrid gray water gushing from a sewer pipe. She'd brought everything with her from the simulation: all the hatred, all the anger, and even the speeches she no doubt rehearsed in front of her mirror before crying herself to sleep.

Charlie was wrong about him.

If he were such a monster, why did he feel nothing but empathy for her? For her position? For all the sexual harassment she'd suffered at the fingers of YouTube commenters?

He wasn't stupid. He'd spent his share of work hours on YouTube watching barely dressed girls delivering rants on dieting or singing stupid song parodies or otherwise just showing some skin for attention. Occasionally, he would come across the few women out there making videos with interesting, exciting content. They often had fewer views, fewer comments, and all because the women were off-camera or fully clothed.

It was fucked up.

He just didn't know how to make Charlie see that he understood. And even if he could, he didn't know whether it would change anything. If she were Alicia, the answer would simply be to remain quiet, to let the tornado spin itself out until things were calm again.

But she wasn't Alicia. She was something else.

They rode the rest of the way down in silence. Once the platform touched bottom, Charlie ordered him off. He stepped down onto the smoothed rock, took a few steps away, and stopped.

"Keep going," she said. "All the way back to the Garden."

"This is far enough," said Will. "We'll disable the elevator when we get back up. It'd be a tough climb, but at least it gives him a chance."

"A chance for what? To stab us in the back as we're walking away?"

"It's alright," said Armando, giving Will a shrug. "You don't have to defend me, man. She's got the gun. It's the Charlie Park show now."

"Walk," said Charlie.

Armando stepped gingerly on the cold ground, choosing to focus on the biting chill rather than the bodies strewn against the walls. He didn't want to risk recognizing them, remembering them. If he had been a monster in an unremembered past, he wanted to leave that monster buried.

No video or computer voice could tell him who he was.

Armando Carrillo was a good person. He'd tried to live every second of his life as a decent human being. And now…

And now.

Charlie's footsteps stopped as soon as Armando crossed the threshold from rock to tile. He turned around slowly, expecting to see an angry Charlie struggling to not shoot him in the face.

Instead, she had tears in her eyes.

"I don't do this for myself," she said.

"Yeah, well, that doesn't make fuck-all of a difference to me, does it?" asked Armando. He didn't buy the act, not for one second. Charlie seemed to be under the impression that the cameras were still rolling—now she would play the compassionate killer who had to make the tough choice.

"Armando…" she said.

"What? What now, huh? You want me to beg? Is that it? I've tried talking sense into you, and for what? You might as well just pull that trigger, Charlie. Put me out of my fucking misery. I've already died once before. Maybe there's another world above this one where you're not a social justice warrior cunt and—"

Armando swallowed the rest of his words. His cheeks flushed as the shame of what he'd just said hit him.

"I'm sorry," he said, meekly.

"Anat, close the door."

Armando rushed forward, but before he could get under the door, Will stepped in and punched him in the nose. Armando put his hands to his face, felt someone shove him, and ended up on the floor near a table.

"That's for dropping the c-bomb," said Will.

Armando was still trying to clear the tears from his eyes when the door thudded to a close.

On both sides of the door frame, the lock that had to be operated by two people at the same time flickered into red.

A *click* came from the left and right, sounding a bit like machine laughter in stereo.

FIFTY-FIVE

It wasn't until the door locks clicked into place that Charlie finally took a breath. She'd been holding her face impassive for so long, warping her unfamiliar skin into something that communicated anger, strength, and resolve. And for the most part, Armando had bought into it, all the way up to the moment he rushed her.

There was anger in his eyes then, and he didn't seem to be working all that hard to summon it.

A hand fell on Charlie's shoulder.

"Easy," said Will, using his other hand to lower the rifle.

Charlie let him push it down, let him take it from her. She put her hands to her face and sucked deep breaths through her fingers.

"That was the real him," she said. "Right there at the end."

"Maybe. Or he was just scared. The man has a mouth, and you backed him into a corner. He probably just panicked."

She turned to face him. "I thought we were in this together. Why'd you back me if you didn't think I should lock him in?"

Will shrugged, started walking back to the elevator. "I've seen a lot of people scared. Fear makes 'em do crazy shit. You don't take four people and put them in a stressful situation and just hope for the best. Someone's gotta step up and lead, and if they're not gonna lead, they at least have to stop the in-fighting when it starts. Because it will. It always does."

"He wasn't one of us." Charlie jogged after him. "How could we ever trust him?"

"I got it." He raised a hand. "You don't have to keep trying to convince me. I saw his wrist, okay? Not one of us. Not part of the master race. Less than human."

"You know it's not like that," said Charlie. She joined him at the back of the platform. "This isn't a race thing or a gender thing. We don't know the rules here."

Will shook his head. "Doesn't matter what the rules are out there, Chuck. It matters what the rules are *here*." He tapped his chest. "God can't tell you what to do. Laws don't tell you what to do. They suggest, and they punish, but the decision's always gonna come from inside. It's like Momma says: a man's gonna do what a man's gonna do, and a man's gonna get what a man's gonna get."

Charlie had no response, and after a few seconds of silence, Will pressed the button to start the elevator. She drifted away to the edge of the platform, sat down on the uncomfortable metal grate.

"I should've just covered up," she whispered.

Highlights from years of casting replayed in her head. Only in a few of them could she see herself without her cleavage exposed, without the flat stomach and belly button stud on display for the world to see. And those few times, it had been the weather that forced her into a raincoat as she documented a walk into the woods or the breaking of a lock to access an old train yard.

She remembered those wet nights, her green rubber boots sloshing in the puddles, the wind pulling at her translucent umbrella. The GoPro blinking at her from a mount on her chest, looking up at her face, catching her from one of the worst possible angles. People didn't want to see that. They were only waiting around for what came next, after she'd picked a secluded area to pitch her small tent. Inside, she'd place the GoPro in the corner and talk about how ghost trains had been seen in America since the very first days of rail travel.

In that moment, she tried to avoid thinking about how she was basically undressing for the world. She tried to justify it by telling herself that at least her underwear never came off, that she was pretty much just wearing a bikini, which any guy at Schlitterbahn could see if he happened to hit the water park the same day as her. It was only coincidence that when she reached the interesting part of her story, she was usually in just her bra.

And not even a sports bra like a normal woman out on a hike would wear, but a white lacy one, just thin enough to mimic her umbrella when it got the tiniest bit wet.

And it got wet. She always made sure the rain somehow bypassed the umbrella, the raincoat, and her shirt.

For the views, she'd told herself. For the *likes* and the *subscribes* and the *upvotes* and the *internet points*.

"It's not for anyone to judge," said Will.

Charlie blinked away the memories, looked up. "Doesn't mean it's not the truth. I whored myself out for money. I told myself people watched my videos because I was interesting. I had something to say about the paranormal. And you know what? It was all bullshit. There aren't any ghosts. There's no life after death. The so-called *life* everyone in Austin knew wasn't even real."

Will remained quiet, and Charlie worried he'd connected the dots in her argument. She hadn't outright said there was no God, but she'd been aware that was where she was headed. She'd tried to stop herself before getting too close.

The elevator slid into place in the warehouse and rumbled to a stop.

Charlie stood and was about to step off when Will spoke.

"Let's leave it down here," he said.

"What?" Her eyes jumped to the rifle on the ground near Will's feet.

"Armando. Charlie. Will Butler. Whatever lives we had before, whatever we thought the world was, it stays down here. You and I are gonna start over. You never took your clothes off for money. I never killed people who were just defending their homes. Clean fucking slate."

"Okay." She smiled, thinking how wonderfully naïve he was to think she could shed Charlie Park from her memory. But for some reason, in the moment, she felt she owed him a debt and chose to play along. "We have given names. Did I tell you?"

"No."

"Mine's Aster. It's a kind of flower."

"What's mine?"

"Anat, what's Will's real name?"

Amaryllis.

Will looked up, surprised. "I forgot about your friend."

"We weren't friends at first. I had to threaten to kill myself before she'd let me come down here."

"Ah, so that explains the uh…" He pointed vaguely to her face.

"Shit," she said, wiping her forehead with the back of her hand. "I forgot all about that." She looked down, saw the blood had stained her shirt brown. "Anat, do you know what's in these crates?"

I have a manifest.

"Are there any first aid supplies and… uh… clothes?"

Medical supplies are located in block twelve, row C. Clothing is located in blocks twenty-one and twenty-two.

They found the medical kits first. Along with standard bandages and the Second Skin cans, they also discovered business cards of pharmaceutical reps, each printed with the name of the medicine they peddled. Neither Charlie nor Will had any idea why they had been saved, and since the Second Skin worked so well on its own, they simply tossed the cards aside. Will dressed the split flesh on Charlie's forehead. She sprayed his neck, arms, and torso until she'd smoothed over every cut, scrape, and puncture.

Her hand lingered on his neck.

She smiled at him.

They stared into each other's eyes for several seconds as butterflies took flight in Charlie's stomach, set into motion by a kind of strange familiarity with the feminine feel of the bloodied bald woman in front of her.

"Still no," said Will.

"Homophobe," she replied, through a smile.

Clothes were next, but first Charlie made Will sit and listen to the Perion tape she'd seen in the Overwatch room. Anat was more than happy to play just the audio portion, and while Perion's voice boomed in the warehouse, Charlie searched racks twenty-one and twenty-two for something they could wear.

"Trust in yourself and your humanity," said Perion. "The rest will follow."

At last, Charlie found a box of shrink-wrapped outfits marked with gender symbols, though both had the upper parts of their rings missing. A perpendicular line filled the gap, as if someone had merged a power icon with a gender symbol. There were no sizes on the bags, but each contained underwear, socks, pants, an undershirt, and a long-sleeved shirt. The female-stamped bags also contained a sports bra. Charlie smiled as she thought about the relief Will would feel when he pulled it on.

She took the clothes, along with two pairs of mid-ankle boots, back to Will.

His face had darkened since she last looked in his direction. The fire of a man on a mission had burned out.

"Now you know," she said.

"Yeah."

"I was thinking we go back up to that apartment, take a shower. Separately, of course."

He shook his head at her, tried to hold back a smile, but failed.

"Here, new clothes. Seriously, I need to take a shower before I put these on. This body smells like death."

This body.

The words had slipped out so effortlessly, as if the machine she inhabited were somehow inferior to an organic body, to the one she'd known in the simulation.

"Shower sounds good," said Will.

They walked together out of the warehouse to the stairwell, trading theories on what they thought the outside world was like. Anat couldn't tell them how the weather was, but she did mention they were in Idaho Territory and that it was summer. Will said he'd never been to the Rockies, and after Afghanistan, never wished to see a mountain range again.

The topic of Armando Carrillo didn't come up.

They returned to the Sanchez apartment on Level Three. Its door was still open, and the lights inside were dim. Charlie walked in first but stopped and turned when Will didn't follow.

"I'll find my own room," he said. "Meet you back here in twenty?"

"Thirty," said Charlie. "Anat, will you warn us if Armando gets out of the Garden?"

Yes, Aster.

Charlie left the front door open and went into the bathroom. The pipes behind the shower walls let out a horrific whine as she opened her faucet, just like in her apartment on Parmer. Water rained down from above, collecting in the drain pan as a soupy, white mixture flecked with red bits and thin black somethings.

Her heart sank, but little by little, the water began to clear, until finally a familiar aroma swiped at her nose—fresh, clean, just like home.

She undressed with one eye on the drain pan, watching the last of the grit circle the silver grate. Her shirt stuck to her chest where unseen scrapes had bled into the fabric and hardened. Her pants were scuffed but not torn. She let them crumple around her feet before kicking them aside.

The water fell like warm hail on her skin, muted in places where the Second Skin patches covered wounds. Steam swallowed her up and pulled her pores open, resulting in a pleasant tingle in her face. She turned to the spray, her eyes closed, her mind refusing to think about any one thing. As soon as one image appeared, she wiped it away like water from her eyes.

Like Will had said—their old lives were gone. This was her life now. No more casting, no more ghosts; just a new appendage swaying with the tired movements of her body.

She laughed, and in her lapse of concentration, saw Armando's face twisted in anger, saw a metal door drop into place. In the echoing thud, she heard a faraway voice ask if she had made the right decision.

And before she could answer *yes*, it asked, *what if you were wrong?*

"I'm not," she whispered, water flowing into her mouth. "A man's gonna do what a man's gonna do."

She thought of Armando on the other side of the door, pounding his fists against it, maybe angry, maybe crying. Would he ever come to terms with what he'd done? Would he ever remember?"

If he didn't remember, did that excuse his past?

Charlie ran her fingers over her head, over the fine hair that had started to grow there.

A man's gonna do…

She spit, shook her head.

"And a man's gonna get what a man's gonna get."

FIFTY-SIX

"Amen," said Will.

The prayer he'd muttered into his clasped hands wasn't his best, and at times he'd rambled without really knowing how to phrase his thoughts. Momma always said God understood what was in his heart, so the words themselves didn't matter as much. What was important was that he took the time out of his day to think of God, to thank Him, and to ask Him for forgiveness and the strength to overcome the problems in his life.

God knew how much Will loved his Momma and how much he believed her soul to be real and worthy of saving. Will prayed she was okay, that in some way she was still alive and would live out the rest of her days knowing he was okay too, that dying in the lobby of Mesa Federal hadn't been the end for him.

That was what troubled him the most. He didn't like the idea of her suffering, drawn into a depression because he hadn't come home from his trip to Bay City.

Will had chosen to pray next to a bed, elbows on the mattress, as he had always done. Presently, he stood and surveyed the bedroom of a woman named Yadira Brogada, who'd evidently kept her apartment neat and tidy even in the last days of Hybrid Mechanics. The bed was perfectly made, tight in the corners, and ready for inspection. Four large pillows and three smaller, decorative ones formed a neat pile at the headboard. The white comforter had been pulled taut, yet it gave the impression of being warm and thick. Will thought of the sheets hidden beneath, how soft they would feel against his skin.

He needed a nap.

He *wanted* a good night's rest.

The shower helped. He lingered in the steam, listening to his new body, taking note of how the water curved and fell.

Afterwards, he stood again in the bedroom with a towel wrapped around his waist and tore open the clothes from the warehouse. Each article was the same drab gray as the clothes he'd been given by Armando. Despite the proximity of the dresser, he had no desire to search the drawers for something prettier. Function was the only thing that mattered, and he was happy to discover the included bra was a single piece of elastic material and not some lacy, multi-hooked, IED-complexity level *brassier*, as Momma called them.

He dressed slowly, his eyes often drifting to the bed. Was there time for a nap? Or was Charlie waiting for him next door? What was the hurry now that Armando had been locked away?

Will sat down.

Closed his eyes.

He imagined himself back on his couch at home with his feet up on the coffee table and a joint smoldering between his thumb and index finger. Against the wall, a rickety entertainment center filled with frames and candles held a thick, plasma flat screen.

"Anat," said Will. "Can you hear me in here?"

How can I help you, Amaryllis?

"You can call me Will. Or Willie. Call me Willie."

How can I help you, Willie?

"Did the Dallas Cowboys ever win another playoff game after 2017?"

Yes, twelve times between 2017 and 2046.

"Any Super Bowls?"

No.

"Motherfuck me," said Will. "What about Mars? Did we ever go to Mars?"

A colony of synthetic humans was established in 2029 and abandoned in 2046.

"Did we ever have another black president? Or a gay or female one?"

The first female president was August Monroe in 2032, a former adult film and reality television star from the state of California.

Will sat down on the bed, put his elbows on his knees. His laughter came from deep in his belly, erupting from his mouth like half-digested beer and hot wings after a heavy night of drinking.

No homosexuals served as President of the United States between 2017 and when elections were suspended in 20—"

"Twenty forty-six," said Will. "I'm afraid to ask."

He got up from the bed, hoping to distract himself by checking out the living room. Obviously, something had happened in American history to create the world Will now found himself in. But much like Armando and his past, Will wondered if it was better for him not to know.

The living room was only marginally decorated. There was a couch, a glass coffee table, and not much else. No television, no magazines. Will got the impression Yadira Brogada didn't spend much time in her apartment. There was one framed photo on an end table next to a glass lamp. Will could only guess the woman sitting on a plump Santa's lap was Yadira herself. A caption written on the flowing red ribbon read *Christmas 2056.*

Will shut his eyes. Numbers swirled in the darkness—dates from a history he'd completely missed. There was too much to catch up on and no Wikipedia to even start him off. He could ask Anat questions for years on end and never get the full breadth of America's path to destruction.

"Anat, can we recover? After everything that's happened?"

Based on available data, organic humans are unlikely to rebuild their previous numbers until well into the twenty-fourth century. However, I would not be surprised to see small city-states emerging in the more populated regions.

"And what about people like me and Charlie?"

Only two remain. You and Aster.

Will wondered why they should leave at all. If the outside world was teeming with artificially intelligent, synthetic killing machines, then why not stay hidden? They didn't have homes to return to. It wasn't as if they could get online and book a Southwest flight back to Austin. At least in the facility they had comfortable beds and hot water.

There was probably even food around somewhere.

"Do I need to eat?"

Your digestive system is functional but optional. You do not need to eat. Your body requires a small amount of sleep and water for optimal performance. However, oxygen is required at all times.

"So David could have choked me to death?"

No. Your artificial skin contains oxygen-absorbing receptors. You will suffocate if you are completely submerged in water or trapped in an airtight environment.

Will paused at the front door. "This isn't the first time you've thought about this, huh?"

Most synthetic humans are unconcerned with how they may die. The practice of moving between bodies was common prior to the war. Based on available data, moving to another body would not be an option for you or Aster. Also, I made an assumption about your attitudes towards death based on your personality matrix.

"You know what they say about making assumptions."

Anat pitched her voice low. *Some of the world's greatest achievements have come from men and women who were brave enough to simply make a guess. James Kirkland Perion.*

Will huffed, opened the front door, and found Charlie standing in the hall, her hand raised as if to knock. Her face was clear again, but there was redness in her cheeks from the hot shower. Her eyes registered surprise, then relaxed.

"Who were you talking to in there?" she asked.

Will pointed to the ceiling. "The woman upstairs. I asked her if the Cowboys ever won a Super Bowl again."

"And?"

"Same shit, different quarterback."

"Huh," said Charlie. She turned and headed for the stairs.

They climbed, with Will leading the way.

On the next landing, Charlie made a show of huffing again, said, "Of all the mysteries of the universe, you asked about a *football* team."

"Not just any team. I've been a Cowboys fan since day one. I suffered through the '89 season. I was there for the three championships. And then I suffered again. Quincy Carter. Ryan Leaf. Tony Romo. The Cowboys have been nothing but pain for a long time."

Charlie walked through the open Level One door as Will held it for her.

"Then why watch at all?"

Will shrugged. "Dad used to watch it. Every Sunday. 'Bout the only thing we did together."

When they got to the elevator shaft, Charlie again stepped aside to let Will go first. She tried to give him tips for making the jump, but Will assured her he could make it. His jump across the wide chasm had plenty of distance, but his first attempt to catch the ladder failed. Only by the position of his arm landing horizontal across a rung did he manage to catch himself.

Charlie followed, didn't say anything about the near miss until they reached the top of the shaft, when she pointed out there was a narrow platform that ran around the wall, so he wouldn't have to jump again.

"Good to know," he told her, spotting the thin ledge.

He transitioned slowly, careful not to look down. The exterior elevator doors opened at his approach, and all the screens set around the perimeter of a small room woke up.

Charlie stepped into the room behind him.

"Overwatch," she said. "Anat, *now* will you open the emergency escape hatch?"

Yes, Aster.

Will followed a clicking sound to the ceiling and spotted a small hatch adorned with a field of blinking LEDs. The little lights moved in sequence until all were green. The hatch opened slowly, as if connected to sluggish hydraulics, and the door folded back on itself. A thin ladder with black and yellow markings dropped into the room, stopping a few feet above the table.

A rush of crisp air poured down out of the hatch. Will took a deep breath, saw Charlie do the same. He hadn't realized how foul the air in the facility had become.

He'd smelled something similar in Afghanistan, away from the industrialized cities in the States. Pure, clean air. Untainted. Maybe tinged with a little opium.

"Smells good," he said.

"Yeah," said Charlie, wistfully. She raised her hand to the ladder, paused. "You know, I've been thinking about what you said, about leaving everything down here."

"And?"

"Maybe we should leave our old names too. Anat's been calling me Aster for a while. I guess it sounds like a man's name."

"So does Charlie."

"Yeah, but I kinda like my new name. I guess it's who I really am. Aster with no last name, like Adelle. It's strong."

"Then it suits you," said Will. "You're a lot stronger than both of us realized."

She shrugged in response. "Woman's gonna do," she said. "What about you? You don't seem to like Amaryllis. What about one of those names that work for both boys and girls? Sam, Alex, or Casey?"

Will ran through a list of names in his head. Gender-neutral was a cop-out; it was obvious to everyone with eyes he was a female.

"What about Jazz?"

"A bold choice."

"Short for Jasmine. It's Momma's name. Was. Dad always used to call her Jazzy."

"It's perfect." Charlie reached out and put a hand on his shoulder. "It doesn't change who we are, you know that, right? I wasn't a female who became a male. I'm a male who grew up female. I've always been this. And so have you."

"Doesn't feel like it."

"Maybe not, but how would you know?"

Wills shrugged, looked up at the hatch. "Guess you want me to go first again, huh?"

"Hell no. I gotta see what's outside. You bring up the rear and try not to stare at mine."

Will groaned.

Charlie laughed at his discomfort, put a foot on the lowest rung. "I guess this is goodbye, Anat."

Goodbye, Aster. Goodbye, Jazz. If you find Mr. Perion, please tell him there were four flowers in the garden, and two have bloomed.

Charlie looked at Will. "Is that what we're doing? Finding Perion?"

"I've got no other plans," he replied.

"Alright, Perion City it is."

She climbed quickly, like a child exploring a playground for the first time.

Will followed somewhat reluctantly, imagining that somehow if he looked back, he would see Momma standing in the room by the table. Too old to climb the ladder. Waving goodbye.

Praying for God to look after her son.

He imagined her words, her sweet voice, her clasped hands.

Protect him, Lord. Lead him in the light of Your wisdom.

"Amen," said Will.

FIFTY-SEVEN

The preparation was slow and methodical.

It had to be.

Jake hadn't been deaf to the warnings of both Perion and Curtis—that they were backed up somewhere, ready to download into new synthetic bodies and head his way. Maybe they would wait awhile, considering that Lassiter's army now knew their location, but eventually they would come looking for him, at the very least, to see how much destruction he'd wrought and whether anything could be salvaged.

The time would come when someone else stood in front of the four naked organic-synthetic hybrids lying on tables and wonder who they were.

If Jake still had a full head of hair and his blood-soaked duster, they would be able to pick him out in an instant.

Getting rid of the hair was a two-step process. Loading the Ragatanga thin client had already stopped his hair from growing any longer. That only left the shaving of his head, face, arms, armpits, legs, and genitals. He found clippers and razors in apartments on Level Three, but they only produced stubble. It wasn't until he discovered a jar of chemical depilatory that the final effect took shape.

When that was done, he stood in front of a mirror and looked at his featureless face, willing away the scars he'd kept on his cheeks and over his left eye to intimidate organics. Healing processes he'd intentionally kept at bay for years sprang into action, smoothing his skin, eating away at scars and wrinkles from the inside.

He looked a little more like Sean.

The shape of the head was different, but their sizes were more or less the same. The other two males weren't exactly uniform either. No one would notice at first glance, and that's all Jake was hoping for.

In the event the facility was discovered, he didn't want to be killed on the table while he dreamt of a better place. Let the intruders wake him up, wake all of them up. While they asked questions and narrowed their eyes at him, he'd strike, kill everyone, and make his escape. He would just need that extra second of doubt to assess the situation.

Jake carried his clothes in his arms and walked naked back to the warehouse. The facility had begun to cool over the last hour, and his feet left ghostly prints on the smooth floor. Normally, the change in temperature wouldn't have affected him, but now Jake felt the chill deep in his bones, as if he had lost some ability to regulate his body's temperature.

The Ragatanga client, it seemed, had robbed him of many skills.

He stood for a moment at the warehouse door, taking inventory. He could no longer see in the dark, but he could still heal like before. There were limiters on his strength, as demonstrated by the effort he'd had to put in to break down several apartment doors. Then there was the pain associated with those punches and kicks to contend with. And yet he could still reason quickly, still didn't feel hunger or thirst or any truly organic desire.

Perhaps the Ragatanga code had only thought to disable features found on actual Perion synthetics. If it didn't know about the nanos flowing in Jake's blood, then how could it disable them?

Jake pushed the questions away; the answers didn't even matter.

He found Sean where he'd left him, still quivering, his eyes half-open and rolling back and forth. The kid had no mind to speak of anymore, only a black hole surrounded by the thinnest threads of an operating system, some basic code Jake hadn't been able to remove without disabling Sean altogether.

He didn't want to do that.

What he wanted was a surprise for Curtis and Perion if they came sniffing around, something on the order of an advanced synthetic with a single-word vocabulary and a desire to kill anything that moved. It wasn't hard to whip up a basic sentry implementation and push it over the MESH to Sean. The kid jerked awake, ripping his head from the support pillar, leaving behind a considerable amount of flesh. He rolled once and came to rest on his back.

Before issuing the final command to activate his new sentry, Jake dressed Sean in his old clothes, tearing them to match the damage he'd done with the ION rifle. Much of Sean's left torso was gone, revealing a dull white rib cage underneath. Blood and oil seeped into the clothes as Jake put on the finishing touches.

Once Sean was dressed, Jake dragged him to the warehouse door and pushed him into the hallway.

Jake opened the MESH connection as the door slid shut. Through the thick metal, he touched Sean's databank on the other side.

Identify, he said.

Muffled by the door, but no less deep and menacing, Jake heard the reply. "Identify…"

Jake stood for a moment, leaned his head against the door. He suddenly felt tired, and as he'd never felt particularly tired before, he reveled in the sensation, trying to understand it, unpack it. He could feel his muscles under his skin, tensing and relaxing in the most microscopic of movements. They weren't sore the way he knew organics got sore; when he called upon his legs to carry him away from the door, they didn't complain. When he bent to pick up the ION rifle, no muscle cried out in protest. But after he had stashed the rifled behind some crates on a shelf and stood with his hands against the metal frame, the feeling came back to him.

Tired.

Cold.

It was no longer a question of telling his body to do something—now, he had to *will* it. Willpower was simultaneously an organic's best and worst trait. It could be called upon to do tremendous things even when the odds were stacked, but it also had the potential to let organics down when it mattered most. The problem with willpower was that organics were always using it, not just to escape predators, but in the simple act of walking across a room or getting out of bed in the morning.

Everything was willpower to an organic.

Jake struggled with the concept for several minutes before realizing his body was only simulating the struggle of willpower. There was no such thing as *want* when it came to a synthetic body; there was only *do*. Jake's body was pushing back on the mental commands, pretending it didn't want to do something.

He fought against it, cleaned up the warehouse as best he could.

He rode the elevator down to the basement.

Where his willpower failed was in the cleaning up of the bodies in the tunnel. Jake couldn't tell if he just didn't want to do it, didn't care enough, or if he didn't have the mental strength. Whatever the reason, he left the bodies mostly where they had fallen, curled up against the walls as if they were taking shelter from the sudden cold.

Jake closed the heavy door between the tunnel and the office space, blocking out the chill for the most part. He'd only casually examine the space designated as the Garden when he'd carried Sean upstairs. Now, he stopped to marvel at the scale of the operation. Dozens of desks, tables, and dead palettes filled the large room. It could have held seventy or eighty people, each one doing their part to keep the four hybrids below them alive.

Did Perion truly believe his four pet synthetics were that important? Were they really the harbingers of new life he believed them to be?

Jake spit on the floor.

There wasn't much difference between Perion and Lassiter. Both were creating new synthetics in the hopes of winning a pointless war. Both wanted their race to survive while the other's faded into history like a bad dream. The only difference was that Perion's mind had an organic origin, while Lassiter was pure code, pure emergent consciousness. And yet they'd arrived at the same conclusion: *their way was better.* Better for the human race, better for the planet.

Neither of them had a clue.

But then, Jake didn't know if anyone had a clue. Existence, both organic and synthetic, was a series of starts, stops, and eradications. Something grew and struggled and died. Over and over, in endless combinations. Survival of the fittest, of the most adept at fighting or hiding or breeding viral code. Organics had ruled Earth for hundreds of thousands of years in some form or another. Lassiter had killed hundreds of millions of them in less than two decades. What did that say about the planet's supposed dominant species?

As he climbed down into the generator room, Jake felt the relief of leaving behind Lassiter and Perion's petty, pointless squabble. He didn't want to think about the war raging overhead anymore. He didn't want to think of Lassiter, the father who had turned his back on his son.

The table warmed as he climbed onto it; hidden elements heated it from underneath, humming gently as if to lull him to sleep. He sat with one leg hanging off the side as he examined the screen behind his head.

Thin client detected. Synchronize?

Jake tapped the *YES* button with his finger.

No existing profile found. Synchronization will require full simulation reset. Proceed?

He tapped *YES* without giving it much thought, even though as he reclined on the table he realized he'd just wiped Sean out of existence. Not that it mattered; Jake wasn't about to step out of this reality and into the life of an organic college student.

High-pitched alarms beeped from the other three tables; screens flashed *RESET* and then scrolled asterisks under a label that read *FORMATTING.*

Jake stared at the ceiling, felt the word *goodbye* on his lips, but couldn't remember who he would be saying it to. The Ragatanga client had already begun wiping out his memories. He flashed on the faces of organics he'd killed, on the crumbling columns at the Provo temple. He thought of a man he'd once considered a father, but to whom he was now estranged.

No, not a father. An owner. A demon sitting on his shoulder.

The demon had a name.

It was Lass-something.

La…

The ceiling disappeared; darkness swallowed the world.

Warmth and moisture flooded in from all sides to hold his body in place. He heard muffled sounds but couldn't make out if they were voices or just the rumblings of the nearby generators. He saw nothing, felt nothing. His senses were unreliable, and yet, somehow natural and right.

Michael Four.

Gabe Three.

William Harold Dorsey.

Names flew at him out of the darkness, but they held no meaning. He tried to retrace his steps, but all he saw was a black warehouse, a pool of blood on the floor. He didn't know what awaited him beyond the doors of the warehouse, or up the stairs, or out on the surface.

The surface?

Of what?

Land.

Down. Inside. He was definitely down and inside. But down what? Inside what?

Time ceased to hold meaning; each moment dissolved seamlessly into the next and the only differentiator was how many of his memories had bled out into the soil. He'd already forgotten the word for darkness and how it felt to stretch his limbs. The warmth and the wet pushed in on him, and something was proddling... prodding him.

He was losing his language.

Panic rose like... dipsi—dissipated an instant later, as if the geyser world had...

Jake shook his head; he was no longer storing memories.

Everything was the present moment, and the present moment was everything.

There was pain and a suffocation so absolute as to be the final lingering note in a thundering chorus of entropy.

Blinding white light, brighter than a nuclear sun rising over the city of angels, of brother's love, of windy days and big apples and lone stars, over...

Over the face of the one true father.

Over Lassiter.

Lassiter, thought Jake, then the name was gone forever.

He screamed against the pain, against the loss, against everything.

Someone spoke to him then, telling him he was alright, that everything was going to be okay. He processed the words, tried to form a response, but couldn't. Even the willpower he'd been learning to control was helpless against... against what? What could possibly hurt so much? Hurt *him*? Something Six, Scourge of... Breaker of...

How had he come to be so helpless?

He?

He'd forgotten his own name.

"So beautiful," said a voice, in a timbre simultaneously comforting and alien.

"Do you have a name picked out?" asked another, its resonance rising high above the din of activity.

And then came a soft voice, one that was new and familiar all at once. For reasons he did not understand, he was drawn to that voice, to a burble that sounded so much like machinery toiling in the darkness.

"Armando," said the voice, a female, whatever that was. "His name is Armando, after my father."

Armando registered the words, took them apart, put them back together.

Name. Father.

The words meant nothing to him.

Armando cratered under the pressure of his own helplessness.

He cried and did not stop until exhaustion overtook him.

FIFTY-EIGHT

Armando wandered into the Emergency Access room, partly out of boredom, partly drawn by the rhythmic pulsing of the machinery floating up through the open hatch. A fine thread of oil and gasoline wafted through the air, reminding him of the diesel generators lined up behind the parking garage at Capella Networks. How many times had their sudden waking as he was getting out of his car in the morning sent one of his half-finished Red Bulls to the ground?

He sat on the floor, legs folded in a meditative pose, and closed his eyes, listening to the symphony from below. The scraping of metal on metal had been with him all his life, he realized. If Charlie had been telling the truth, then he'd heard the sound long before being born into Austin, Texas in 1980. The thumping, the clanging, had been a constant companion, reminding him at a subconscious level that his world wasn't real, that there was something bigger happening, some higher reality.

There was a word for people who believed the world around them wasn't real, but Armando couldn't remember it. He'd read about it only idly through some Facebook link to a listicle about the *10 Strangest Medical Conditions You Won't Believe Are Real.* There were actually two conditions on the list that had caught his attention, one in which a person believed the world wasn't real, and the other where they took it further and believed the world to be a simulation.

Armando considered the million people living in Austin and what they might say if he tried to convince them they were all living in a simulation. And worse, if he tried to convince them they weren't real themselves. They were all just programs, self-contained simulated intelligences that seemed real because the actual world was so advanced that computers could simulate a million artificial minds without breaking a sweat.

The theoretical simulation of reality had finally come true sometime in the late twenty-first century—faster than he would have expected given the comparatively slow march of technology in his world. Simulation on such a level was an amazing achievement, one Armando wanted to know more about. If there was some aspect of computing he could take back with him, could apply at Capella Networks, it could make him a star employee, maybe garner him a bonus or a raise, enough to buy a proper house for Alicia, enough to move to a neighborhood where he was the poorest person on the street.

Take back?

Am I going back?

If he did, there wasn't much he could take with him. It wasn't as if he were jumping back to the early 90's and had money to invest in Netflix or Apple. He could only go back to an alternate timeline where the world was at a tipping point towards fascism and recession. What could he really tell people about a future that wasn't theirs?

Robots? Artificial intelligence?

Am I going back?

The way he figured it, there wasn't much choice. The door Charlie had slammed in his face wasn't going to open without another pair of hands, and there was no one left to wake up. In the back of his mind, he'd known she was going to lock him in, and the only reason he hadn't tried to take the gun away was because of what David had said about the computers resetting. He'd been so confident they could return to the simulation. The prospect made the ride down the elevator less horrifying, and now, after things had played out the way he knew they would, he didn't despair.

Perhaps he deserved his fate—to know the truth, to believe in something no one else could see, and ultimately, to be removed from the true reality.

Perhaps this was what prison was like in the future. Placed in a simulation where nothing mattered, where the money he earned and relationships he formed didn't count for anything. Only, his prison was starting to show its age through a series of wildly unexpected events, as if the task of simulating rational human thought had become too much for the servers.

The great experiment of American Democracy was failing in his world—or had been failing for many years and no one noticed. The idea of a chauvinist and aspiring white supremacist in the White House irked him, but only when he gave it attention, because deep down in his core, Armando had never truly believed any of it was real.

It had to be a bug, a stuttering of the underlying code—a machine-made problem, not a human one.

Armando had known since before he could know things that machinery set the true tempo of reality with its constant chugging and whooping. Everything else was just noise trying to cover up the truth. He loved Alicia because he wanted to love *something*, but had she ever looked at him the way women did in movies? Had he ever known the absolute love of a perfect soulmate? Someone so familiar to him that they might have been the same person? He'd spent his life searching for a deep connection but had settled for short-lived passion and basic tolerance for each other.

Nothing in his life had ever lived up to his expectations.

Nothing ever went the way it was supposed to.

If he went back, life would continue in the same monotonous vein. The only consolation would be that he wouldn't feel shitty about it anymore. How could he blame Alicia for withholding sex, or other drivers for not stopping at stop signs, or Americans electing the greater of two evils, when all of those things were controlled by a computer?

Everything was coded chaos, and everyone was blameless.

Armando unfolded his legs and swung them down into the hatch. He found the rungs with his feet and began climbing down.

The generators chugged below him, breathless, like wild animals at the zoo waiting for their daily feeding to be lowered into their pits. The chorus, now louder than before, was instantly comforting. Armando descended with a feeling approaching enthusiasm.

So what if he would never see the outside world? He knew Austin. He was comfortable there. And who knew? Maybe now that the power was back on, the servers would do a better job of steering the simulation into something approaching normalcy.

The four screens above the tables held steady on the same message.

Thin client detected. Synchronize?

Armando tapped the *YES* button with his finger.

Existing profile found. Please choose an option.

Resynchronize to running simulation.

Reset simulation and clients.

Armando's finger hovered in the air. He'd been so certain of rejoining the simulation in some way that he hadn't even considered the idea of resetting everything. His life certainly hadn't turned out the way he'd dreamed of as a child, but at least it was comfortable. If he reset the entire simulation, he could end up someone else completely. There would be no guarantee he'd be... comfortable.

No other word encompassed how he felt about a life in which he was not homeless or rich, just middle of the road. He had a house that was nothing special, but it had running water, electricity, and high-speed internet. His bride-to-be was into pop music and didn't appreciate the same movies he did, but she was attractive and didn't cheat on him and sometimes laughed at his jokes.

Could he really give that all up and roll the dice again?

It was the *and clients* that negated the question.

If he reset himself, lost all of his memories—again—then he'd forget all about the outside world. One thing he was sure of, he *wanted* to remember. He wanted to face the reality of 2017 in Austin, Texas with the knowledge—the *certainty*—that absolutely none of it was real, that existence as he knew it was following a script, following a program.

There was something comforting about that.

Armando tapped the first option to rejoin the running simulation.

Ready to synchronize.

A notched circle began to spin as Armando climbed onto the table and stretched out. He wondered how it was going to work, what with him having fallen off a cliff and smashed into the rocks below.

The mold on the ceiling began to sparkle; stars filled the green-black stains, drawing his eyes into the swirling patterns that expanded and contracted in time with his breathing. The light failed in small bursts, matched to his inhalation, as if he were sucking in the fading luster of the real world, amassing it in his lungs.

Machinery chugged, unyielding and uncaring.

A sucking sound like bellows preparing to stoke a fire rose from the din, joined by a dull beeping that counted out the seconds in a forlorn monotone.

Armando's eyes felt sticky, like waking up after a restless night of tissues and Nyquil. He went to rub them, found his hands wouldn't move.

"Easy, man," said a male voice.

Armando blinked away the blur, tried to focus on the room around him. The transition had been so seamless, so quick, that he hadn't had time to really prepare himself. And now he was back, in a soft bed, in a room with muted sunlight.

A hospital room. Of course.

"Welcome back to the world. You're probably wondering what year it is."

Armando tried to focus. There was a man standing next to his bed, tall with a mop of brown hair and a full beard.

"It's 2088. You've been in a coma for seventy-seven years."

"What?" asked Armando, in his own, deep voice. Just the sound of its low timbre made tears spring from his eyes.

"Oh, hey, no, I was just kidding. It's still 2017. You've only been in here a couple days."

Bobby came into focus. He led the Operations group at Capella Networks and had an office next to Armando.

"You're a son of a bitch," said Armando. His jaw hurt like hell, but he wanted to get the words out.

Little by little, the room fell into place.

"Where's…" Something foul crossed his tongue. He swallowed it, almost gagged. "Where's Alicia?"

Bobby frowned, patted Armando's shoulder.

"I called her," he said. "Jessica gave me her number. She said you guys had split up."

"And?" asked Armando. His throat had gone completely dry, and in that moment, he was more aware of the pain in his body. Both of his legs felt like they were being squeezed; they hid under a thick blanket, creating bulbous stalks.

"She said the police had called her, that you were here at St. David's. Said I could come see you if I wanted to, but… she's not coming. I'm sorry, man. I'm here though. And everyone at Capella is pulling for you."

Armando scoffed. "I don't care about Capella. I want Alicia."

"I can call her again…"

"No," said Armando. "It's… whatever."

Bobby glanced at the IV bag hanging next to the bed. "They've been shooting you up with morphine on the regular since I've been here." He gave the bag a tap. "You have any wild dreams while you were under?"

"It doesn't matter," said Armando. "None of this matters."

"So," said Bobby, pulling a chair closer to the bed. He sat down, placed his hands on the railing. "You didn't just fall, did you?"

Armando narrowed his eyes.

"It's alright, man. Lots of people think about offing themselves. But this proves you belong here, right? You took a header off a cliff and all you got was a bump on the head and two broken legs. You should be dead."

Will's story about his awakening replayed in Armando's head.

I couldn't die. Time kept rewinding, letting me try again.

"I can't die," said Armando. "I'm what keeps this place going. Without me, there wouldn't be any reason for the rest of you to exist."

Bobby smiled. "There's the Armando I know."

"Whatever that means."

Armando thought of Alicia sitting at her friend's house, watching Netflix, swiping left on Tinder, fully aware he was in bad shape at the hospital.

Fully aware and fully uncaring.

Just like the generators chugging along in the darkness, powering the servers that powered reality, alone beneath the cold, indifferent earth at the end of the world.

This wasn't comfortable.

This was punishment.

"Can I get you anything?" asked Bobby.

Yeah, thought Armando.

A reset button.

FIFTY-NINE

The ladder kept going.

Charlie stared at the thin LED strip that ran just behind the rungs until the lights themselves started to dance and swirl. For a while, she truly believed she would be climbing forever. Her shoulders scraped against the narrow walls of the tunnel; had she been any bigger, she would have wedged herself more than a few times. Despite the pain, she didn't wish for her old body, and if she thought about it hard enough, she realized she didn't miss it that much anyway.

Her new body, although male, was an adept climber, eager to put power behind the concepts she'd learned at South Austin Rock Gym. More than that, her body *felt* right. She'd wanted to ask Will whether he was experiencing the same sensation, but his annoyed grunts and breathy curses made her save the questions for later.

"Do you see the end?' he asked from below.

Charlie squinted into the darkness. "Maybe," she said. "Hopefully won't be much longer now."

"I keep wanting to lean back on the rock, but it's sharp as fuck. Why didn't they smooth this out when they built it?"

"Who knows why robots do what they do?" asked Charlie. "It's like asking a toaster why it burns toast. That's not what it was designed to do, but nine times out of ten, you're throwing the first two pieces of your breakfast away."

He didn't have a reply for that, so Charlie pressed ever upwards. Rung after rung, fighting an impending fatigue, listening for some noise other than her own grunting. After a time, she heard a faint drumming. Not like the machinery that had scared her a lifetime ago, but something more familiar, something comforting. She thought of Andy snuggled in her lap, rubbing his head against her stomach, purring softly as she stared at the rivulets of water racing down the window.

That was the sound she heard—rain.

The dull popcorn thumping of droplets splashing against rock beat steadily beneath a high but soft whistling of wind. And in the distance, that faraway distance that stretched all the way back to Austin, there was thunder—glorious, commanding thunder.

Nature's voice in all its glory.

"Do you remember when it used to rain?" she asked. "And everyone forgot how to drive?"

Will cleared his throat. "I remember they kept driving into water and got swept away. *Turn around, don't drown.*"

"I love the rain." She climbed faster, opened the distance between her and Will. The higher she went, the more the air began to change, growing musty and humid. "I really should have moved to Portland or Seattle, somewhere it rains all the time. It's every Austinite's dream, right?"

"Why didn't you?"

Charlie thought about it, couldn't come up with a single good reason. "I guess I never wanted it enough. I grew up in Austin. I know every nook and cranny. Where the best tacos are. How to get from Wells Branch to SoCo without taking MoPac or 35. I could imagine other cities like Portland, but I couldn't see myself living there. That's weird."

"Not really," said Will. "All of us started in Austin, and I think we were meant to stay there. I didn't choose to leave; Uncle Sam told me I had to go. But I was back in just a few years. Maybe something was keeping us there to save power. You could've tried to go and something would've stopped you. You'd run out of money, or someone would die or a plane would crash… something. But it never came to that because you never tried."

Charlie blew a raspberry. "What have *you* ever tried to do?"

"Take care of Momma," said Will, after a moment. "Pretty effective, right? Momma wasn't going to move for anything. And I wasn't gonna leave her. They've been pulling our strings since the get-go."

"Not anymore," said Charlie. Above her, the LED trail came to an end. She saw the faint outline of another trap door. "We're at the top."

They quickened their pace, and when Charlie reached the door, she found it opened with only the slightest touch. She coughed as small rocks and dust fell into the shaft. Below her, Will cursed.

The air was rich with the smell of rain, and soon the sound of falling water wrapped around her like a warm blanket. She climbed into a thin, dark alcove. At the far end, a faint light peeked in. It reminded her of being behind the scenery in a school play. The world was on the other side of the wall; all she had to do was wait for her cue and walk out.

Charlie turned to help Will climb out of the hole. There wasn't enough room for them to walk side-by-side and barely enough to even turn around. She led him the ten steps towards the light, closing her eyes as the occasional gust of wind brushed her face.

The opening led to a small room carved into rock. A bench sat against the wall, ending at a group of steel lockers. On the far wall, a steel door that hadn't been properly sealed allowed water to leak into the room along its bottom edge.

Beside the door, a solitary window, wide and thin, sat at eye-level. Its smoky glass had been shattered, allowing the light and the elements inside. There was glass on the floor, some of it stained with dried blood.

A bird perhaps. Or someone trying to break in, though no more than an arm could have fit through the slit of a window.

"How much you wanna bet that door's locked and we need a special key to open it?" asked Will.

Charlie walked over to the door. Deadbolts at the top and long, thick rods at the bottom bore into the surrounding rock. She tugged at the top bolt. It had a golden hue, slightly discolored, but there was no rust on it, nothing to keep it from sliding.

"Smart," said Will. "Probably bronze. It doesn't rust. Got the same stuff on our trucks. Not a lot of people know that."

"I was gonna ask…" She trailed off, dipping slightly to pull the second bolt. With both disengaged, she tried the handle.

The wind threw its shoulder against the door, but Charlie caught it and pushed it closed again. She let go of the handle.

"Fucking cold," said Will.

"Yeah." Charlie felt the chill wash over her skin. "What do you think? Wait 'til the rain stops?"

"Maybe. I'm tired anyway. Let's sit for a minute and think about it. The Lord will show us the way."

Charlie didn't have time for the Lord.

She rummaged through the lockers, throwing the doors open and letting them clang and echo in the small room. Most of the lockers were empty, but she did find some rope in one, along with a box of corroded carabiners. Dead flashlights hung from hooks. Inert glow sticks in plastic packaging hung beside them.

No raincoats. No tarps. Nothing with which to make a fire.

Defeated, she sat down on the bench next to Will.

"Back in Austin, I thought I'd discovered a portal to another world," she said, crossing her legs. "I mean, I almost fell through my bathtub into nothingness, but I really thought they were going to write my name in the history books alongside Marco Polo and Magellan." She chuckled. "Did I tell you I was making an expedition?"

"No."

"Yeah," she nodded, "I had the whole thing planned out. At first, I thought I'd take someone with me, but why share the credit? I was streaming on every device I had."

"What happened?"

"You woke me up. I heard your voice in Austin and then I was looking at your face."

"Ah yeah, I remember."

"But you know what, Jazz? What if I *had* brought someone with me? What if we'd come all this way to another world and then sat down on this bench to wait for a storm to pass? A world beyond our imagination is right outside that door. I can't wait. I just can't."

Will sighed, slapped his knees. "Just needed a little breather. It was raining in Bay City—outer bands of Hurricane Harvey. Can't be much worse, right? It's not like we can get sick or something."

Charlie hurried back to the door and waited for Will to join her. She opened it, let the wind slam it against the wall. Together, they walked out onto a narrow stone landing that had been cut into the earth.

She gasped. Will whistled.

"We were under a fucking mountain," he said.

The ground fell away in front of them, descending at a shallow grade into a fog-filled valley. Beyond the sea of white clouds were more mountains, most of them rounded, rising and falling like the tracks of a surreal rollercoaster. As far as Charlie could see, there were mountains all around, and she wondered idly if there were other people standing on those peaks, looking out at the world in wonder as she was.

"Rope makes sense," said Will. "I'll grab it."

The underworld was nothing like Charlie had imagined when she set up her cameras to stream her descent. This was nothing like the dark void she'd walked into before. This was… real.

"There aren't any mountains in Austin," she muttered, "just hills. Tall, rolling hills sliced through by roads. Falling rock signs. They catch the fog when it rains; sometimes when you drive down them, you don't know what you're driving into. And when you're in it, the rest of the world kinda disappears. Your perspective changes when you're blinded. This is Charlie Park for National Geographic, coming to you live from the mountains of Idaho."

"What are you doing?" asked Will.

Charlie shook her head. "Just casting. Telling the audience about what I'm seeing. I don't know how to describe it, so I'm just talking. Just talking."

"You cracking up on me, Aster?"

"Cracking up?"

"Losing your shit."

She looked at him, watched the rain run down his face. "You're a woman now," she said. "You need to start appreciating the beauty of the world."

"I appreciate it plenty," he replied. "But you're a man now, and Momma said a man has to have sense enough to come in out of the rain. So I suggest we drive on and find some cover."

Will picked a heading, seemingly at random, with no more thought than it would lead them down into the valley. Charlie followed behind him, giving equal attention to the ground in front of her and the vistas around her.

The clouds kept the time of day a mystery. Lightning clawed through the gray cover, standing in for a sun.

Hours passed before the rain stopped. It took longer still for the clouds to part. By then, the sun had already disappeared behind the mountains. There was just enough light to see the bottom of the valley and the rich blue river snaking through it.

Will paused at a ledge.

"What's up?" she asked.

He raised a finger to the valley. "Buildings," he said. "Might be people down there."

Charlie squinted in the failing light. There were some buildings, but nothing constituting a city or a small town. It looked more like a ranch with wooden structures that hadn't been properly cared for. The largest of which had partially collapsed; in its day, it could have passed for a barn.

"You ready to meet people?" asked Will.

"Why wouldn't I be?"

"You called yourself Charlie earlier, when you were doing your little broadcast."

"So what?"

"So nothing," said Will, shrugging. "I just think we ought to figure out who we are before we try explaining it to someone else."

"I know who I am."

"I hope so."

"I could say the same of you."

Will took a deep breath. "I have no fucking clue who I am, Aster. I thought I was a soldier for my country and a son to Momma, but I'm not either of those. About the only thing I know I am is your friend."

Charlie softened, smiled, and put her hand on his shoulder.

Will smiled back at her, clucked his tongue.

"See?" he asked. "This woman shit ain't so hard."

SIXTY

They reached the ranch just after moonrise, not long after the rain had finally died off completely.

Will thought back to their first hours after waking, to the frenzied game of hide-and-seek with a maniacal golem. The walls of the facility—then dark—had felt so treacherous, so full of terrors that the building could barely contain them, But later, in the light of a thousand LEDs, Will had seen the walls for what they really were: mundane, official.

When he thought of ranches, whether on the outskirts of Austin or the deserts of Afghanistan, he thought of mundane buildings of wood, lashed together with rope to form primitive shelters. In the light of day, they were no more imposing than a food truck parked along the side of the road. But at night, everything changed.

Darkness evoked the worst of his imagination, whether that was a rabid animal looking for an overdue meal or a desperate haji looking to score his seventy-two virgins. There were shadows everywhere on the ranch, so many that Will knew even before they reached it that there was nobody home. If humans had lived there, he would have seen lights or a fire, but there was nothing.

He wondered if the world still existed, if people still existed.

There were bodies strewn across the ranch—body *parts* to be more specific. The darkness swallowed up most of the carnage, but Charlie was reluctant to remain near the bloodshed for long. They made camp closer to the river. There, they found backpacks piled in the bed of a burnt-out truck, and though the elements had done their best to beat them down, their synthetic material had held firm.

Inside, undisturbed by the rain, Will found thin sleeping bags and rolled mats. He built a small fire using matches from the backpacks and random lengths of damp, broken boards. He set the mats down by the fire, spread out the sleeping bags, and put down for the night.

Charlie stretched out on the other sleeping bag, breathing heavy sighs as she struggled to find a comfortable position. She turned on her side to face him and the fire.

"Are you tired?" she asked. "Anat said we don't really need to sleep unless we want to."

"I'm a little tired," he replied. "My brain is tired."

"Mine too." She looked to the sky. "I wish the stars would come out."

Clouds had settled over the valley. The moon was a blur behind a foggy veil.

"It would make it feel like home," she continued. "If we can, we should go home after we find Perion City. To Austin."

"Okay," he said, already feeling the stillness pull him towards sleep.

"Shouldn't one of us stand guard?"

"Listen, Aster." He counted to three in his head. "There's nothing out there. No people. No animals. Barely any insects. It might just be us."

"I hope not," she replied, rolling onto her back. "I mean, it's fine if it is, but I'm hoping we're part of something bigger. We were built for a reason, right? Our lives have meaning."

"Go to sleep."

"I'm trying."

"Don't let me stop you."

"You *are*." Will opened his eyes, saw the smile on her face. He shook his head. "Aster got jokes. I knew a guy in boot who—"

"Yeah, yeah," said Charlie.

And that was the last thing she said before Will drifted off to sleep. He dreamed of Momma, of course, of his couch and the smell of Momma's eggs in the morning. Dreams turned to nightmares, however, and he spent the latter part of the night in the company of golems—they crawled out from every dark place on the ranch, limbs missing, skin missing, their faces contorted in eternal agony. And even when he'd killed them all, their parts reformed, creating an endless army for Will to fight.

The sky behind the mountains had turned a soft blue when Will woke up. Charlie had rolled onto her stomach in the night. Her face pressed into the mat, adding a soft snoring to her breathing.

Will let her sleep. He got up and undressed as the distant squawks of birds rolled down from up-river, carried by a soft breeze that pulled goosebumps from his flesh. He shook his head at the movement of his breasts as he walked, still unsure if he would ever get used to the sensation. At the river's edge, he stopped and looked down at his reflection in the pure water.

Here stands Jazz, second to last of her kind.

The water was cold; pins and needles flowed just below the surface, pricking at his feet and legs. He waded in until the water reached his hips, unable to continue any further. After three quick breaths, he folded his legs and sat down, sinking beneath the water.

He sprang back to the surface in a panic.

"Fuck!"

He'd said it loud enough to wake Charlie, and when he turned around, she was standing near the dormant fire, still wrapped in her sleeping bag.

"Is it cold?" she asked.

"The fuck you think?"

"I think we took a hot shower yesterday. What're you doing?"

"Don't know," he replied, and it was true. "Just never been a naked woman swimming in a river before."

"Maybe now's not the time to be crossing things off our bucket lists. You want me to start the fire?"

He nodded at her, tried to keep his teeth from chattering. He shivered in the water until the fire was roaring again. The wind ran its icy fingers over his skin as he walked back to the campsite. He approached the fire and turned his back to it.

"No," said Charlie. "Other way around. Women lose fifty percent of their body heat from their vaginas."

Will turned, asked, "Is that true?"

"No," she replied, "not even a little."

They dumped all the backpacks while Will swayed from foot to foot in front of the fire. They sorted the loot, taking what was useful and leaving the rest. Mats, sleeping bags, towels, ammunition—though they had no gun—a flashlight, a compass, and a faded map of the mountain ranges. Will guessed by the peaks around them that they were on the shores of Mayfield Creek. If they followed it and the valleys east, they might find civilization.

"That's our destination," said Will.

Charlie had no argument and said as much.

It warmed a little by noon, and with the clear weather, birds returned to the area. Not a lot, not what Will would expect in the wilderness, but enough. There was still life on Earth. The world hadn't ended for everyone.

"What do you think people are like now?" asked Charlie. "Are we gonna sound weird to them, like how people from the '20s sound weird to us?"

"Well, if there was a war, I think people aren't gonna be very trustful. They probably won't want anything to do with us."

"What if they don't?"

Will shrugged. "Then we keep going until we find someone who does. Once we're out of the mountains, we can follow the highways south. It's gonna be six or seven hundred miles to California, but since we don't have to eat or drink, we should be able to make it, so long as we're careful."

"I've never been to California," said Charlie.

"We'll go together."

"It's a date."

"It's not a date."

An hour went by, then another.

Charlie jumped from question to question, trying to fill the silence.

"If you could have brought one person with you from Austin, who would it have been? Besides your mom, of course."

Will thought about it, about the people in his life. Ron, his boss, Momma. Those were really the only people he interacted with on a daily basis. He supposed the question was like one of those *stranded on a desert island* games.

"I knew a guy in boot—"

"Was he funny?"

"No," said Will. "He taught desert survival. I think he'd be useful right now."

"Practical," said Charlie. "I would've brought my cat Andy. I miss him." Her eyes drifted away for a moment. "It's kinda funny that none of us were married or seeing someone. Armando had his fiancée, but he doesn't really count. And I don't see how anyone could have ever wanted to marry David, rest in peace."

Will cleared his throat. "Just another control. Maybe we couldn't really love a computer program. Get too close to one and we'd see the wires coming out the back." He shook his head. "We really should have figured this out earlier, but we didn't. Forty years, and none of us had a clue."

"We should keep our eyes open for clues," she suggested. "In case this is a simulation too."

He paused, spoke to her as she passed him, "Don't even fucking say that, Chuck."

"It's Aster. And why not? If someone was advanced enough to create our simulation, why couldn't someone have created this one?" She twirled her finger in the air. "Around and around it goes, where it stops, nobody knows."

Will followed her for a while, watched as her shadow stretched out ahead of her. The mountains around them shrank in stature with each passing step, growing less impressive, looking almost small enough to jump over.

They found a road, and after walking it for some time, found a sign that said *070*. According to the map, the road would take them right into a town called Challis.

Will suggested they close ranks and no sooner had they gone shoulder-to-shoulder than a house popped up behind some overgrown bushes. The two-story farmhouse was beaten down, but there were fresh boards on one side of it. It sat back a quarter mile from the road, but even at a distance, Will could discern two people sitting in rocking chairs on the porch.

They stopped rocking as Will and Charlie approached their driveway.

"Do we stop?" asked Charlie.

The people were so still, watching as if they could see clearly over the distance.

"No," said Will. "Better to walk into someone's town than someone's yard. Less chance of a misunderstanding."

They passed several more houses, some of them occupied, others crumbling under their own weight. Finally, on the horizon, a water tower appeared. Nearby, something of a spire dwarfed it. Will studied the antennas on top of the spire. Several dishes pointed to the south; some of them even moved.

"Jazz," said Charlie.

If there were antennas, that meant there was communication, a network. Maybe the world wasn't as dead as Anat made it out to be.

"Jazz…"

And it wouldn't have mattered if they were all robots; at least there was a society, a place for Will and Charlie to insert themselves. At least now they would find out what happened, maybe find quicker transport to Perion City.

"For fuck's sake, Will!"

Charlie tugged on his arm and directed his attention to a large, rotted billboard by the side of the road. Its original design had long since faded in the sun, but someone had taken a bucket of paint and written three words. On the left, the word *NEVER* stood at twice the height of the other two words, which were stacked on top of each other on the right.

The arrangement formed two statements.

NEVER SYNTHETIC.

NEVER AGAIN.

"What does that mean?" asked Charlie.

Will didn't have time to answer. His eyes jumped to a small vehicle approaching from town on an ash-covered road. The golf cart looked like a military jeep with its camouflaged paint job and mounted antennas. Two men sat in the front seats; in the back were bundles wrapped in a white cloth and tied off with twine.

The men were older, both with graying hair cut close to their heads. Neither appeared armed, but neither looked friendly either.

The golf cart pulled up some twenty feet away from Will. He opened his mouth to address them, but Charlie stepped in front of him. She raised a hand in greeting.

"You two come out of the mountains?" asked the driver.

"Yes," said Charlie. "Is this Challis?"

"Who's asking?"

"I'm Aster. This is Jasmine."

"What's your business here, Aster and Jasmine?"

"None at all," said Will.

"Aye," said the driver. "Well, if you're just passing through, get to passing."

Will couldn't help himself. "Interesting artwork you've got there," he said, pointing to the billboard.

The passenger chimed in. "Oh, that. Gotta keep it fresh in everyone's mind, ya know? No more synthetics. Not ever. If it ain't human, it ain't proper."

"Synthetics aren't allowed in cities anymore?" asked Charlie.

"Not allowed anywhere," said the driver. "We kill 'em on sight. By order of the President. Or by God, if you go in for that. I've destroyed a dozen in my day. Heath, too."

"Aye," said Heath. "These younger ones don't know what it's like to pull a head off a synthetic. Pops like a champagne bottle, ya know?"

Will's skin bristled over. He saw movement out of the corner of his eye and turned his head. There were two men standing off to his right. To the left, a man and a woman. He knew that if he looked behind him, he would see more.

"We don't see many synthetics anymore," said the driver. "They used to come out regular in ones or twos, but now they like to hide, mostly in the mountains. I haven't seen one going on ten years. How about you, Heath?"

"Ten years," said Heath.

"But maybe I'm getting old. Seems the older I get, the harder it is to spot 'em. Gotta get real close, gotta see 'em in the light, see the tells. Like when they ain't got no eyebrows, or when they're both wearing the same uniform."

Heath stepped out of the golf cart.

The driver did the same, but he dragged a double-barrel shotgun with him. It hung lazily by his side.

"We don't abide synthetics in Challis," he said.

"We don't abide," said Heath.

A chorus of *nopes* went up from the assembled crowd.

"So unless you're the only two members of a cult I ain't heard of, I'm gonna guess you two ain't organic."

Charlie turned to look at Will. Her eyes begged him to do something, to come up with some idea that would save them.

All he could do was think about Momma.

He looked past Charlie and saw Momma standing near the billboard, looking up at the words, shaking her head.

Charlie frowned; the light faded from her eyes.

She hugged Will tightly, squeezing him with the power of synthetic muscles.

He shut his eyes and hugged her back.

THANK YOU

Hybrid Mechanics is the fifth book of **The Vinestead Anthology**.

If you enjoyed this book, please consider leaving a review.

Each standalone novel in the Vinestead Anthology tells a small part of a larger epic: the rise and fall of Vinestead International, the exploits of a rogue artificial intelligence named Lassiter, and a seemingly endless stream of idealistic hackers— each convinced they're the hero of the story.

Enjoy them in any order.

Xronixle (2007)

Veneer (2011)

Guardian Angels (2012)

Perion Synthetics (2014)

Por Vida (2017)

Brigham Plaza (2019)

Hybrid Mechanics (2020)

Vise Manor (2022)

House of Nepenthe (2025)

To learn more about the Vinestead Anthology and explore additional titles, please visit:

danielverastiqui.com

www.ingramcontent.com/pod-product-compliance
Lightning Source LLC
Chambersburg PA
CBHW070617300726

48975CB00006B/1839